TOGETHER *for* GOOD

TOGETHER *for* GOOD

A NOVEL

MELANIE DOBSON

Kregel
Publications

Together for Good: A Novel

© 2006 by Melanie Dobson

Published by Kregel Publications, a division of Kregel, Inc., P.O. Box 2607, Grand Rapids, MI 49501.

Scripture taken from the King James Version.

Library of Congress Cataloging-in-Publication Data
Dobson, Melanie B.
    Together for good : a novel / by Melanie Dobson.
        p. cm.
    1. Adopted children—Fiction. 2. Loss (Psychology)—Fiction.
    I. Title.
PS3604.O25T64 2006
813'.6—dc22   2006007930

ISBN 0-8254-2444-5

Printed in the United States of America

06 07 08 09 10 / 5 4 3 2 1

David and Renee,
you've inspired us with your faith.

Laura and Lynn,
you've blessed us for life.

Acknowledgments

I once believed that writing was a solo profession.

I was very wrong.

I'm grateful for the many people who've helped and encouraged me during the past seven years as I struggled to learn the art and craft of novel writing. Without them, this book never would have been born.

Thank you—

To my parents and cheerleaders, Jim and Lyn Beroth, who cried after reading each of my many drafts (I hope it was a good cry), gave me lots of hugs, and entertained our girls while I worked. I couldn't have finished this without you.

To the best in-laws in the world, Dobby and Carolyn Dobson, for your love and grace and countless hours you've spent caring for our family.

To my dear friend and sister-in-Christ, Tosha Lamdin Williams, who championed my dream as she read hundreds of pages of my writing (work no one should ever have to read). Where would I be without you gently and consistently inspiring me to press on?

To an incredible group of readers and editors—my sister Christina Nunn, Michele Heath, Vennessa Ng, Chip MacGregor, Lisa Bergren, Sarah Hamaker, Ginger Adams, Betsy Holt, Yvette Mihaly, Pamela Gregory, Allison Nelson, Susan Nikaido, Chris and Marji Cyrul, Bob McPeek, Kelli Standish, and Cheryl Dunlop. Your honest input and critiques have been invaluable. Thank you for believing in this book.

To Davis Bunn and the Mount Hermon Writer's Conference—the place to make incredible friends and learn how to excel as a writer.

To Dr. Rusty Whiteamire, who helped me get my brain back.

To Kregel Publications: Jim Kregel, Dennis Hillman, Steve Barclift,

Janyre Tromp, Amy Stephansen, and Moriah Sharp. Thank you for giving me the opportunity to share this story. I've loved working with you.

To my girls, Karly and Kinzel, for your inspiration and constant delight.

To my amazing husband, Jon, who has encouraged this dream of mine since we walked down the aisle in a Colorado lodge eight years ago (did I mention he was amazing?).

And to my Savior, Jesus Christ, who planted this story in my heart and gave me the words in spite of myself. I'm eternally grateful.

Prologue

May 11, 1986

"No!" the girl screamed as she collapsed against the glass.

But no one helped her. They were stealing her baby, and no one cared.

She pounded her fists against the hospital window, but they couldn't hear her cry. Would they tell him how much she loved him? That she never wanted to let him go?

Her stomach cramped, and she bowed over with pain. Losing him hurt worse than the contractions. Worse than the labor. Worse than her parents slamming the front door. Worse than her boyfriend never coming back.

It was more than she could bear.

Her hands pressed against her belly, but the baby was gone. Two days ago, she'd felt him growing and rolling and dancing inside her. Just hours ago, she'd snuggled him close to her chest; playing with his tiny fingers, stroking his dark crown of hair.

The nurses took him away and never brought him back. One kiss, and her boy disappeared.

She scraped her fingernails across the glass, squinting to see his crinkled lips and soft blue eyes as they carried him across the parking lot below.

No one believed her, but she would've taken good care of him. She would've loved him more than anyone else could ever love him. She would have been a good mom.

The man who'd taken him tucked a blanket around his legs; the wife kissed his cheek. How dare that woman kiss her baby!

She was his mom! She'd taken care of him for nine months and anguished through twelve hours of labor to deliver him into the world. She'd borne this child, so much a part of her even after he was gone.

Would she ever see her boy again? Not for a minute did she want to let him go. Surely they'd tell him she hadn't wanted to give him away. That she'd love him for the rest of her life. That she'd done this for his own good.

If only she could run down the hospital stairs and rip her baby from their hands. If only she could take care of him by herself.

"Stop!" she yelled at the glass. *Stop those thieves.*

As the woman opened the car door, the girl's fingers trembled. Her nose pressed against the cold glass for one last look before the couple stole away her son.

Part 1

The only feelings that do not
heal are the ones you hide.
—Henri Nouwen

Chapter 1

Twenty Years Later

Abby Wagner smoothed her tailored skirt before she knocked on her boss's closed door. Blanche Nulte was a player in the public relations world, but new business at Nulte P.R. had waned over the past year. Not good for the firm, and especially not good for anyone meeting with Blanche on a bad day.

Abby wished there was a Blanche meter beside the door to gauge her boss's mood. If a client was upset, Blanche was irate. If a client was happy, she was tolerable. Most days were a combo of highs and lows. The wise employee waited for one of the high moments before delivering bad news.

Blanche's disposition didn't seem to matter to their clients. She was a professional. She got results. And she'd succeeded at building her company over the last seven years into a firm that competed with agencies in New York City and L.A.—the ones that billed hundreds of dollars an hour and powered through lunches with politicians, celebrities, and CEOs. Nulte P.R. was only a few steps behind.

Abby had been in the trenches with Blanche from the beginning, first as her only employee—executive assistant and chief gopher. Now she was a vice president, and in spite of her boss's rants, she intended to be here until she retired.

Abby knocked.

"Come in," Blanche shouted. Edging the door open, Abby walked in and slipped into a black leather chair.

Pictures of aspen groves and mountain peaks plastered the brick walls, and behind Blanche's handcrafted desk was a long window framing the

range of white-tipped Rocky Mountains. Blanche's peach-painted nails skimmed across the *Denver Post* on her desk as she finished reading the article. Pearls lined her long neck, and her fiery red hair was pulled tight.

"I've got a potential client that I want you to pitch." Blanche reached for a green file. "We're competing with the big boys on this account."

Abby released her breath. It was a good day.

"What's their story?" Abby leaned forward in her chair to see the stack of papers Blanche was spreading across the desk.

"It's a national adoption agency that's based here in Denver."

Abby gulped air and held her breath. An adoption agency? How many national adoption agencies were based out of Denver? Hopefully there was more than one.

"They've got a new president who wants to update their old-fashioned image, but it's a huge, cumbersome organization. A lot of people to move into this century. They've got sixty-plus offices across the country placing infants in—," she held up a paper of statistics from the adoption agency's Web site and read, "'. . . placing every needy infant into a loving home.'"

Blanche tucked the page back into the file. "The agency has been around for forty years, but Harold Rogers wants to generate more exposure for them as well as educate potential adoptive parents on the simplicity of the process."

Abby steadied her voice and lied. "Sounds like an admirable cause."

"Harold believes that more people would adopt if they connected with a reliable agency. Heartsong Adoptions is the agency people can trust."

Heartsong Adoptions. Abby hadn't heard that name in years. The familiar surge jolted her hands, and she clenched her fingers into fists. Not here in her boss's office! She couldn't start shaking now.

Blanche didn't miss a beat. She handed a booklet to Abby. "Here's their current brochure. Awful, isn't it?"

Abby clamped onto the brochure with her thumb and stared down at the cover. Grainy photos. Cursive fonts. Splashes of mauve and baby blue.

She opened the fold. Was that child wearing white jelly shoes?

"Needs some work, doesn't it?" Blanche asked.

Abby slowly nodded her head. Her eyes caught the small picture in the left-hand corner. A perfect baby boy with blond hair and blue eyes. He looked just like her son.

"I think we can create a real story here." Blanche made a note on her legal pad. "With infertility rates up and couples waiting until later in life to have kids, Heartsong wants to present adoption as a viable option to expensive infertility treatments. They also want to encourage girls from rough home situations to consider giving up their babies to a loving family instead of opting for an abortion."

Was Blanche still talking? Her words muffled like they were caught in a drum.

"Heartsong is working with treasures, family treasures. Do you like that: 'Heartsong Adoptions . . . Treasuring the Heart of Family'?" Blanche asked. "We'll have no problem getting the national media onboard if we can convince Harold that we're right for this job. What do you think?"

The irony stung. Abby Wagner promoting the good works of Heartsong. What was God trying to do? How could she tell the world about Heartsong's "treasures" after they'd destroyed her family?

Abby shut her eyes briefly, begging the darkness to flee.

"Are you with me, Abby?"

She struggled to focus on her boss's stare. "Just thinking. Is there a downside?"

"You have less than a week to get us ready for the pitch."

"No problem."

"Go get started then." Blanche dismissed her with a wave. "We're meeting with them on Wednesday."

Abby grasped the leather arm and maneuvered herself out of the chair. Her heart pounded so hard that she thought Blanche must be able to hear it as she walked across the room and reached for the doorknob.

"We need this account," Blanche said before Abby shut the door.

Hunched over the bathroom sink, Abby splashed cold water on her face. This was ridiculous. She hadn't had a panic attack in seven years.

She had to get over this insanity. Too much time had gone by for this to happen again.

Someone knocked on the door. "Abby, are you in there?"

She splashed one more handful on her face and opened the door.

"Are you okay?" her assistant, Maggie, asked.

"I'm fine."

"Well, you look awful."

Abby had to smile. She'd marveled for years at the consistent polarization between her assistant's disheveled appearance and her meticulous organizational skills. Today Maggie's powder blue suit needed to be cleaned, blood red lipstick oozed down toward her chin, and her hair begged for a decent cut.

She must really look bad.

"*Good Morning America* just called," Maggie said. "They want to do the interview."

If it was an hour earlier, she would have cheered. She'd been pitching the morning show for two weeks on a feature story, an in-depth look at preserving Colorado's decayed mining towns. Different angles. Back and forth. New footage. Old footage. And an interview with Ted Zant, one of their top clients, the man leading the charge. Ted would be thrilled.

"That's the best news I've ever had," her assistant prompted her, squeezing her arm. "You deserve a raise just for delivering it."

"You're right, Maggie. You're the best."

"How about that raise?"

Abby caught a drop of water with her sleeve before it dripped off her chin. "If you deliver this news to Blanche, she might give you one."

"You're leaving for the weekend or I will visit Blanche and tell her to send you home." Maggie paused. "Seriously, are you okay?"

Another tremor raced through Abby's arm. "I'll be fine."

Chapter 2

The winds were perfect—blowing eighteen knots from the southeast. Damian De Lucia edged the sailboat's silver wheel starboard to race past Orcas Island, the breeze propelling their uncharted course.

He hadn't sailed *The Drifter* in four days. No sailboat should be tied to a slip for that long. Freedom is what she deserved, roaming and gliding and drifting across the water like she had fins instead of a sail.

"Prepare to tack," Damian shouted to Marc Cartwright, his sole crew member for the day. Marc braced himself against the traveler, grasping the jib sheet. Even though the kid was only nineteen, he'd already mastered the art and science of sailing.

"I'm ready," Marc yelled.

Damian turned the wheel starboard, tacking *The Drifter* as he scanned the horizon. "Trim the sheets!"

Marc pulled in the sail, and the two men flew back into the wind.

Damian headed up and then bore back down into the breeze—dancing a steady tango with the wind and the sea. The San Juans, a colony of almost five hundred islands off the Washington coast, had been his home for the first twenty-four and the last three of his fifty-three years. Tucked into the surreal Puget Sound, the islands were a haven for wildlife and an escape for people. Only a few of the islands were accessible by ferry; you needed a private boat to visit most of the Sound.

When he worked for the International Whaling Commission, the IWC, during his twenties and thirties, Damian pretended not to miss Washington's coast. Exploring the seas around exotic countries like Finland, Saint Kitts, Italy, New Zealand, and Indonesia had captured his attention for years, but when the mystique of each new place wore off, he yearned for the quiet inlets and beaches of home. When he finally

returned to the San Juans, he realized that the novelty of sailing through them had never disappeared. This is where he belonged.

The coastline of Orcas emerged before them, its jetted rocks wrapped tightly around the shore. Damian crossed the boat through the breeze and tacked back toward the sea, the navy yarn on the mainsail fluttering up and down. Riding the wind calmed and thrilled him at the same time, like napping through the fierce crashes of a thunderstorm.

"Does it get any better than this?" Damian shouted.

Strands of Marc's black hair blew across his forehead. "Not in this life."

Damian scanned the shoreline. The marina to the right harbored the swanky yachts with their walnut interiors, Jacuzzi tubs, and vintage wine cellars. Compared to these floating manors, his thirty-two-foot boat looked like it had been crafted from scrap metal.

He scrubbed a black grease mark off the white hull with a towel and wiped his hands on his shorts. *The Drifter* could sail with the best of them, though, and probably better than some of those multi-million-dollar works of art. Fortunately, you didn't need a million bucks to dance with the wind.

As they sailed around a bend covered with leafy maple trees and a few pines, Damian fervently searched the water's wrinkled surface for Puget Sound's most famous resident—the black and white orca.

Nothing. They'd keep sailing until the sun went down.

It was already the middle of May and time for the killer whales to come home to the Sound. In the next week, tourists would pack Orcas Island—filling the inns and restaurants of the island's three villages. Most of them came specifically to catch a glimpse of the whales breaching the cold Salish Sea, and as the owner of a tour boat company, it was his job to deliver this popular entertainment.

Every year it became harder to spot the whales. In the past, visitors were almost guaranteed to spot at least one pod, but the orca population around Puget Sound was dying out.

Weaving by another inlet, Damian peered up a rock wall at a yellow bungalow needing new paint, a new roof, and probably a complete renovation. Tall sprays of lavender and white hollyhocks sprung up in the midst of the weathered grasses. Clematis had overtaken the side of the house, and ivy curled around the porch. What had once been a spectacular island garden had grown into a wild jungle. He couldn't imagine what was growing inside the house.

Years ago, he'd spent long summer days jumping off the dock below the house and into the clear, cold water. He and Abby Taylor would anchor his boat on the coast, climb the steep stairs embedded in the stone, and eat homemade ice cream with strawberries and chocolate sauce.

Surely the Taylor family would sell the cottage before it passed into complete ruin. He had assumed they'd liquidate the property when Mr. and Mrs. Taylor died a few years back, but a "for sale" sign never emerged. And the two Taylor daughters never seemed to come home any more.

Damian turned the rudder and the boat flew south, the wind carrying them away. "Look to port at ten o'clock," Marc yelled back at him, and Damian flung his head left.

Three harbor seals popped their pudgy heads out of the water, their spotted gray coats gleaming in the sun. They clapped their flippers as Damian and Marc sailed by, and Damian waved at the mammals like they were friends. They dove under the water, trailing a path of ripples behind.

Damian squinted, straining his eyes as he searched the horizon.

They sailed past tiny Shaw Island. Last year, he'd spotted an entire family of orcas in this exact area. He hauled boatloads of people here over the summer, and every few days, they'd get a new show. The whales loved entertaining as much as the onlookers enjoyed watching the show. The orcas would whistle and squeal and shoot towering sprays from their blowholes like they'd spent days in rehearsal.

Damian trimmed the sail, and they sailed around a bend and into a cove. Marshy grass towered over the still water, and driftwood blanketed the ground. Beer-colored foam lapped onto the shore and coated the wet sand.

"What's that?" Marc pointed to a giant black hump ahead of them.

Panic clutched Damian's gut. On the beach lay a whale.

Chapter 3

The humidity warped Jessica Wagner's straight hair into a mass of frizz, and the stifling hot air smelled like chlorine. She gathered her damp tendrils back into a black band and leaned against the plastic chair, watching her boyfriend race to the pool's tile wall, flip, and propel himself back down the middle lane in one fluid move.

A dedicated shelf in Brett's dorm room was crammed with trophies and blue ribbons from more than a dozen swim meets he'd won in high school and college. He planned to add Olympic gold to the shelf before he retired his collection.

Jessica flipped the page of her textbook and tried to concentrate on the description of the American Revolution. "These are the times that try men's souls," she read. Who said that again? She reviewed her notes—oh yes, Thomas Paine, an instigator of the American Revolution and author of *Common Sense*. Would she ever get these names straight?

Her mother prided herself on being a straight-A student, but Jessica was lucky to get Bs and Cs. The truth was she simply didn't care about the founders of the Revolution, the theorems in differential calculus, or even the nuances of English literature that her mom loved. The only classes she enjoyed were the two mornings a week spent studying plant and animal life in biology. She didn't even mind cramming for her biology exams. Every other subject seemed dull compared to the colorful world she'd discovered on Tuesday and Thursday mornings at nine.

Brett propped himself at the side of the lap pool and hopped out. Jessica threw him the red and white striped towel he'd strung over the chair, and he wrapped it around his waist. Water dripped off his toned arms as he waved a quick good-bye to one of the other swimmers—a slender blonde with a body cut perfectly for her suit.

"Who's that?" Jessica asked as she tucked the history book into her bag.

"I didn't expect to see you here." He ripped off his cap and rubbed his matted hair.

She sighed. "We're supposed to go to dinner tonight."

"I forgot again, didn't I, Jess? I'm sorry. Give me three minutes to change."

She watched him walk into the locker room. He'd forgotten the last two times they'd made plans, and yet here she was again reminding him that they had a relationship after he'd finished swimming for the night. The future for her and Brett was obviously fizzling, and neither of them had the guts to initiate an end.

Jessica gazed down at the beautiful blonde swimming another lap.

It wasn't worth it. Swimming was his first love—and perhaps there were other new loves in his life. The girl surfaced in a perfect breast-stroke and dove back under.

The strange thing was, the expected jealousy didn't pang against her heart. Relief, maybe, but no apparent pain at losing him. That couldn't be healthy, could it? If she loved this man, she'd want to be his sole focus . . . or at least, his partial focus. She supposed she wanted what every woman wanted—to be cherished and loved. Brett just seemed to tolerate her.

He emerged from the locker room, dressed in his green UC sweatshirt and long shorts. "You ready to hit the cafeteria?"

Another romantic evening with her boyfriend. "I guess."

"I heard sloppy joes is the main entrée tonight."

"My favorite."

Brett glanced back at the girl in the pool, and she waved again. Jessica was tempted to wrap her arms around her boyfriend and kiss his lips, fanning the glorious flames of a burning plane before it crashed. Instead, she strapped the book bag over her shoulder and followed him outside.

When Brett had asked her out the first time, she'd wondered if his friends thought he was "dating down." She wasn't especially popular, an amazing athlete, or a stellar student. Just plain Jessica Wagner—a girl who'd much rather be playing outside than imprisoned in a classroom or

rec center. Her workout choice? She preferred biking a mountain path or swimming across a lake instead of being confined to a treadmill or an indoor pool.

Five months ago, she'd been elated when this good-looking athletic guy had asked her to dinner and the student production of *West Side Story*. They'd met at a Fellowship of Christian Athletes event, and she'd been intrigued by his faith . . . and his popularity. She loved water. He loved water. For weeks, it had seemed like a dream, but the dream had faded to black. She didn't doubt his commitment to God—just his commitment to her.

Cottonwoods shaded the winding path as they walked toward the cafeteria. Brett waved to a couple guys from the football team who were huddled around a bench and stopped to talk sports. Jessica glanced at her watch. If he didn't hurry they'd miss dinner, and she really didn't want to eat cheese crackers from the vending machine again.

He slapped one of the guys on the back and caught her eye. "Guess I'd better go," he muttered. "Don't want to get in trouble."

"When are you going to break free?" One of the guys laughed, slugging his shoulder.

"She's not so bad." Brett put his arm around her. "You guys are just jealous."

Words spoken from a man in love, she thought. One of them needed to put their wounded relationship out of its misery.

"See ya, Jess," the same guy said as they walked away. "Call me if you ever get tired of him."

Not in a million years.

"You're in quite the reflective mood tonight," Brett said.

"I've got a lot on my mind."

"Thinking great thoughts, huh?"

She stopped walking and faced him. She'd once been intimidated by the strength in his green eyes and the allure of his smile. She couldn't pinpoint when the chemistry between them faded, but probably about a month ago—the first time he'd forgotten to pick her up for a movie date. There were signs before then, of course. Promised calls. Tardy dates.

Brief apologies. Her awe had dissipated rapidly until now . . . it was completely gone.

"This isn't working, you and I," she said simply. "We both know it, but neither of us wants to talk about it."

His face relaxed. Was that relief in his eyes? Why hadn't he done something about this before if he knew it wasn't going to work? The frustration inside her boiled.

"We can talk about it if you really want to."

"I do, Brett. I can't take this anymore. I could blame you for forgetting our dates and ignoring me for days, but you'll say you're busy training and trying to maintain good grades, and I should understand. The thing is—I do understand. If I fit into second or third or even fourth place in your life, I'd be okay. The thing is, I barely fit into last."

He tugged on her arm when a group of students approached them, pulling her off the sidewalk toward a bench.

"You want to break up," he said.

She nodded her head.

"Then I guess I'll have to concede."

"Concede? This isn't a swim meet, Brett. This is our relationship. Don't you want to fight for it?"

His silent response answered her question.

"Then you really don't care," she replied quietly.

"We haven't been working for a long time, Jess. You know that."

She should cry or beg him to stay or something, but she didn't really want him to stay. She didn't even feel sad.

"What happened?" she asked simply as the lights along the walkway flashed on.

"We never really seem to talk. I need to be with someone who has a little more fire."

"Excuse me?" Since when had her athletic boyfriend wanted to talk about fire?

"It's not your fault. You get it honestly."

"Get what honestly?" She stood up. "I don't know what you're talking about."

"You never get angry or happy or jealous or excited or anything." He picked his book bag off the ground. "No offense, Jess, but you act like you're too good to feel passionate about anything."

"That isn't fair." She snatched up her bag.

"It's the truth."

She didn't look back as she ran. She crossed the grassy slope toward her dormitory, but she didn't go inside. Her roommate would ask about her dinner with Brett, and she needed to be calm.

She collapsed on the grass.

She'd spent her life hating her mom's avoidance of the tough talks, dodging everything from the death of her husband to the anger she felt toward her boss. It had frustrated Jessica her entire life.

Now her ex-boyfriend was accusing her of being cold . . . just like her mom!

Her cell phone rang. She glanced down at the number and answered. "Hey, Mom."

"What's wrong, honey?" Abby asked.

"Nothing."

"What did Brett say?"

Jessica watched a group of students walk up the cement steps and into the dorm. "Things just aren't going that well."

"You deserve better, Jessica."

"You always say that about my boyfriends."

"Brett's so focused on swimming that he doesn't have any extra time for you."

"He has to spend a lot of time preparing for his meets."

"I think you should break up with him."

"No worries, Mom. We just broke up."

She waited for her mom to ask how she was doing. Wasn't that what mothers were supposed to ask at a time like this? They were supposed to comfort their daughters and empathize with their pain.

Tears filled her eyes.

"You'll meet the right guy when you're a little older," Abby said.

"I don't know."

"When are you coming home?"

"As soon as my finals are over."

"I'll grill you a steak if you come this weekend."

"I've lost my appetite."

"Then tell me what you're reading in English class."

She sighed. "I'm not really thinking about English right now."

"I bet it's something good. *Pride and Prejudice,* maybe?"

Jessica groaned into the phone.

Chapter 4

"Call the Coast Guard," Damian commanded, stripping off his shirt and shoes. A wave rocked the sailboat, and he steadied himself as he climbed the rail.

"We found a beached orca on Shaw Island," he heard Marc say into the radio. Damian didn't wait for a response. He dove into the icy water and swam toward the beach and the whale. If she was still alive, he might be able to save her. He couldn't let another one die.

Damian ran onto the sand. The cold air didn't make him shiver. It was the stench. He didn't need his degree in marine biology to recognize the smell of death. The lifeless eyes of a carcass stared back at him.

When he'd worked for the IWC, Damian had seen a dead whale almost every week, but that was in third world countries, places where whale meat fed an entire village. He didn't want to see one here.

In seconds, he circled the mammal, searching for a sign of injury. A bite or a mark or something to show she'd been wounded. Nothing.

He collapsed on a sandy rock and threw a stone at the water. Fewer than a hundred of the resident whales returned to the Sound each year. Now another one had succumbed to toxic chemicals. Another poisoned whale.

When he was a kid, he'd explored what seemed like a hundred of these coves hidden among the San Juans. On every beach, he'd imagined a band of pirates burying a chest of gold or hiding out as they prepared to plunder an unsuspecting ship or just lounging against the hot rocks, carving grainy pictures with their swords. He'd wanted to find buried treasure, not a rotting whale.

The wind shifted and the pungent stench of decay blew out to sea.

Twenty minutes later, the white Coast Guard cutter zipped around the bend. Damian stood on the rock, waving his arms in the air like they hadn't already spotted his sailboat or the black mass on the sand. The patrol boat picked up Marc from the sailboat and sped toward the cove.

Before the boat brushed up on the sand, four men hopped out into the water. Marc tossed Damian a beach towel while two coastguardsmen dressed in navy blue uniforms anchored the boat.

"Hello, Dr. De Lucia." The man who greeted him had a thinning goatee and wore an oversized windbreaker and khaki pants. Dr. Neven was Seattle's chief expert in marine toxicology, yet the two of them had never quite agreed about the threat of toxins in the Sound.

"Kyle Neven." Damian shook his hand.

"Haven't seen you in a long time." Kyle glanced over Damian's shoulder at the whale.

"I've been busy."

"I heard you retired." Kyle lifted a black bag out of the boat like a physician making a house call.

Damian clutched his fist, quietly reminding himself that he and Kyle were on the same team. "I don't have time to retire. I'm running a whale watching business on Orcas."

"I'd give anything to spend more of my days on the water." Kyle nodded toward the water.

"If the orcas don't return this year, I may have to start running dinner cruises."

Kyle laughed. "Maybe I wouldn't give *anything*."

"That's what I thought."

Kyle pointed toward the arrow-shaped scar on the whale's dorsal fin. "Do you recognize her?"

Damian shook his head. "I only know a few of them by sight."

"Her name's Macy, from the L-pod. Twenty-six years old. No one saw her last year, but she's been returning to the Sound since she was born."

"I wish she hadn't returned this year." Damian kneeled beside her. He wanted to pet her, massage her belly until she came back to life. Instead he watched Kyle slip plastic gloves over his hands to examine her.

"She doesn't appear to be injured." Kyle looked up at Damian. "But you already knew that, didn't you?"

"A lab assistant could tell you that."

"And your preliminary diagnosis?"

"PCB toxins killed her at sea, and she drifted to shore."

"Let's see if science concurs." Kyle took several vials out of his bag and punctured her blubber with a needle.

"You already know the answer, Kyle."

"I'll run some tests." He held up the clear tubes.

Marc stepped up beside Kyle. "How do the toxins kill these whales?"

"The whales gorge on salmon, and if the salmon have a high level of polychlorinated biphenyls, it can kill the whales."

Kyle packed his samples into tiny, padded slots before snapping several pictures of the whale. "Even with environmental regulations, we haven't got a handle on it."

"No wonder," Damian mumbled.

Sewage and pollution from both the United States and Canada collided right here in the pristine San Juans. If they didn't clean up this water, the whales would stop coming home to Puget Sound. They'd stay up north or simply go out to sea. Their disappearance would be more than just bad for his business, it would be the end of an era. The beautiful whales were part of the island's heritage. Part of what made it Damian's home.

"Unfortunately, these chemicals stay in the water for years," Kyle told Marc as they walked back to the boat. "It passes through the females to the next generation."

"It's unstoppable?" Marc asked.

"Not necessarily," Kyle replied. "We just haven't found a way to block it yet."

Damian hopped onto the boat. "Locals should be demanding that someone clean up this water."

"I'm in your choir, Dr. De Lucia." Kyle scrambled into the boat beside him and stored his bag under a bench. Damian and Marc followed him into the cutter, and they sped toward the sailboat. "There are just too many things vying for support right now."

Damian and Marc climbed onto their boat and waved good-bye to the coastguardsmen and Kyle Neven.

"That's not exactly how you wanted to find a whale this season," Marc said as he prepared the sail.

"I've seen hundreds of dead whales, but it never seems to get easier." Damian pulled his T-shirt over his head. "If someone doesn't do something, there won't be any whales left in the Sound."

"Why don't you do something?"

"I don't think so."

"Why not? You've worked with whales for years."

Damian tied his shoes. "My crusading days are over."

"But it would be for a good cause."

Damian didn't say anything. The last time he'd done an interview was four years ago when he was still the director of the Seattle Aquarium. He almost threw a chair at the TV reporter after she implied that he'd partnered with whale killers because he'd worked for the IWC. The final story hadn't been pretty, and the board politely asked him to delegate future interviews to another member of the staff.

"Didn't you do interviews when you were with the aquarium?"

"I hate being in the spotlight."

"Too bad for the whales," Marc muttered as they sailed home.

Chapter 5

Abby unlocked her office door a few minutes before seven and dumped her briefcase onto a padded chair. The agency was completely quiet, but the silence wouldn't last long. Monday morning frenzy would overcome any hint of the calm by eight.

She needed the quiet right now. She had two hours to immerse herself in Heartsong's background, to convince herself that she could succeed. Two hours until Blanche would open her door and expect her to optimistically declare that she'd divide and conquer this publicity campaign.

She set her latte on the desktop and sat down. The wall beside her desk was filled with a collage of local Public Relations Society of America awards and framed newspaper clips from articles she'd pitched as she pursued a public relations career. She still loved the rush when she scored a huge hit for a client. They needed her to promote their work, cheer for their causes. She just wasn't sure she could be the cheerleading captain for Heartsong Adoptions. They needed someone who actually believed in adoption. Someone who thought it was the right decision for the parents and the child.

Centered on Abby's desk was a picture of her daughter. It was her favorite picture. At just four years old, Jessica was grinning as she sailed across Washington's Puget Sound with her dad, her hair pulled back in a ponytail and the tip of the mainsail plastered against her hand. According to Scott, their daughter had contented herself for days paddling alongside the fish in the frigid Pacific water and sailing across the inlet beside their family's bungalow, pretending she was either a mermaid or Peter Pan.

Those trips were father-daughter getaways. After what happened to her on Orcas Island, Abby never went back to the cottage. Twenty years had gone by since she'd canoed across the bay or gazed out at the dark pods of whales gliding through the inlet. She missed the water, but she'd never return.

Her daughter was finishing her freshman year at the University of Colorado up in Boulder . . . the same age Abby had been when she met Scott. Where had the years gone? Losing her son. Welcoming her daughter. It all seemed like yesterday.

Focus. She had to keep her mind engaged on this task. It never paid to let it wander back. The memories made her lose control.

Blanche had neatly stacked materials on her desk to review, and Abby pulled out a clean legal pad to make notes. She was a professional. This proposal would be no different from the hundreds of others she and Blanche had pitched over the past seven years.

Thumbing through the Heartsong brochure, she cringed again at the outdated pictures and blocks of brightly shaded copy. An intern must have designed it twenty years ago. She jotted a note—updating the brochure would be at the top of their priority list. If Heartsong expected someone to pay $20,000 or more to adopt a child, their clients would want them to be up-to-date.

Abby set aside the brochure and opened their royal blue information packet. Heartsong placed 2,100 infants a year. They worked solely with domestic adoptions, leaving international adoptions with other specialized agencies.

What makes Heartsong different from every other adoption agency?

She skimmed a series of direct mail pieces. Hundreds of agencies focused on domestic adoptions, and Heartsong's marketing pieces showed nothing to make them stand out from the rest. Maybe it was time for Heartsong to get personal.

She sipped her creamy espresso as Blanche opened her office door.

"Good morning, Abby." She buttoned her tan blazer. "What's the status on the *GMA* interview with Ted?"

"Everything's set up for two segments."

"Good. Did you recover this weekend?"

"I just needed a little rest."

"Well, no more time for rest. I'm ordering subs for lunch and Chinese for dinner."

Blanche knew Chinese food made her nauseous, but her boss always ordered it anyway.

"We'll be here all night if we have to," Blanche said. "I want this Heartsong presentation to be one for the history books."

"I'm on it," Abby said. "We'll wow them on Wednesday."

"Of course you will. You always do." Blanche spun around, not even bothering to shut the door.

Abby didn't mind competing with other agencies for clients, but she hated competing with her own boss. She'd applied for an administrative position with Blanche five months after she'd launched the company, and Abby had slaved beside her to build the fledgling firm into a respected agency. Yet, even with all their successes, the tension never went away.

She sighed and concentrated again on the stack in front of her. Even if Blanche secretly wanted her to fail, she'd push ahead on this project no matter what the toll.

She scribbled another note on her pad. *Adoption encompasses every facet of the prospective parent's life—financial, spiritual, physical, and emotional. Heartsong must prove they can succeed in every one of these areas. They must not let their families down.*

To have a successful campaign, she needed to demonstrate that Heartsong valued adoptive couples by giving them the correct information and then struggling with them through the long, involved process of placing a child. And she needed to demonstrate it with a straight face. No one could know that it was a lie.

She'd have to put her personal feelings aside and show that Heartsong cared.

Abby leaned back in her chair. If they got the contract, this would be the toughest campaign she'd ever overseen.

Nine hours later, Abby, Blanche, and four others gathered in the agency's rustic conference room. The hand-carved table was bulging with laptops, notepads, folders, and coffee mugs. Maggie had lined up a golden and red parade of tiny cartons, and the buckets of moo goo gai pan, Szechuan beef, and kung pao chicken quickly disappeared.

"Nothing beats Chinese," Curtis Parks, their chief staff writer, said as he pushed back the cardboard tabs on the carton he snatched.

Abby ripped open a packet of cheese crackers, trying to ignore the odors—hot mustard, peanut sauce, chili pepper. She should have ordered Italian.

"Let's do this," Blanche said, scooping a bite of her spicy chicken and rice. "I can't afford to feed you breakfast too."

"To a short but brilliant night." Curtis lifted his Dr. Pepper can for a toast. Two other people raised their soda cans in salute.

Blanche pointed a chopstick toward Abby. "Why don't you get this party going, Abby?"

She nodded at her cue to take the lead. "I've got a long list of where I think we need to take this campaign. First of all, we need to update the very outdated image of Heartsong, and then we need to promote this image like we're launching a brand new agency."

"Obviously," Blanche said. "But how do you propose we do that?"

Abby grabbed her typed notes. "A massive media push to start. Once we've determined our specific news angles, I want to pitch the story at the national level as well as in the top twenty-five markets.

"Alongside the media blitz, I'm proposing that we do very specific public service messages on the topic of adoption, image-based advertising in women's magazines, a four-color promotional piece to send to prospective parents, and, of course, an updated Web site and brochure. We need to oversee the evolution of Heartsong from simply a professional agency to a personal one."

Abby stopped to sip her soda. Next on her agenda was an in-depth plan of market-specific programs, the overall costs, and the targets they needed to reach.

"That's nice, Abby." Blanche barely suppressed a yawn. "A real solid campaign. The challenge is that in order to win this campaign, we need light-years above solid. We need brilliant."

Didn't Curtis just use that word?

Abby took a deep breath before continuing her presentation, but she didn't get the chance.

Blanche waved her chopstick, a conductor prepping her orchestra. "Any ideas?"

Curtis sprang into the conversation like he'd been flicked.

"I think we have to present Heartsong as *the* place to go if you want to have a successful adoption," he said. "Adoption is a complicated and often confusing process. Heartsong takes the pain out of the process."

"It isn't surgery," Abby muttered, but Curtis ignored her.

"How do you propose we do that?" Blanche shoved the half-filled carton of food away and leaned back to listen.

"We do the national blitz like Abby said, but we do it in style. We train a local spokesperson in the top thirty markets to do national media and conduct public forums to simplify the process—a presentation that is more fun than a stuffy seminar."

Abby crossed off a bullet point on her notepad. Only five hours ago, she'd written: *Simplify. Conduct seminars to make adoption easy for people to understand.*

Did Curtis really believe adoptive couples wanted to come to a seminar to have *fun?* Abby wondered if he even had a clue as to what he was proposing or if he'd copied his ideas from a textbook.

"We can take these same people," he continued, "and feature them in our advertising—directing potential clients to a Web site that has compelling copy and an easy step-by-step list of the adoption process. I think we can say that while adoption isn't guaranteed until it's final, Heartsong will guarantee that they will do everything they can to make it happen."

"Now that's what I'm talking about," Blanche approved. "Let's brainstorm."

The team worked until 3:15 AM, but Abby didn't say another word.

Chapter 6

Damian and Marc motored *The Drifter* slowly into the Westsound Marina and docked in the slip between *Weekend Warrior* and *Serenity Now*. Damian named his boat *The Drifter* before he became a Christian, years before he realized that roaming the sea wasn't going to give him the peace he craved. Still a drifter at heart, Damian prayed daily that God would send the wind to guide his course, blowing him toward His will instead of letting him run.

Securing the rope around a metal cleat, Damian knotted it into a hitch. Marc shoved his hat on and hopped out of the sailboat, a cooler in one hand and his windbreaker in the other.

Three days had passed since they found the dead whale. They still hadn't found one alive. "We'll try again tomorrow," Damian said as the two men walked down the rugged dock toward town.

"The orcas always come back."

"I don't remember a summer where at least one of the pods haven't returned by the end of April." He looked down at the date on his nautical watch. "May ninth. It's way past time for them to come home."

"Did you hear from Dr. Neven yet?"

"Not a word. Said he'd call me by yesterday, but I bet he won't even bother."

Damian De Lucia was a washed-up marine biologist in the eyes of the professional world. A has-been. No one needed to report info back to him anymore.

Sweet cigar smoke wafted across the dock, and Damian glanced up at the top level of a classy yacht. Two men were leaning over the rail, their tanned chests sagging over Bermuda shorts. One of them lifted his cigar in a half-hearted salute, and Damian waved back.

The yacht appeared first-class with its elegant teak hull and parade of sails. Yet what good was it to own a piece of paradise if you were too scared to take it out? Damian never understood experiencing the water from a crowded marina when there were thousands of coves and inlets to explore.

"Let's start at seven again tomorrow," Damian said as their feet hit the freshly tarred pavement.

"No problem." Marc rolled the combination to unlock his rickety bike from the grate, the spokes groaning as he propped himself up on the torn seat. "Do you need help at the restaurant tonight?"

"Vincent's got it under control," Damian said. "Go be a kid for a few hours."

As Marc's bike creaked out of town, Damian strode quickly through the village, glancing at the newest displays that decorated the shop windows. Pastel lollipops and saltwater taffy floated inside the candy store's front window. Coffee-table books with photos of splashing whales and sunsets were propped up in the bookstore's display. An art store had modernized its window with four black and white photos framed in steel.

Only a few tourists roamed the streets this early in the season, but that would change in a week or two. He'd soon have to jam through the hordes before climbing up the hill. Hordes that had come to see the Sound's famous killer whales.

Damian ascended the wooden stairs to De Lucia's white clapboard restaurant. The aroma of garlic and basil settled on the wide porch that overlooked the harbor and drifted down into town. During all his years of roaming, the poignant scents of stewing tomatoes, roasted peppers, and red wine instantly reminded him of home.

He opened the heavy front door and glanced around the dimmed dining room. Sixteen round tables, clothed in white, dotted the hardwood floors. Only half of them were set for dinner.

He'd moved back to Orcas Island under the guise of helping his Uncle Vincent at the restaurant that Vincent and Damian's father had started in 1965. Damian came back home three years ago when his father died, but both he and Vincent knew the restaurant was only an excuse for him to be back on Orcas Island. Too many hours confined inside any building sent Damian racing for fresh air.

He and his uncle had reached an agreement. Damian volunteered to help at De Lucia's each spring until Vincent picked the best and the brightest for the summer staff. Damian focused on his own business during the summer months. The truce seemed to work for the first two years, but by year three, Vincent seemed to have forgotten his nephew was a volunteer.

"It's a beautiful night," Damian said as he walked into the kitchen.

Vincent De Lucia was stooped over one of three stoves that had been in operation since the restaurant opened. A splattered apron dangled from his thick neck and green splotches of pesto dotted his white hair.

"Andiamo!" He exclaimed, lifting the handle of a long wooden spoon, stained rusty red, and pointing toward the dining room. "We're opening in ten minutes."

"I guess that means you need my help tonight."

Vincent grunted as he adjusted the heat for a steaming pot of ravioli soup. "Not until you get rid of that seaweed smell. *Per favore.* You're contaminating my kitchen."

Damian grinned at his uncle's tone as he swiped his finger through the pesto sauce. Vincent swatted him with the spoon.

Vincent De Lucia never cushioned his words. He excelled at warding off sales calls, confronting the town's council about rutted potholes, and scaring trick-or-treaters when they knocked on his front door. Fortunately, Damian didn't have any children for him to frighten.

In spite of his edge, Vincent treated his customers like royalty.

"Don't you think the guests would appreciate a little variety?" Damian joked.

"Now you've got nine and a half minutes."

Damian shrugged his shoulders and strolled up the kitchen's back stairs. Damian's father had been the same way. When he was a kid, Damian had learned to duck when his father's barrel of fury was pointed at him and to laugh instead of cry if one of the bullets hit hard. Years into adulthood, Damian quit trying to exceed his father's expectations. He finally realized if a degree in marine biology and a successful career

with the International Whaling Commission and the Seattle Aquarium didn't please his father, then nothing would.

The man had died unhappy and heartbroken. When he turned seventy, his wife left him for the East Coast's cosmopolitan life and a wealthy New Yorker born twenty years before her. His father had never recovered from the divorce.

Damian pushed open the cracked door to his uncle's living room. Strewn across the plaid couch and coffee table were neckties, dishtowels, and stacks of torn *National Geographic* magazines. A thin coat of dust clung to the television set, and a vine of cables connected the VCR, DVD player, and satellite box. When Vincent wasn't running the restaurant, he planted himself on the stained couch and watched old Westerns, *Happy Days* reruns, and Oprah.

While Vincent was a master at restaurant management, he'd never learned the art of homemaking, or even the science of keeping a house clean. It drove Damian crazy. The restaurant was spotless, but Vincent's apartment was covered in grime.

Damian grabbed his standard uniform from the messy closet—a starched button-down shirt and black pants that conformed to hosting, waiting tables, cooking, or bussing for De Lucia's fine dining. He scrubbed off the clinging sea salt in the shower and combed his fingers through his dark hair. When he left his desk job with the aquarium, he'd let it grow back into a grungy summer mop that dragged against his shoulders on land and sailed in the wind when he was at sea.

Nine minutes after he'd left the kitchen, he buttoned the stiff white shirt, knotted a black tie around his collar, and then walked back down the stairs to greet a young couple in the lobby. They were holding hands and muttering something to each other that he assumed was sweet. Honeymooners.

"Is this a dinner for two?" Damian asked, and the woman giggled as they followed him to a table by the window, the water below sparkling from the sun's rays. He handed them menus before quickly setting the empty tables around them with china plates, linen napkins, and freshly polished silverware.

The door opened again, and Damian turned, blinking his eyes twice in disbelief. Her chestnut hair was shorter and straight, and she'd gained ten pounds or so since he saw her last, but her grin hadn't changed a bit.

"Laurel Taylor!" He kissed her cheek and shook the hand of her husband, Davis, and their son, Travis, who sported a cowboy hat and a goatee. He glanced behind the family to see if Abby was with them, but they were alone.

"The Taylors haven't graced our presence in . . . how many years?"

"It hasn't been that long," Laurel laughed. "You just haven't been around."

"I've been back on Orcas for three years."

"And I've been Laurel Taylor Graham for twenty-three years." She winked at Davis, and her husband grinned back. He was at least four inches shorter than her and wore starched khakis and a polo shirt. Just what Laurel needed—a buttoned-up guy. When she was a teen her world was always falling apart.

"Mom says you serve the best Italian food in the world," Travis said as the family followed Damian to a table.

"You've never been to De Lucia's?" Damian whispered, hoping his uncle wasn't listening from the kitchen.

"Too young to remember."

"I promise you won't forget it after tonight," Damian said. "I don't know if we're the best in the world, but definitely on the West Coast."

"Is the restaurant business good on the island?" Davis asked.

"It's been good to my uncle. He's been operating this place for forty years."

Davis pulled a chair out for his wife and scooted it in behind her.

"I'm sure you're still a sailing guru," Laurel said as she took a maroon and gold menu from Damian.

"I actually sailed by your cottage yesterday."

"It's just awful, isn't it?" Laurel sniffed as she flipped through the ivory pages. "An absolute jungle."

"I keep trying to talk them into selling," Davis said. "But Laurel won't budge, and Abby won't even discuss it."

How is Abby? The question played on his tongue, but even as he rehearsed the inflections in his mind, he knew it wouldn't come out right.

"I know it's ancient, but that house is still perfect for weekends." Laurel's hand flew down on her silverware, knocking her fork on the floor. She leaned over to pick it up.

Davis opened the menu. "And that's why we're staying at a bed and breakfast this week."

Laurel ignored him. "Besides, all our family's summer memories are scrunched into that one place, and I'm purely selfish. I don't want anyone else enjoying themselves where we had so much fun."

"See what I mean?" Davis shrugged his shoulders. "Nothing I can do."

"I feel for you." Damian winked before he disappeared into the kitchen to ice three glasses. He filled them with water and placed them on a tray.

Could he casually ask about Abby? Was it even right to ask about her? After all, she was a married woman now, had been for years. Better to steer clear of that topic. Maybe they should stick to the weather.

"Who's that family out there?" Vincent asked, his forehead saturated in sweat from the kitchen heat.

"Laurel Taylor. You remember the Taylor family, right?"

"Of course I do. Laurel used to work for me." Vincent ripped off his apron and wiped his face with it. He took the tray from Damian and headed into the dining room.

"A beautiful family," Vincent said as he delicately placed each glass on the table like they were goblets of wine. "De Lucia's is a fine tradition to pass down to your kids."

Laurel laughed. "Did you know Davis proposed to me out on your porch?"

"Superb!" Vincent flung his free hand. "Dessert on the house for all of you."

Laurel thanked him, and he left for the kitchen with as much fanfare as he arrived with. Damian stepped forward, pulling a small notepad and pen from his shirt pocket.

"You ready to order?"

Davis stuck his nose into the menu as Laurel studied Damian's left hand.

"Don't tell me there's still an eligible bachelor on this island?"

Damian laughed. "And not one unattached woman left."

"An expert chef like you . . ." Laurel sipped her water.

"That's my uncle, but he's not interested in marriage."

"Well, you should try it."

"I was never in as high demand as you Taylor girls."

Davis closed his menu. "I couldn't help myself," he joked as he reached for his wife's hand. "Laurel lured me into commitment."

"Seems like both the Taylor women made good matches," Damian said.

Laurel's dark eyes erased his grin. "You don't know, do you?"

Damian shook his head, his pulse racing. *What was there to know?*

"Abby's husband died almost ten years ago from colon cancer."

He almost dropped his notepad as his hands fell to his sides. "I'm so sorry," he paused. "How is she?"

"Just fine," Laurel said quickly. Too quickly.

A hundred questions popped into his mind. *Where was Abby now? Was she the same girl? Does she still love to sail? Did she get remarried? Does she remember who I am?* But instead of asking another question, he recited the daily specials. Better to operate in auto mode.

"We've got fresh mozzarella, flown in from Italy, and homemade marinara sauce. If it's Italian, Vincent can make it for you, but I'd recommend the manicotti or eggplant parmesan."

Travis ordered plain spaghetti, Laurel decided to try the lasagna with pesto sauce, and Davis stuck with the recommended manicotti. Damian took their order to the kitchen and told the cook to rush it through. He opened the pantry door and sat on the lid of an old flour barrel.

Poor Abby. Maybe it was time for her to come home.

Chapter 7

Subtle light drifted through the windowpanes and softened the sage and cream colors in Abby's bedroom. A finch chirped at her from the windowsill, and she groaned, flicking off her alarm clock before it was supposed to ring. It was too early to get up.

Pulling her comforter to her shoulders, she propped herself up on her pillows and gazed out the tall Palladian window at the Front Range. The early sun had settled on the mountains, transforming them from a dark green into a hazy blend of pinks and oranges.

She rubbed her eyes. Scattered beside her on the queen-size bed were blue and yellow index cards, scribbled preparation for today's pitch. Working almost around-the-clock the last two days, her team had researched and planned. Then Abby took the ideas from their staff meetings, combined them into a *brilliant* proposal, and submitted it to Blanche before dinner.

Apparently Blanche hadn't thought it was quite as brilliant as the team had. She'd handed her back ten pages of scratch marks, arrows, and scrawled notes. If Abby were still in college, Blanche probably would have awarded her a solid C- or D.

Abby had finished the changes sometime after midnight and raced home to sleep a few hours before she and Blanche met with Heartsong. If the birds weren't so jovial, she could probably convince her body to sleep at least a half hour more.

Abby leaned her head back against the maple headboard. Today was May tenth—Hunter's twentieth birthday. Somewhere in the world, her son was probably preparing to celebrate this new decade of life. At least she hoped he was. A lot can happen in twenty years.

She forced herself out of bed and slipped on a pair of white socks and the satin robe looped over her bedpost. She couldn't think about Hunter right now. Today could be a red-letter day for her career, and she wasn't going to ruin it with an agonizing trip down memory lane. She needed to concentrate, focus on the carefully crafted plan she'd be communicating in a few hours. It would be her best presentation yet.

The strong aroma of Sumatra coffee floated up the stairs, and she followed it down the spiral staircase and under exposed beams and the two skylights filtering enough light to show off the stone fireplace that anchored the living room. The builders had used wood from a dilapidated Pennsylvania barn to accent the timber frame structure of the house and for the weathered hardwood across the main floor.

She turned into the kitchen and slipped a bottle of Advil out of a cupboard before filling her coffee mug. She gulped down two caplets, took a sip, and leaned back against the kitchen counter. A doe and fawn meandered through the tall grass on the back of her property, and she watched them leap over the fence and bound away.

It was the not knowing what happened to her son that hurt more than anything. If only she knew he was okay.

The twenty years had passed quickly. If she closed her eyes, she could still see the gentle folds on Hunter's neck and his long lashes that forced themselves open even when his tired body so wanted sleep. A determined little guy with a smile that melted her heart.

Abby reached for the coffee pot and spilled it on the tile floor as she tried to refill her cup. She couldn't do this today. She wouldn't.

She jolted herself with another shot of caffeine and rushed back upstairs to shower. With a quick twist, she blasted steaming water from the showerhead, and the hot stream running down her hair and shoulders cleared her mind.

She'd have to prove her worth to Blanche without stepping on her toes. She didn't like the feeling of having to compete with her boss, yet lately Blanche had ramped up the rivalry between them. It wouldn't be a small feat, but she could make both Blanche and their potential client happy today. She just couldn't predict the future if Blanche continued to lose money. Her vice president's salary would probably be the first one cut.

Abby knew it was up to her. If there was something she could do well, it was a killer pitch. She and Blanche had won eleven national accounts over the last few years by blowing away the ideas of larger agencies. They'd do it again this morning.

Abby dried her light brown hair before wrapping it behind her head and clipping it tight. She smoothed sheer black hose over her legs and dressed in a salmon blouse, a black blazer, and a matching skirt with black heels. Then she wrapped her note cards with a rubber band and threw them in her briefcase.

When she reached for her laptop, the power cord dangled onto the floor in front of her. *Oh no!* The charger was supposed to be connected to the wall, siphoning electricity all night. She couldn't remember how much power she had left—twenty or maybe thirty minutes. Not enough time for even a partial presentation on the battery.

She wound the power cord and stuffed it in her bag, followed by her laptop. She'd deal with it when she got to the meeting. Checking her watch, Abby rushed out the door to meet Blanche.

Ten minutes behind schedule, Abby rushed through the office doors and stopped. Curtis was in the lobby, dressed professionally in a gray pin-striped suit with his coal black hair slicked behind his ears.

She heaved a deep breath after her run up the stairs. "You're looking quite dapper today."

"Just trying to impress our clientele," he said with a smile.

She hesitated before asking, "Who exactly are you trying to impress?"

"Heartsong Adoptions, of course."

Abby opened her mouth, then quickly shut it. She opened it again. "Blanche didn't tell me you were going to the presentation."

"I don't tell you everything, Abby." She turned to see Blanche step from the hallway into the small lobby. "I asked Curtis to tag along. He's had the best ideas, and I'm relying on him to be able to answer any specific questions that might emerge."

"I'm prepared to answer anything," Abby said.

"I know that, but it can't hurt our pitch to have several experts in the room." Blanche turned on her heels, and they followed her out the door and to the parking garage.

What was her boss trying to prove? That Abby was still a peon in her hierarchy? That she wasn't really needed? Since when did someone with six months experience at Nulte get to pitch a potential client? This was ridiculous.

Blanche's Mercedes was in front of them, and Abby hesitated at the passenger door. Curtis stopped beside her like he expected to sit in the front seat.

You've got to be kidding! Abby met his intense stare and upped the ante with a smile. She refused to crawl into the tight back seat in her slim-fitting skirt and heels.

"Be a gentleman, Curtis." Blanche unlocked the doors with a click, and Abby opened the door. "It's bigger than it looks."

"Of course I'll do the honors," he said before slithering into the back.

Chapter 8

Damian strode across the weathered dock, its wood smothered in spongy moss and dew. A thin layer of gray hovered above the marina, but according to the weather report, the clouds would dissipate in the next hour or so with blustery winds from the east. Another good day for sailing.

"Good morning, Bob," Damian greeted a rugged man sitting at the edge of his lawn chair, a fishing pole strung off the back of his old boat and into the water.

Instead of lifting his ball cap like he did most mornings, the man sprang off his worn chair, his crusty hands reeling in the line that battled for cod or salmon. Damian shook his head and laughed, wondering what Bob ate when a fresh breakfast eluded him. Probably canned tuna or Spam.

The aromas of fresh paint, fish, and sweat stifled the cool air. Sailors rationed their fresh water, hoarding it for cooking and drinking instead of showering. Someone needed to douse the whole place with a bucket of soap and water.

Damian romanticized the sailor's life until he became a sailor himself. After two decades of traveling the waters around the world, he craved calm . . . most of the time. Sometimes he still longed for the freedom he'd lost when he returned home, but that freedom seemed as foreign to him these days as some of the harrowing journeys he'd taken when he worked for the IWC.

Now, instead of rocking to sleep at night with the waves, he returned to the cottage he'd built on the island, rinsed off the Sound's brackish spray in his hot shower, and crashed on the feathered top of his bed. Not a bad life.

Marc waited for him in the hull of the boat, a khaki outback hat covering his dark hair. "Fair day for sailing," Marc said as Damian hopped into the boat.

"I said you didn't have to be here until seven."

"Didn't have anyplace else I needed to be."

The kid was always early, raising the mainsail before Damian arrived. Damian told him almost every day that he didn't need to get there before sunrise, but Marc never listened.

"Happy birthday." Damian held out a plastic box filled with donuts. "I should have brought candles."

"I was just thinking I was hungry."

"Do you want me to sing?"

Marc laughed as he opened the box and plucked a chocolate-filled donut. "No thanks."

"It's no small feat to make it to your twenties."

Especially considering that Marc had to pull himself out of the ghetto to attend college, Damian thought. The kid wasn't given a chance in life yet he somehow managed to not only overcome his tough childhood; he thrived on it. God rescued the boy from the dark Seattle projects and brought him into Damian's life. It was ironic that Marc was the one to show Damian the light. He could only imagine how many other people Marc would introduce to Jesus Christ.

"It's delicious," Marc mumbled with a mouthful. "Thank you."

"Vincent made them for you last night, and he's also planning on having you as his guest for dinner tonight."

"I'll be there."

Damian leaned back against the hull and bit into a donut. "So what big plans do you have for year number twenty?"

Marc shrugged his shoulders. "Finish my sophomore year."

"Did you declare your major yet?"

"I'll do it in the fall. Marine biology."

"Good for you."

The kid was planning to use his passion for the water as an inroad into other cultures. He wanted to practice marine biology in a foreign country while he shared the love of Christ—a tentmaker, just like the apostle Paul, offering a needy people both his service and his faith.

"I suppose it's too much to hope that you're going to return every summer to help me."

"I'd like to."

Marc was just being nice. Damian knew his first mate would be gone after he finished college. "God has something bigger in store for you than giving island tours."

The plank groaned beside him, and Damian glanced up on the dock.

"I thought I smelled something sweet," Bob said.

Marc held up his doughnut, chocolate oozing out onto his fingers. "We've got plenty if you're hungry."

"Maybe just a bite."

"I thought you had a fish," Damian said.

"So did I."

Marc handed him the box, and Bob took one donut, flashed a quick smile, and took one more.

"What are we celebrating?" Bob asked as he finished the first donut in a single bite.

"Marc's birthday."

"You drinking age yet?"

"No, sir."

"Too bad." Bob climbed back off the boat. "Are you going in search of the whales again?"

"We'll keep searching until we find them," Damian said.

"I don't know if they're coming back this year." Bob wiped his fingers on his stained shorts. "Bad for your business."

Damian shrugged his shoulders. "We still have a great tour through the islands. Lots of seals and coves and bull kelp to show off."

Bob muttered in response as he walked away. They all knew the truth. The whales were the primary reason the tourists filled their boat each season—the suspense capturing their minds. A whale-watching business hinged on the big question of whether or not they'd see the orcas perform that day, not the playful seals or jungles of kelp.

As the chief narrator for his tours, Damian always described in glorious detail the last time they saw the whales gliding through the water.

The entire group would watch and wait. Whether or not they actually found the whales on any given trip, their passengers felt like they'd at least come close. Actually finding them was the reward for his daily game of hide-and-seek.

Damian lifted the floorboards and checked the bilge and pump. "I think we're ready."

Marc started to walk toward the bow of the boat and stopped. "I almost forgot . . ."

"What do you need?"

Marc pulled an envelope out of his pocket and flashed it toward Damian. "I'm supposed to mail it this morning."

"We've got time."

Damian didn't let Marc hear his sigh when he jumped out of the hull and rushed toward the mailbox at the end of the dock. Most parents celebrate their kids on their birthday. Instead Marc spent his twentieth birthday caring for his mom.

Chapter 9

"What's the mission of Heartsong?" Blanche asked as she sped Abby and Curtis toward the agency's main office.

"To make adoption available to both infertile couples and to pregnant women in unfortunate situations," Curtis shouted over Abby's shoulder like he was on a game show.

Blanche turned west on Alameda, and they wound through an industrial park. "How many offices do they have?"

"Sixty-seven. More than one in every state," Curtis said. "And they have the highest success rate of adoptions in the country."

"Very good. How many adoptions do they coordinate each year?"

Abby looked out the window as her boss continued to quiz them like they were in grade school. Why did she let Curtis tag along? It had always been the two of them, she and Blanche, flying off to New York or Los Angeles, or simply driving across Denver like today. They'd been a dynamic team, winning over clients by promising them personal attention and fast results, something the bigger agencies couldn't always do. Now their dynamic team had a sleazy sidekick trying to usurp their campaign.

Blanche drove onto Heartsong's crowded parking lot. The manicured lawn beside the silver building contrasted with the crumpling warehouses on both sides of the property. Pink and white petunias huddled together at the base of the office, and the downtown skyline reflected in the building's six stories of glass.

Abby grabbed her leather briefcase and climbed out of the car. The three of them crossed a wooden bridge and entered Heartsong's airy atrium, decorated with waxy trees and potted plants. A well-dressed but imposing man with dark hair and skin greeted them near the glass door. She bet people always listened to what this guy said.

"You must be from Nulte P.R." He extended his hand toward Abby, and Blanche reached over to shake it. "I'm Harold Rogers, the new president of Heartsong."

"It's our pleasure," Blanche said, still shaking his hand. "I'm Blanche Nulte, and these are two of my associates, Curtis Parks and Abby Taylor Wagner."

"We're looking forward to your pitch," Harold directed them to the open staircase in front of them. "The team's upstairs."

They followed him into a stuffy conference room on the second floor. Crammed around the plain white table were eight men and women who immediately stopped chattering when Harold entered.

As Harold introduced the management team, Abby placed her laptop and mobile projector on the table and scanned the wall for an outlet. None by the table. If only she'd checked the charger on her laptop last night before she fell asleep.

It was a small room. She didn't need the projector to show the team their slides, but she definitely needed her computer. She started her laptop—only fifteen minutes of power remaining. It would die long before she finished their PowerPoint presentation.

She looked to her immediate left. Nothing there. As she smiled confidently at the group in front of her, adrenaline shot through her veins. She would figure this out. Blanche's introduction should last a good five minutes, and she could stall a bit more if necessary.

Blanche started the pitch, briefly covering Nulte P.R.'s history and successes and explaining that they were the right agency to make Heartsong succeed. Abby had heard the spiel a hundred times.

"Excuse me," she whispered. Two men scooted in their chairs and she slid behind them, but the wall was bare.

"With the precision of our targets and direction of our proposed campaign, we believe Nulte P.R. will catapult Heartsong into a household name," Blanche explained to the group.

Abby only had two minutes left before Blanche expected her to move

seamlessly into the PowerPoint presentation. Curtis motioned to her from the other side of the room and pointed toward the wall.

Curtis Parks to the rescue.

She clenched her fists and then released them as she ducked gracefully in front of Blanche to cross the room. She should be grateful for Curtis's help, but she didn't need him to be her hero. His intentions were far from pure.

Well, at least she had an outlet. She quickly plugged in the projector and her computer.

"And now, our vice president, Abby Wagner, is going to demonstrate how we'll help you take Heartsong to the next level," Blanche said in perfect time. She folded her arms and leaned back against the wall.

Abby stepped to the front of the room to begin her speech, flipped on the projector, and clicked her mouse. She almost sighed in relief when the title slide appeared on the blank wall.

"Heartsong has excelled as an adoption agency—simplifying the process so more couples can adopt newborn babies as well as helping birth mothers reach the decision to give their child up for adoption."

Abby made firm eye contact with Harold and his team. "We plan to springboard from Heartsong's extraordinary reputation and develop a campaign that will demonstrate not only Heartsong's strong history and successes, but your ability to implement this knowledge and expertise to adoption today.

"There are many reasons why infertile couples don't pursue adoption." She clicked the mouse and a list of bullet points flew onto the wall. "They're often worried that they won't bond with an adopted child like they would their biological baby. The mounds of paperwork and legalities are expensive and intimidating. And they're also afraid that the birth mother will change her mind, and they won't be able to handle the emotional anguish of giving back their child."

Abby breathed deeply as she changed the slide. Actors and politicians buried their true emotions when they spoke to the public. She could do the same.

"We've all heard the horror stories of failed adoptions, but as you know, these stories have usually been exaggerated along the grapevine or the media is only reporting half the story. Most adoptions are successful, and we plan to position Heartsong as the premier adoption agency for information and success."

Abby glanced over at Blanche, ready for her to jump into the pitch, but Blanche let Abby's words resonate a moment before she picked up the speech.

"Over the next six months, we will establish a grassroots campaign by utilizing the stories of adoptive couples in top markets like New York, Dallas, Chicago, and Denver," Blanche said. "We'll help them learn to communicate their personal story, focusing on the reasons why they're thrilled they chose Heartsong, and then we'll use these couples to conduct educational seminars and do media interviews. They'll be able to answer the tough questions while encouraging other couples to adopt."

Abby clicked to the next slide as Blanche continued speaking. A family of six smiled back at the audience—their children a cultural mix of Hispanic, Caucasian, and African American.

"We believe if we can take the fear out of the process, we can be a part of creating hundreds of new families across the country, and children will find a loving home with parents that adore them. We want the country to know that Heartsong treasures these children and these families. You are the avenue to adoption, and you help couples maneuver every unexpected turn and detour along the way. We need to communicate that you will be there for them no matter what."

Abby reached into her briefcase and removed a stack of bound proposals. She handed them to Curtis, ignoring his passing glare as he crunched the materials between his fingers before distributing them around the table.

"We have developed a detailed plan," Abby continued, "of exactly how to update Heartsong's image across the country, and as a result, bring not only new couples to you but birth mothers as well."

Plastic covers crackled as the team opened the proposals in unison and skimmed the cover page. She couldn't afford to lose them yet.

"As part of this campaign, we want to use every form of media to communicate your message. We will develop public service announcements for radio stations, image advertising for selected publications,

Web-based articles directing readers back to the updated Heartsong site, and a grand reunion of Heartsong's adopted families at Central Park in New York City. We're confident that the national morning shows will want to cover this amazing event as a top feature story."

Abby took a deep breath. The finish line was closing in.

She highlighted the major details of the costs and the markets they would target. She mentioned the shows they would pitch and the numbers they'd calculated about the potential reach of this massive campaign. A few heads nodded in her small audience. They were listening and understanding. She motioned to Blanche to bring the pitch home.

"At Nulte P.R., we are devoted to working for you and your campaign," Blanche's voice intensified for the finale. "We know we're not in New York, and frankly, we like it that way. We can give you something no other agency can give you—personal, undivided, expert attention.

"While we have a wonderful team of people working with us, Abby and I will answer your questions personally, and we will personally guarantee you results."

Abby hated it when Blanche used the line. They usually delivered on their promises, but there was never any guarantee in the unpredictable world of public relations. She'd learned early—you never make assumptions when you're convincing the public through messages and media instead of buying advertising or other promotions. They could deliver on a solid plan, but there was never any certainty about the results.

"Any questions?" Abby shut the lid on her laptop as hands sprung up around the room. She pointed toward a woman in the back.

"Our company has spent the past forty years building a reputation that I'm not convinced we want to change." The woman took off her glasses. "I'm not arguing against using new ideas and new media. I'm just curious as to why we need a different image when we've already proven we can excel with the image we have."

Abby glanced over at Blanche, who nodded for her to take the question. No one had told her management wasn't onboard with the idea of updating Heartsong's image. If that was the case, they needed to do more than beat other agency pitches. They needed to gently but firmly convince the Heartsong team that they needed a makeover. But who wants to hear that they look bad?

"You're absolutely right. Heartsong does have a stellar reputation." Abby paused as she configured her response. "It's just that with so many new agencies vying to place kids for adoption, Heartsong needs to have more than a solid history. We need to demonstrate that you have a phenomenal future as well. We want people to know that Heartsong can relate just as well to people today as they've done for forty years and will do for forty more.

"Next question?" she asked, pointing toward Harold.

"I wish we could promise a hundred percent success rate with our adoptions," the CEO said, "but unfortunately, we can't. What do we say about the birth parents who've changed their minds and taken the children back?"

What do you say? Abby wanted to ask. She'd really like to know.

What would they say to a mother who adored her baby boy, who fell instantly in love and cared for him like her own son? What would they say to her heart that had been yanked out of her chest when they pulled him out of her arms?

They'd told her that Stacie was certain; that they'd done everything they could to ensure the adoption would move forward. They'd let her fall in love with Hunter, develop a bond that could never be broken. How could they have lied to her? How was she supposed to stand here and act like nothing had gone wrong?

"Ms. Wagner?" Harold asked.

Abby blinked and glanced around the room. Everyone was staring at her. Waiting for her response.

"I'm sorry," she said. "Could you repeat that question?"

"That's not necessary," Curtis said, sliding in next to her.

What was Curtis doing? She started to say something, but held her tongue when she caught Blanche's glare.

"Of course we'll be honest about not being able to guarantee the success of every adoption, but we won't dwell on it," Curtis explained. "We'll say that Heartsong counsels every birth mother and gives her all of her options before she decides on adoption, and then you counsel her until the process is complete so she knows she made the right decision.

"Heartsong can't guarantee a birth mother won't change her mind, but we'll explain clearly that Heartsong does everything possible to ensure a birth mother only proceeds with adoption after she determines she's ready."

Harold nodded his head and made a note. "I want to be clear. Heartsong certainly needs exposure, but our primary goal is to make adoption a viable option for both infertile couples and birth mothers who are in difficult situations, not to become media hounds."

"We want to take the mystery out of the adoption process, but we also have a tight line to walk as we balance our relationships with both adoptive parents and the birth parents."

"We couldn't agree more . . ."

"Our job is to communicate your vision, Harold." Abby cut Curtis off. She didn't care what Blanche said; she wasn't going to let Curtis steal her show.

"We will take that vision and use every possible means to share it with your target audience. We're on your team."

A few more hands went up, and Abby managed to answer each question succinctly before Harold called a wrap.

"You've obviously done your homework," Harold told Blanche. "We've already heard pitches from several firms, but we're really hoping to use a local agency. If you could give us a few days to review all of the materials and budgets we've received, we'll call you with a definite answer."

"Absolutely," Blanche said as she shook his hand. "We'd be honored to work with your team."

The drive back to their office was unbearably quiet, Abby silently counting the telephone poles that lined the road. When they pulled into the parking lot, Curtis hopped out and rushed to open the elevator door.

"I'm sorry if I seemed distracted," she whispered to Blanche before they got in the elevator. "I just lost my focus for a moment."

"Go home, Abby."

"Excuse me?"

"Go home and find your brain. See a doctor or something if you need to, but don't come back to the office until Monday."

She'd seen a doctor years before, but the medication they gave her made her feel foggy, confused. "I don't need a doctor."

"Whatever," Blanche said before she stepped into the elevator. "And while you're at home, you'd better ask your God to give us this job."

Abby nodded her head as she turned back toward the parking lot, but she didn't tell her the truth. She'd stopped praying a long time ago.

Chapter 10

Abby raced down I-25 in her Navigator, the city's malls and industrial centers blurring by her. She may have escaped the office, but the onslaught of memories mocked her resolve. If only there was a pill she could take, a memory eraser that would make it all disappear. Nothing the doctors gave her made the pain stay away for good.

Minutes outside the city, Abby exited the interstate at Surrey Ridge and wove west. As she steered her SUV up a pine-covered butte, she reprimanded herself over and over for being distracted. Harold had asked a simple question. How hard was it to give him a simple answer?

Just stay in the game.

Blanche probably thought that her only vice president was on the verge of a nervous breakdown. She wasn't losing it . . . was she? What was wrong with her?

Turning left into her steep driveway, she passed two acres of scrubby oak trees, piñon pines, and golden grasses before she reached her home. Ten years ago she'd created this retreat, a mixture of dusty-colored stucco, river stone, and worn timber. The rounded mountains of the Front Range sloped just a mile or so in front of the house, jagged white peaks jutting up in the distance. With the surrounding hills and trees, she couldn't even see the city lights at night.

Abby shut off her truck, bolted into the house, and rushed back up the spiral stairs. She flew past the maple walls lined with classic books and into the master suite, tossing her briefcase onto the bed and throwing her pantyhose, suit, and silk blouse on top. The dry cleaner could deal with the wrinkled mess later. She eyed the novel on her nightstand, but even if she tried to immerse herself back into the story, she wouldn't be able to concentrate on a word.

She needed to hit the trail.

Pulling on cotton shorts and a navy T-shirt, she tied her running shoes and jogged back down the stairs, out the front door, and onto the wooded path that lined her property. Fresh air, a clear mind . . . a place to escape.

Stomping the crisp needles that covered the trail, Abby tried to control the thoughts swarming through her mind. She just needed to run faster, harder. Surely the memories, the anger, the pain would disappear. She'd make it disappear.

She ran past her neighbor's decaying barn and fence and tried to think about preserving Colorado's mining towns. The *Good Morning America* show she'd arranged for their client would lead to other national media, newspaper stories, and magazine features.

Once she pushed the ball forward, it would roll and roll until the entire country knew about their cause. The exposure would pressure government officials to act, and they'd be fighting on several levels to save a bit of America's history and heritage. The client would be pleased, and Abby could hang another plaque or two on her office wall.

Helping a client should be her top priority, but she couldn't focus right now.

Where was her little boy? Was he living in poverty? Was he being loved? Was he even still alive?

Year after year the questions persisted, driving her crazy. You'd think after all this time it would just go away, but she couldn't bear to think of him living in a loveless home when she loved him so much. Today he turned twenty—a young man.

She had wanted to celebrate his high school graduation, his first date, his flight to college. She longed to be the one to wrap her arms around him when he was hurting and tell him his mom would always be there. No one could possibly take care of him as well as she had, especially not a sixteen-year-old girl.

Hot tears poured down her cheeks as the sun bore down on her. She coughed to dampen her crusty throat and clenched her trembling fingers. She wanted to punch something—hit and hit until her own anger subsided. Until the shaking stopped.

The back of her hand erased the tears cascading down her cheeks. This was ridiculous. She could usually suppress her emotions like a pro. She would not let her bitterness destroy her or her career. She'd worked too hard to put a lock and key on the past and move ahead.

As she pushed herself ahead on the trail, she actually considered asking God to take her anger, heal her pain. But she'd prayed so often and so hard in the past, and He never listened. Her words seemed to evaporate before they reached the Lord's ears.

Abby ran for three more miles until her muscles demanded a break. With the sun edging over the mountains, she rushed home to her kitchen and gulped down a glass of water. Collapsing onto a kitchen chair, she gazed out the wall of windows to the endless mountain view.

No one had understood why she couldn't let go of Hunter, but they couldn't possibly comprehend what she'd been feeling. She may not have carried him in her womb for nine months, but she'd held him in her arms for four entire months before he was ripped away. He was her son.

When Scott told her that God had a plan for their lives and for Hunter's, she blasted her optimistic husband with the truth. What if God didn't have a plan? What if He wasn't in control? She'd decided then that if God wasn't going to direct her life in a loving way, she would take back control. She'd never let it go again.

Chapter 11

Damian muddled through a stack of paperwork inside the musty boat-house that doubled as his summer office. Docked outside the window was his other office, a fifty-two-foot tour boat with a canopy that covered the back deck, an open front deck, and enough seats to escort forty-five passengers on four-hour weekend excursions. He hoped the tours would turn into seven days a week when the whales returned.

When he decided to leave Seattle three years ago, he purchased Orcas Island Expeditions from Kendall Blake, a high school friend who retired after thirty years of touring Puget Sound. The only reason Damian had stayed in Seattle for so long was because of Christina. When they broke up, he moved back to Orcas Island. Home. The tour company allowed Damian to cruise the waters by day and sleep in the same bed at night. An ideal life, he'd decided. Fifteen years globetrotting followed by a decade of stifling office confinement had culminated in this perfect job.

But when they opened for business this past weekend, it hadn't been good.

The phone rang beside him, and Damian propped the handle against his ear.

"Hello," he said as he tallied the weekend numbers. They were 30 percent lower than normal . . . no surprises here. People weren't as inclined to go whale watching when there weren't any whales to see.

"This is Frank Slater from the *Seattle Times*." The man spouted the words like he had a hundred other things he'd rather be doing than talking to Damian.

"You're up awfully early," Damian said as he checked his watch. It wasn't even eight yet.

"I'm doing a short story on the whale you found beached on Shaw

Island, and I wanted to see if I could get a quick comment or two from you."

"You really should talk to Dr. Neven," Damian said as he punched another set of numbers into his calculator.

"I already talked to him."

"Good. He specializes in marine toxicology, so he should be able to answer your questions."

"The whale's PCB levels checked out high," Frank pressed. "Seems like she might have died from pollution out at sea."

"That makes sense." Damian studied the Excel chart in front of him. Could they make it an entire season without the whales?

"Aren't you worried about the pollution?"

"Of course I am. The levels have been high for thirty years."

"What will happen if the water doesn't get cleaned up?"

"Didn't you ask Kyle these questions?"

"I'd like to get your opinion as well."

Damian sighed. "If it doesn't get cleaned up, even more of our sea life will die from contamination."

"You're a former marine biologist, aren't you?" Frank asked.

"Technically I'm still a marine biologist—at least, that's what my degree says."

"But you're guiding a tour boat instead of practicing biology, aren't you?"

"I'm a boat captain and an educator, but I don't understand how that has any bearing on your story."

"Just curious," Frank raced through his words like he'd already missed his deadline. "You used to work for the International Whaling Commission, didn't you?"

"You've done your homework."

"My homework tells me that you used to kill whales, so I'm trying to figure out why all the sudden you're interested in saving them."

Damian slammed his fist against the desk, scattering papers on the floor. "I never killed a whale in my life."

"But you helped kill them."

"I made sure that whale hunters didn't kill too many."

"Interesting career."

"Any more questions about the orcas?"

"Have you studied the local pollutants, or are you just guessing the PCB levels are high?"

Damian glared out a cracked window at the Sound. How dare this guy question his credentials? Evidence of toxic chemicals in the Sound was fact. He didn't care where the pollution came from—legal sewage, illegal dumps, or one of the many factories dotting the coast. He just wanted it treated properly so the PCB toxins wouldn't spread through the water and kill all of their sea life. A decent reporter should be able to find out who was contaminating their water.

He was barely sounding an alarm for the orcas, but the reporter was right. Even if he had spent most of his life defending sea life and regulating whale hunting, no one would sympathize with someone previously involved with the whale industry. They needed a lifelong environmentalist to triumph this cause to the national press.

"Information about these toxic chemicals is public record," Damian spat. "Maybe you need to do a little undercover work and find out what isn't public. I'd look on the coast of Washington. Pageant Industries for a start."

"Are you saying Pageant Industries is doing something illegal?" Frank asked.

"I'm not accusing anyone," Damian insisted, "but the orcas seem to be dying out, and I'd suggest that you stop questioning me and ask someone who knows why."

"Got it." Frank actually sounded pleased.

Damian slammed down the phone.

Chapter 12

On Monday morning, Abby left for work before the sun came up. She couldn't stand the thought of spending one more minute at home alone. She'd called Jessica three times over the weekend until her daughter had told her she had to study for finals. She glanced at her calendar. In seven more days, Jessica would be home.

Her office phone rang at 8:30 AM, and Abby jumped, shoving aside the press release she'd proofed four times.

"It's the producer at *Good Morning America*," Maggie announced over the speakerphone. "Returning your call."

She let out a moan. She wasn't in the mood for a fight, but she didn't have a choice. The *GMA* producer had e-mailed her late Friday, stating simply that they had decided to cut one of the segments they'd coordinated for Western Mining Preservation. She'd written that Ted Zant only needed to be prepared to talk for one segment instead of two.

Abby didn't have the nerve to tell Blanche about the change. Instead of facing her boss's wrath, she decided to try to convince the morning show that they needed two segments to tell the story.

"Hey, Gloria," Abby forced a casual tone. She didn't want the producer to sense her desperation even if she was wearing it on her sleeve. She'd beg if she had to. At least she could tell Blanche she'd done everything she could.

"Just got your e-mail about cutting Ted's interview, and I totally understand," she breezed through her prepared speech.

"Glad to hear that," Gloria replied. Abby heard her typing on a keyboard.

"The thing is we've been able to acquire some great footage from several mining towns across the state," Abby continued. "This story is really heating up, you know. We've got an entire group of people wanting to tear down these remarkable pieces of our history and replace them with expensive real estate. You've got it all—a great story, a little scandal, and killer footage."

"We couldn't agree more, Abby, but my boss thinks we can cover this story adequately in about three minutes. Your client will have his say, we'll show a few clips of your footage, and then we'll get some feedback from the other side."

No one had told her there would be opposition. This was supposed to be a friendly feature on America's dying towns. Were they planning to surprise Ted with this confrontation on air? Their media trainer needed to prepare him for a fight.

"In that case," Abby proposed, "you might want to have a lively debate between Ted and the opposition. Maybe Ted can tell the stories of a few of these towns in the first segment and then debate the importance of preserving these structures in the second."

"We'll consider it, Abby, but I can't make any promises. Why don't you tell Mr. Zant to be prepared for the two segments, one of those being a debate, but if we have hot news, I'll have to cut it short."

"Fair enough."

Abby hung up the phone. There was nothing else she could do. Of course they'd have urgent news. There was always a story to be told. At least the producer had hinted at doing two segments. She'd just have to make an excuse to Ted when his interview was sliced in half.

She blitzed off a message to their media trainer, Marcia, to prepare Ted for a debate.

The downside of this business was the lack of control. She could persuade, charm, and explain why she thought the morning show should do a longer segment, but she certainly couldn't force them to listen. On days like these, she wished she'd chosen advertising for a career. If she paid for the time, her message would definitely air. In the publicity business, there were no guarantees.

Returning her attention to the press release in front of her, she crossed out an entire quote filled with words like "exceptional," "amazing," and

"superb." This type of hype should've been squelched in Public Relations 101.

The exuberant writing was her fault; she'd assigned the release to a junior staff member instead of to Curtis. Purely vindictive, she knew, and extremely juvenile, but right now, she planned to avoid Mr. Parks at all costs. If she kept ignoring him, maybe he'd go away . . .

She rolled her eyes at herself as she jotted a note in the margin. Maybe she should just go to the principal's office and have the kid expelled.

Blanche swept into her office, and Abby jumped when her boss clapped twice.

"We got it!" Blanche slid into a chair. "Harold just faxed over the contract."

Abby tried to muster enthusiasm. "Fantastic. When do we start?"

"Right away," Blanche answered. "They love the idea of a reunion of their adoptive families in Central Park, and Labor Day weekend would be ideal."

Abby silently calculated the deadlines. It would be tight but . . . "We've got three months to pull this off."

"Think you can do it?"

Abby ignored the not-so-hidden doubt in her question. Of course she could do it.

"The impossible makes this job fun," she replied as she scribbled down the dates.

This would be huge. Lots of work ahead, but the pay-off would be amazing. Not to mention the job security.

Blanche stood up and leaned across Abby's desk. Abby met her eye.

"We've set their expectations high."

"We'll get results, Blanche." Abby glanced at the stack of press releases she needed to edit. She'd finish those at home. "I'll move the team into action right now."

"Good." Blanche turned toward the door and stopped, turning her head back toward Abby. "And I want Curtis to be the lead strategist on this campaign with you."

Abby hesitated. "Don't you think it'll be too much to have two people in charge?"

"Oh, don't you worry." Abby shivered at Blanche's crass laugh. "You're still in charge. I just want Curtis to be your right hand man."

"No problem."

"Didn't think it would be." Blanche backed out. "Let's meet this afternoon to see where we're at."

Maggie called together the team, and within minutes two publicists, three coordinators, and her director of media crowded into her office, bright coffee mugs and yellow legal pads in their hands.

Three of them were young, just a few years out of college and filled with youthful enthusiasm for their jobs. She had two middle-aged employees who'd lost their excitement for the business, but knew exactly how to run a smooth campaign.

And then there was Curtis Parks. She didn't know his exact age, but he seemed to fall in between the two categories. He knew what he was doing yet he was still excited about his job . . . a little too excited.

"Good news," Abby began. "Heartsong has given us the thumbs up for their campaign and now it's time for us to run with it."

Applause.

"Janie, I want you to develop media lists both nationally and in the top thirty markets for interviews."

The publicist nodded to her as she made notes.

"Marcia, we're going to need to train thirty adoptive couples to do media in these markets. Some of this you'll obviously want to freelance, but I want you to develop the questions and oversee their training. It's huge, I know, but you're more than capable of managing it."

"When will I have the names of these couples?" Marcia asked.

"Call Harold Rogers's assistant at Heartsong and tell her you need the list in two weeks. Three max."

"Got it."

"And, Dustin," she continued, "I want you to start working on the logistics of coordinating a national event in Central Park over Labor Day weekend. Plan on going to New York in the next week or two to meet with city officials and get this ball rolling."

She smiled as she watched Dustin try to stifle a grin. He was perfect for this assignment—the kid had conquered the Big Apple on multiple

weekend getaways, and the place didn't intimidate him like it did some of her team. She had complete confidence in his ability to get this mammoth task done.

"How much can I spend?" he asked.

"Think big," she replied, "and then give me the budget. We've got a healthy retainer from Heartsong, and they're expecting to spend a lot on this reunion. I'll present the plan to them, and we can trim it from there."

Blanche would expect her to spend the retainer and pour on hundreds of billable hours after that. With the extent of this campaign, she had no doubt the thick invoices to Heartsong would meet her boss's approval.

"I will have a bulleted draft of our talking points and media hooks by tomorrow. In the meantime, let me know if you have any questions."

Her e-mail box would be full of questions by day's end.

"Curtis, can you stay so we can discuss the press kit?" she asked.

"You bet."

The team marched out of her office like soldiers ready to level the enemy. She knew they'd work around the clock to complete their tasks. They'd fought hard to win their competitive jobs and weren't about to let them slide away.

Curtis pulled his chair close to her desk and set his leather-bound portfolio on top. As he opened it, Abby eyed him warily. She knew she had to call a truce in her mind to make this work. They needed to partner together to move ahead, and, as the senior employee, it was her responsibility to take the initiative to meet him in the middle.

"I need you to outline the components for a press kit," she said.

"Already done." He slid a typed outline across her desk.

"But how did you . . ."

"It pays to be prepared," he said. "Before we send out a kit, though, I want to put a release about the new relationship with Nulte P.R. and Heartsong on Business Wire."

"Good." She checked the item off her list.

"And then follow it up with a release about updating Heartsong's image."

"Hmm," she started. "Not so good. I think I want to be a bit more covert about this image campaign. We need to just do it instead of announce it."

"But this would be good publicity for us as well as our client." He didn't blink as he stared her down.

Only one dog, she decided, could be the leader of this pack.

"I understand that, Curtis, I just think we may ruin a few media opportunities if we concentrate on the image campaign. We need to focus on the great news angles instead."

"Okay, what exactly are the great news angles?" he asked.

"First of all, adoption is a pertinent topic right now." She glanced down at her notes. "There are almost two million adopted kids in the U.S., and as more couples wait until later in life to have children, some are choosing adoption when they can't get pregnant. People are talking about it. Popular television shows are featuring it. The topic's already out there, we just need to expand on it."

"That's great, but passé," Curtis said. "I need something flaming hot to make this work."

Hot, Abby scribbled on her notepad and then flooded her page with raging flames.

"You must have something in mind," she said, flinging him the bait.

"Let's do something no one ever talks about." He eased closer to her desk, his intent gaze focused and his words strong. "Let's do the research and figure out how many adoptions don't work, and then compare those numbers with the successes of Heartsong. Just think of the human angle of this story. The anguish that these couples have experienced would slice the hearts of television viewers. We could play it out for weeks, maybe months."

Abby's fingers shook, and she clutched the top of her desk. She'd slice the heart out of him if he had a heart.

"That's so much more than we signed up for," she said. "The research could take years, and the stats will be different in every state. Birth mothers have to relinquish their rights in twenty-four hours in some states, while others get to drag the process along for months. The research won't be accurate or consistent."

"I disagree," Curtis said. "We can compile a solid average and

really hit this angle hard. Maybe we can do more than just publicize Heartsong. Maybe we can position them as being the vanguard of adoption reform."

Abby sighed. It was like trying to explain addition to a child.

"That is not what we told them we would do. If you remember correctly, they don't want to reform adoption. They want to offer it as an option for both couples and birth parents. That's what we need to focus on."

"It's a great angle, Abby."

"Maybe it is, but it's not what we're pitching. Go back to the drawing board and brainstorm some hot ideas that will actually work."

"This will work."

"Let's meet again tomorrow morning," she clipped, the meeting done. "And plan on bringing some viable options with you."

He mumbled an obscenity as he rushed out the door.

Chapter 13

Jessica lugged a duffel bag out of her ruby red Honda CR-V and threw it on the cold cement floor behind their home's third garage door. She tugged on a desk lamp, its cord draped over the back seat and looped under the front. Propping the lamp under her arm, she reached for a stack of books and carried them into the garage, haphazardly tossing both the books and the lamp onto the heaping pile.

Clothes, pillows, and random shoes were strewn across the dusty interior of her car. She'd ditched the concept of neat packing and dumped all her belongings inside when she left her dorm an hour and a half ago. Most of it she'd probably throw away by the end of the summer anyway. It was useless college stuff.

Two weeks had passed since she and Brett broke up, and he hadn't even called her once. Six months of her life stolen from her. An entire school year wasted.

She packed an armful of clothes against her chest and deposited them inside the house on the couch. Then she walked back to her car for another load.

She'd never once questioned Brett's dedication to swimming, nor would she have if their relationship had continued. It wasn't his concentration on the sport that had pulled them apart. True love, she'd decided, should inspire a couple to focus on their own dreams, and the pursuit of their individual dreams should bind them together, not rip them apart. The trouble with her and Brett was that she hadn't discovered her dreams while he had a sheer determination to win Olympic gold.

Jessica nudged the last box out of the hatch, shoved it into the two feet of remaining open floor space, and sat down on the rough set of stairs leading into the house. That was it. Her entire freshman year stacked into the corner of the garage.

She clutched her knees to her chest, waiting with the garage door open for her mom to come home from work.

She didn't really miss Brett. She'd enjoyed his attention during the first few months they'd dated, but now that they'd broken up, she felt relieved. Confident was what she was. She felt confident that God had a real plan for her life even if she wasn't sure what it was. It appeared that His will for her life didn't involve Brett Anderson, and she was okay with that.

A blurry trail of dust weaved up the long driveway, and her mother pulled her Navigator into the garage.

Abby jumped out of the SUV. "Welcome home," she said as she enveloped her in a hug. "I didn't think you'd be home for another hour."

"I was pretty ready to come home."

Abby hugged her daughter again and let go. "Let's go celebrate in style."

"I'd rather stay home and celebrate in sweats and a T-shirt," Jessica replied as she followed her mom through the tiled mudroom and into the kitchen.

"Sounds like a great plan," Abby agreed, pouring two cold glasses of lemonade and setting them on the taupe marbled counter.

They both grabbed their drinks and walked into the great room. Jessica shoved aside her stack of clothes before collapsing on the couch and stretching her arms over her head. Abby sat in the leather upright.

"Were finals as bad as I remember?" Abby asked.

"It may be months before I recover." Jessica flung the back of her hand to her forehead in mock dismay. "At least without Brett around, I had plenty of extra time to study."

"Good riddance is what I say. That boy was never good enough for you anyway."

"There isn't a guy alive that you think is good enough for me . . ."

Her first real boyfriend hadn't had enough ambition. The basketball player she dated in high school was too snobby and rich and, according to her mom, liked the sport of womanizing more than he liked basketball. Then, big surprise, her senior prom date didn't meet her mother's fashion standards. He'd fled after her mother's comment on his poor taste in evening attire.

She'd yet to date a guy who met her mother's approval, and she'd yet to meet a guy who would put up with her mother's cool edge.

"Won't you miss college life over the summer?" Abby asked, ignoring her daughter's words.

"I don't think so."

"Surely you'll miss your roommates just a bit."

Jessica shrugged her shoulders in response. Her dorm had been a place to live; she spent most of her time hanging out with either Brett or her girlfriends.

"Well, you'll be ready to go back to school after a long summer hanging out with me."

Jessica elbowed herself up on the cushions and planted her socks on the hardwood floor.

"I'm not planning on returning to school."

Abby positioned a coaster on the coffee table in front of her and set her lemonade down. "You've always wanted to go to college."

Jessica sucked a piece of ice out of her glass and crunched down on it. She could feel the heat rising, and she prepared herself for the volcanic eruption—her mom was about to blow.

"I hate to dash your dreams, Mom, but you're actually the one who wanted me to attend college and then pretended it was my idea," Jessica said.

"But you love to study."

"Hardly, Mom. I love to be on the water."

Abby's voice brightened. "Well, I guess we've got all summer to think about it."

Jessica crunched her ice louder. This discussion was about to get even hotter.

"Why don't we go back to Orcas Island this year?"

"We don't have time to go to Washington," Abby said.

"You always say we don't have time to go home, but this summer is perfect."

"Why don't we take a trip to North Carolina in July? We can hang out at the beach for a few days."

"I won't be here in July," Jessica stated simply.

Abby bit her lip. "Are you planning to run away?"

"I'm serious about Orcas, Mom."

"We're not going."

"You may not be going, but my flight to Seattle is next week."

"What?" She looked stunned.

"I'm going to spend my summer on Orcas Island doing what I love. I can't hide out here any more."

"Are you kidding me?"

"I may have been only eleven when we moved to Colorado, but I remember Grandpa and Grandma begging us to stay in Seattle. You ran away from home and took me with you."

"You don't know what you're saying."

"Then tell me, Mom. Tell me what happened before we moved."

Abby turned to look out the window instead of meeting her eye. "How are you going to pay for your vacation?"

"From the dream fund that Dad left in my name. He said I could use it anyway I like, and I want to go to Orcas."

"You're abandoning me?"

"Hardly. I'm just going for a few months, not the rest of my life. It's in my blood, Mom, just like it was in Dad's veins. He would have wanted me to do this."

Jessica stared out the wall of windows, at the prickly crests of pine trees rising above the porch, as she waited for her mom to answer.

"Have you called your aunt?" Abby asked.

"Of course not. I was going to tell you first, and then see if you'd ask Aunt Laurel if I could use the cottage."

"This is a horrible idea." Abby shook her head as she swept her lemonade glass off the coffee table and turned toward the kitchen.

"Why don't you go with me for a few weeks?" Jessica prodded. "We could enjoy the island together."

Abby refused to meet her eyes. "There's no way I can support this," she managed. "You'll have to call Laurel yourself."

Jessica punched the pillow beside her. "Fine, Mom, whatever. I don't get this. I want to, but I don't."

Chapter 14

Abby clicked on the button to check her e-mail again. It had only been five minutes since she'd checked it, but she couldn't wait. Surely she had a response by now. The clock on her computer screen spun slowly as she distracted herself by skimming through the press kit Curtis had written.

When the clock timed out, she glanced at her inbox. Nothing.

She clicked open the carefully constructed message she'd e-mailed yesterday to a staff writer at *USA Today*. An exclusive story is what she'd offered if he'd respond in twenty-four hours . . . but he hadn't written back yet. Ten more minutes and she'd call and explain her proposal via phone.

Only a week into this project and she was already pitching the national press.

Abby leaned back in her chair. *I'm going to spend my summer on Orcas Island.* Jessica's words rang in her head. How could her daughter betray her?

Jessica knew Abby would never set foot on Orcas Island again. There were so many beautiful beaches on the East Coast they could visit together—why go back to that awful place?

Abby's office door opened, and she braced herself for Blanche's onslaught. Maggie entered instead.

Her assistant eased into a leather chair. "So . . . did Jessica come home last night?"

"Yes." Abby wouldn't meet her gaze.

"What exciting things do you two girls have planned for the summer?"

Abby's eyes didn't move from their focus on the computer screen.

"Jessica's decided that she wants to go to Washington State this summer and play in Puget Sound."

"How fun!"

"By herself," Abby moaned.

"That's what children are supposed to do, hon. Grow up and fly away."

Abby punched a few words on her keyboard. "She's too young to fly away."

"Heavens, Abby, your little girl is nineteen. You're supposed to encourage her to pursue her dreams so she remembers to fly back to the roost for Christmas. If you're lucky, she'll come home an occasional July Fourth or Labor Day too."

Abby watched Maggie stand up and march back out the door. Her assistant may be fifteen years older than her, but that didn't mean she was wiser. Jessica was way too young to be out on her own.

She rechecked her e-mail and a note popped up from Gloria at *Good Morning America*. Ted Zant's interview was confirmed for Friday. At least one thing was going right today.

She flipped through Heartsong's bulging file. After days of deliberation, she and Curtis had reached a compromise about the angle of the Heartsong pitches. They decided to focus first on the successful adoption stories of Heartsong—the stories of families who'd adopted fifteen or more years ago. They'd discuss a hotter angle if this conservative one failed, but failure wasn't an option for Abby. If she couldn't turn this angle into a successful campaign, Curtis won.

She armed herself with statistics that triumphed the positive aspects of adoption—more than twenty thousand infants were placed in the U.S. last year, studies showed that adopted children were just as well adjusted as non-adoptees, and adoptions were up in some cities by 25 percent over the past year. Solid numbers for her to pitch. The kind of data that would sit well with the mainstream press.

With Harold's help, Abby had handpicked six couples around the country who'd parented talented, successful adoptees. One of the adoptees featured in their media pitches was a Rhodes Scholar at the University of Oxford and another was crowned Miss Tennessee last year.

Abby uncovered a story about a twelve-year-old girl who had a recurring role in an off-Broadway show and another of a nine-year-old boy who'd spelled his way into the national bee.

Abby had pitched a few key media—offering a story before the masses received a kit. Her *USA Today* pitch focused on the family of the current Miss Tennessee. The girl would retire her crown in just a month, but she'd spent the past year championing the adoption cause. When Abby's staff researched her platform, they discovered that none of the national papers had picked up her story. It was the perfect angle.

Her parents had not only adopted her through Heartsong, but they'd adopted two other children as well. One of these children was a seventh grade honors student and the other, a junior in high school, was a pianist who played with the Knoxville orchestra. They were the model family for this cause.

Abby checked her e-mail again. Still no response from *USA Today*.

She grabbed her phone as she weighed desperation against determination. She wouldn't beg, but the writer should know this story was hot. If he didn't pick it up, someone else would.

She dialed the newsroom, and she tapped her toes against the wood floor as it rang once, twice, three times.

Victor picked up after five rings.

"Hey, it's Abby Wagner," she began.

"Abby . . . I was just thinking about you." She heard the rustling of papers. "Now the e-mail I've so eloquently written will have to be trashed."

Abby laughed. She could play this game.

"Don't you dare throw away a single word until you tell me exactly what it says."

"Something about liking your idea, blah, blah, blah. The end."

"I'm a little curious about the 'blah, blah, blah' part of your note."

Abby drew a huge circle on her notepad, dotted the eyes, and curved a smile. Ripping it off the pad, she scrunched it into a ball and tossed it into the wastebasket. Her score was about to tick onto the board.

"Well, it's like this," Victor said. "My editor has asked me to write an unusual feature on family, and I can run any direction I choose. I like the adoption angle—with a new twist, of course."

"Do you want me to arrange an interview with Miss Tennessee?" she asked, calming her voice. She held her breath as she waited for his answer.

"No, too high profile for what I want to do," he explained. "What I'm thinking is a feature with two families. One where adoption has worked and one where it hasn't."

Curtis will be thrilled.

"I need both sides of the story, Abby, and if you can give it to me, I promise to mention Heartsong."

"When do you need this info?"

"Yesterday."

"How about by tomorrow?"

"Close enough," he laughed. "Can I get their names and numbers by three?"

"It's done."

"For a publicist, you're not so bad." He hung up the phone.

Her hands trembled slightly as she started an instant message to Blanche.

Why does it keep coming back to this issue? Failed adoptions happened, but why did it seem like suddenly everybody wanted to talk about it? A printed version of this sorrow seemed so crass, yet here she was, trying to coordinate a story about a family whose heart had been shredded and then handed back mangled and worn.

Birth mothers had total power—they could break an adoptive mother's heart or make it whole. No parent should have to lose a child and then talk about their broken heart, especially with the national media. Of course, Curtis was right—negative angles make for the best stories, but a feature on a failed adoption wasn't just a story. It meant exhuming a heartbreak that should stay buried.

"Why are you doing this?" she snarled at the computer screen. Like dumping salt water into an open wound, God kept burning through the gash that should have healed by now. All she wanted was for it to stop festering and disappear.

"Are you okay, Abby?" Blanche asked warily from her door.

Abby's eyes met hers in a silent challenge. Blanche had caught her wallowing again, and she certainly couldn't be honest with her boss about the source of her recent episodes. She had to check her emotional state before Blanche thought she'd lost her mind. Or maybe it was too late for that.

Blanche's perfectly plucked eyebrows scrunched into a V, and she looked like she might dive for the phone and call for backup.

"I've got good news, actually," Abby said. "*USA Today* is going to feature Heartsong and several stories on adoption."

"What's the catch?"

"How do you know there's a catch?" Abby squirmed behind the safety of her desk.

"I hope there's one or I'll be wondering why in the world you didn't call me the second you found this out."

"I just secured it seconds ago, and yes, there's a slight catch. They want stories of both a successful adoption and a failure."

Blanche walked into the room and leaned over Abby's desk. Her stare was unnerving.

"And do you think this will be a problem?"

"No. I'm sure we can get the information from Heartsong."

"Of course, we can get this from Heartsong, and we'll spin it with a twist sweeter than lemonade."

"I don't know . . ."

"Abby, dear, don't you lose your edge on me. I need your expertise, and the exposure it brings."

Maggie buzzed her line—an urgent call for Blanche.

When her boss deserted her office, Abby swiveled in her chair, gazing out at the range of cream-covered mountains in the distance. If Blanche lost faith in her work, she'd be yesterday's news in this agency. An old, crumpled story tossed out with the trash.

There were other places she could work, but she liked the atmosphere in a boutique agency. At a larger company she'd be downgraded instantly from a vice president to a director, and she was too old to claw her way back to the top. Once she fell, she'd probably stay down for life.

She couldn't imagine Blanche firing her now. She oversaw too many major accounts and harbored too many important media contacts. If she kept the major profiles like *USA Today* and *Good Morning America* rolling in, Blanche would sacrifice her personal feelings and keep Abby at her right hand.

Abby walked to the door and motioned Maggie over from the copy machine.

"Get Harold Rogers on the phone, please, and cushion this for me," she said as her assistant wheeled her chair behind her desk. "Tell him I've got great news."

Chapter 15

When Marc plopped the *Seattle Times* onto his desk, Damian jumped, splashing drops of coffee across a nautical chart. "A knock might have been appropriate."

"Sorry." Marc wiped up the spill with a paper towel. "Thought you'd want to see this ASAP."

"The article on the orcas?"

"You don't happen to take blood pressure medicine, do you?" Marc asked as he took off his soaked rain jacket and flung it across a chair.

"For high or low pressure?"

"What do you think?"

"It can't be that bad." Damian glanced down at the teaser and turned to the second page.

The story started with information from Kyle saying the toxin level in the deceased whale was high, but it was no guarantee that the PCBs caused her death. Fair enough, Damian thought. The man had to cover himself.

A quote from Damian followed: "If companies like Pageant Industries don't clean up their act, our whales will disappear."

"I didn't say that," Damian mumbled at the paper.

Marc threw the towel into the trashcan. "I warned you."

The newspaper followed his misquote with a quote from Colt Dantzler, a vice president at Pageant Industries.

"'Odd that a former whale killer is suddenly interested in saving whales,' Dantzler said."

"How dare he!" Damian almost threw the paper across the room.

"There's no need for him or anyone else to conduct an undercover investigation," the quote continued. "Mr. De Lucia is welcome to view our research and regulations at any time, and it would be a lot easier for him to come through our front door than conspiring to find it secretly. We'd hate to arrest him for trespassing when he's got an open invitation to visit anytime."

"'I'm too busy giving tours to practice biology,'" De Lucia said. "'My previous work has no bearing on your story.'"

Damian tossed the paper onto the ground and stomped on it until the black and white lines blurred into gray under his wet boots. He didn't need to read anymore.

How dare that gnarly little reporter make him look like an idiot. He knew exactly what he was talking about. The pollutant levels were raging through the Sound, and obviously someone was trying to keep the information under wraps. Why couldn't people see what was going on?

He picked up the telephone and dialed the newspaper office. The operator sent him into Frank Slater's voice mail.

"I don't know what you're trying to do," Damian said. "But most journalists actually search for the truth."

He hung up.

"Pretty harsh," Marc said.

"Someone needs to give him a reality check." Damian grabbed his yellow slicker from the antique coat rack at the side of the room. "Can you man the office for me?"

"Sure, but where are you going?"

"I've got a little visit to make."

Marc glanced out the window. "It's pouring outside."

"I won't even notice."

Rain soaked Damian's hair as he rushed out of the office, and he pulled the hood over his head. No sail necessary. He'd power his way to the mainland.

In a quick sequence of well-oiled moves, he tilted the motor back on his boat, set the choke, and adjusted the throttle. A few squeezes primed the fuel system, and he pressed the start button.

Minutes later, he was motoring out of the inlet and into the open water. He'd be at Pageant Industries in an hour.

His fist clenching the wheel, he prayed as he hit wave after wave.

Keep me calm, Lord. Please give me the wisdom to speak Your words.

He was convinced that his heavenly Father cared about the whales even more than he did. God asked man to care for the mammals, but men weren't doing their job.

Damian motored the boat in front of the imposing industrial area known as Pageant. He thought he'd be able to dock alongside the corporate headquarters, but a huge ship was already parked outside, a handful of men loading it with a crane.

He watched a dinghy leave the shore and speed toward him. So much for any element of surprise.

The man who pulled up beside him wore an orange rain slicker and hat. Damian couldn't even see his eyes.

"This is private property," the man said.

"I realize that. I'm here to see Colt Dantzler."

"Most visitors come by car."

"I'm a truck man, myself."

The man finally met his eyes. They were the same color as the gray sky. "Don't really care. Is Mr. Dantzler expecting you?"

"I have an open invitation. Name's Dr. Damian De Lucia."

The man radioed something to the corporate office.

"He said he wasn't expecting you so soon."

"I'm a fast guy."

The man coughed. "I'm supposed to escort you inside."

Damian anchored his boat and climbed into the dingy. The man quickly docked the small boat and led Damian down a cement walkway and into a warehouse packed with pallets of shrink-wrapped boxes. A forklift whizzed up behind them, and Damian jumped out of the way.

Drenched and cold, Damian followed the man up steel blue stairs and into a makeshift lobby decorated with a stained couch and two folding chairs.

"Mr. Dantzler will be here in just a minute," the man said, pouring thick coffee into a Styrofoam cup.

Ten minutes later, a man with a wrinkled suit and ruddy skin entered the room. He didn't shake Damian's hand.

"You work fast, Mr. De Lucia," he said.

"Actually, it's Dr. De Lucia."

"Why are you here?"

"I read the paper this morning and wondered if Frank Slater misquoted you as badly as he misquoted me."

"He only polished my words a bit to make them better."

"I see," Damian said as he pulled a small case of vials from his pocket. "In that case, I have a few tests I wanted to do while I'm here."

"Excuse me?"

"Your quote clearly said I have an open invitation to visit."

"That's true, and here you are. Welcome to Pageant Industries."

"You also said there's no need to conduct an undercover investigation, so I'm ready to test the plant's water for you."

"The reporter may have taken my words slightly out of context in that last quote."

"So you won't let me do a little research?"

"We already employ a team of top researchers, Mr. De Lucia. Your little experiment won't change a thing."

Chapter 16

Abby tapped her foot impatiently as the kid behind the café's counter chatted with a friend. She checked her watch. She had forty-five minutes before she needed to be back at the office, but the guy wasn't in any hurry to make her lunch.

As the line inched forward, she eyed the rack of newspapers from across the country and picked up the *Chicago Tribune,* perused the headlines, and set it back down. Her eye caught today's *Seattle Times,* and she reached for it.

The headlines were typical—Seattle's City Council was debating over road repairs, there was a new report on crime downtown, and she saw a feature story on the local production of *Music Man.* Nothing that interested her.

The espresso machine buzzed beside her.

Another Orca Dies in Puget Sound. She reread the headline.

The barista cleared his throat. "You going to order?"

Was he peeved at *her?*

"A tall caramel latte and a grilled mozzarella and tomato sandwich on foccacia bread."

"$7.50," he barked before looking down at her newspaper. "Are you buying that?"

She shrugged her shoulders. "Sure."

Sighing, he rang the total again.

Carrying lunch in her hands, Abby clutched the *Seattle Times* under her arm. She stepped out into the heart of downtown Denver and checked her watch again as the traffic rushed by her.

Rounding the corner, she strolled under a wrought iron arch, ivy draping over the top and weaving down the posts to the grassy ground.

Today a mix of daffodils and tulips paraded in straight lines along the gravel walkway that led to the pond. It was her favorite place to lunch on a warm spring day.

Sitting down on a bench, she watched the fountain spurt into the air. She had arrived in time for the half hour water show. As she sipped her latte, Abby laughed at a toddler waving his hand through the rippled water and racing back to his mother. The woman kissed his cheek, and then he ran back to the pond again and proudly repeated his brave act. He was probably imagining a giant fish was going to gobble his hand or a mammoth submarine was about to emerge and attack.

Abby admired the boy's bravery. He apparently thought he was doing a remarkable feat every time he soaked his fingers in the tiny waves. The courage of a child.

She leaned back against the hard slabs of the bench and folded back the white paper wrapped around her sandwich. Biting into the soft mozzarella and bread, she opened the *Seattle Times* again and skimmed the first few lines of the story on the orca. She wondered how the writer would make the old "save the whales" angle fresh.

Frank Slater briefly described the demise of the Sound's best-loved mammal, and the recent death of a beached whale out in the Sound. How sad! She'd loved watching the killer whales when she was young. They were intimidating and overwhelming and absolutely majestic. She had a healthy fear of the beautiful creatures . . . and a sense of camaraderie with them. She, too, had loved the waters where they lived.

She read further. There was a quote by a specialist who had examined the mammal, countered by the reactions of a government official and an executive of a Washington-based textile plant called Pageant Industries.

"The levels of PCBs in the Sound are below legal limits," said Colt Dantzler, Pageant's vice president of environmental protection. "Just because there was a trace of PCBs in the orca doesn't mean the pollutants caused her death. Another animal or a fishing boat may have injured her, or she just may have died of old age."

Abby sat straight up. A simple autopsy would have shown if any of those caused the whale's death. Colt Dantzler would have known this—

his quote was classic diversion. She wondered what the problem was with the truth.

She continued reading.

"'This is obviously a cover-up,' Dr. Damian De Lucia, former marine biologist, said. 'A little undercover work at places like Pageant Industries would reveal the truth.'"

Damian De Lucia? Abby smiled at the black and white print in front of her. The name was too unique to be anyone other than her old sailing pal. She hadn't seen him for so many years that she'd almost forgotten what he looked like. Thick, dark hair—it used to ruffle in the wind as they sailed around the island. After she started dating Scott, Damian stopped coming around.

Damian had probably gotten married and fathered four or five kids by now. He'd always been a good guy—a real gentleman, which had seemed normal until she went to college and realized how rare that was.

"'Odd that a former whale killer is suddenly interested in saving whales,'" Dantzler said." *What was that supposed to mean?* She skimmed down the lines.

"'I'm too busy giving tours to practice biology,' De Lucia said. 'My previous work has no bearing on your story.'"

Abby folded the paper and sipped her now tepid latte. No matter how well Damian was or wasn't doing, he obviously wasn't very good at talking to the press. His quotes made him look like a washed-up biologist, and he'd always been sharp.

She remembered the hours and hours of sailing lessons he'd given her. He'd simplified the complicated sport into a beautiful dance. She'd never met anyone as passionate about sailing as Damian. He'd been an expert teacher, and he'd taught her how to ride the wind.

If she ever went back to Orcas Island, she'd give him a crash course in media training before he talked to a newspaper again. No matter how well you knew the information, a savvy reporter could make the finest expert look like a sap. All they needed to do was get their subject irritated, and then move in for the kill.

She'd seen it happen over and over in her career. She'd tell her clients to stick to their message and never, ever let the media coerce them into saying something they didn't mean. Sometimes they listened and sometimes . . . well, they always regretted it when they didn't listen. They stuck like glue to their message on their next interview.

It was too late to redeem this story, but the next time she saw Damian, she'd help him before he completely ruined his reputation and determination to save these whales.

Abby's cell phone rang, and she set down her paper to answer the call.

"I've found two perfect couples for you," Harold Rogers announced. She pulled a pen out of her purse to write their information on the newspaper.

"I'm ready." She glanced at her watch. It was almost one o'clock. She'd have the good news to Victor two hours before he asked. That's how she liked to do business.

"The success story is of a couple up in Rochester, New York," he explained. "Heartsong was actually a last ditch effort for them. They used several other agencies before they called Heartsong, desperate for a baby. They'd had so many false hopes and starts, and they were emotionally exhausted.

"Three years ago we found them an infant girl, and every year on her birthday they send both our corporate and local offices a bouquet of flowers and updated pictures. They'll have nothing but good things to say about their experience."

"Excellent." Abby jotted their name and number and looped a wide circle around the information.

"Don't worry about calling them," Harold said. "I prepped them last night."

Abby didn't tell him, but she would have her media trainer call them right away just to make sure they were prepared for any surprises. She liked Victor, but she never trusted reporters. If they weren't careful he'd turn this into an adoption exposé, and she had no desire to clean up that kind of mess.

"And now for the story that wasn't a success," she prodded.

"This couple might surprise you," Harold replied. "Tom and Briana Duncan are their names, and they're an absolute delight. They're in their

thirties, living just south of Denver in Littleton. You'll love talking to them and so will the writer."

"This is the story of a failed adoption?" She'd been there, and there was no delight after losing an adopted child.

"Right," he continued. "Five months ago the Duncans received a baby boy, and, of course, they bonded with the baby immediately as most adoptive couples do. Everything seemed to be fine at first, but then the birth mother's parents talked their daughter into raising the baby herself. Two weeks after the Duncans received the baby at the hospital, they had to return him.

"It was just horrible for all of us involved, yet they are both Christians and seem to believe that if they wait on God, He will bring the right baby to their family," Harold cleared his throat. "I sure hope there's some divine intervention on their behalf. They have amazing faith in spite of what happened, and I'd encourage anyone scared of the adoption process to talk to them."

"That sounds like the positive spin we're looking for," Abby said even though she knew it wasn't possible. No one who lost a baby could possibly recover in months. It was too fast.

"The only catch is they want to meet with someone at Nulte P.R. before they talk to the reporter. I promised that you or Blanche would go down and walk them through this before they do an interview."

"No problem," Abby said. "I'll tell the reporter to call them tomorrow so one of us can visit with the Duncans tonight."

She hung up the phone and scribbled a wave of lines across the newspaper. It sounded like the Duncans were the ideal interview for *USA Today*, but she couldn't coach and train them on sterile things like simplifying their message and developing unforgettable sound bites. She was too close to their story to help. She could do more than sympathize with them; she could wholly empathize if she were willing to expose her pain. She wasn't prepared to do that.

Abby finished her sandwich as she rushed back to the office.

Harold's words intrigued her. This couple's core had been shaken, and if Harold was right, they still clung to their faith. But how could they still believe? She'd accepted Christ into her heart when she was twenty-five, and she still believed in God. She just couldn't accept the fact that a loving God would take her son away. Not if He really cared about Hunter . . . or about her.

How had the Duncans reconciled what happened to their baby with their trust in God?

When she reached her desk, Abby sent an instant message to Blanche asking if her boss could meet with the Duncans tonight before they interviewed with *USA Today.* She may be intrigued, but there was no way she could face this couple and their pain.

Blanche replied back seconds later, her misspelled note perfectly clear. She most certainly could not meet with the Duncans, but Abby would make it fit into her schedule.

The thought of sending Curtis in her place flew in and out of Abby's mind. She would not give that man any more control over the campaign. She reminded herself again that she was a pro. This was a professional visit, not a personal one. She could talk about a failed adoption without treading through her own nightmare. She could avoid memory lane.

She buzzed her assistant. "Maggie, could you set up a meeting with a couple in Littleton this afternoon? Their names are Tom and Briana Duncan." She quickly recited the number Harold gave her.

"Consider it done."

Abby pulled out her computer keyboard from the ledge under her desk and typed a quick e-mail to Victor with the names and numbers of both couples, adding a short PS that the Duncans wouldn't be available to talk until tomorrow. Victor shot her a quick reply—the story was a go. Her pitch was done.

Maggie flung her head inside Abby's office door. "Just talked to Briana Duncan and set your meeting up for five o'clock. She's the sweetest girl. Said she's looking forward to meeting you, et cetera, et cetera."

"You're a gem," Abby said, noting the meeting on her calendar like she might forget.

Chapter 17

Jessica packed her last textbook into a box and heaved it from the garage, down the long staircase, and into the basement. The door to the storage area was usually shut, but she'd been carrying stuff up and down the stairs all afternoon so it stood wide open. One day the piles of stored junk might just wake up and take over the house.

Papers and manila files, and a hodgepodge of other clutter, spilled over the scattered white and brown boxes. No wonder her mom never wanted anyone else to see the mess. She prided herself on being a neat freak, and this hidden area was out of control.

Jessica had no desire to organize the chaotic piles, though every once in awhile she liked to rummage through them. Most of her childhood was stored in this one room. Her mom was notorious for recording their lives, which included keeping every picture Jessica had drawn, every sloppy craft she'd made in Sunday school, and every school paper with a big red "A." The many Bs and Cs, and her embarrassing D papers, were actually thrown away.

She heaved a large box off the shelf and tucked her smaller box of textbooks behind it. She'd probably forget where she stored it, but it wasn't like she'd need the books anytime soon. Hopefully, she would forget where she put them.

She glanced down at her watch before replacing the large box. Her mom wouldn't be home from work for a few more hours. She had time to look inside.

Flipping back the cardboard, she inhaled the musty smell. Then she gently removed the web of tree ornaments that she'd made from Popsicle sticks and decorated with a messy combination of glittery red and green. She dug under the pile of ornaments and unwrapped a plate that she'd used as her canvas when she was five. She'd outlined her hand with purple paint and spelled her name in pink. Her parents had sent it away, firing her painting into the ceramic, and they'd displayed her masterpiece on the dining room wall for years.

A flurry of papers were scattered under the plate, selected pieces torn from her collection of coloring books. She'd always been a little crazy with crayons, valuing speed over quality. The scribbled attempts at art were a mess. She set them aside and dug deeper.

Under the jumble of crafts was a framed portrait of their family when she was a kid. A sterile studio shot of the three of them dressed in matching navy attire. Her mom's hair was teased high, and her dad's hair was feathered perfectly over his ears. She must have been somewhere between two and three, sporting a simple jumpsuit, black leather shoes, and pigtails with bows.

Grasping the picture, she sat down on the cold cement and stared into her father's eyes. She missed him terribly at times. As much as she loved her mom, she'd always been a Daddy's girl. She wished she could run to him right now for his honest advice.

What would he have told her? He probably would have looked her straight in the eyes and said in his deep voice, "Jessie, you have to chase your dreams."

She could envision him packing their things and taking her to Orcas Island for a few weeks no matter what her mom said. Of course, if he were still here, they never would have left Seattle in the first place.

Everything had changed after he died.

She tucked the framed picture back into the box and hurried upstairs to retrieve her last two duffel bags from the garage. She wanted to finish sorting and packing before her mom came home. She'd probably freak if she saw Jessica preparing to leave for Orcas.

She still didn't understand why it was such a big deal. Most of her college friends were traveling to different places this summer. It wasn't like she was going to Asia or South Africa. Washington was only a few states away. She wished she knew why talking about that island made her mom lose her mind.

She lugged the duffel bags up the grand staircase to her room, propped them on the bed, and dumped their contents on the comforter. She bundled her skiing gear and the dorm bedding into her arms and deposited it onto the floor of her walk-in closet. She'd deal with that stuff later.

Summer T-shirts, shorts, and three bathing suits were jammed into her bags, and she added a couple sweatshirts for cool evenings, a pair of her cargo pants, and jeans. She wouldn't need much variety since she planned to spend most of her days in and on the water.

With a loud swish, she tossed the duffel bags into her closet and opened the drawer of her nightstand. She pulled out the sheet of Orcas Island restaurants she'd printed off the Internet last night. She'd call every one of them until she found a job as a hostess or server or even bussing tables so she wouldn't spend all of her dad's money in one summer. Besides, work meant she could meet some local friends and learn where to sail.

She dialed the first number and listened to a long recording about the Mexican restaurant's hours and their specials for the night. She hung up, dialed the second number, and took a deep breath when a brusque voice answered the phone.

"Vincent De Lucia."

"My name's Jessica Wagner," she said. "I'm coming to Orcas for the summer, and I wanted to see if you had any summer jobs available."

"You a college student?"

"Yes, sir. My family has a cottage on Orcas, but I haven't been on the island in a long time."

"I've owned this restaurant for over forty years," Vincent said. "I'd bet money that I know your folks."

"My mom is Abby Taylor Wagner, and my aunt is Laurel Taylor Graham," she explained as she paced the bedroom.

He laughed. "Your aunt was one of the most scattered waitresses I've ever had, but the customers loved her. I haven't seen your mother in years."

"She doesn't visit Orcas any more."

"I've got one server position left that needs to be filled. When are you coming?"

"Late on Monday."

"Why don't you stop by Tuesday and apply in person?"

"I'll be there."

"Ciao," he said and then hung up before she thanked him.

Jessica sprung onto her fluffy goose down comforter and kicked her legs in the air. Yes! Doors were flying open already. She balled up the listing of restaurants and threw it toward the trashcan. She wouldn't need to call anyone else. She was an inch away from having a job.

For a quick moment she thought about calling her mom with the good news, but she beat that thought back the instant it occurred to her. Her mom wouldn't be happy—she'd be horrified.

She grabbed a pillow from her bed and crushed it under her chin. Her mom's stubbornness just didn't make any sense. Jessica and her dad had gone to Orcas almost every summer when she was a child, but her mom always refused to join them. After her dad died, her mom still wouldn't go back. She'd seen albums filled with pictures of her mom growing up on the island. She always looked happy and content—like she loved being near the water. What had gone wrong?

She leaned toward the window and looked out at the layers of rugged pine forest and imposing rock formations carpeting the mountains.

Was it okay for her to leave this summer without her mom's blessing? Guilt! She definitely felt guilty about leaving her mom here alone all summer. If only she wasn't so stinking stubborn. Her mom would be lonely and sad, and she'd blame Jessica for her sorrow.

Yet she felt like she was supposed to go to Orcas, at least for a few months. She didn't understand why her mother was taking it so personally. Maybe her mom actually needed some time alone.

"Please help her understand," she prayed.

Chapter 18

Winding through a maze of identical streets, Abby found Tom and Briana Duncan's home hidden among a thousand similar houses dotting the Denver suburb. She pulled into the driveway and examined their light yellow paint, manicured lawn, and obligatory white fence. Perfect in every way.

She strapped her purse over her arm, but didn't move from the truck. She couldn't go inside. No matter what Harold said, the pain this couple faced would be unbearable. It wasn't fair to come into their home as a consultant and suddenly break down in tears. It would be better to restart her truck and slam it in reverse.

But Blanche would explode if she backed down now. This was her job. She'd pitched this article, and she was responsible for carrying it through.

She slowly opened the door and climbed down to their driveway. If she focused on Tom and Briana's story, she could stay above her emotions. She'd simply answer their questions and then escape the instant they were prepped for the interview.

She plodded to their front porch, breathed deep, and rang the bell.

"You must be Abby," Briana greeted her as she opened the door. Briana introduced her to Tom, who was holding the collar of a yellow Labrador in his left hand.

Abby shook both of their hands as they invited her inside. Briana was dressed in stylish black pants and a white blouse, her long hair pulled back in a classic twist. Tom's chin was sanded with light stubble. He wore a navy collared T-shirt, black leather shoes, and dark Hilfiger jeans. The ideal American pair.

This couple should be wallowing in grief—it had taken her almost three months before she was motivated enough to get dressed again and go outside, years before she could welcome company into her home. What was wrong with these people? Or maybe she should ask—what was wrong with her?

"Don't you love spring?" Briana asked as she led Abby into their formal room. The scent of vanilla settled on the room, probably from the candle burning on the fireplace mantle. Beside the candle Abby saw a family picture of Tom and Briana holding a baby boy. How could they possibly look at that every day?

"I always get the itch." She forced a smile. "I'm dying to be outside."

"Me too," Briana said as she motioned for Abby to sit across from her and Tom on a floral-covered couch. A tea set was centered on the glass coffee table between them, pink cups and saucers on a sterling silver platter.

"My tulips and daffodils are blooming, and it makes me want to plant more and more," Briana continued. "Is it possible to have too many flowers?"

Tom laughed. "You certainly don't think so."

"Are you a tea drinker?" Briana asked, holding up the silver teapot. "It's Earl Grey."

"I'd love some."

Briana poured them each a cup of tea and then stirred a cube of sugar into her own.

Abby sipped the hot tea. "Harold said he explained the concept of the *USA Today* story to you."

"He did," Briana said. "We don't mind doing an interview if you and Harold feel comfortable with our story. We'd love for thousands of people to know how God worked in our lives."

"And how exactly did God work?" Abby asked. She'd never felt anything but anger after God stole Hunter away.

Tom leaned back against the ivory chair and crossed his legs, like an elderly college professor preparing to expound on a complicated theory. She almost expected him to pull out a gray-flecked cardigan and a corn-cob pipe.

"On our third wedding anniversary we decided that it was time to start a family." Tom glanced over at Briana, who gazed back with admiration. Abby wasn't sure she could handle their affection on top of their obvious denial.

"We were elated at the thought of having a little Duncan scrambling around the house." He snapped his fingers. "Just like that, we ran to Babies R Us and shopped for cribs and blankets and baby clothes. Briana picked out the colors for a nursery, and we thought we'd better go ahead and paint it while we had time.

"We organized and painted and dreamt about our baby—all before we actually conceived. Weeks and then months went by, and nothing. We were surrounded by close friends with babies, and it seemed like they just thought about getting pregnant and suddenly they were giving birth. We'd assumed this would happen to us too, but a year passed and we still weren't pregnant. We prayed, our friends prayed, our family prayed . . . and then it happened."

Tom paused as a wave of sadness flickered across his face. Abby had almost begun to believe they weren't human.

"We got pregnant," he explained as he grasped Briana's hand. "There's never been a couple more excited than we were. The instant the doctor confirmed we called everyone we knew. We rejoiced, and our church family rejoiced with us. A miracle had occurred, and we wanted to announce God's goodness to the world."

Abby watched as tears tumbled down his cheeks. She wanted to take both of their hands and say she understood, but they'd already faced enough pain without having to relive hers.

Briana rubbed their dog behind his ears and took over for her husband. "Two months into the pregnancy, I doubled over with stomach cramps," Briana explained. "Tom rushed me to the emergency room where I miscarried.

"I've never felt such agony. Physically, I felt like I was about to die, and my emotions were shattered. I thought it was the most awful experience of my life . . . until the doctor told us we may never be able to get pregnant again."

"Why not?"

"My egg count was low, and he said the odds of me getting pregnant the first time were extremely low. The odds of me getting pregnant again without medical help—near impossible. We were devastated."

"I bet."

The Labrador crossed the room and brushed against Abby's skirt before draping himself over her feet.

"Come here, Amos," Tom said.

"He's fine." Abby smiled as the animal pawed her hose. She bent over to pet his fur.

"We researched infertility treatments right away. We tried artificial insemination for six months, but nothing happened, so we upped our chances of getting pregnant with in vitro fertilization. You know how that works?"

"I do, and I also know it's expensive."

"We had money saved and decided that this was the best way to use it," Tom said. "So we went to a specialist and proceeded. We were convinced that this would work."

"It didn't?" She knew the answer, of course. This story was too familiar to her.

"Two eggs fertilized, and they implanted them. We were so hopeful that one or even both would make it. We would have loved to have twins. Briana was such a trouper—taking two shots a day, resting her body," he continued, his voice drenched with admiration. "We both sank into a state of depression when the doctor called to say the in vitro didn't take."

"Our savings account was dwindling fast, and so was our hope of having a baby." Briana set her teacup on the table. "Then our pastor asked if we'd considered adoption. We'd talked about it briefly, but we so wanted to have a baby of our own that we hadn't seriously considered it."

"We prayed and prayed," Tom continued. "And that's when God changed us. We thought we knew what He wanted, but we realized that God might have a different plan for us. We had just enough money left to pursue either another in vitro treatment or adoption. We felt that God wanted us to pursue adoption."

"That's when you approached Heartsong?" Abby set her teacup back on the coffee table.

"Exactly. We researched several agencies and decided that was the right place for us. In two weeks we completed all the paperwork and put together a photo album that they show birth mothers. The birth mothers choose an adoptive family from the pictures and profiles. Heartsong believes it helps the women feel better about their decision."

"And you were chosen."

"Three months later. We met the birth mother and really connected with her. She was due in a week but gave birth fifty-two hours after our meeting, so we didn't have much time to prepare. We went to the hospital right away and picked up our son—Samuel Thomas Duncan."

Abby clutched her hands together as the dog's rough, wet nose rubbed her foot. She knew that unspeakable joy of holding your baby in your arms for the first time, cuddling close to his face, smelling the baby powder, kissing his sweet nose.

She knew this couple's story by heart. She'd lived it herself, and it had consumed her.

"We'd had the baby for two weeks when the birth mother suddenly changed her mind. We were told that her parents wanted to keep the child even though Samuel's young mother was returning to college. The grandparents promised to raise him, so after some haggling, Samuel's mother called the agency and told them she didn't want to proceed with the adoption. Since she hadn't relinquished her rights yet, we had no legal ground to fight it."

Abby wanted to hug them both and sob, but she held back. She wasn't about to share her story with anyone, especially a couple she didn't know. Yet, she so wanted to tell them how much she hurt for them. She'd been right there, but she couldn't offer them hope. It didn't get better. Sure, the pain subsided, but like an old injury, it flared up unexpectedly—never really going away.

"How do you get by?" she asked.

"Harold probably told you that we're Christians," Tom explained. "There's a verse in the book of Psalms that says if we wait on the Lord, He will strengthen our hearts. We've been praying every day that God will strengthen us."

"But surely you must still grieve for this loss." Abby struggled to keep skepticism out of her voice.

"We do," Briana said. "But alongside our grief is an amazing strength and faith that can only come from God, and this is what we want to tell the reporter from *USA Today*. We're waiting on the Lord to see what He has in store for our family."

"If Harold feels comfortable with you describing your faith to the newspaper, then I certainly do too."

"Wonderful." Tom reached out to shake her hand. "We're thrilled to be able to share what God has done for us."

What God has done for them? Taken away their baby, destroyed their hearts, ruined their lives. She picked up her teacup again and gripped it. She was here to talk about media training, not to counsel them or seek counseling from them. If they believed God was working for their good, who was she to tell them the truth?

"When you talk to Victor, I'd like you to focus on the fact that you are planning to adopt again and hopefully soon. Heartsong's working hard to find you the right child for your family."

"We're just waiting for the call," Briana said. "Our home and our hearts are ready for another baby."

"That's what I thought, and that's the perfect quote. Say those exact words to the reporter."

"Okay. What else should we do?"

"Nothing. You've described your story like a pro. Keep it concise and to the point, and be just as honest as you've been with me."

"We want to represent Heartsong well," Tom said.

"There's no reason for either of you to be nervous—you've got nothing to hide."

Chapter 19

Marc Cartwright bumped down the winding gravel lane less than a mile out of town and pedaled under a line of sloping trees that reminded him of a long wind tunnel. This was home for the summer. The perfect location with easy access to work and church.

Damian had come back from his boating excursion this afternoon in a somber mood though he hadn't told Marc where he'd been. It wasn't hard to guess. Marc asked him why he'd gone to Pageant Industries, and Damian grunted in return.

His boss and friend was a crusader at heart, but crusaders often acted before they figured out the best approach. When Damian was passionate about something, he didn't think about consequences. Ready. Set. Action. Actually, nix the ready. Damian just jumped into action.

Marc checked his watch—six o'clock. He had an hour to eat and be back at the dock. He and Damian were hosting a sunset cruise tonight for a group from Seattle.

He parked his bike behind a white clapboard house complete with dark green shutters and ruby red clematis crawling up the sides. He climbed the shaky metal stairs at the back to the third floor and opened the door under the cracked awning. For the last three summers, he'd rented this room and made it his home.

The place was tiny but neat. He rented it furnished with a green and blue plaid couch, worn leather chair, kitchen table, and single bed in the far corner of the room. The kitchenette had yellowed Formica countertops and a baby blue tiled floor.

In New York, this would have been called something glamorous like a studio. It wasn't glamorous, but it was a decent place to eat, sleep, and study . . . and much better than the dirty, cramped space in Seattle that his mother still called home.

He threw his backpack on the couch as the phone rang. Probably a friend from college or someone from church.

"Hello."

"Collect call from Stacie Cartwright," the operator barked.

He braced himself. "I'll take it."

"Hi, honey. It's, uh, Mom." A nervous laugh. "But of course you already knew that. Who else calls you honey?"

He sighed. Somehow she'd managed to get alcohol again. He'd done everything he could to keep her away from her addictive drink of choice, vodka straight up, but she always seemed to find a way to get the stuff.

"Hey, Mom." He never asked how she was.

"Happy birthday, honey. I'm a little late, huh?"

Two weeks late. "A little."

"I'm so sorry. I've been busy, but I love you so much."

"I know you do, Mom."

He could strangle whoever gave her the alcohol. Didn't they know they weren't helping anything? His mother had no money, yet she always found a way to get her drink.

"Whatcha doing?"

"I just came home from work."

"You're such a good worker. My boy was always the best worker there is. I'm so glad you work."

Here it comes.

"Did you get paid today?" she asked.

"Every other Friday," he said like he hadn't told her this ten times.

"When you get paid this week, could you send me fifty dollars? That's all I need to pay my rent and stuff."

It was the "stuff" that concerned him. He and Uncle Sam already covered the rent.

"I'll send you another grocery certificate on Friday."

"You're such a sweet boy." She coughed. "All I need is a little cash too."

Marc looked out the window to the forest of trees behind the house. "I'm not paying for your alcohol, Mom."

"I won't use it to buy al—" She coughed again. "Alcohol."

"Are you hungry?"

"No." She hesitated. "But I don't feel so good."

"That's because you've been drinking again."

"I haven't. . . ."

"I love you, Mom. I only want you to get better."

"Just twenty dollars then . . ."

"Sleep it off, Mom. I'll call you tomorrow."

"But. . . ."

"Good night."

When the dial tone came back on, Marc called the manager at the grocery store near his mom's apartment.

"Dennis, it's Marc Cartwright."

"Hi, Marc. Your mother was in here today."

"Please tell me you didn't let her use the grocery certificates to buy booze?"

"None of us let her use those for alcohol, but I can't argue with cash."

"Where is she getting the money?"

"No idea."

Marc groaned. His mom was dangerous when she used her brain. She was too smart and too strong to let the alcohol win.

"I appreciate you watching out for her," Marc said.

"We do what we can, but we can't make her stop drinking. She'll get the stuff someplace else if she doesn't buy it here."

"It's not your responsibility." Marc sighed. "Can you mail me another round of gift certificates?"

"A hundred bucks again?"

"Exactly."

"Your mom's a great woman when she's not drinking. She talks about how proud she is of you every time she comes to the store."

"Thanks, Dennis."

Marc hung up the phone, walked over to the kitchen, and poured himself a glass of orange juice.

Ever since he was a child, he'd been competing against alcohol, and he knew he'd probably never win—his mom would rather spend her days drinking than spend time with him. For his entire life, he'd craved a real family with loving, sober parents like the families he knew from church.

He lay down on the couch and propped his feet up on the armrest. He had to give his mother credit for church. She insisted he go every Sunday even though she never went. In her own way, she'd introduced him to Christ and encouraged him in his faith. She just wasn't interested in giving her life to the Lord.

How was he supposed to spread the gospel around the world when he couldn't even save his own mom?

Chapter 20

Tom clutched their dog's collar as he and Briana waved to Abby from their front porch. She lifted her hand in a slight good-bye as she backed out of their driveway and wound back through their suburb.

She missed swerving left at an intersection and whipped her truck around a quick U-turn before heading north again toward I-25. The streets were fairly quiet as she found her way back to the main road—an occasional garage door slid up and a few children cruised down the sidewalk on roller blades. Not much action on this end of town.

She decided the Duncans were nice enough . . . just a little too cheery. They obviously hadn't realized yet how this loss would impact the rest of their lives. No other baby would ever be able to replace the love they had for their first child.

It still amazed her how quickly it had happened with Hunter, the bond that tied her and her son. She'd been so nervous about being a parent, nervous that he wouldn't want her to be his mother, nervous that she'd realize instantly that she couldn't be a mom. But the second she held him all her nervousness disappeared, melting away when he snuggled against her chest, content to be in her arms.

Sitting in the hospital she remembered thinking that the courts may not have finalized the process, but in her heart, the adoption was complete. Hunter was part of their family before he was born. A treasured gift from God.

Her shaking hands clung to the steering wheel as a sob escaped her lips. If she didn't get a grip, her tears would spiral out of control.

Ever since she took the job with Blanche, she'd been able to appear strong. Now she was suddenly cracking in front of her boss and clients.

Who knew where she'd lose her composure next? She needed to get it together, and soon.

To her right was a neighborhood playground filled with rusty picnic tables, a bright red swing set, and an empty pavilion. She pulled her Navigator into the almost vacant parking lot and clicked off the ignition. A few kids poured down the giant slide, and two young moms strolled across the paved trail beside her truck, pushing dual jogging strollers as they chattered.

She couldn't escape! She squeezed her eyes shut, leaning her head back on the seat.

The night they got "the call" was burned into her brain—not the call that told them the agency had a baby. It was the call that said they were taking him away.

They'd been visiting her family's summer cottage on Orcas Island. She was in her bedroom, blowing kisses on Hunter's belly, and he giggled for the first time. She hollered to Scott, and he rushed into the room to tickle him again and again. Together, they kissed Hunter and rattled his favorite toy, savoring his sweet laugh.

They'd been absolutely and completely in love with their son.

They were still tickling him when the telephone rang, and Scott ran out the door to pick it up in the living room. She heard him greet Julia from Heartsong.

Then she heard the long pause.

"She can't do that!" he finally bellowed before his voice turned into a whisper. He strung the phone line toward her and slammed the bedroom door.

She clutched Hunter to her chest as she strained to listen, but Scott's muffled voice remained low.

What were they saying? Her mind raced through the horrible possibilities. It had been four months! Surely, they were too far along in the process for anything to go wrong.

Scott hung up the phone, and she carried Hunter into the hall. She heard the sobs before she saw Scott huddled on the couch, bawling into his hands.

"What happened?"

He shook his head, tears shelling the wood floor.

"Tell me what's wrong!"

He finally looked up at her with sad, desperate eyes, his cheeks streaked red. "Stacie's changed her mind."

Abby collapsed onto the couch beside him, her body shaking as she gasped for air. "She can't do that!"

She'd wake up, and this would be a nightmare. The call an awful dream.

"Apparently she can," he whispered. "She never signed the relinquishment papers. The agency thought she was just procrastinating—Julia said they had no idea she would renege."

"But the court hearing is this week. Everything's supposed to be done."

"She's not going to court."

"It's too late." She squeezed Hunter so hard he cried. "He's our son!"

Scott reached out to hug her, but she pulled away, grabbing the telephone beside him with one hand while grasping Hunter with the other.

"Don't, Abby!" Scott said, but she didn't listen. She dialed Heartsong's number.

Julia answered on the first ring.

"You're not taking him," Abby lashed at her as Hunter released another scream. "We're going to fight this, Julia. We'll sue you. We'll sue Stacie. We'll do whatever we can to keep our child."

Scott reached forward and jerked the phone cord out of the wall. Then he reached for Hunter, taking him from her trembling arms.

"You're not helping things." He patted Hunter's back. The baby took a deep breath and nuzzled his head into Scott's shoulder.

"We're going to fight this." She clenched her fists, waiting for him to say "yes," but he didn't reply. "We are going to fight this, right?"

"We need to pray about it first," he said.

"I don't need to pray. This isn't right."

"We've got to consider what's best for Hunter," he mumbled. "If we go to court, we may not get him back until he's three or four."

"You've just got it all figured out, don't you?"

"He wouldn't even know who we are."

"We would remind him."

"Let's pray," he begged. "Maybe Stacie will change her mind."

Abby fled outside, leaving the screen door wide open behind her. How could her husband not fight for their baby? What was wrong with him? She'd fight until she died to keep her boy.

She raced down the steep steps to the dock and fell onto the weathered slabs, pounding them with her fists. She'd promised Hunter that she'd never let him go. She'd promised she would take care of him for the rest of his life. How could she break her promises to her son?

Abby's cell phone rang La Traviata on the leather seat beside her, wrenching her back to reality. She grabbed it and looked down at the office number on ID. She'd call them back.

She gazed out her front window at a group of toddlers playing in the sandbox. Why couldn't she rid herself of these agonizing memories? After all, it had been twenty years since she'd said good-bye to her baby. She should be able to let it go.

She had to admit that she admired the Duncans' honesty. She'd never been honest with anyone about Hunter. Not about her anger at God or the pain or the guilt of letting him go. After they took Hunter back to the agency, her heart turned cold. It hurt too much to care.

If only they hadn't waited years for a child. If only he hadn't been so perfect for them. If only he hadn't stolen her heart . . . if only she could have faith like the Duncans so she could say a final good-bye, knowing God was in control.

But they'd only had Samuel for two weeks. Maybe they'd be just as angry as she was if they'd had their son for four months. Maybe they would still be mad at God twenty years from now.

She groaned. Their impenetrable faith probably wouldn't crumble if they'd given Samuel up after a year.

She closed her eyes again. One prayer wouldn't hurt her.

"God," she whispered. "After all these years, I need to know why."

The two mothers circled the path again with their strollers, one of them stopping to retrieve a pacifier catapulted from under a navy-toned visor.

Maybe it was time for her to be proactive. She'd run for so long from

the memories and yet they kept confronting her. Maybe it was time for her to confront the past.

Her phone rang again, the office number lighting up the small screen. She sighed as she picked it up.

"Abby, it's Blanche," her boss clipped. "How did it go?"

She hesitated as she dug through the glove compartment for a napkin to wipe her nose. "Good. Really good. They hardly needed coaching."

"Are you crying?"

"I'm fine. Just a little emotional today."

"They've got pills for that kind of stuff, Abby."

"I know. Probably just a little menopausal."

Blanche didn't respond.

"Anyway, I'm coming back to the office. I'll be there in thirty minutes."

Blanche coughed. "I've got some bad news."

Abby held her breath. She couldn't take any bad news right now. Her emotions were already teetering on the edge of a meltdown.

"What is it?" she asked.

"Your producer friend, Gloria something, called from *Good Morning America*. She said they're canceling the show on preservation."

"What? I just talked to her yesterday, and everything was fine. They were considering trimming the interview, but they were excited about the material."

"Well, something obviously happened in the last twenty-four hours, and Ted is irate. I think he may be having a breakdown too."

"Don't worry about it, Blanche. I'll handle it. We just need to work with them to get what they need."

Blanche paused again, and Abby's gut sank. Something else was wrong.

"You need to take some time off, Abby."

"I'm fine, Blanche. Really."

"I don't think that you are. I want you to rest and recover for a few weeks, or maybe even a month or two, so you'll be able to dive back into your job with all that fervor and passion and focus that we're used to. Curtis Parks will oversee the Heartsong account until you return.

"I'm not laying you off," Blanche continued. "I just want you to take a break."

"I don't need a break."

Blanche ignored her comment. "We'll talk at the end of June. Five weeks for you to relax."

Abby threw the phone onto the seat, turned the truck ignition, and drove back toward the highway. She'd gather her things, and then go home.

Chapter 21

All the cubicles were empty when Abby returned to the office. It didn't appear that anyone had stayed to say good-bye. How many of them knew about her mandatory vacation before she did? Curtis Parks was probably the first to know, and she assumed he was off celebrating—drinking toast after toast in her name.

Abby turned the corner to find Maggie sitting at her desk, tears filling her bloodshot eyes.

Maggie reached for a tissue, blew her nose, and raced around the desk to squeeze Abby. "I don't know what's happening around here."

Abby backed away, clasping Maggie's hands. What was she going to do without her?

"Go home," Abby said. "I've only got a few things to pack."

"I'm helping you."

Abby shook her head. "This is only temporary, you know."

Maggie nodded her head in agreement, but she didn't look convinced. She hugged her again, grabbed a few items from the top of her desk, and fled. Abby watched her dash down the hall, her huge purse flailing behind her. Of everything she'd miss here, she'd miss Maggie most of all.

She flipped on the light and glanced around her office. She'd spent so many late nights and early mornings plugging away on a project at this desk, concocting ideas in her P.R. lab. Others may look at their office as a prison, but hers was a harbor, a safety net that protected her from life's pressures. With no warning, her secure cage had been blown away. Her predictable path veered off course. Not even the diverging road stanzas from Robert Frost could cheer her up.

She'd try to enjoy her few weeks of rest. Maybe she and Jessica could rent a cabin for a few weeks near Telluride and roam the Rockies. There were novels she wanted to read and museums she wanted to explore. She'd either talk Jessica into staying in Colorado or tempt her with the offer of spending the summer at some lake out east so her daughter wouldn't have to use the money in her dream fund.

She pulled a cardboard box out of the closet, unloaded it, and threw her framed photos and awards inside. Then she tugged open her desk drawers—only a few of the contents were actually hers. There was a pricey Mont Blanc pen she'd been given by a grateful client, her old Day-Timer, and a file of professional photos she'd had taken over the years. She didn't know what she'd do with this stuff, but it was hers and she wasn't about to leave it for the scavengers.

She sat down in her chair and wakened her laptop with the mouse. Zipping through her directories, she printed several public relations plans for her records and deleted a folder with all her personal documents.

The telephone rang, and Abby waited for Maggie to answer it until she remembered she'd sent Maggie home. She picked up the line.

"Hi, Abby," the deep voice greeted her. "It's Harold Rogers. I just wanted to see how your meeting went with the Duncans."

"They were fantastic." She'd leave the news of her vacation for Blanche to report.

"Do you think their story will work?"

"Absolutely," she replied. "It's heartfelt and real and filled with hope. It'll be great exposure for you."

"Excellent."

Abby hesitated. This might be the last chance she had to talk to Harold as a client for a month. If she called him back, she'd have to tell him the truth.

"Before you go." She took a long breath. "I have a few questions to ask you."

"Sure. Whatever you need."

"What if the Duncans decide fifteen or twenty years from now to find out what happened to Samuel? Could Heartsong track down the information for them?"

Abby braced herself when he didn't reply. Had her voice betrayed her? Did he know this was really a personal question?

Harold cleared his throat. "We would never guarantee we'd have that information, but we may be able to contact the birth mother and ask if she'd be comfortable passing along information about her son."

"That makes sense." Abby's mind raced with possibilities. Maybe she could find out what happened to Hunter, just enough information to know he was fine.

She put a file into her briefcase. "But what if, say, someone adopted from one of your satellite offices, maybe from Seattle. Would they have the same policy there?"

"Yes, it would be the same, but I would really hate for the reporter to give false hope to adoptive families. It's incredibly unlikely that an agency would be able to locate a birth parent after so many years, and if they do find them, the birth parent might not want to give out the information. It's an angle that I'd like to avoid."

"No problem." Abby shut down her computer and stood behind her desk. "I won't focus on it. I just want to be prepared to give the writer all the facts."

"Let me know if you need anything else," Harold said before he hung up.

"How's it going?" Curtis Parks asked from her open door. *The scavengers had come.* Of course, this scavenger wanted more than her office supplies. He wanted her job.

"I'm fantastic." She picked up the cardboard box and walked toward the door. "How are you?"

"I'm sorry to hear what happened. I told Blanche it was a bad idea," he said like he'd been begging Blanche to let her stay.

She turned off the light as she squeezed by him. "Vacation is never a bad idea."

"We're going to miss you," he said solemnly.

She turned to face him. "Don't you worry about it, Curtis. I'll be back in no time."

Chapter 22

Damian crossed the short plank and walked onto the back of the tour boat.

"Evening, folks," he said to the small group onboard. A few of them nodded back in response.

The team of insurance professionals had converged on Orcas Island for their annual convention, and they'd hired him to help with the playing aspect of their retreat. This one cruise would pay his expenses for the week . . . maybe he should just ditch public tours and focus on charters. If the orcas didn't return soon, he wouldn't have a choice.

He ducked under the low doorway into the heated wheelhouse, snatched his navy and gold captain's hat from a hook, and planted it on his head. He was now the official tour guide. Signaling through the window to Marc, he watched his first mate shove the plank away from the boat, throw in the rope, and jump aboard. They were ready to cruise.

Damian started the engine, and as he steered the boat out of the harbor, he flipped on the microphone beside him and held it up to his lips. He could do this tour in his sleep.

"Captain Damian De Lucia speaking," he said in his perfected tour guide voice. "We're glad to have you aboard for this fine evening of cruising the Sound."

He turned the giant wheel portside. "We've got calm seas tonight, so I don't expect we'll need life jackets, but just in case we do, my first mate will show you exactly where we've hidden them."

Right on cue, Marc waved at the small crowd and opened a closet door to display a rack of faded orange and green jackets.

"Puget Sound is filled with mysterious legends and lore, but if you get tired of me gabbing, you're welcome to take a swim. We'll come back and pick you up in an hour or two."

They passed a seventy-plus-foot yacht starboard.

"You may see a pirate or two on our cruise today. Off to the right, you'll see the Sound's most famous pirate ship."

The crowd managed a slight laugh. Good enough for him. He didn't think the line was that funny either, but it was tucked into Kendall's thirty-year-old script. Usually he mixed up the traditional tour spiel for variety, but when his improv clearly stunk, he reverted back to the script he'd inherited.

"Puget Sound is home to otters, porpoises, eagles, seals, salmon, and some of the largest octopuses in the world. It's also home to bull kelp, which is the fastest growing seaweed in the world. The kelp usually grows to thirty feet in length though it's able to grow to 120 feet in a single season.

"If we look hard enough, we should see plenty of sea life this evening . . . and if we're lucky, we'll even see the island's most famous mammal—the killer whale."

A half hour into the ride, Damian handed the wheel off to Marc so he could mingle with their guests. He'd barely stepped out onto the deck when a man sporting a black leather jacket and a gray ponytail stopped him.

"Do you think we'll see any orcas?" The man tugged on the chain by his coat pocket.

"They're late coming back this year, but you never know."

"I read your story in the newspaper."

Damian looked over the man's shoulder to see if anyone else wanted to speak with him. No one was there.

"It wasn't my story."

The man propped his boot up on a white bench. "Well, you had an awful lot to say."

Damian looked for a way around the man, but he was blocking the walkway. "Are you enjoying the boat ride?"

"Do you really think Pageant Industries is polluting the water?"

"I'd rather not talk about it."

"You're going up against a giant, my friend."

Damian met his eye. "What do you know about Pageant?"

"They're our biggest client."

"And yet you still chose to take my cruise."

"I don't think anyone else knows."

Just great. Damian turned around and went back to the wheel.

A quarter till ten, Damian entered the front door of De Lucia's. The servers were cleaning the tables as lingering guests finished dessert and coffee. Of course, they hadn't seen a whale on their ride, and the insurance man cornered him again when they docked. Colt Dantzler probably sent him over to annoy Damian and disrupt his tour.

Well, Pageant Industries was in the wrong here. He shouldn't be the one worrying.

Vincent was scooping the remaining minestrone into a Tupperware bowl when Damian walked into his kitchen. The aromas of onion and spicy pancetta filled the hot room.

"Can I help you clean up?" Damian asked.

Vincent rubbed his nose. "You need to clean yourself up."

"I guess that means you have it under control." Damian grabbed a rag and wiped off the red-stained counter.

"Did you know Laurel Taylor had a niece?" Vincent asked as he turned off the oven.

Damian's back stiffened, and he turned to stir a pot of mussel soup left on the stove.

"I guess I did." He smoothed the wooden spoon through the cream. "Abby Wagner's daughter, right?"

"Exactly. Didn't you sail with Abby before you went prancing around the world?"

"A very long time ago."

"Well, her daughter's coming to Orcas next week and is looking for a job. I wonder if her mom's coming with her."

Abby back on the island? His mind raced. He didn't actually want to see her again . . . did he? He could try to avoid her, but the island was too cramped to play an extended game of hide and seek. What would he say if he saw her?

"Are you giving her a job?" Damian asked.

"Of course I am. Locals first, you know."

"She's hardly a local, Vincent."

"Doesn't matter. As long as she's a decent waitress, she can work here all summer if she'd like. I always liked those Taylor girls. Thought you'd marry one of them."

So did I.

Damian powered the mussel soup around at full speed. Vincent reached down and plucked the spoon from his hand. "Please stop blending my soup."

"Just trying to help."

Vincent tossed him a clean rag. "I'll take care of the food."

Chapter 23

Abby crumpled newspaper onto her fireplace grate and added a tower of oak. She flicked a match, and when she lit the paper base, the wood erupted into an inferno. The chilly spring nights would soon transform into warm summer evenings, and she'd miss the weekend fires that calmed her after a hectic week of work. Not that she had any hectic weeks ahead. Her busy life had hit a wall.

She closed the mesh screen and stepped back to watch the blaze. Besides the hum of the crackling fire, the house was still. Jessica had escaped an hour ago to see a movie with friends. Neither of them had said much during the muted commercial breaks as they watched the evening news, pretending to be consumed by their cuts of microwave chicken, carrots, and roasted potatoes.

Abby tried to tell Jessica about her mandated "break," but she never got the nerve. Who wanted to tell their daughter that they'd failed? With the money from Scott's life insurance, she didn't have to work, but she craved purpose. She needed someone to need her.

She sat down on the couch. For the past seven years, her passion had been cause P.R. She'd fought battles to educate parents on healthy foods for their children, reclaim Colorado's unsafe mining lands, and warn families about the dangers of debilitated fire alarms. Where would she focus her passion now?

Leaning back, she sipped hot blackberry tea as she picked up her book. She'd decided to tackle a classic tonight—one of her favorite books from college. Delving into a novel always distracted her from reality.

Opening the crisp pages of *The Count of Monte Cristo,* she read the first lines of Edmond and Dantes sailing into port at Marseilles. Their captain had died at sea. She should be intrigued.

But she'd barely read through the second page when her mind wandered from the story. As hard as she tried, she couldn't concentrate on the text.

Jessica didn't even need her anymore. If her daughter did what she threatened, Abby would be alone all summer in this huge, quiet house. She supposed she could travel—maybe tour New England or even Western Europe for the next month. But Jessica wouldn't understand why she would travel east and not come west with her.

Maybe it was time to come clean with Jessica and tell her the reason she didn't want to return to Orcas Island. Her daughter was certainly old enough to handle it.

She'd debated this many times over the years—first with Scott and then with herself. Scott had wanted to tell Jessica about Hunter when she turned five. He'd prepared a short speech about how they'd adopted a little boy at one time, and even though he wasn't around anymore, they still loved him and wanted her to know. He'd insisted the best way to approach this situation was to make their loss as normal as possible for their daughter. Tell her directly so she knew and then let it go.

Abby had insisted they keep Hunter a secret. She never wanted Jessica to feel inferior, measuring herself against this invisible brother, or being afraid that her parents would have to give her up too. Her daughter didn't need to feel even a portion of the pain they'd experienced. Abby simply wanted their family to forget about their past and move on.

Yet Hunter kept creeping back into her life . . . and it was too late to tell Jessica the truth.

She wondered what the Duncans would do when they got a new baby. Would they tell their child about the adopted baby they lost, or would they keep it a secret? They probably would tell him or her, and they would do it in an absolutely perfect way.

Wrapping her fingers around her warm mug, she watched the dancing flames perform in front of her. Like a perfectly choreographed show, the blaze leapt and twirled and then bowed to silent applause.

If only God had choreographed her life as well as He did fire. She'd heard repeatedly that God was orchestrating her life and using every facet of it for good. Yet where was God when her life was spiraling out of control? He could wipe clean the painful memories of Hunter. He could pull a string or two to change Jessica's mind about leaving this summer. He could make Blanche realize her error and bring her back on the team. After all, hadn't God changed the hearts of kings? Her desires must seem piddling in comparison.

Maybe that was it. Maybe her needs were too insignificant in the course of the world. It wasn't worth God's time to mess with the trivial fragments of her life.

She sighed as she stood up and added another log to the fire. She sat on the Oriental rug in front of it and pulled her knees close to her chest. She glanced up at the open beams and the darkened skylight above. Lonely . . . she felt so terribly alone. The huge house would engulf her if she stayed in it for long.

She took a deep breath. Wallowing on the floor wasn't helping her a bit. She needed to talk to a friend.

She reached for the cordless phone on the end table and held it for a moment before dialing Laurel's number.

"Hey, Sis," she said when her younger sister answered her call.

"Abby, wow! Hold on a sec."

The phone clunked. Abby heard the commotion of loud voices competing in the background. Someone hollered. Davis broke into laughter. She almost wished she were playing games with them.

"Sorry," Laurel huffed. "I'm running up the stairs to get away from all this craziness."

"I don't want to interrupt you."

"Friday night's our family night, and you're part of the family so it's actually quite perfect. How's my favorite niece?"

"She's home from school and getting ready to launch out on her own for the summer."

"I'd say good for her, but I'm guessing it's extra tough for you."

Abby slid into a smooth leather chair and propped her soft moccasins on the coffee table.

"No single mother wants her only child to grow up and go off on her own."

"Knowing Jessica, I'm sure she's doing it in the nicest way possible."

"That's the thing," Abby said. "She's asked me to go with her, but I haven't decided yet what to do."

Abby heard a "whoosh" and assumed her sister had jumped onto her bed.

"Well, go with her, you silly chick. That invitation may only come around once."

Abby switched the phone to her right ear. "She wants to go to Orcas Island."

Abby straightened, preparing herself for a huge gasp and then an on-slaught of questions. But Laurel only choked down a cough before she replied. "The old cottage is a disaster, but you should go to the island."

Abby wanted to hug her sister for overcoming her shock and the hundred questions that must be swarming her head. But maybe she was the only one who thought it was strange to go back to the place where she lost Hunter. Maybe a visit to the old cottage would help her heal. She could spend a few more weeks with her daughter . . . and find out what happened to her son.

"How much of a disaster?" she asked.

"We went to Orcas a few weeks ago and stayed at an inn."

"Pretty bad, huh?"

"Nothing a little cleaning won't cure. You know that's not my gift."

To say the least. Her younger sister embraced life and left the mundane tasks of cleaning and repairing to fend for themselves. Fortunately, she married a man who had both feet planted on the ground.

"So it's okay with you if we brave it?"

"Of course it is. Davis will be thrilled to have you use it. He's been threatening to dump it for years." Laurel covered the phone and shouted to someone in the background. "But don't feel guilty if you sleep at a bed and breakfast."

"A little dirt won't kill us."

"Well, if you get in over your head, you can just come stay with us in Seattle for a few weeks. It would be just like old times."

Abby thanked her and hung up. She walked across the room and opened the sliding glass door. Stepping onto the porch, she gazed up at the expanse of stars. A gorgeous, cool, clear night. She folded her arms and breathed in the cold air.

She could do this. Orcas Island was only a place—surely a lot had changed since she'd been there last. She'd hoist a sail and see where the wind blew.

Jessica tiptoed into the living room around midnight, and the staircase creaked when she started to climb.

"Did you have fun?" Abby asked quietly. Her daughter gasped in surprise.

"Are you trying to kill me?"

"Your heart is young." Abby sat up on the couch.

"What are you doing up so late?"

"I fell asleep waiting for you. Apparently, I'm no longer a night person." Jessica sat on the stone hearth in front of the smoldering fire.

"You haven't waited up for me in a long time."

Abby smiled. If that's what Jessica thought, she'd let it go. She'd spent more sleepless evenings than she could count waiting in her room for Jessica to come home from a date or a ball game. When the garage door opened and closed for the final time on Friday and Saturday nights, she'd finally fall asleep.

"I wanted to talk to you about something."

Jessica leaned forward, her elbows resting on her knees. "Okay."

"I've been doing some thinking tonight," she paused. "And I wanted to see if the invitation was still open for me to visit Orcas with you."

"Of course it is!" Jessica shrieked and leaped forward to hug her. "Does that mean you're coming?"

"I talked to Laurel tonight. She said no one is staying at the Orcas cottage this month. I thought I could go with you for a few weeks and then come home."

"That would be awesome. But what about your job?"

"Blanche has given me an unexpected vacation."

"It's about time she gave you some time off."

Abby managed a smile. She wished she could look at it the same way.

"So when are we leaving?" Abby asked.

"My flight's on Monday."

Part 2

But oars alone can ne'er prevail
To reach the distant coast;
The breath of Heaven must swell the sail,
Or all the toil is lost.
—William Cowper, *Human Frailty*

Chapter 24

The 737 banked left above Seattle's crowded skyline. Abby fidgeted with her book, unable to concentrate on its words. Today, after all these years, she might actually get some answers.

"Look at the Space Needle," Jessica blurted, her nose scrunched against the cold glass, her eyes engulfing the sights.

Abby glanced at the spindly tower to the right and then looked across the aisle at downtown's silver skyscrapers, the arches and slopes of the buildings creating a bumpy line above the harbor.

She knew the downtown streets by heart. Raised in a quiet suburb northeast of town, she and her sister had spent most weekends visiting Seattle's restaurants, museums, and art shows. Her father had been an English professor, a stuffy man with old family money, and her mother an art teacher at the local high school, creative and bright and fun. Together, they'd instilled a passion into their daughters for learning, but in spite of all her education, Abby had been the happiest when she became a mom.

"We took you up the Needle for the first time when you were four," Abby said.

"I remember." Jessica's gaze focused out the window. "I was terrified until we got to the top. Then I was mesmerized by the sails below."

"You begged your dad to let you sit on his shoulders so you'd be the highest one there."

"I probably thought I could see even more."

Abby laughed. "You probably wanted to dive off the deck and into the water."

The plane looped over the busy Elliott Bay, cargo and cruise ships plugging through its waterways, and then descended toward the runway.

The in-flight air was stuffy and warm, and Abby was ready to be on the ground, enjoying Seattle's rare sunny day.

Catching a crowded bus from the airport, Abby and Jessica rode to the Avis lot and rented a sporty red convertible. They had it planned. Abby would use the car for three weeks and return it to the lot when she left for Denver. Jessica would spend the rest of her summer exploring the island by bike.

"Do you remember the seals and otters at the aquarium?" Abby asked as they drove north on Interstate 5.

Jessica nodded her head. "And all the tropical fish."

"Do you want to visit while we're here?"

"Sure. Do you want to stop?"

"Why don't I drop you off while I get some groceries?" Abby suggested.

"Cool."

Abby curved through the downtown streets, passed Pier 59, and stopped by the aquarium's front doors.

"I'll pick you up in two hours or so."

"Take your time," Jessica said as she hopped out of the convertible. "I could spend days in this place."

Abby drove south, past three grocery stores and a food mart.

Even though she and Scott had only visited the Heartsong office a few times during their adoption process, she remembered exactly where it was. She turned onto Madison and then Eighth Avenue. The building came into view.

A plain white sign stuck in the narrow lawn announced that it was the Seattle division of Heartsong Adoptions. Inching back and forth, Abby steered the rental car into a parallel space and parked crooked by the curb.

She stared at the simple office beside her. Housed in a boxy brick building with a flat roof and peeling flower boxes under the two front windows, there was no glamour about the place. Most people who visited only spent minutes here, maybe an hour—a brief stop that would change their life. Time stopped for her the last time she visited; her life had never been the same again.

Scott had asked her to stay home that day and let him take Hunter back alone, but she refused. She wanted to hold Hunter until the very last moment, hoping . . . praying Stacie would see them together and change her mind.

As she sat in the car on that misty day, she contemplated all the places she could run with him. It wouldn't be hard. They could hide in Canada or Europe or New York City, for that matter. It wasn't like anyone was going to chase them. Stacie wouldn't have the money to pursue them. Heartsong wouldn't want the bad press. The government couldn't care less. They could be a family anywhere, just as long as they had their child.

Scott said she was being ridiculous. He hadn't spent all these years building their lives to run like fugitives, and it certainly wouldn't be fair to Hunter. Abby called him selfish, but he held strong. For years, she wished she had run away with Hunter and left her husband behind.

Abby closed her eyes. She'd clung to Hunter until Julia took him from her arms. She returned her son like he was a Christmas present that was the wrong size.

She'd fled outside and collapsed on the back floor of their minivan, heaving heart-wrenching sobs the entire trip home, trying to purge herself of the unbearable pain.

Abby looked back up at the building. A girl, about six or seven months pregnant, walked out beside a woman in a business suit. Abby wondered if this girl knew what she was doing or, like Stacie, she'd change her mind. Adoption was a wicked game of guesswork, all the parties trusting their hearts to someone they hardly knew.

She tentatively opened the car door and coasted up the cracked sidewalk like she was in a trance.

She stopped and stared again at the brick front. What was she doing? She shouldn't be here, trying to relive her past. Why couldn't she leave Hunter alone and move on?

Stepping back, she debated why she should and shouldn't proceed. If she found out something bad had happened to him, her heart would break again. Her mind envisioned a thousand horrible scenarios, but she needed the truth to let go of Hunter permanently. If she didn't do it now, she'd never come back.

Gulping a deep breath, she willed herself to move ahead and open the screened front door. Thankfully, they'd redecorated the lobby since she'd been here last. The walls were a light peach with a border of grapevines draped around the top. The furniture was a mismatch of pastel colored chairs and two couches around a coffee table.

No one sat behind the open receptionist window, so she walked over to a row of photos lining the walls. She hadn't made an appointment, afraid they'd reject her before considering her request. In-person was always best when you were asking the impossible.

She examined the smiling faces in the pictures—all successful matches of adoptive families and their beautiful children. The Wagner family photo was probably buried in a vault.

Leaning around the corner, she glanced up a hallway with six or seven doors.

"Hello," she called down the empty hall.

A tiny woman wearing a headset over her straight brown hair peeked out of a doorway. She pointed toward her ear with one hand while she covered the mouthpiece with the other. "I'll be done in a minute."

Abby nodded and backed toward the lobby.

She sat on a padded chair and looked down at the *USA Today* spread across the glass table. Picking up the newspaper, she scanned the headlines. Then she pulled out the Life section and saw the smiling picture of Tom and Briana Duncan along with their yellow Lab. Front page, above the fold—not bad. She breezed through Victor's story. Not bad at all. He'd done his homework, portraying the Duncans as a brave couple, strong in their faith instead of weak. Very courageous of him.

"Children are a gift from God," Briana said in the article. "We're just waiting until He blesses us with another child. We were sad when our first adoption didn't work, but we're confident that God will bring us a baby in His perfect time."

Heartsong should be a very happy client right now. National exposure and the negative aspect as polished as Briana's silver.

Abby heard a swish of light footsteps rush down the hall.

The woman removed her headset as she walked into the lobby. "I'm so sorry to keep you waiting."

"It's no problem." Abby pointed at the newspaper she'd dropped on the table. "Nice article."

"Thanks. You never know how a story is going to turn out."

"You should be pleased," Abby said.

"We were pleased and pleasantly surprised that they picked Heartsong. There are so many adoption agencies out there."

Abby thought briefly about the hours her team spent developing the story and distributing it to the right people, but she didn't say anything. The allure of P.R. was that the end result seemed effortless. Even Heartsong's employees thought the story just happened. Snap . . . and it appeared.

"But you're not here to talk about newspaper articles, are you?" The woman stuck out her hand. "I'm Chloe Meyers."

Abby introduced herself, and Chloe invited her back to her office.

"Tell me what I can do for you." She shut the door and sat down behind her black metal desk.

"I have an odd request." Abby sat down in a folding chair and faced Chloe. "It's extremely hard for me to ask."

"Believe me, Ms. Wagner, I've heard about everything in this office, so please don't think I'll be shocked by anything you say."

"I guess it's not shocking," Abby sighed. "I'm not pregnant or anything."

Chloe smiled. "Last month I placed a baby from a forty-seven-year-old woman who called her doctor a pervert when he told her she was expecting."

"I'm surprised she was able to speak."

"Me too," Chloe laughed. "So what can I do for you?"

Abby took a deep breath. She could do this.

"Twenty years ago my husband and I adopted a boy from this agency."

Chloe started to offer her congratulations, but Abby waved her hand to cut her off.

"The birth mother changed her mind four months after he was placed in our home, and we had to give him back."

"Oh no." Chloe leaned forward on her desk.

"It's been a long time, but I need to know what happened to him. I don't know if it's possible for your agency to track him and his birth mother down, but I'd be so grateful if you'd try."

Chloe folded her hands on the table, silently considering her appeal. Abby would have begged if she thought it would help, but it was up to Chloe and her superiors to make this decision. It wasn't a good business decision—they wouldn't make a cent off the hunt. But it would be an honest work of compassion if they'd help her.

"That is an unusual request, but I understand why you'd want to know." She thumped her fingers across the keyboard, typing Abby's name.

She scanned an Excel chart. "Your file's in storage, but we'll dig it out. I'll call the birth mother's number to ask if she'd be willing to pass on any information."

"I appreciate it," Abby said.

"We've never done this before, so I can't predict the response."

"I understand." Abby scribbled her cell phone number on the agency's letterhead and passed it to Chloe.

"Ms. Wagner," Chloe said softly. "I really am sorry this happened to you."

Abby's throat choked as she stood up. She wished the agency had said that years ago, but it was still nice to hear those simple words today.

"Thank you." She turned and rushed to her car.

Chapter 25

Marc slipped an old black baseball cap on his head as he stepped off the sailboat. He and Damian had taken a short afternoon ride around the island, another failed scouting trip in search of the orcas. He had a feeling they'd sail at least once a day until they spotted the whales, and he was okay with that. No place he'd rather be than on the water.

"Marc!" he heard someone shout as he secured the boat to the slip. When he turned, he saw a gaunt woman running his way. He did a double take. Her chestnut hair was pulled back in a ponytail, and she wore faded jeans and a blue flannel shirt that hung off her arms like a scarecrow's garb.

"Mom?"

"Hi, honey."

She hugged him for so long that he wasn't sure she'd let go. It was his third summer on the island, and she'd never come to visit him before. For all he knew, she hadn't even known where Orcas Island was.

He finally backed out of her bony arms and took a deep breath. "What are you doing here?"

She grabbed his hand, and her fingers trembled against his. He was afraid he'd break them if he squeezed.

"I just wanted to see my son."

He examined her eyes. They were the crystal green color that he knew from her good days, but by the look of her yellowed skin, she hadn't gone long without a drink.

He heard Damian's footsteps behind him.

"Mom, I'd like you to meet my boss, Damian De Lucia."

She let go of his hand to shake Damian's.

"Actually, I'm more of a friend than a boss, but Marc is the hardest

working kid I know. Can't tell you how grateful I am to have him work-ing for me."

"My boy's always been a hard worker. Takes good care of me."

Damian managed a sad smile. "I bet he does."

"What are you doing here?" Marc repeated.

"Can't a mom miss her only son?"

Marc shrugged his shoulders. He knew his mom missed him, but driving from Seattle to the ferry and then crossing the Sound was a huge feat for her.

He took her elbow. "Let's get dinner. Damian owns a great Italian restaurant in town."

"Actually, it's my uncle's restaurant," Damian said. "But it's the best food on the island."

"I can't." She shifted her denim purse from one arm to the other. "I just came for an hour."

"You can at least spend the night," Marc insisted as he escorted her down the dock, but she shook her head.

"Hey, Marc!" Damian called to him, and he walked slowly back to-ward the boat.

Damian pretended to re-knot the rope Marc had tied.

"You okay?"

Marc didn't meet his eye. "I'm going to take my mother back to the ferry."

Grasping Marc's shoulder, he whispered. "Alcohol is a cruel master."

Marc nodded his head before joining his mom at the end of the pier.

Her clunky blue Chevrolet was illegally parked in a fire lane, and he glanced around for a cop. Fortunately there was no officer to write a ticket.

The seat was cluttered with crumpled newspapers and a fast food bag, so he pushed the stuff onto the floor and slipped inside.

"I'm glad you came to visit," he said as she tried to start the car. It fired on the third attempt. "But I can't believe you're only staying for an hour."

"I have to get home tonight."

The sun was descending slowly over the water as they drove back toward the ferry terminal at ten miles below the twenty-five-mile-per-hour limit.

"Why don't you stay with me for the summer?" he asked. "You could get a job at a restaurant or the marina."

She shook her head like she always did when he suggested this plan. Marc knew exactly what she was thinking. He'd never tolerate alcohol in his apartment. She was embarrassed about her problem, but not embarrassed enough to stop.

She turned into the terminal, strands from her ponytail falling over her eyes. "Do you have a few dollars with you?"

Marc groaned. Of course it came down to cash. Why else would she travel to the island? Since her telephone begging hadn't worked, she'd resorted to an in-person sales pitch. She must be desperate.

"I'm not giving you any money."

"Just a little for the ferry ticket, honey. Nothing else."

He hated this.

"How did you get the money to get over here?"

"Borrowed it from a friend, but I have to pay him back tomorrow."

He sighed as he pulled out his wallet and handed her two twenties.

"This is to cover the money you borrowed and the gas to get you home."

"Nothing else," she said, crossing her heart with a bony finger.

With a thousand broken promises cramming their past, she'd never given him the chance to believe.

"I'll come visit in a few weeks," he said as he kissed her cheek.

She wouldn't be able to get alcohol when he left her at this terminal. Hopefully she didn't know about the liquor store on the other side.

Chapter 26

Four hours after Abby picked up Jessica at the aquarium, she drove the convertible onto the crowded deck of the ferryboat headed to Orcas Island. Before she even set the parking brake, Jessica jumped out of the car and ran toward the railing. Abby locked the doors and propped herself up on the trunk to gaze out at the choppy sea.

The meeting with Heartsong's local office went much better than she'd imagined. She'd been afraid they would remember her story, her anger. She'd been afraid that after all these years Julia would still be there, and after the horrible things Abby had said to her, the adoption coordinator would scorn her pleas and tell her to go home.

She shivered and pulled her jacket tighter around her shoulders.

Chloe had been young but helpful, even remorseful over what had happened. That's all she needed—a little heart.

Jessica turned toward her, eyes lit from her grin. "This is awesome!"

"Do you want to take a nap?" Abby asked as a cloud of car exhaust drifted through the cramped tier.

"Are you kidding me?"

"It's an hour and a half to Orcas."

"I couldn't sleep if it was ten hours."

Abby smiled. She'd never been able to sleep on the boat ride either.

"Then let's go inside and enjoy the ride from a warmer deck."

With a forward jerk, the ferry left the Anacortes terminal, and Abby and Jessica edged through the tight lot of vehicles and up the narrow stairs.

The main deck was enclosed in windows, large cushioned booths lining both sides. The cafeteria was dark, closed for the night, so Abby fed two dollars to a vending machine and bought a Diet Coke for herself, a regular Coke for her daughter.

As Abby slid into a booth beside Jessica, the ferry passed a power plant with thousands of orange lights glowing in preparation for sundown. Small waves lapped against the sides of the boat as they rode out into open water.

"Are you up for a game of rummy?" Abby asked.

"Sure."

Abby dug through her purse, pulled out a deck of cards, and shuffled. She'd probably spent a hundred hours on this boat as a child playing card games with her sister or reading Nancy Drew.

She dealt them each seven cards, centering a stockpile in the middle. Then they began a silent battle of gathering, matching, and discarding. Abby won the first game; Jessica won the next two. Jessica shuffled the cards and dealt them again.

The ferry made several island stops as the sun faded behind the fog, but Abby and Jessica continued to play their hands.

"Does the ferry bring back memories?" Jessica asked as she placed a run of royal blacks by her side.

"A few, but I remember most the stories your dad would tell me after he brought you to the island. He said you'd stand out on the deck and scamper like a puppy from side to side so you wouldn't miss a thing. You haven't changed much, you know."

"Hopefully, I've grown just a little in the last ten years."

"You've grown so much that I'm going to have to use my broomstick to ward off all those boys on the island."

"I don't think you have to worry, Mom."

Abby grunted in response. She didn't believe that for a second. Abby would have to lock their doors to keep the boys away.

"Dad used to talk about Orcas all the time," Jessica said as she deliberately displayed a set of tens.

"Before we got married, I used to say that the only reason he proposed was so he could spend summers at our cottage. He was always begging me to come out here."

"Is that why you stopped coming?"

"Digging right down to the heart of the matter, aren't you?"

"I'm just curious. You never let me come back here after Dad died."

Abby displayed a lousy set of threes. Her daughter was going to cream her on this round.

"I suppose that was one of many reasons. Sometimes it's important to let our good memories rest as we move on with life."

Abby watched Jessica analyze her cards. Until she became a mother, she'd never understood the pain of losing a child. The cottage had been her haven, a sanctuary for their family. When the call came from the adoption agency, she'd wanted to stay on the island. Taking Hunter back to the mainland, to the agency, was like attending his funeral. He hadn't passed away, but her heart felt like he'd died.

Abby had sworn she'd never go back to Orcas, and yet here she was traveling across the Sound, playing cards, pretending nothing was wrong.

The alarm on her watch interrupted her thoughts and their game.

"We're almost there," she said as she gathered the cards into a neat stack.

"You set your alarm?" Jessica stared at her like she was insane.

"When Laurel and I were kids, we got so involved with our card game that we almost missed this stop. We rushed downstairs to find our parents steaming in their car, a line of other vehicles honking behind them. Ever since then, I've paid attention."

"So how long do we have to get to the car?"

"Two minutes, if the boat's on time."

Abby stood up as the ferry brushed against the dock. She held onto the table to steady herself.

"We're on time."

Engines revved across the deck as the bridge connected their boat to land, and minutes later, Abby and Jessica's convertible joined the string of cars driving onto the island.

As their wheels hit the pavement, Abby looked at the line of cars waiting to get on the boat. Some of them had probably been there for hours. Monday night wasn't a bad night to catch the ferry, but if it were Friday or Saturday, some of these people might be spending another night on the island.

Abby blinked.

To her left was an old blue Chevrolet with an emaciated woman in jeans and a flannel shirt sitting on the hood. Abby shuddered. It was uncanny. The woman's chestnut hair was back in a ponytail, exactly how Stacie had worn her hair at the agency. The woman's face was several decades older, but her arms and legs were just as thin as Stacie's had been on the awful day that Abby returned her son.

The truck behind Abby honked.

Twenty years ago, everyone seemed to look like Stacie. It figured the mirage would appear tonight since she'd been thinking about Hunter and his birth mother all day.

"What are you doing, Mom?" Jessica asked, and Abby hit the gas.

"I thought I saw someone I knew."

"I bet you know a lot of people on the island."

"Maybe." She glanced in the rearview mirror. The woman had disappeared.

"I know one person who knows you."

Her daughter's statement pulled her back to the present. "Who?"

"Vincent De Lucia."

"How do you know Vincent?"

"I'm going to work for him this summer."

"What? You didn't tell me that."

Jessica shrugged her shoulders. "I need a job."

"I used to know Vincent's nephew."

"Maybe he's still on the island."

Abby ignored her daughter's arched eyebrows and studied the road in front of her. She didn't tell Jessica that according to the *Seattle Times*, Damian De Lucia was on the island.

The convertible's headlights seemed like a dull flashlight ray struggling to illuminate the dark island road in front of them. Copper-colored Pacific Madrona trees lined both sides of the pavement, their dramatically curved trunks resembling spooky, hand-sculpted pieces of art in the dim light.

They passed the marina, but it was too dark to see any of the boats and the outline of the water barely shimmered in the sparse light. Abby turned into their wooded driveway and zigzagged up a winding road fenced with maple trees and bushy grass.

"I can't believe we're finally here," Jessica said as Abby parked the car in front of the cottage.

Built from simple slats of aging wood, the house was two stories with a covered entrance and a porch loaded with firewood. The only out-building doubled as a storage area and garage. Abby doubted there was actually any space inside the garage to park their car, but she'd wait until tomorrow to check. She didn't want any surprises on their first night.

Jessica leapt out of the car and grabbed a suitcase from the trunk. She rushed to the front door and jostled the knob.

"Key's under the flower pot," Abby called as she unloaded a cooler filled with their groceries and then pulled out a suitcase.

Jessica tipped back the clay jar and held up the key.

Not really a brilliant place to hide a key, but break-ins around here were so rare that no one seemed to care about security. The fact that it was so difficult to flee the island probably deterred criminals. Who wanted to break into a house, steal the valuables, and wait for an hour or two to get on a ferry?

Jessica wrestled with the rusty lock until it cracked open. She flipped on the porch light when she went inside.

At least we have electricity, Abby thought. She hoped the water was running too.

Abby flung the leather strap of her suitcase over her shoulder and followed her daughter into the house. She wished she shared Jessica's enthusiasm at being back. Maybe she could muster excitement after a solid night's sleep. So much had changed since she used to beg her own parents to come to the island . . .

Abby pushed open the door with her foot and coughed. Jessica was already roaming through the rooms, kicking up the dust. Abby looked in horror at the thick coat of dirt on the coffee table and bookshelves. Laurel wasn't kidding—the place was buried in filth. Tomorrow, she'd tackle the cleaning with force.

"It hasn't changed at all," Jessica shouted from one of the three bed-rooms. "This dresser even has some of my old clothes in it."

Abby looked into the paneled room—the same room she'd been sit-ting in when they got Julia's call. The last time she'd been here, she was holding Hunter in her arms.

Jessica picked up a plaid jumper and a pair of girl's shorts. "Don't you think it's time to give these away?"

Abby's stomach felt nauseous as she backed out of the room.

"Isn't this fun?" Jessica called after her as Abby entered the open kitchen. The entire wall over the sink and counters was windowed, the dim kitchen light reflecting in the glass.

"A blast," Abby drawled.

"I'm going to take a shower."

Abby pulled the teapot off a shelf and rinsed it. Thankfully, they had water along with the electricity. She filled the pot and turned on the stove to boil the water for tea.

A scream erupted from Jessica's room, and Abby ran to find her daugh-ter in the bathroom, two towels wrapped around her shivering body.

"C-c-cold," she stuttered, pointing to the shower.

Okay, so they didn't have hot water. A minor inconvenience.

"You're supposed to feel it before you jump in."

"I thought it would warm up."

"I'll call the plumber tomorrow."

Abby left Jessica hidden under a pile of thick blankets in her bedroom.

She poured a mug of hot tea before collapsing on the stained yellow couch in the living room. A cloud of dust puffed up around her, and she sighed. She didn't know if she was up for this adventure, but for Jessica's sake, she'd try.

Chapter 27

Abby awakened to a stream of light spilling across her room. She reached to shut off her alarm clock before it rang, but it wasn't there. She bolted upright, her eyes flying around the dark paneled walls and the green-checkered curtains to her side . . . she was back on Orcas Island.

She threw back the plaid comforter and glanced over the loft railing. Light filtered through the dramatic windows that reached up to the cathedral ceiling and saturated both her room and the living room below. Rubbing her eyes, she looked across their long back yard at the seawater sparkling below the house, crisp dark waves framed perfectly by the red cedar trees.

She blinked. What had happened to the yard? It was cluttered with dandelions, weeds, and enough grass to cover half the back yards in Denver proper. She'd focus on cleaning the house first, and then she'd do something about the overgrown jungle outside. If she didn't, the plants would overtake them in their sleep.

Abby pulled her hair back in a ponytail and changed into a burgundy cotton shirt and Bermuda shorts. She started her climb down the narrow stairs, but three steps down, her foot wobbled on a rotten board and pressed through. She pulled her foot back in horror and stared at the broken step. She and Jessica may have to rent a hotel room if the house continued to crumble around them.

"What are you doing up in the loft?" Jessica asked as Abby limped down the remaining steps. Her daughter's legs were up on the end of the couch, and she was gazing out the window at the water and the forested hills across the bay.

"I like how open it is." Abby sat down on the bottom step, pulled off her sock, and rubbed her sore ankle. It was scraped, but no blood. "Did you end up sleeping out here?"

"No, I crashed in my old bedroom." Jessica nodded toward the window. "I'd forgotten how incredible it is here."

"Me too," Abby replied. "Though I don't remember the house being on the brink of collapse."

"You're exaggerating."

She pointed up to the broken step. "I'm not so sure."

"I think we'll make it, Mom."

Abby stepped into the hall. "Do I smell coffee?"

"Fortunately, the coffee pot still works." Jessica smiled as she lifted a steaming mug to her lips.

Abby padded to the kitchen, poured a mug full of Tulley's coffee, and added two spoonfuls of sugar with a dash of cream. She was grateful she'd already stopped for groceries. One less thing to worry about today. Now she just needed to get the hot water turned on, a new set of stairs installed . . . and a blowtorch to sterilize the entire place.

The faint tune of La Traviata played in the distance, and Abby rushed toward the hallway to find her phone.

"I've got it," Jessica hollered from the living room. Abby heard a loud "ouch!" as Jessica raced up the stairs to the loft.

"Don't answer that!" Abby yelled back. Her daughter didn't respond.

Surely, Heartsong wouldn't call her back so quickly. It hadn't even been twenty-four hours.

Her hands shook, and coffee splashed on the hardwood floor. Thirty seconds passed . . . sixty. She realized she'd been holding her breath as she wiped up the coffee with a paper towel.

Jessica appeared in the arched hallway, her hand covering the phone's receiver.

"They tracked you down," she whispered.

"Who is it?" Abby tossed the paper towel in the trashcan.

"That adoption agency."

Abby grabbed for the phone.

Jessica took a step back. "What's wrong with you?"

"Just give me the phone."

Jessica huffed. "I don't know how you're going to take a vacation if your clients keep calling you."

Clients? Of course. Abby smiled in relief. Heartsong was technically still her client.

"I'm sorry, honey. I'm sure they just have a quick question."

She grabbed the cell phone, walked into a bedroom, and shut the door. Her face flushed and sweat soaked the palms of her hands. Surely the news was good or they wouldn't have gotten back to her so quickly.

"Is this Abby Wagner?" the woman asked.

Abby recognized Chloe Meyers' voice. She swallowed hard, keeping her voice low so Jessica wouldn't hear her conversation through the door. "How are you, Chloe?"

"I wish I had good news."

Abby's shoulders slumped. She'd set her hopes too high. "I dug through Stacie's file and called her old number. The man who answered had never heard of her. She probably moved years ago."

Abby sank down on the flimsy double bed. If she'd been honest with herself, she would've known this was a dead end, but she'd still hoped God would help her find her son.

"I know this isn't a typical request," Abby's voice trembled. She wouldn't let herself cry. "But is there any way I could get her last name? I think I could track her down pretty easily online, and I'd let someone at your agency make the actual call."

"I'm sorry, Abby. Stacie has a legal and moral right to her privacy, no matter how long it's been."

"What if I paid you to find her?"

"I can't imagine how difficult this is for you, but if Stacie wanted to be found, she would have notified the agency when she moved."

"Thank you for trying." She folded her phone and tucked it into her pocket.

"Everything okay?" Jessica asked when she came back into the kitchen. She appeared to be chomping down on a salami sandwich for breakfast.

"It's fine," Abby lied.

"Good." Jessica leaned over to retie her shoes. "I'm outta here."

"Aren't you going to help me clean this place up?"

"I'll help later." Jessica jogged toward the front door. "This morning I've got to check on my job."

Abby watched her daughter pull an old red bicycle out of the shed, pump up the tires, and pedal down the driveway.

Abby sat back down in a chair with the cold coffee in her hand. Why had she agreed to come? She'd been happy and satisfied with her life before Blanche had asked her to work on the Heartsong campaign. Okay, maybe not actually happy, but everything had been fine. She had a gorgeous home, a good job, and a life she'd created for herself in Denver.

It was time to stop dwelling on the past. If Heartsong couldn't help her, it was time to move on. She could do this.

She set down her coffee a little harder than necessary, pulled a towel out of the hall closet, and walked into the bathroom, twisting the shower dial as far left as it would go. Maybe, just maybe, the cold water turned lukewarm overnight.

Abby stuck her fingers under the flow and icy water chilled her hand. She sighed as she undressed and climbed into the shower.

She scrubbed her skin in record time and jumped back out seconds later. Wrapping herself in a warm towel, she raced back into the kitchen and sipped hot coffee to thaw.

The instant her shivering stopped, she picked up her cell phone and checked for new messages. There were none.

She'd thought that Blanche would have called by now to congratulate her on the *USA Today* article or at least ask a few questions about one of the current campaigns.

But not a word from Denver.

She might as well start cleaning. At least the house needed her.

Chapter 28

Marc smoothed his paintbrush over a black streak on *The Drifter*, dipped the brush back into the bucket, and wiped the white paint across the hull of the boat again to cover the mark.

He hadn't heard from his mother since she left last night even though he'd asked her three times to call when she got home. He almost tried to call her this morning, but he'd beat himself up for a month if she was drunk.

He'd been up most of the night anyway, debating whether he should have tempted her with hard cash. It was the first time he'd given her money since his freshman year in high school when she'd "borrowed" ten dollars for dinner and spent it on vodka within the hour.

The grocery certificates he bought her and the monthly payment to her landlord kept her fed and dry. Somehow, she managed to get the money for her electric bill . . . and something to drink on the side.

He was swiping another coat of paint on the sailboat when someone caught his eye. It was a girl with dusty blonde hair brushing against her shoulders as she stopped along the pier to look at each boat like she was a critic working an art show. She wore a red and white striped tank top, white cargo pants, and red Converse sneakers—proper attire for a college kid.

He caught himself staring and refocused on the scattered clouds above him instead of on her. A bald eagle flew through the maze of masts beside him and up into the forest. He kept looking up to see if the bird would fly his way again.

"Great day, isn't it?" he heard her say, and he met her light blue eyes.

"Gorgeous." He stood up beside the boat, paint dripping onto his army green shorts. "You look lost."

She grinned. "I'm trying to rent a sailboat."

"You like to sail?" He dropped the brush on a plastic sheet and wiped his hands on a paint-splattered towel.

"I used to, but it's been awhile."

"Well, there are plenty of boats around here to rent." He pointed to a shack at the other end of the pier. "Go up there and talk to a guy named Bert. He'll hook you up."

"Thanks."

Marc watched her walk toward the end of the pier. He'd spent the past three summers working on Orcas, and he'd never seen her before. Probably just a vacationer. In a week or two, she'd be gone.

Draping a rope across his shoulder, Marc looped it under his arm until it was wound tight. He tucked it into the boat's lazaretto.

Damian walked down the pier and stopped in front of him, nodding toward the girl. "Who's that?"

"No idea." Marc shrugged. "She was just asking about sailing."

"Hmm . . ." Damian replied as he climbed onto the deck of *The Drifter* and started unfurling the tightly wrapped sail.

He hopped over the side of the boat to help Damian ready the sail.

"How did it go last night?" Damian asked as he guided the sail with his gloved hand.

Marc shook his head. "She wanted money."

"I hope you didn't give her any."

"Forty bucks to cover the ferry and gas."

Damian didn't say anything.

"You don't know what it's like," Marc said.

"You're right."

"I don't want her to drink, but she's my mom."

"An impossible situation."

Marc nodded his head.

"I want you to know I haven't stopped praying for your mom," Damian said.

"Thanks."

Damian raised his head and whistled softly. Marc followed his gaze and elbowed him when he saw the girl walking back to them.

"What are you doing?" Marc hushed him.

"She's the spitting image of her mother."

Marc wanted to ask who she was, but the girl was already at his side.

"Thanks for the tip," she said. "That's exactly what I was looking for."

"Bert's a good guy." Marc grinned down at her. "He'll treat you right."

Damian cleared his throat and stuck out his hand. "I'm Damian, and this is Marc."

She smiled again. "I'm Jessica Wagner."

"Are you a local?" Damian asked.

"My mom is. I'm just here to work and sail."

"Where are you working?" Marc asked.

"I just interviewed with a weird guy named Vincent De Lucia. Do you know him?"

"He's my uncle," Damian laughed.

Her face turned pink. "He was more nice than weird."

"I'd stick with weird if I were you." Damian took a half step toward her. "I have to ask. You look exactly like an old friend of mine—Abby Taylor."

"That's probably because I'm her daughter. You must be the nephew she used to know?"

"That's me. Please tell her I said hello."

"Why don't you come and tell her yourself?"

Damian lifted the sail. "I might have to do that."

He glanced over at Marc and back at Jessica. "Would you like to sail with Marc and I this morning?"

Jessica stepped toward the boat, and Marc thought she might actually climb aboard. *Thank you, Damian!*

"I'd love to, but I can't today. Could I take a rain check?"

Marc caught Damian's eye. "I'm sure we'll be sailing again tomorrow morning."

"Well, then, how about tomorrow?" Damian asked. "We'll sail to your house around eight."

"Sounds great. You know how to get there?" At Damian's nod, Jessica waved as she walked back toward the town.

"Danger, my man," Damian whispered, handing Marc the clew of the sail.

Marc hoisted the mainsail along the boom. "Do you think your uncle needs any more help this summer?"

"I'm telling you, those Taylor girls are trouble."

Marc tugged the sail up. "I thought she said she was a Wagner."

"Well, she's got a good dose of Taylor blood."

"Are you scared of Jessica's mom?"

"Are you kidding me?" Damian took the wheel, backing them away from the slip.

"Maybe terrified is a better word."

"You do realize that I'm more than thirty years older than you."

Marc laughed. "That's a pitiful answer."

"I'm only sounding the alarm."

"Did Jessica's mom break your heart?" Marc asked.

Damian steered the boat toward open water. "I've never had success with romance."

"Didn't you tell me that you once faced Indonesian natives with harpoons and lived to tell about it?"

"I never should have told you that story."

"And ran from the Russian mafia?"

"I exaggerated that just a bit."

"And braved Grenada's parliament to convince them to impose a moratorium on whale hunting?"

"Your memory's going to get you into trouble."

Marc laughed. "These are good questions."

"Save your questions for the classroom."

They breezed out of the marina and cut through the steady waves, water glistening against the pastel blue sky. He couldn't see another sailboat on the horizon.

"You told me once that I have to face my fears head on." Marc said.

"I don't remember that conversation."

"Mrs. Wagner can't be that scary."

Damian sighed as he turned the wheel. "You have no idea."

Chapter 29

Abby stretched her fingers and toes to reach the coastal paintings on the wall and brush off the thick dust settled on top. She smoothed the strands of hair escaping from her ponytail and tucked her shirt back into her shorts before wiping the brown muck off the living room's white wicker furniture and its pastel yellow and blue cushions.

Laurel may not be interested in cleaning, but Abby didn't know if she'd be able to sleep again without an overhaul. Who knew what creepy things hid under the furniture? After years of growing and reproducing dirt and mold, this house was a horror flick waiting to happen. Freddy Krueger was probably hidden under the mounds of clutter.

Well, dirt be warned. It may have called this place home for a decade, but not only was she ready for battle, she was determined to win.

She threw a stack of papers into a box. She'd attack the cleaning of the cottage like she'd attack a P.R. campaign—scheming, strategizing, and conquering. With a quick glance around at the smeared coffee table, scraped paint, and cracking wood, she sighed. Even if she worked twelve hours a day, it would be weeks before this place was decent enough to call a home.

She sipped a glass of watery lemonade, beads of moisture dotting the crystal sides, and Chloe's words repeated themselves in her mind. Even a filthy house couldn't distract her. Finding Hunter was hopeless if Heartsong wouldn't help her.

Her hands shook as she soaked an old dishrag. She needed to do something. Anything to redirect her disappointment. Anything to distract herself from the truth that Hunter was lost for good.

Surely, a little detective work would uncover Stacie's whereabouts.

This was the age of the Internet—easy research at the fingertips of one Chloe Meyers.

She wrung out the rag. Chloe hadn't tried very hard to find Stacie. People just didn't disappear these days without a lot of money and motivation. She couldn't imagine that Stacie had either.

A dead end, and she'd slammed into it. Heartsong had reimbursed most of their adoption fees when she realized she was pregnant with Jessica in 1986, and since she wasn't paying the agency for their services now, she had no right to demand. They were simply doing her a favor, and she couldn't ask any more. It was done.

She lifted a framed picture as she brushed the damp cloth across the corner table, and a cloud of fine dirt swooshed into the air. She glanced down at the photo of the entire Taylor clan and stared at her parents, Scott, Laurel, and Davis huddled together on the dock. This picture was taken before the kids were born. Back when they had high hopes for the family to come.

She remembered that summer week vividly. She and Scott were newly married, and they'd whispered that within the year, they'd have a child. It was their secret. Something they'd never doubted would happen soon.

Of course, the baby didn't come. Six more years went by before they brought Hunter to the island.

She centered the frame on the glass-topped table and scrubbed an oval mirror hanging on the wall. Her parents had purchased this cottage as a summer getaway back when the island's main industry was fishing and real estate was cheap. When she and Laurel were young, they'd spent every summer in this house. Her parents had updated some of the décor before they passed away. The couch, two of the beds, and the kitchen table were new. Everything else looked pretty much the same as when she was a girl.

Strange what happens when you turn into an adult. She'd never particularly cared before about the cleanliness of the cottage . . . only about the water below. In fact, she remembered begging her parents to leave just a few days earlier than they'd planned each summer so she could get a jumpstart on the sailing and swimming and canoeing across the bay. They patted her on the head and left when they were ready.

She practically counted down the minutes until her family drove away from their Seattle home. The moment her family arrived in Orcas, she leapt out of the car and raced down the rocky staircase to the dock. Exhausted by dusk, she'd collapse into bed at night not noticing if the house was overrun by mud or dust. She was certain her mother had kept it decent, but she'd loved the water as much as Jessica did and would hardly be confined inside a few walls.

Orcas Island was another world to her when she was a child—a glorious, beautiful, magical world filled with endless adventure and intrigue.

Abby picked up two rugs from the living room floor and stepped outside, following the flagstone path that meandered through wild patches of orange, purple, and yellow flowers to the top of a cliff.

A slight breeze blew and rustled the webbed maple leaves around her as she shook the rugs over the cliff, dust scattering in the wind. She leaned back against the peeling bark of a cedar tree and watched the water below her ripple across the bay and smack against the crags. The only boats in the bay were a sailboat and a canoe being paddled steadily around the shoreline.

With both rugs under her arm, she trudged back through the tall flowers and weeds and walked inside the house. Next on the agenda was to sweep and mop the hardwood and tiled floors, scrub every fixture in both bathrooms, and wash the bedding on at least her and Jessica's beds. Booked solid until dinnertime.

She set down the rugs. When she opened the coat closet, a broom fell off a hook and banged her head. Startled, she jumped back, her arms raised in defense, and then she laughed at herself. She'd probably be seeing ghosts in no time.

The vacuum cleaner was hidden in the far corner of the closet behind a pair of galoshes that her brother-in-law probably used for trout fishing. She pulled out the vacuum and plugged in the old cord. Bracing herself, she flipped the switch, and waited for it to explode. Nothing blew as she swept across the hardwood floors.

Someone needed to replace the old furniture and wall hangings with cleaner, modern matches. If only that someone could eliminate the memories with the dirt.

When she finished sweeping the living room and kitchen, she searched the coat closet and the pantry for a mop or bucket. Nothing. If it wasn't hidden in the attic, she'd make a quick trip to town and buy one. She had a long list of things she needed to clean and conquer.

She checked her watch. It was almost noon.

On second thought, she'd send Jessica back to town so she wouldn't run into anyone who asked about her son.

Chapter 30

Jessica pressed her bike through the waterside village of Westsound, wind whipping her hair across her eyes as she heaved great breaths of clean air. She felt free! No books or classes or Brett to tie her down. It was just her and God . . . and her mom, who would probably spend the entire month fixing up a cottage she didn't even like. Oh well. Jessica wasn't going to let that stop her from enjoying the island.

She pedaled by a row of bright candy-colored shops, tourists gazing in their windows and streaming out their front doors with armfuls of white boxes and green plastic bags. She rode back past De Lucia's Italian Restaurant and its row of rickety stairs that led up to the white clapboard building.

When she'd walked through the dark red doors this morning, she immediately liked the restaurant's homey feel with its pine floors, blue-tinted curtains, and the scent of lemon furniture polish mixed with garlic and tomato sauce.

An older man with graying black hair and a full face had greeted her, asked if she'd ever waited tables before. She said no, but he still hired her on the spot, starting that afternoon. She'd never quite had a job interview like it, but no matter how quirky Vincent De Lucia was, she was grateful for the work. Her mornings were free, and after this week, she'd have Monday and Tuesday nights off. Perfect!

She rode past the city limits sign and into the countryside. The road was at least thirty feet above the water, and as she pedaled, she watched the waves crash against the rocks below.

The summer was coming together just as she'd hoped, and now she had an offer to go sailing. Could it get any better? Twenty more hours, and she'd be out exploring the Sound.

She rounded the corner toward the cottage and slowly rode up the gravel driveway. She didn't want to go inside, but her mom needed her help.

She opened the door and glanced around at the wicker furniture in the living room. It was actually white!

"Hey!" Jessica shouted when she didn't see her mom.

"I'm up here." Abby's face appeared over the loft railing. Her nose and cheeks were smeared with dirt.

"What are you doing?" Jessica asked.

"Cleaning."

Jessica bounded up the narrow stairs two at a time, barely missing the step with the gash. She waved her hand toward downstairs. "It looks like you hired a maid."

"Do you think I made a dent in it?" Abby asked as she opened a closet at the side of the room. Something loud clattered inside, and she jumped.

"A huge dent. The living room almost looks clean."

"I'll take that as a compliment."

Jessica lay down on the bed and propped her feet up on a pillow. "Any luck with the hot water?"

"I called every plumber on the island and only one said he might be able to come next week."

"The sea water's warmer than our tap."

"You wanted an adventure."

Jessica nodded toward the closet. "What are you looking for?"

"A mop."

"Up here?"

"It's definitely not downstairs," Abby pointed toward the nightstand. "Next stop is in there."

"Where?"

"Behind the stand."

Jessica stood up and moved the piece of green-painted furniture. Behind it was a small door in the paneling, barely big enough for her to crawl through. "I didn't know this place had an attic."

"It was always top secret." Abby shut the closet door and handed her a flashlight. "Too dangerous for kids."

Jessica knelt down on the worn shag carpet and clicked open the latch on the door. "I'll search for the mop."

"Thanks, honey."

Jessica grinned. "By the way, I met your old friend today."

"Who's that?"

"Damian De Lucia, and he's pretty good-looking . . . for an old man."

Abby rolled her eyes. "Damian was my sailing instructor, and he's not an old man. He's just a couple of years older than me."

Jessica raised her eyebrows with a clear but silent "I told you so." Abby rolled her eyes before Jessica squeezed into the secret space.

A tiny stream of light shone through a rounded window at the far end, and Jessica squinted. This place was creepy but cool.

She flicked the silver flashlight on as she stood up. The attic room was filled with cardboard boxes, trunks, scattered papers, and old magazines. It reminded her of their storage area at home—a museum of memories, all contained in one place.

No wonder they didn't tell her and her cousin about this place when they were kids. They'd get lost for days in this maze of boxes.

She shined the hazy light across the room. Rafters framed the ceiling and extended to both ends, canvassing the mounds and mounds of stuff. Testing each floorboard in front of her, she walked slowly across the worn wood and held her breath as the boards groaned back at her. She whispered an apology for waking it up, and then reminded herself that if it could hold all this junk for so many years, surely it could hold her too.

Peeking behind a row of boxes, she looked for a mop. Nothing.

A corridor of boxes enclosed her as she moved across the room. It was like she'd walked into the Taylor family's own in-house junkyard. Her mom might be more organized with her stuff than her Aunt Laurel, but they both kept everything. Her grandparents had created one out-of-control collector and one collector control freak.

Jessica laughed as she lifted out a pair of bellbottom pants in a strange orange plaid from the pack of clothes. Under the pants were a puffy lace blouse, an evergreen-colored vest, and a pair of clogs. Trying on the shoes, she admired herself for a moment in a cracked mirror before throwing the clogs back inside and opening another box.

This one was filled with stained Tupperware and a few baking tins. Why in the world had her family kept this junk? Some people might call it a time capsule, but this kitchen plastic was hardly educational. It had been used and then stored, she supposed, just in case they'd ever need it again. Of course, they'd never needed it. It was easier to buy more Tupperware instead of searching for this used supply.

Her light exposed a slim wooden handle standing in the corner with a gray bucket beside it. She grabbed the mop. Mission accomplished.

As she crept back toward the hobbit-sized door, she spotted a navy photo album sitting by itself on the floor. Strange. Why wasn't it in a box?

Directing her dimming light onto the worn leather cover, Jessica opened the album and stared down at the yellowed page.

There were three pictures of a couple at the cottage, a baby cocooned in the woman's arms. She squinted her eyes at the grainy photos. It was her parents! She smiled at them doting on her as a baby. Her mom wore a long, crinkled skirt and lacy blouse. Her dad sported a mint green polo shirt and white pants.

She turned the page. Close up shots of her in a blue blanket. Why would they have wrapped her in blue? Maybe these were photos of her cousin, Travis.

She turned the page again and squinted at a collage of grainy shots. Her mom smiling down at the child lying in a white bassinet. Her dad feeding the baby a bottle on their old checkered couch. Both parents putting the baby into a minivan.

Her parents looked so happy together. When were they happy? When she was a girl, they always seemed to be fighting.

Turning the page, she saw blue streamers strung from the ceiling and china plates with cake crumbs scattered across a party table. It was obviously a baby shower with her aunt and grandparents and her cousin who was just a few months her senior. Travis was bundled in a baby blue

blanket, and Aunt Laurel held him out on display for the camera—obviously proud of her firstborn.

Then she saw a huge sign strung across the door. Block letters screamed *Welcome Home, Hunter* in bright crayon colors.

Hmm . . . Maybe it wasn't Travis in the picture.

She whipped through page after page of the packed album searching for a baby picture of her. Not a single one.

"Any luck?" her mom called from the attic entrance.

Jessica jumped.

"Yeah," she replied, staring at the page in her lap. "I found a mop and bucket for you."

With the worn album under one arm and the mop handle and bucket in the other, she crawled out of the attic space and faced her mother.

"Thanks," Abby said as she took the mop.

Jessica held out the photo album, and her mom's eyes froze on the cover.

"Who's Hunter?"

Chapter 31

Jessica's question rang in Abby's ears as she braced herself against the bed, her gaze locked on the navy blue photo album. With one hand, she reached out and touched the cracked leather like it might disappear.

Could it be?

No. It couldn't be the same album. Scott had destroyed it twenty years ago.

She remembered shouting at him, yelling that if he was going to throw away their son, he might as well throw away all his pictures too. Scott said he would take the pictures out with the trash. She never had any reason to believe he'd done anything else.

"Are you going to tell me?" Jessica asked as she handed over the album.

"Just a second," Abby whispered as she sat down on the bed. She wiped her fingers across the cover warily and opened it, staring down at a picture of her carrying Hunter home from the hospital.

Scott hadn't trashed the memories of their son.

She turned the pages again and again. Scott must have hidden the album up in the attic until she was ready to look at them again. Of course, she'd never been ready. Grateful . . . she was actually grateful to him that he hadn't done what he said. Grateful that he'd lied.

A photo from July 4, 1986, captured her attention. She'd dressed Hunter in blue pants, a white shirt, and a red-tipped hat to celebrate the holiday. It was a grainy picture—a snapshot that barely clipped the event.

They'd eaten barbecue on the back porch of the cottage with her family that year and then taken the boat out to watch fireworks from across the bay. Hunter was captivated by the exploding lights, laughing as their

tails spun across the night sky. He'd reached up like he could put them in his mouth. He was always putting things in his mouth.

Abby jumped as Jessica leaned over her shoulder and gazed down at the photos.

What is my daughter going to say when she hears the truth? She could lie and say it was someone else's child. A friend? A relative?

But then she turned the page again, and they were back at their Seattle town home, holding Hunter on the couch while he snuggled with a teddy bear.

This wasn't someone else's child. He was obviously their son.

"Who is he?" Jessica repeated. Abby met her gaze.

She was completely unprepared to have this discussion . . . but it was time to tell Jessica the truth.

"Before you were born," Abby said as she leaned back against a stained, pale blue cushion, "your dad and I had trouble getting pregnant."

She took a deep breath. "We tried several different treatments and finally ended up pregnant, but I miscarried the baby a few months later."

"I'm sorry, Mom." Jessica sat down beside her and pulled a pillow to her chest.

"We didn't know what to do because we wanted a family so badly. Since your dad had a close cousin who'd been adopted, he knew a little about the process, but I didn't know anything. We found a Seattle adoption agency and asked them a thousand questions. We prayed about it for almost a month, and it seemed like our only option."

Jessica waited stoically for her to continue.

"We blazed through all the paperwork, and it seemed like it was only weeks before the agency called to say they had a baby for us to adopt. We were ecstatic. After our frustration with the infertility treatments, adoption seemed like a sure thing."

Abby cleared her throat. "Do you want a drink or something?" she asked her daughter, but Jessica shook her head.

"Okay," Abby continued, breathing deeply for the air to feed her resolve. Maybe God would help her do this.

"It's so strange. I haven't really spoken about it with anyone since Scott . . . since your dad died."

She looked down at the yellowed pages again and blinked back tears.

"Okay," she repeated. "Twenty years ago, we brought home an amazing little boy from the hospital. His birth mother had been young and decided that she couldn't take care of her child."

She wouldn't tell Jessica, but they'd lavished the best of everything on Hunter. She knew that he'd be spoiled, but at the time, she didn't care. She hadn't anticipated having any more kids.

"We loved this boy like our own child—we thought he was our own. We took care of him for four months and watched him grow into a little person as he smiled and laughed and talked to us in his own way."

"What happened?" Jessica asked, looking down at the photo of Hunter lying on top of a blue afghan and grinning at the camera.

"The birth mother changed her mind. She was supposed to relinquish her rights a month after Hunter was born, but she never signed the paperwork. I guess she panicked when the agency set a court date. She was supposed to go before a judge and officially relinquish everything, but she couldn't."

Abby had never understood how any mother could relinquish her parental rights. She remembered looking at Hunter in his crib and wondering how Stacie could possibly give him away. Abby would have done almost anything to keep this boy. When Stacie changed her mind, Abby had understood why she wanted Hunter, but that didn't make it fair.

"We were staying here when the agency called and said we had to bring him back. It was a horrible time in our lives."

Abby smiled. "Then, five months later, a miracle occurred. We discovered we were pregnant again even though we hadn't used a single treatment. You were growing and living inside me, a real fighter, and when you were born, we never tried to adopt again."

There it was; she'd told her daughter the truth. The seconds dragged as she waited for her daughter's response. The silence was unbearable. Abby swallowed hard and willed herself to look at her daughter.

"Wow," Jessica finally said as she released the pillow in her arms. "I can't believe you never told me about this."

"We loved you so much, and we didn't want you to worry that we might have to give you back too."

"That's crazy, Mom."

Abby shrugged her shoulders. She hadn't meant to keep the memories of Hunter from her daughter. She'd only wanted to protect her from the truth.

"You were planning to keep this brother a secret for the rest of my life?"

"Yes."

"So everyone knew about this baby except me?"

Abby fidgeted with the edge of the plastic page. "Travis would have been too young to remember him."

"But Grandpa and Grandma and Aunt Laurel and Uncle Davis knew all about him."

"I asked them not to tell you."

"I think this is one of those things that you're supposed to tell your only child before someone else lets it slip." Jessica paused. "But maybe that's why you moved us to Denver after Dad died."

"It was one of many reasons."

"What happened to Hunter after you gave him back?"

Abby clutched her shaky hands. "No idea."

"That's rotten." Jessica took back the photo album and flipped through its pages again. "Surely you had some rights."

Abby glanced out the tall window in front of her. She'd been irate at Scott for letting Stacie tromp all over them. In her mind, Stacie's indecisiveness was only a glitch for them to overcome. A fair judge would see it their way. A good, solid family with the resources to raise a child versus a sixteen-year-old drunk without a home. The decision should have been easy for the courts, but they'd never given the judicial system a chance. If Scott really loved their son, he would have fought.

But she couldn't say that to her daughter.

"We debated about what was best for Hunter," Abby said, trying to overcome her bitterness. "We decided that it wasn't in anyone's best interest to tie up the case in court for years. Stacie probably would have kept Hunter until the case was closed, and there was no guarantee that we would win."

"That must have been awful for you."

"It was . . . but then you came along, and we were so grateful to have you."

Abby hugged her daughter. She wished she could tell Jessica that her birth had erased the pain.

Chapter 32

Stacie Cartwright hauled a bottle of cheap wine to the front counter at Haggard's Grocery and casually presented it to the cashier with her grocery card. The store didn't sell hard liquor, but wine would do. She hadn't had alcohol in twenty-four hours, and her fingers shook from withdrawal.

The cashier called the manager to the register, and they whispered as she waited. Dennis didn't even smile, but his eyes were full of pity when he turned toward her. She wanted to slap him, tell him he didn't need to bother with sympathy. If he let her buy the alcohol, he wouldn't have to feel sorry for her at all.

Dennis handed her back the grocery card. "You know we can't sell you this, Stacie."

"But it's as good as cash."

"Good as cash for any groceries you want to buy."

"Please, Dennis. I don't need food right now."

He swiped her drink off the counter and hid it under the register.

Why was he tormenting her? Did he really think she'd feel better if the bottle was out of her sight?

"I need it, Dennis."

"No you don't."

Her eyes filled with tears. "You don't understand."

"Let's go outside, Stacie."

"I'm not moving until you give it back to me."

Dennis skirted around the paper bag bin and grasped her elbow. She shook her arm loose, but he grabbed it again.

"Let me help you out," he commanded.

"I don't need help."

"Just to the sidewalk."

"You afraid I'll make a scene?" Only one time had she yelled at him, and he'd never let her forget.

"To the sidewalk, Stacie," he said. She followed him outside and sat on a wet bench.

Her head pounded. Didn't he know that she needed to drink? Some people needed money or cigarettes or drugs, but liquor was her lifeline. Without a buzz, it was impossible to survive.

Rain drizzled from the gray sky, and she covered her head with a newspaper, trash someone had left on the bench. Water ran over the sides of the paper and onto her jeans.

It wasn't fair. Right inside those doors were shelves packed with booze, and they wouldn't give her a sip. How dare Marc put a condition on his card? Who gave him the right to judge? He was her son, and she'd been a good mom to him.

For the first five years of Marc's life, she hadn't even taken a sip of beer. She'd cared for her baby the best she could, just like she'd promised the social worker. She worked late into the night, and during the day, Marc played in his crib until she woke up and they would laugh and sing and build towers with soup cans. She loved to play with him. She loved her son.

But it wasn't like it was always fun. Stuff happened that would have made anyone turn to alcohol . . . like the night she almost lost Marc in a fire.

After all these years, she could still smell the wall of smoke that choked her when she opened the apartment door. Marc was asleep on the kitchen tile when she arrived home that night. He'd climbed out of his crib, put a jar of mustard into the oven, and turned it on high. If she'd come home seconds later, the entire apartment would have been gone . . . along with her son.

The next morning, she took Marc to her parents' house and asked for help. Flat out begged. Her own mother took one look at her only grandson and told her the family brownstone was no longer home. When her mother slammed the door shut, Stacie stood outside the picture window,

clutching her baby as she watched a party of snobs toasting each other with flutes of champagne.

Still she didn't drink.

She found a neighbor to babysit Marc, and she slaved every night for tips that barely paid the bills. None of the money went to alcohol . . . until Marc turned five years old, and she turned on the late night news.

Her older brother was on the TV screen with a giant smile, accepting the job as assistant mayor of Seattle. He was only twenty-nine. Local officials raved about his talent and potential and future. Her parents stood behind the podium, grinning at the camera like it was their show.

She looked around at her grimy furniture and leaky ceiling and dirt-caked floor, and she grabbed Marc's hand, marching him down to the corner store.

She didn't remember much about that night. Marc must have taken off her shoes and helped her into bed, because she woke up the next morning with a liter of vodka on the pillow beside her head.

Marc had been such a good boy. He was still a good boy. He just shouldn't judge what he didn't understand.

A man in denim overalls and cowboy boots sat down beside Stacie. He mumbled to himself, and then he turned toward her.

"You need help?" Strands of greasy hair clung to his face, and he reeked of sweat.

She scooted away from him. "Nothing you can do."

"I don't know about that," he said, eyeing her like she was candy.

Her fingers shook harder as she met his gray eyes. She'd been here before . . . maybe it wouldn't hurt to negotiate.

His nose was in her hair. "You obviously need somethin'."

"Maybe."

"I think we could strike a deal."

She crammed her hands into the pockets of her jacket and felt one of Marc's crisp twenty-dollar bills. She'd promised him that she would use it to pay back the money for the ferry ride and gas.

Maybe she didn't have to break her promise. She could get the alcohol now and pay her neighbor back later when she got some extra cash. Marc would understand.

She stood up and the man grasped her arm, pulling her toward him. His rancid breath steamed across her face, and she almost gagged. She pulled the money from her pocket and clenched it in her fist as she pushed him away.

"Not interested," she said as she turned back toward the store.

She wouldn't have to negotiate today.

Chapter 33

Abby poured the fresh Colombian coffee into her mug and savored the scent. Leaning against the cold tile on the kitchen counter, she glanced out the window at the crisp blue sky. It was a perfect day to be outdoors, yet she'd barely been motivated enough to climb out of the soft folds of her bed. She certainly hadn't been motivated to dress, tugging on a sweatshirt and leggings for her climb downstairs. She'd taken two steps into the bathroom and then stepped back out, opting to down some hot coffee before she braved another ice cold shower.

She'd slept so well last night that even caffeine wasn't rousing her like it usually did. She felt relaxed, dazed. She didn't have to be afraid anymore that Jessica would find out about Hunter. After so many years of tiptoeing and sidestepping around the truth, Jessica finally knew.

The bedroom door creaked open. Abby heard Jessica clip clop down the hallway until she reached the kitchen. Her daughter's hair was pulled tight in a ponytail, and the strap of her emerald-colored bathing suit slipped out from under her navy T-shirt. She wore dark jean shorts, yellow-tinted sunglasses, and flip-flops that displayed the glittery green polish on her toenails.

"Apparently, you have plans today." Abby filled a bowl with Special K, poured skim milk over the cereal, and topped it with sliced strawberries. She sat down at the kitchen table and took a bite.

"I'm going sailing."

"By yourself?"

Jessica stuck her head in the refrigerator, and Abby heard her rummaging through the food. She looked over the top of the door.

"Did you get any donuts at the store?"

"You don't need to eat donuts."

Jessica shook her head and dug back into the refrigerator until she found a pint of yogurt. She slammed the door shut.

Abby ate another bite of cereal. "Who are you sailing with?"

"Your friend, Damian, and Marc."

"You don't even know these men!"

"I thought you liked Damian."

"I said he was a good instructor." Abby set down her spoon. "Who's Marc?"

Jessica sat across from her, scooping the blueberry yogurt into her mouth.

"I think he works for Damian."

"And . . ."

Jessica shrugged her shoulders. "And, what?"

"That's all you know about him?"

"He seemed nice. Besides, Damian was the one who asked me to go with them."

Abby trusted Damian completely, but she didn't know the other man.

"Aren't you going to ask me about my job?"

Abby sighed. Later she'd revisit the topic of her daughter sailing away with men she didn't know.

"Okay, I'll just tell you." Jessica took another bite of blueberry yogurt and made a funny face. "Mr. De Lucia is brutal. He had me waiting tables solo by the end of the night. I forgot an order and dropped a glass, but the other servers backed me up. I made sixty bucks in tips."

"Are you going to save that money?"

"I figure I'll use my tip money on the sailboat lessons and rental, and I'll use Dad's money for food and other stuff."

"About your father's money . . ."

Jessica stiffened. "Dad told me I could use it for whatever I wanted."

"Of course you can," Abby said. "It's just that I don't want you to have to use it this summer. Save it to go to Europe or someplace else next year, and I'll pay for your food while you're on the island."

Jessica stared at her like she'd gone mad. "When did you decide that?"

"Last night. It's the least I can do."

"I don't want you to feel guilty about Hunter, Mom. You were just waiting for the right time to tell me."

"It's not that," she protested a bit too hard. "Let me be your mom for just a few more months. You're growing up so fast, and I'd like to pretend for one last summer that you're my little girl."

Jessica reached across the table and squeezed her hand.

Out the kitchen window, Abby watched a white sailboat breeze into their bay and then disappear from view as it sailed under the cliff wall that protected their cottage from the water.

"Looks like they're here." Jessica took one last bite of yogurt and wiped her mouth on a paper towel.

"Who's here?"

"Marc and Damian."

"I thought you were meeting them at the marina."

"Nope."

Abby glanced out the window again, quickly running her fingers through her flat hair. "Thanks for the notice."

"You look fine, Mom."

"I don't care how I look."

"Whatever." Jessica strapped on her backpack, opened the side door, and walked outside.

Abby sat at the table, pretending that she really didn't care how she looked. So what if Damian saw her like this? It wasn't like he hadn't seen her without makeup before . . . of course that had been almost thirty years ago when she didn't need it like she needed it now.

Two heads popped over the rocky staircase that rose up from the water, and Abby raced for the bathroom. She brushed her hair and her teeth and quickly applied a round of mascara and lip gloss.

"Mom?" she heard Jessica call from the living room.

She set down the blush case, took a deep breath, and opened the door. She glanced down at her stained gray sweatshirt and wished she'd at least put on a decent shirt and jeans. A cold shower would have been nice, a little more makeup. Damian would notice every wrinkle under her eyes, not to mention the age spots dotting her cheeks.

She stopped and looked out the window. Damian and Jessica and the guy she assumed was Marc stood around the picnic table in the back yard. She'd expected someone older—Marc was just a kid.

She leaned toward the glass. Marc and Jessica were talking animatedly like they were old friends. She wasn't surprised at the boy's attention toward her daughter; Jessica seemed to attract young men wherever they went. She was surprised at Jessica, grinning back at him like a puppy dog. So much for just sailing. . . .

She watched the boy for another moment. His hair was shaggy with layered bangs, his eyes barely peeking out from under them. He was tall and wore long khaki shorts and an olive-green shirt. Way too handsome to be any good.

She slid open the screen door and stepped outside.

"Abby!" Damian greeted her with an awkward hug. "It's been too long."

"It's good to see you." She pulled away from him and the blast of warmth that shot through her arms. His dark hair was rugged and peppered with gray, his smile even more confident in his older years.

"Abby, this is Marc Cartwright," he said, and the boy shook her hand like a gentleman.

"Pleasure meeting you." Marc smiled and nodded toward her daughter. "I was hoping to take Jessie out sailing this morning."

Jessie? She glanced at her daughter for reaction, but her daughter only grinned.

"Jessica was going to help me work on the house today," Abby said, but Jessica ignored the threatening look in her eyes.

"No, I wasn't, Mom. I just told you I was going sailing."

Abby stared at the boy, warning him with her glare to take a step back.

"I don't know, honey," she hesitated.

"Marc's like a son to me," Damian vouched. "Why don't you let the two of them go play, and I'll help you around the house for an hour or two?"

"Don't you have to work today?" Abby asked. She didn't take her eyes off Marc.

Damian shrugged his shoulders. "We're still on a weekend schedule—funny how people expect to see whales on a whale watching tour."

"Funny," Abby replied.

"We'll only be out for a few hours," Marc said.

When she didn't protest, Jessica and Marc rushed toward the stairs. Jessica playfully punched his arm, and he laughed, raising both his fists like he was about to rumble. Abby heard them chattering about tides and winds and different kinds of sailboats until their voices faded down the cliff stairs.

Was this what her own mother used to do? Watch her and Damian sprint toward the water and wonder? They'd been the best of friends, laughing and playing and joking like nothing else mattered. They'd developed their own language, a labyrinth of unique stories and experiences, a bond she'd never thought would break.

"I don't know about this," Abby whispered.

"They'll be fine."

"How do you know?"

"He's a good guy, Abby, and your daughter seems just as strong as you."

Abby wasn't convinced but she turned toward the cottage and took a deep breath. "Do you want some coffee?"

"Sounds good," he said as they started toward the house.

She watched his gaze as they entered the kitchen, looking at the antiquated refrigerator door, rusty oven, and cracked porcelain sink.

"I haven't been here in almost twenty-five years."

"Probably hasn't changed a bit, has it?"

"Not at all . . . and you haven't either."

She handed Damian his coffee without meeting his eye. "So tell me about this boy that I've entrusted with my daughter's life."

"You really don't have to worry about him, Abby. He's as straitlaced as they come. Going to be a missionary someday."

"You know what they say about pastors' kids?"

Damian chuckled. "His home life isn't anywhere close to being religious."

That's supposed to keep me from worrying?

She took a sip of her tepid coffee. "How do you know him?"

"Through a friend." He paused. "He grew up in her church in South Seattle and happens to love the water."

"You've been happy with him?"

"He's a godsend."

"Well, I'm glad you can trust him," Abby muttered.

"She's fine, Abby," he repeated. "Marc may have had a tough home life, but he inspires just about everyone he meets."

They were both quiet as Abby rinsed her mug in the sink. She and Damian used to banter nonstop when they were teens, but it had been a long time since they talked. She didn't know what to say.

"So, what can I do to help you get this place back to its old glory?" he asked.

She looked at the mess around them. "Not a great place to entertain, is it?"

"It's always been a great house for entertaining," he said. "It just needs a little facelift."

"I don't know where to start."

"Just give me a task or two."

"Don't worry about it."

"C'mon, Abby," he insisted. "I may not be the best carpenter, but surely there's something I can do to help."

She hesitated. "Well, you can take a look at the hot water heater, if you don't mind. The plumber's booked for a week."

"Let me at it."

He opened the utility closet and knelt down to look at the base of the heater. Then he stood and turned and grinned at her.

"I don't know if you can afford to have me fix this," he joked.

"Can I talk you into a trade?"

"What did you have in mind?"

"You fix my hot water heater, and I'll help you recoup your image after that awful *Seattle Times* article."

He grimaced. "So you read that, huh?"

"Glad to see you got the exposure, but the guy must have riled you up."

"He was a jerk."

"Yeah, he's paid to be a jerk. Your job is to be the nice guy no matter what he says."

He looked down at the aging stove. "I don't care a bit about my image."

"Are you really a whale killer?"

He looked down at her, his eyes a mixture of anger and hurt. "Of course not."

"Then my guess is that you care a lot about the whales."

"You know I do."

"Then I'll start a media campaign for you and the whales as soon as I get this house whipped into shape."

"Tell you what." He leaned against the closet door. "If you throw your mom's famous chicken cordon bleu into the mix, I'll get you some hot water and help you repair the rest of the house."

"Do you know how to fix a broken step?"

"I think I can manage."

She threw out her hand to shake his. "Well then, your whole family is invited for dinner."

"Do I have to invite my uncle?"

She laughed. "No, I meant your wife and kids."

He knelt down in the cramped utility room.

"Do you have a match?" he asked.

"What?"

"I need a match to light your pilot."

"Then I'll have hot water?"

"Yep."

She laughed. "You're going to have to fix a lot more to earn your publicity work plus dinner."

"Now you're adding strings to our little agreement?"

"You have to earn your keep, Dr. De Lucia."

"Gladly."

Chapter 34

The Drifter swayed with the waves, its anchor resting on the sand several yards from the shore. Jessica followed Marc onto the pebbled beach. They stepped over a sharp boulder and around a pile of driftwood bleached a grayish white from the sun.

"How do we get to it?" Jessica asked, scanning the shore for a dinghy to row them out to the sailboat.

"We wade," he said as he held out his hand. She took it.

Seaweed brushed her ankles as they trudged toward the boat, and icy water lapped against her calves and knees.

"We're almost there," Marc said as the salty spray soaked the hem of her denim shorts. She waded the final steps on tiptoe.

Marc pointed to a set of stairs at the back of the sailboat and lifted her up by the waist to reach the bottom step. She clutched the metal rail as they rode over a wave, mounting the slippery stairs carefully so she didn't fall back into the bay.

Jessica waited for Marc on the bow, the boat rocking gently, sun rays warming her chilled skin. Several white sails glided in the distance, but there was no one else in the bay. The only sound was water skimming over the beach and spraying the stone wall.

"Have you ever sailed before?" Marc asked as he handed her a fire red life jacket. She pulled the yellow bands tight around her chest and snapped them into place.

"When I was a kid, my dad and I used to sail every summer. I haven't been out since I was like ten." *Six months before Dad died.*

"It'll come back to you in no time," he said as she sat down in the stern.

Marc pointed out the mainsheet, jib sheet, and traveler. He defined

each edge of the sail, showed her where to brace herself when the boat was heeled over, and demonstrated how to trim and ease the mainsail.

"Port means your left side, and starboard is your right." He wiped his forehead with his sleeve.

She nodded. "It sounds good now, but I'll forget everything you just said when we get out to sea."

"I have a feeling you won't forget a thing."

Jessica smiled at him. Another sailing instructor might have shown off his boating skills, trying to impress her with his knowledge. Marc simply explained the basics. She understood exactly what he was saying. No pretense involved.

"I think I'm ready," Jessica assured both herself and him when he finished the first lesson in Sailing 101.

"Alright." He reeled up the anchor. "Let's sail around the bay until you get the hang of it."

The wind guided them slowly away from the bank. Marc grasped the tiller, turning the rudder and watching Jessica man the sails.

For an hour, they practiced—heading into the wind and then bearing away from it as Jessica concentrated on trimming the sails, matching the wind angle to prevent them from luffing.

"I'm impressed," Marc said as they successfully turned the boat toward the wind again.

"I love this!"

"It's obviously in your blood."

She felt the heat in her cheeks as Marc steered the boat toward the open waters. She threw back her head, the breeze cooling her face and blowing through her hair.

This was exactly what she remembered. This heavenly experience of flying over the sea. She felt exhilarated . . . *free*. At Marc's command, she trimmed the mainsail again and waved good-bye to the cottage as they sailed past the cliffs that guarded the entrance to the bay.

Within minutes, they were jaunting across Puget Sound.

She was away from the pressures at the cottage, away from the talk about a brother she never knew. She didn't understand why her mom hadn't told her the truth, but it explained a few things. For her entire life, she'd been competing against a brother she didn't even know existed. A baby who'd been too young to be anything but perfect while she, on the other hand, had nineteen years to prove how truly imperfect she was.

Two gray dolphins sprang out of the water beside them, and one did a somersault in the air.

She never wanted to go back to Colorado. She never wanted to go anywhere else, for that matter. She'd been created to be on the water. It was in her blood.

Jessica smiled at Marc, and he grinned back before jerking his eyes away from hers to focus on the wind.

Three hours later, Marc and Jessica climbed back up the steps to the cottage.

"Do we have to eat?" Jessica asked again. She would have sailed until the second she had to leave for De Lucia's, but Marc insisted they give it a rest.

He smiled. "I do."

Jessica opened the screen door. "It seems like a waste of time when we could be on the water."

"We'll go out again another day . . . if you want."

"Definitely."

Her mom was waiting for them inside, a bag of deli ham in one hand and a block of cheddar cheese in the other. Jessica wondered how long it took her to get from the kitchen to the living room when she saw them walking across the yard.

"Didn't think you two were going to come back," Abby said.

Jessica ignored her sarcasm. "It was amazing, Mom! Marc's a pro."

"Don't you have to work tonight?" Abby asked as she followed Jessica toward the kitchen.

"I don't have to leave for awhile."

"Good. I need some help with laundry."

Jessica rolled her eyes and turned on the kitchen faucet. Warm water flowed out.

"Yes!" she screamed as she washed her hands.

"Damian fixed our broken step and our water heater."

"Where did he go?" Jessica dried her hands on a towel.

"I took him back to the marina an hour ago."

"He's probably working on the boat," Marc said. "The man never goes home."

"I bet his family doesn't appreciate that."

"It's just him." Marc washed his hands. "He's never been married."

"But . . ."

Jessica threw the towel to Marc. "What, Mom?"

"Nothing. He wanted Marc to motor the sailboat around when you got back."

Jessica smiled. "I'm sure he wouldn't mind if Marc ate lunch first."

"Just a quick bite, and I'll take off." Marc dried his hands. "Your daughter's a great sailor, Mrs. Wagner. In no time at all, she'll be out on her own."

"My daughter's always liked to be on her own."

Jessica snatched the ham out of her mom's hand with a glare. "You want a sandwich?" she asked Marc.

Marc looked back and forth between the two women. "I think so."

Jessica brushed mayonnaise and Dijon mustard on the bread and added ham and cheese. As she melted the cheese in the microwave, Jessica grabbed two cans of soda and handed one to Marc.

"Let's eat on the patio." She took the sandwiches from the microwave and the two of them walked back outside.

They sat down across from each other on the picnic table benches, and Jessica handed him his sandwich. "I'm sorry about that."

"Don't worry about it. She's just being a mother, trying to protect you and all."

"Overprotect is more like it."

He bit into his sandwich. "Is it just you and your mom?"

"Yeah. Dad died when I was eleven, and we don't really talk to his family anymore. My mom's sister and my cousin live in Seattle, but other than that, it's just the two of us." She popped the lid on her soda can. "How about you?"

"It's just me and my mom, too. Never had any brothers or sisters, but my pastor practically adopted me into his family. I hung out with his three children during my teen years, and it made all the difference in my life. Now God's given me Damian as well. He never had kids, but he treats me like a son."

"What about your father?" Jessica asked.

"Never knew him. My mom said he died before I was born."

"You sound like you don't believe her."

He crushed the icy Coke can in his hand and tossed it into a tin garbage can. "Mom's not the best at telling the truth."

Jessica ripped open a bag of Doritos and handed them to Marc.

Why did parents try so hard to annihilate the past? The navy album appeared again in Jessica's mind, its dust covering a secret that shouldn't have stayed hidden for so many years. Was honesty really that difficult?

"So you're in college?" Marc asked as he ate a chip. She nodded—she was for now.

He deepened his voice. "And what do you want to be when you grow up?"

"The dreaded growing up question," Jessica laughed. "My answer is I have no idea, but I'm hoping God's going to show me soon."

"You're a Christian?"

"Since I was eight."

Marc leaned back on his chair. "I started my journey with Christ when I was young too. My mom never went to church, but she thought it was a good idea for me to go. The best decision she ever made."

"Do you know what God wants you to do with your life?" Jessica asked.

"Something with marine biology. I can use my research to get into a country that might not welcome missionaries. Wouldn't that be amazing? Sharing Jesus' love with a culture that might never have heard of Him before?"

Jessica stared at him. *Is this guy for real?*

"I'm not sure exactly what that looks like yet," he continued. "I'm just waiting to see where God leads me next."

"I wish I could believe like that," she sighed, contemplating the odd workings of God in her life. Surely He had a plan for her if she kept pressing ahead with what she thought was right. She wished He would spell it out for her or even just hint at what was at the end of the pitch-black tunnel. Everything seemed so dark and hazy and downright scary.

"What are you studying?" he asked.

"Nothing specific right now. The only class I like is biology."

She didn't tell him that if she stayed in college, marine biology would be her major of choice.

"That's a good trek to go down."

She shrugged her shoulders. "My mom wants me to major in education or English."

"She obviously cares about you."

"I suppose, but it's not what I want."

Jessica glanced down at her watch and jumped up.

"I have to be at work in an hour." She reached for the plates. "Thanks for an amazing day."

He stood up beside her. "Would you like to go snorkeling sometime?"

"I'd love to." She smiled at him before he turned to walk toward the dock.

She rushed inside, and her mom was standing in the kitchen, eating the last bite of her sandwich.

"What are you trying to do?" Jessica said as she dumped the plates into the sink.

"I just wanted him to know that I was watching out for you."

"You couldn't have been more rude."

Abby rinsed off Jessica's dishes.

"You need to be nice, Mom."

Abby turned to face her. "I need to take care of my daughter."

Chapter 35

Marc hopped on his bike and hummed as he rode away from the marina. Where had this girl come from? Out of nowhere she appeared. And, not only did she intrigue him, she loved God and the water.

A potent combination.

As he pedaled his bike through the village, he prayed. He certainly needed help. He wouldn't let anyone distract him from his focus . . . but a partner would sure be nice.

He shook his head. He couldn't even begin to think like that.

Jessie was right. It had been an amazing day. And Jessie's mother was also right. He was way out of his league.

They were too different for anything more than a taste of friendship. Jessie's family owned a beautiful summer home on Puget Sound that they rarely used—he couldn't even imagine what their winter home looked like. Until he left for college, he lived with his mom in a filthy apartment, one of a hundred in a building that he kept waiting for inspectors to condemn before it fell down. Jessie would be shocked if she ever ventured into his neighborhood. He'd give her a medal for bravery if she had the guts to brave the projects and meet his mom.

He sighed. He'd relish their friendship for the summer. She'd go back to school in Boulder and he'd return to Washington State.

Leaning his bike against the bushes at the base of De Lucia's restaurant, he bounded up the stairs, two and three at a time. When he reached the door, he tried to push it open but it was locked. He pounded on the wood and then flipped open the doorbell cover and rang twice. Vincent De Lucia finally opened the door.

"Is there a fire?"

"Mr. De Lucia . . . I'd really like to work for you this summer."

"But you already work for Damian."

Marc nodded. "Yes, sir, but just during the day. I'd like to work for you at night."

Vincent glanced down both sides of the wide porch. No one was there.

"This doesn't have anything to do with the arrival of that Taylor girl, does it?"

"No, sir," Marc retorted and then grinned. "Okay, maybe a little."

Vincent shook his head. "I suppose I could use the help."

"Good."

"As long as you can keep your mind on your work, consider yourself hired. If you mess it up, your night job's history."

"Got it."

"You can start on Saturday."

Marc hesitated. "And can I have Tuesdays off?"

"One of our servers already has Tuesdays off . . ." Vincent arched his left eyebrow. "But you already knew that, didn't you?"

Marc shrugged his shoulders and tried to act nonchalant, but his smile crept back onto his face again.

"Alright," Vincent said. "Tuesdays are off, Mondays we're closed. Every other night you're here—no matter what."

"Thanks!"

Marc bolted down the stairs without looking back.

He pedaled rapidly toward home, swerving to miss the shiny yellow-backed snake on the road. Fresh crabapple flowers lined the driveway to the house, and the pink and white buds were so sweet that it smelled like he was riding through a candy store.

He propped his bike by a woodpile when he heard his phone ringing from the top floor. He rushed up the stairs as he fumbled with his house key, opened the door, and grabbed the receiver.

"Hello."

"Hey, honey," his mom said. "Whatcha doing?"

His stomach clenched. Had she even made it home before she spent his money on vodka? Or did she bum booze off someone on the ferry?

"I've been trying to call you all day."

"I just got another job, Mom."

"Good. Oh, that's so very good, honey. I'm so proud of you."

He collapsed on the couch. "Where did you get the alcohol?"

"I don't know what you're talking about."

"Did you use the money I gave you for ferry money and gas?"

"I don't need gas right now."

He threw his keys against the wall. He wanted to be a good son; God knew he loved her. But he couldn't spend his money helping her kill herself. "I don't have any more money to give you, Mom."

"But maybe with this new job . . ."

"I love you Mom, but I can't send you anything else."

"Please, Marcus. I need your help."

"I'm sorry," he mumbled as he hung up, acid erupting in his belly.

Why did his mother always corner him into such an awful place? Mrs. Wagner may not like him, but at least she cared about her daughter. He couldn't remember one time during his teenage years that his mother cared for him like that.

He knew she'd sacrificed for him, and he appreciated it. Twenty years ago she'd given up her own dreams of college to take care of her son. She'd given up everything to raise him, and he wanted to give back to her, show her that he loved her. But he couldn't support her drinking habit.

He clenched his fists together. How could such a good day end so badly?

He bowed his head. *God, what am I supposed to do?*

Chapter 36

With a mug of hot chamomile tea in her hand, Abby shivered inside her bulky wool sweater as she strolled barefoot through the tall grass and down the cold stone stairs. The evening was chilly; the sweet scent of a burning woodstove permeated the air. The glassy bay below reflected the rays of the setting sun.

She should have worn shoes, but for some reason, it just seemed wrong. As long as her fingers warmed themselves on the toasty sides of the ceramic, her feet would be fine.

They'd been back on Orcas for an entire week, but she'd only left the house once—running into town for food and supplies when Jessica was at work. She'd stayed busy, trying to keep her mind off of her job and Hunter. Only three more weeks left for her on the island, and then she'd be back in Denver, buried in the sweet relief of work.

Abby stepped over a rock when she reached the bottom of the stairs, pebbles biting her toes as she walked over the beach. Bulbs of dry, wilted kelp were strewn on the narrow shoreline in front of her alongside knotted driftwood and jagged rocks.

She strode carefully onto the dock and over the wooden planks, and then she sat on the edge of the dock, looking down at a burnt-orange starfish that clung to an underwater rock like it was an anchor.

She trailed her toes through the water, the cold shock thrilling her, making her feel alive.

Her search for Hunter had slammed into a wall, and she wanted to let it go. Why couldn't God take this burden away? If only God would take her pain away once and for all. Memories of Hunter—she wanted to keep those. Just not the agony that attached itself to them.

When she'd accepted Christ into her life more than twenty years ago, she'd honestly believed God would take care of her needs. Yet the road had been more rocky than smooth. She still believed in God, just not in His ability to care. Where was He in the midst of all her loss? Why had He disappeared?

She had to hang onto the thread of hope that there was a God and a heaven. If there was a God, maybe her family would be reunited one day. Maybe she'd be able to give Hunter a giant hug and listen for hours to the story of his life.

A blast of cool air hit her, and she shivered again. This was crazy. What was she doing out here in the cold? She could think just as well inside as she could here.

But, in spite of the cold, this dock was her refuge, her place of escape. She craved fresh air, breathing it deeply as it cleansed her from the inside, stress blowing away in the wind.

She gazed across the bay to see if she could spot an orca. The whales used to hide in the bay when she was a girl. She'd watch them from the cliff top, and she remembered feeling guilty, stealing a glance at their private time. They'd seemed so carefree together, like a human family who enjoyed playing together at home.

Maybe she really could help Damian with this campaign. He was certainly passionate about the topic, and she also wanted the orcas to return to Puget Sound. Surely she could get some media interested in the missing whales.

She glanced down at her watch. Almost nine o'clock in Washington. Ten in Colorado.

What was going on in the office while she was gone?

Most of her staff would be home by now, but Curtis was probably still in the building, rummaging through her files to find the next step for the Heartsong campaign.

She'd expected Blanche to call by now, begging her to return early. When the call finally came, she'd coyly consider the offer for an hour or two. Then, of course, she'd go back. They needed her . . . and she needed a job.

The sky darkened, and she stood to go back inside. A flash of brown caught her eye, and she squinted to see a seal dive behind a rock. The seal waited a few seconds before peeking out from behind its hiding place and skimming across the water to another rock. Then he glanced back out at her again. Abby laughed out loud at him as she waved. If only she had someplace to hide so she could play the game.

"Abby?" She looked up to see Damian's head craning over the top of the cliff. "Are you down there?"

She waved to him and started climbing the damp stairs. He'd stopped by twice over the past week to help her fix the house, and she still hadn't made him dinner or started on his publicity campaign. She could use a break from cleaning for a few days.

She reached the top of the stairs and leaned against a tree.

"Where are your shoes?" Damian laughed.

She looked down at her mud-streaked toes and grinned. "I forgot them."

"Looks like you haven't checked your mailbox since you've been here." He handed her a stack of letters.

"I wasn't expecting anything."

She flipped through the generically addressed direct mail pieces and credit card offers before seeing a letter from Nulte P.R. She caught her breath.

She turned the envelope over to open it, but she tucked it into her back pocket instead to read later. There wasn't a single good reason why Blanche would send her something via snail mail to the temporary Orcas Island address.

"Shouldn't you be at the restaurant tonight?" she asked as they walked toward the house. She tried not to think about the envelope wrinkling in her pocket.

"Vincent fired me again."

"What?"

"Every year I get fired when he gets enough summer help. Fortunately, that happened this week."

"So I guess I should be congratulating you?"

"Exactly."

"I'm glad you stopped by."

Damian stuck his hands in his pockets. "I wanted to make sure your water heater's still working."

"Still hot, and I'm still grateful."

"Wonderful," he said as she slid back the door. "Mind if I come in for a few minutes?"

"Not at all. Do you want some hot tea?"

"Sounds perfect."

When they walked into the kitchen, she put the kettle on the stove and turned it on.

"So when am I getting my chicken dinner?" He pulled out a cane-covered chair and sat down.

"How about tomorrow night?"

"Perfect."

"I guess I won't be inviting your family to dinner after all," Abby said.

He shrugged his shoulders as she pulled two bags of Orange Spice out of the cabinet.

"I figured you got married right after college."

"Considered it a few times," Damian said. "But it never worked. I traveled constantly when I worked with the International Whaling Commission, so it really wasn't conducive to family life."

She poured hot water over the tea bags and handed him a mug. "That crazy, huh?"

"Some days. I moved back to Seattle about ten years ago to work at the aquarium."

"Sounds like a pretty stable job to me."

"Met a girl, thought I'd settle down . . . but it didn't work out." He stirred his tea and set the bag on a saucer. "So here I am, a bachelor for life."

"It's not such a bad life, huh?"

"It was exactly what I wanted for a long time."

She decided not to ask him what he wanted now.

"Do you realize how odd it is to make you dinner when your uncle owns the best restaurant around?" she asked.

"I suppose, but Vincent's not nearly as attractive as you."

Abby fidgeted with her tea mug. "My cooking's not great."

"I don't believe it. The stars wouldn't be aligned properly if the daughter of Fran Taylor wasn't a fine cook."

She tried to remember the last time she made a decent meal. It was probably the time she'd entertained Blanche and her latest boyfriend, making them a mediocre roasted duck, tomato salad, and a mushroom soufflé. The boyfriend had been polite, saying it was the best he'd ever tasted. Blanche hadn't commented at all. The evening ended in disaster when she served sour cheesecake for dessert. She'd forgotten to add the sugar.

She rarely ate, let alone made, a real meal. Her "cooking" was usually a slab of meat on the grill or take-out on her way home from work.

"So, tell me more about your campaign to save the whales?" she asked, leaning toward him.

"It sounds so pithy, doesn't it, 'saving the whales.'" He drank his tea and sighed. "I'm not here to start an international campaign—I don't even want a career of saving the whales. I just want to rescue the orcas right here, around the Sound, and be done. This is their home, you know, their feeding grounds. They've always been protected here."

She shoveled two spoonfuls of sugar into her tea.

"What's changed?"

"The toxin levels."

"I read about the PCBs in the *Seattle Times* article."

He nodded. "They were used in different industries along the Sound until they were banned in 1977."

"And now they're back?"

"They stay in the water for a long time without breaking down, and when they do break down, the whales digest them from eating salmon. When the cows give birth, they often pass the toxins down to their first-born calf."

She sipped her tea. "How can you stop the PCBs from poisoning the water?"

"The levels should be fading out, but that's the strange thing. They're not."

"So someone's putting toxins back in the water."

"Not sure." He shrugged. "It could be done unintentionally through raw sewage or industrial waste, or someone might know they're dumping PCBs but they don't care."

"A great case for Erin Brokovich," she joked. Damian didn't even smile.

"I don't know if there's a conspiracy here. I just think our country needs to be concerned if this whale population dies out . . . not to mention the host of marine life that would follow." He stared down into his tea cup as if he could see the death of the ocean creatures in the brown liquid.

"Sounds like you need a national spotlight on this." Abby turned off the burner under the simmering teapot.

"That would be ideal, but I don't know where to start. The media certainly wouldn't listen to me."

"Why not?"

"Part of my job with the International Whaling Commission was to regulate the number of whales killed. The obvious perception is that I was responsible for their deaths even though I was trying to keep whale hunting under control."

"Well, that's where I can help you," Abby said. "I've spent the last seven years of my life drawing attention to important issues, and I think I could get you an interview or two with some national press in a way that shows you're passionate about keeping the whales alive."

Damian pressed his fingers against the bridge of his nose. "I don't know . . ."

"I'd prepare you for it."

"I've never done well talking to the media."

She smiled. "I'll get you ready."

He stood up, and she walked him toward the front door. Working on a campaign for the orcas would be the perfect way to spend her last two weeks on the island.

"Let me think about it," he said as he stepped outside.

"I can at least send out a press release and see what happens."

After she said goodnight, Abby locked the door. She leaned back against the wall, reached into her back pocket, and removed the dreaded envelope.

Her address was printed on Nulte P.R. stock. It looked very official. Unnerving.

She ripped it open. The letter inside was addressed to "Ms. Wagner." *Not good.*

She read the short note quickly, blinked twice, and read it again.

> *Dear Ms. Wagner,*
>
> *Thank you for your years of service with Nulte P.R. Due to a recent decline in work, I regret to inform you that we no longer need your services at our firm. We appreciate your expertise in the past and hope you will find suitable employment soon.*

Abby collapsed on the couch.

Short and sweet. Blanche had signed the impersonal declaration with her firm, professional hand. With one swoop, she'd fired her vice president and probably hadn't looked back. No phone call. No note of apology. No bouquet of flowers for seven fine years of work. Not even an extra hour to say good-bye to her staff and client friends. With a quick flick of her wrist, she'd established that Abby wasn't good for the agency's bottom line.

The least Blanche could do was send her off with a parting cake and a few nice words. Pretend she was retiring or making a wise career move or something other than firing her.

Abby turned to the next page, but the words blurred as she tried to read the details of her termination. Something about two weeks notice and four weeks of pay. Whatever . . .

Blanche obviously sent her away "on vacation" so she wouldn't make a scene at the office. She probably had already written the letter . . . she certainly hadn't wasted any time sending it to her.

She walked to the kitchen, opened the door under the sink, and threw the letter away. She wouldn't be needed back in Denver in two weeks after all. This was the end of her career in public relations . . . at least, the end of her work with Nulte P.R.

Chapter 37

Jessica watched Marc unload an indigo-colored kayak from the bed of Damian's truck and slide it over the toasted sand until its nose touched the saltwater. He'd picked her up twenty minutes ago and introduced her to one of the best-kept secrets on the island—a private beach hidden behind a grove of pines. Island visitors rarely caught a glimpse of this enchanted bay, found only by accident if they happened to meander down the dusty gravel road omitted from tourist maps.

She squeezed into the cramped kayak seat as he handed her a paddle.

"You ready for this?" he asked.

"More than ready." She trailed her fingers through the frigid water. She'd never kayaked before, but she didn't doubt for a second that she'd love it.

Marc waded into the water beside her, launching her small vessel out to sea. Then he crammed into a red sea kayak and followed her. They paddled out over the gentle waves and into the bay, a giant horseshoe accented with chiseled charcoal cliffs and wiry evergreens.

"What do you think?" he asked as he rode the waves beside her. The rhythm of their paddling ceased, innate quiet enveloping them.

"It's so peaceful out here," she murmured. "Otherworldly."

"You'll never want to go back to the big city after this summer."

"I decided I wouldn't be going back the moment Mom and I drove off the ferry."

"Where are you going to go?"

Jessica closed her eyes, breathing in the salty scent of the sea and the sweet aroma of the pines looming above. The rocky shoreline around them swept up into forested hills and then crested back down like a tidal

wave into random flats of beach. With the exception of a flock of black birds circling overhead, they were alone.

"I may just stay right here."

He grinned. "Works for me."

They rowed steadily across the bay, the breeze sifting through her hair.

Jessica prayed softly. The quiet hand of God was displayed in the soft rhythm of the waves; His steady Spirit was revealed with every stroke of her paddle gliding across the water's crisp cap. There was so much more to life than sitting in a classroom with useless material being drummed into her head. This was what was important to her—fresh air, peace, contentment, and the gift of freedom.

Marc paddled up beside her as a forest of leafy green sprigs appeared on the surface in front of them. They crossed slowly over the giant leaves and bulbs.

"What is this?" she asked.

"A bull kelp forest—the fastest growing algae in the world."

"It looks like it's taking over," she said as her paddle swept through the long stems and she tugged to release it from the heavy weight of the fronds.

"Bull kelp grows about two feet a day," he said. "If we sit here long enough, we can probably watch it spread."

"Amazing," she said as she squinted her eyes, trying to see beneath the surface. "What's underneath?"

"All sorts of sea life. They hover here for protection and food. It's pretty incredible."

She squinted again, but the sunlight reflected off the water, and she could only see a few inches below.

The kelp disappeared behind them as Marc led the way toward a narrow cove, the edge carpeted with wild grass and wind-blown pockets of sand. He beached his kayak, lifted himself out, and waded onto shore. Jessica wedged her boat into the sand next to his, and he tugged the kayak onto shore as she hopped out, damp sand mashing between her iridescent pink-painted toes. Squishy and soft.

She glanced around her. They'd landed on a secluded inlet, surrounded by a labyrinth of thick mustard yellows and dusty greens. Alone—with Marc. She'd paddled to a deserted beach with a man she hardly knew. Her mom's fears pervaded her thoughts for a moment; she should be afraid.

But when she looked down at him dragging her boat onto higher sand, she wasn't frightened at all. Marc Cartwright wasn't like any other man she'd ever met. He'd take care of her.

"Where are we?" she asked.

"No one's ever named it," he said solemnly. "The only real way to get here is by boat. If you tried to walk, you'd need a machete to chop your way through the forest and then you'd have to cross a river, no bridge, before climbing over the sheer cliff that guards this place."

"I'm glad we kayaked in."

Marc opened the lid on the back of his kayak and pulled out two nylon bags filled with snorkeling gear.

"This place deserves a name," Jessica said, brushing her hand over the soft grass.

Marc set the black bags on the sand and stood over her. "What do you propose?"

She glanced up at the deep forest overseeing the tangled masses of brush that surrounded them. Sunlight wrapped itself around the fir and the pine trees, glittering like tinsel on a Christmas tree.

"I'll think of something," she said as she took the snorkel and mask that Marc held out for her.

"Jessie's Cove," Marc pronounced with a wide grin.

"Very funny."

He shrugged his shoulders as he slipped his diving knife into a band secured around his calf. "I'm serious."

"What's that for?" She nodded to the knife.

"Just in case."

"Of what?"

"An emergency. If one of us gets tangled in something, I can get us out."

"You're not taking me into dangerous waters, are you?"

He shook his head as he handed her a slippery neoprene jumpsuit.

"The water's freezing," he said.

"Where am I supposed to put this on?" She glanced around the thorny brush on both sides.

"Just pull it over your swimsuit."

She tugged off the shorts on top of her suit as Marc busied himself with his own gear. Then she struggled into the insulated wetsuit and zipped it up.

"I feel like an alien," she said as she flopped across the sand with her fins, the wetsuit plastered to her legs and arms.

"You look like you're ready to explore."

"Let's go." She bit into the flimsy mouthpiece of the snorkel and tasted chlorine. It probably had been soaking all winter in a pail, eating away the bacteria from someone else's mouth. The nasty taste was at least a reminder that the rubber was sterile.

"Spit in your mask," Marc said as they waded out into the bay.

"You're kidding!"

Marc spit and spread the saliva across the silicon faceplate. Then he rinsed it in the water.

She shook her head and just rinsed her mask. No way she was going to spit in it. She pulled it back over her face, and they lowered themselves into the cold water.

Through the haze, she saw Marc's hand signal underneath the surface, and she swam hard, following the streaks of his black fins toward the cliffs. Beneath her were speckled rocks, sharp and threatening. Tiny fish nibbled at the mossy fuzz of algae that grew up between the rocks and swayed with the current.

They swam over a maze of embedded rocks and tangled seaweed before the sandy floor dropped away. They were gliding over a world she only knew existed from TV. Tall, stringy grass danced smoothly with the tide, and a school of tiny silver fish swam an arc around them.

Spectacular!

Together, Jessica and Marc passed tall boulders that harbored secrets too deep for them to explore without diving gear. A bold yellow fish swam in front of her and seemed to watch her with as much curiosity as she watched him. She reached out to touch the fish, and he bolted away. Then he swam back, watching her again from an arm's length away.

Her mask slowly fogged over until the entire underwater world blurred. She burst up through the surface, spewing out her mouthpiece to get a full breath of air. Marc's head popped out right after her.

"What are you doing?" he asked as she rinsed off her mask again in the seawater.

"I can't see."

"Give me your mask," he said, his arm extended toward her.

"Why?"

"Just hand it over."

Reluctantly she gave him her mask. He spat in the surface, washed it off underwater, and then handed it back.

"That's disgusting."

"At least you'll be able to see."

She wrapped the rubber around her ears and the faceplate stuck to her forehead. When she dropped underwater again, her view was crystal clear.

In front of her, Marc dove down through the rocks. She held her breath, following him eight feet or so below the surface. Brilliant blue and orange coral swayed with the water, creating a shimmering display. Massive boulders stood staunch behind the coral with honeycombed ledges that climbed each side.

A white fish peered out of a shadowed ledge, and then ducked back into the cave. When she reached out to touch the ledge, her hand floated by it, the water messing with her sight.

Marc turned his head to check on her, and she waved at him. It was miraculous—the simplicity of the ocean floor contrasting with the complexity of its marvelous life. No one else was here except her and Marc and the curious fish. A world of their own to explore.

She popped her head back out of the water, and Marc followed.

"You okay?"

"I thought of a name for that little beach," she said.

"I liked 'Jessie's Cove.'"

"You can call it that, but I'm naming it Coral Spit."

"Rather appropriate," he laughed. "Are you ready to swim back?"

"Nope."

"Well, Vincent might bless us both with a comment or two if we don't get to work in time."

Jessica reluctantly followed him back to the kayaks beached at Coral Spit, and they paddled to the truck. She wanted to stay—relishing this silent, beautiful world for hours.

For a moment she regretted her decision to take a job. She could stay out here all day if she didn't have to be at the restaurant by four.

But the restaurant money would support her sailing obsession. And, now that Marc had joined the wait staff, it was extra incentive to hang onto her summer job.

They shoved the kayaks into the flat bed of the truck, and Marc drove them back toward the cottage.

"This day is going down in my personal history book." She pulled her wet hair back into a ponytail.

"How's that?"

"As the most perfect day ever."

He grinned. "Does that mean you enjoyed yourself?"

"Just a little."

When Jessica walked into the cottage, she waved at her mom in the kitchen before rushing into her bedroom and slamming the door. She jumped on the soft comforter, the pillows bouncing like balloons. It had been the best day of her life. She wanted to pull the curtains tight, lock the door, and hide under the cotton sheets, relishing every moment she'd had with Marc.

Tires spun on the gravel outside and she peeked out her window between the wooden blinds as Marc drove away. She contemplated going back out to the kitchen, but her mom would see the goofy grin oozing across her face and ask questions. Better to stay in her room and pretend she was dressing for work.

Hugging a ragged teddy bear in her arms, she stared at the ceiling and dreamed about the future like a silly schoolgirl. The possibilities looked much more pleasant with Marc involved.

A knock on her door, and Jessica sighed before telling her mother to come in.

Abby leaned against the doorframe and stared. Jessica could almost hear the silent critique in her mom's head. Jessica's soaked hair was plastered to her head. Her T-shirt was drenched. And she was grinning like a Barbie doll.

"How was your date?" Abby asked, her arms crossed so firmly that someone would have to pry them apart.

"It wasn't really a date—we just went snorkeling." Jessica felt guilty for a second that she'd had so much fun. "Are you ready for your date?"

Abby's shoulders stiffened. "Clever," she replied. "Damian and I are friends from way back."

Jessica crossed her arms like her mom. "Friends like Marc and I."

"Something like that," Abby mumbled. "Let's concentrate on Marc."

Abby sat down beside her daughter on the comforter.

Red flags. Warnings. Flares. They were everywhere. Jessica didn't want to talk to her mother about Marc. She'd ruin her perfect day.

"Not much to discuss."

"You only met this boy a week ago," Abby said. "You don't really know anything about him."

Jessica bristled at her mom's tone. "I know he's a nice guy. I know he's been respectful and kind and has a relationship with the Lord. Not a bad start."

"Have you met his parents?"

"His mom is in Seattle."

"According to Damian, not a very nice place in Seattle."

"Well, that hasn't stopped Damian from hiring him or becoming his friend. I've decided to make him my friend too."

"Be careful, Jessica."

"This is ludicrous, Mom. It's the twenty-first century. People are allowed to change and excel far beyond their circumstances if they're given the chance."

"I'm not saying he's not allowed to change. I hope for his sake that he does. That doesn't mean I want him dating my only daughter."

"I've got to get ready for work." She hopped off the bed and walked

into the bathroom. She turned on the shower's hot water and stepped inside. Why did her mom always try to ruin her life?

Be careful, Jessica.

Of course she'd be careful.

Chapter 38

Abby pounded the dough for homemade croissant rolls as she watched Jessica leave for work on her bicycle. Usually she baked bread that had been pre-rolled at a factory and stuffed into a can, but if Damian wanted a Fran Taylor meal, she had to make homemade.

Less than an hour ago, she'd watched her daughter pull into the driveway with Marc, splats of mud coating the sideboard of Damian's white truck. The two kids had been talking just as fast as when they'd left. What did they find to talk about?

Marc jumped out to race around the front of the cab and open the passenger door. As the two of them headed toward the front door, she'd pushed herself up on her toes to see if they were holding hands. She couldn't tell, but he was certainly much too close to Jessica. Any closer and she would have marched out and said a thing or two.

Life was spiraling out of her control. She had to do something about Jessica and Marc, but what? She'd hinted to Jessica that this relationship would never work, but obviously her daughter wasn't listening. Jessica would be crushed when they broke up, and she didn't want to see her girl get hurt again. If only there was something she could do to stop this before it was too late.

Maybe she'd simply tell Marc to stay away, or she could make up a shocking story or two about their family. Just enough to scare him. Jessica may kill her now, but she'd thank her in a few years when she met the right man. She may have failed Hunter years ago, but Abby wasn't about to fail Jessica. With no job waiting for her in Denver, she could stay on the island as long as she needed to protect her girl.

A knock on the door interrupted Abby's thoughts, and she walked

across the house to answer it. Damian smiled back at her. He was almost an hour early. "Is that an apple pie I smell?"

She planted her hands on her hips. "Yes, and it's the only thing that's done."

"I'll take apple pie for dinner."

"I've got a lot more planned, but I'm not even close to being ready."

"Good." He stepped into the house and slid off his shoes. "I was hoping to help."

They worked side by side for the next hour until she served him a plate of baked chicken overlaid with sliced prosciuto, fresh green beans soaked in bouillon, and croissant rolls.

"I have to say—" he swallowed slowly, relishing the creamy chicken before he took another bite— "this is even better than your mom's."

"You're very kind," she said as she scooped up another bite of beans, "and a very bad liar."

He grabbed his heart like she'd just delivered a blow. "I would never tell a lie—especially in regard to food."

"You're a mess."

He met her eyes and held her gaze. "It must have been hard to lose your mom."

"Some days, I really miss her," she sighed. "A few months ago, I actually picked up the phone to call when it hit me again that she wouldn't be answering."

"You've lost several people in the last few years," he said.

"It's been almost ten years since Scott passed away."

"You say that like it explains everything."

"There's not much else to say. It's been a long time."

"Do you still miss him?" he asked as he buttered a hot croissant. She leaned back against the hard cane on the seat, her fork resting on the plate in front of her.

How could she be honest with Damian about this? It seemed so cold-hearted to say no, she didn't miss her husband. But she didn't miss him like she missed her son.

"It's been a long time," she replied simply. "So you had a girlfriend in Seattle?"

He nodded. "Christina was a flight attendant. We actually met while I was working in South Africa. Her transfer to Seattle was the main reason I came back."

He put down his fork and knife. "When she became a Christian, I wasn't the least bit interested in her faith. I'd seen too much suffering in my travels through third world countries and had already decided that a loving God could never exist."

"I can understand that," Abby mumbled, hoping she didn't sound as bitter as she felt.

"But then, in a twist that I can only describe as a miracle from above, Christina married a pastor in Seattle. She called me three years ago to say there was a boy in her church that wanted an internship. She gushed and gushed about what an amazing kid he was, but I didn't hire him for an aquarium position. Instead, I called Marc and asked if he would work with me on the island."

"Apparently, Christina was right."

"Marc's a great worker, and he did what no one else has ever done. He listened to me rant about all the wrongs in the world, and God somehow used his story to guide me to the truth."

Abby carved through her chicken and took several bites. She twitched uncomfortably in her chair as she searched for what to say next. Could she trust Damian? She wanted so much to talk to a friend about this persistent pain that kept flaring up in her soul.

But she couldn't do it. How could she trust an old friend when she couldn't even trust herself?

"What truth is that?" she finally asked.

"The truth that the result of sin in this world is grief. The truth that I needed Christ even though I was irate at the injustice in the world. And the truth that God is indeed love, and He could save me in spite of my own many sins."

Damian bit into his buttered roll again. "I used to think I could only be free if I was traveling and sailing and exploring, but it was a trap. The only freedom I've ever been able to find has been through Christ. I'm still a drifter at heart, but now I try to let God take me where I need to go."

"Sounds like you have it all figured out."

"Does it?" He grinned. "Most days I don't feel like I've figured out a thing."

"I envy your faith."

"What happened to your faith?" he asked.

"I still believe in God." She played with the pieces of chicken left on her plate. "He's just let me down over and over the past twenty years."

"Are you sure?"

She looked at him in surprise. Of course she was sure.

"Do you still want apple pie?" she asked as she stood up and took her plate to the sink.

Abby's telephone cord draped over a kitchen chair and around the corner to the wall jack. She studied the screen of her laptop, jotting a few notes on the notebook beside her. Then she rubbed her eyes and glanced up at the clock in the corner of her screen—12:36 AM.

She hit the button for another Google search, and an error message popped up on her screen. She sighed. It was the fourth time in the last hour she'd lost the connection. She'd pay top dollar to connect via cable or satellite, but dial-up was her only option at the cottage and it was slow, slow, slow.

Over apple pie, she and Damian had discussed the publicity campaign to present the orcas' plight to the world, and he'd agreed to do an interview or two. Now it was time for her to act.

After five hours of searching, she'd unearthed enough material to corroborate Damian's concern that PCB toxins were killing off their population of orcas. She also discovered that, contrary to what Damian thought, several media outlets had already expressed concern over their demise—it just hadn't received the national attention to make a difference.

Sipping her lukewarm blackberry tea, she read that one gram of PCBs was enough to make one billion liters of water uninhabitable to marine wildlife.

"Orcas eat up to one-twentieth of their body weight each day," the article said. "In a twenty-day span, they can eat the equivalent of their own body weight."

Abby scribbled another note. If this massive amount of food contained traces of PCBs, it could kill a whale.

The more she researched, the more she realized that Damian was right. Raw sewage or illegal industrial waste could contaminate the entire Sound. The orca that he had found on Shaw Island had more than 800 parts of PCB toxins per million, busting the average of 58. Something was definitely wrong, and someone needed to trumpet this cause.

Who better to talk about this than a Puget Sound resident who loved the water and its sea life . . . and had earned his doctorate in marine biology? With a little training, Damian would be the perfect spokesperson for their campaign.

The clock on her screen blinked 1:14 AM.

Where in the world was Jessica? She said she'd be home late, but it was way past late. Surely she'd walk in the front door any moment.

Abby clicked on a new link. Several factories on the Washington and British Columbia coastlines could be guilty of releasing these deadly toxins, including the Pageant Industries that Damian had blasted during his *Times* interview. She wondered how she could put the spotlight on Pageant and other factories without actually revealing their names. Give reporters the taste of a good story and let them do the undercover legwork. Surely there was a reporter at a national show or paper who had a passion for the environment and the guts to confront some bigwigs at these companies, asking the really hard questions.

She wrote the headline for her press release: *Dead Whales Haunt Puget Sound*.

She deleted the words. Too hyper. This was a serious story. She needed a good hook and an inspirational lead that didn't sound sensational. If only she could hand this over to Curtis to write.

Yikes! Did that awful thought just cross her mind? The man had cost her a job and here she'd lapsed into wishing he could write for her. For a brief moment she wondered what was happening back at the Denver office, but then she stopped her mind from wandering down that

dangerous path. It didn't matter what was happening there. She was no longer on the staff.

She plugged ahead with her copy, her words forming faster than she could type. She'd come back to the headline when she finished the press release.

Another half hour rushed by as Abby edited and reedited her release, striving for perfection. It was an important issue, but more important to her, it was Damian's issue, and the release should be impeccable before she sent it out. She wanted to score national coverage for him, the whales . . . and herself.

A blast of wind shook the kitchen windows, and Abby pushed back her chair, shutting the cover on her computer. It was after two, and she wouldn't be able to sleep until Jessica arrived home.

Abby wrapped her long raincoat over her sweatshirt and leggings and walked out the door.

Chapter 39

Marc winked at Jessica when she rushed into De Lucia's hectic kitchen, dressed in her plain black skirt and white shirt with her hair tied back in a ponytail. She rolled her eyes at him as her right foot slid underneath her. Grasping the counter edge, she balanced herself, then reached down and snatched the fork someone had dropped. Only an hour into her shift, and she was ready to go home.

"You okay?" he whispered as he passed her with a full tray of food.

"I'll be better if the silverware stays off the floor."

And if her hose would stop rubbing her sunburned legs raw.

Marc grabbed the fork from her hand, tossed it into the sink, and sped out the door to deliver his food.

"Two plates of spaghetti with clam sauce," she told the chef as she slid him the order and watched him add it to a long line of crinkled papers.

Turning to the next counter, Jessica straightened her skirt before filling a platter with iced water. Until she took this job, she couldn't remember the last time she'd worn a skirt, and she hadn't worn a pair of scratchy hose since . . . well, she couldn't remember that either. Both felt strange, and the last six nights she'd raced home and replaced the awful uniform with an extra large T-shirt and gym shorts.

Marc blasted back through the swinging doors and smiled at her again before picking up another tray loaded with manicotti.

It was odd to act so professional around someone she'd just talked heart and soul with hours before. Funny, she thought, how you could be snorkeling one morning with a friend—feeling incredibly close and connected. Then that same evening, you dress up and admire each other from afar, the closeness erased in a chalky cloud of professionalism.

Their relationship was a blank blackboard waiting for colorful pictures, and tonight she could only draw with black and white.

She steadied the tray across her forearm and walked toward a family sitting at a prime table that overlooked the moonlit bay.

Focus, she reminded herself again. Vincent would fire her if she kept tripping, or heaven forbid, found herself sprawled across the sticky floor.

Without even looking toward his section, Jessica knew Marc's eyes were focused on her again. She'd caught his glimpse tonight more times than she could count, and it both thrilled and unnerved her. She felt like she was starring in her own *Truman Show* with a dedicated audience of one.

Removing a pad from her front pocket, she announced the night's specials and prepared to take the family's orders.

"Just wanted you folks to know that you have De Lucia's finest waitress serving you tonight," Marc said from behind her. He stood directly over her shoulders, grinning down at the poor family who stared back at him stunned. "Only a special few get this privilege, and you were chosen."

The kids at the table giggled as a warm tide of red crept up her neck. She almost stuck out her tongue at him, but instead, she faced the small group with a nervous smile.

"Ignore him like the rest of us do." She clicked her pen.

Marc gave the table a thumbs up before he turned to leave.

With the kids still chuckling, Jessica scribbled down their orders and then rushed back to the kitchen. If nothing else, Marc made the eight hours of work fly by. It was midnight before she realized how quickly the evening had passed again. At this rate, the summer would vanish in a blur of watery days and exhausting nights.

With the last tablecloth stripped, tips counted, and the floor swept, Jessica paused by the front door and glanced around the room for Marc. He must have left before her, and she couldn't blame him. He was probably at home in bed.

She walked outside, the sliver of moon casting its light across the sea. Vincent's floodlight illuminated the long set of white-painted stairs in front of her, and she strolled down them. Her calves and biceps were throbbing, but the tips stuffed in her sweatshirt pocket eased some of the pain.

She could see her bike in the shadows, locked to a tree trunk at the bottom of the steps. If she rode fast, she'd be snuggled into her warm bed in twenty minutes.

"Jessie!" Footsteps pumped down the stairs and she turned around.

"Are you going home?" Marc asked as he caught up with her.

"Planning to." She looked down at the hazy street lamps below them. Most of the town's store lights had darkened hours ago. "Not much nightlife."

"You need loud music to have fun?"

"No," she huffed. "I was thinking more about a movie or a coffee shop or even pizza. Does everything close around here at 9 PM?"

"Pretty much." He sat down on the chipped step, and she sat beside him. Flakes of white paint on the railing beside her had been stripped away, and the wooden step under her chilled through the thin nylon of her hose.

"So what do you do around here in the evening when you're not working?" she asked.

"Incredibly exciting stuff," he laughed. "I'm usually in bed by ten since Damian has me working at dawn."

"I guess it's worth it to be on the water all day."

"My exact thoughts."

She breathed in the chilly night air and hugged her arms tight to her chest. "I had a blast today."

"Me too."

He started to say something else, but someone closed the door above them and started down the stairs. They each edged to the sides, and Jessica leaned back against the railing until it wobbled. She bolted back up. It would be a long plunge if it broke loose behind her. The server squeezed between them.

"Good night, you two," the girl said, waving back. "Looks like you're shutting the place down."

A gust of wind breezed through the railing, and Jessica shivered as she pulled her sweatshirt tight around her arms.

"Let's get you home before you freeze," Marc said.

"I'm fine." This was nothing compared to the winter evenings in Boulder when she had to walk back from classes. Besides, hot or cold, there was no place else she'd rather be.

"Did your mom say anything about our day together?"

"Not much," Jessica said. "My dad and I used to talk all the time, but there's this odd barrier between Mom and me that I've never been able to cross. It's better not to say anything at all."

"Do you know why?"

Jessica shrugged. "She wants me to be like her, so she's not really interested if I want something else."

"Her expectations are too high?"

"Unbelievably high and completely unattainable. She wants more than the best for me. She wants the impossible."

They were quiet for a moment as the clouds darkened the moonlight, relishing each other's company in spite of the cold wind.

"I haven't talked to my mom in a week." He paused.

"Did she call you?"

"Yeah. She wanted money."

"For what?"

"She says it's for food, but my mom has a problem with alcohol. If I give her the money, she'll run down to the liquor store and drink until she turns crazy."

Jessica felt sick for him. Some days were rough with her mom, but she had no idea how she'd respond if her mother called her, begging for cash. What a horrible place to put your child.

"So you said no?" she asked.

"I didn't know what else to do. I gave her money last week, and she spent it on booze."

"So neither of us can make our parents happy."

"I guess not."

Clouds eased over the stars and moonlight, turning the night to pitch black. Jessica scooted closer to Marc, and the minutes disappeared like grains of sand stolen by the tide.

Jessica had no clue what time it was when a car slowly drove up to the restaurant's steps and stopped. She squinted into the bright headlights as she heard the door open and slam shut.

"Jessica?" her mom called.

She didn't move. "What are you doing here?"

"I was getting worried. It's almost 2:30."

Jessica sighed as Marc gently took her hand into his.

"I'm sorry, Mrs. Wagner," he said. "We lost track of time."

"I'll be down in a minute, Mom."

His fingers were calloused, but strong. She liked how they felt weaved through her hand. She didn't want to move.

"It's a good thing she came along," Marc said.

"Why?"

He hesitated. "Because we would have talked all night and I have to meet Damian at six."

"Right."

He squeezed her hand and let go. "I'll see you tomorrow night."

"See ya." She stood up and started to walk down the stairs.

"Just a sec," he said.

She turned back to him, his face lit by the headlights. Why couldn't her mom at least turn them down a notch?

"I'd like to take you on a real date," he said simply.

She paused for only a second. "Okay."

"Maybe on Tuesday afternoon?"

"Sounds great."

She turned again, concentrating solely on climbing down the narrow stairs without tripping. She wanted to shout and laugh and twirl around.

So this was what it was like. She'd heard about the fuzzy emotions of falling in love, but she'd always thought it was a fabrication—wild stories from women trying to convince themselves that they'd found their man.

Maybe the fairy tale was true.

She opened the passenger door of the car. "I can ride my bike home."

"I'll bring you back tomorrow to get the bike," Abby said.

Jessica shrugged her shoulders, climbed in, and slammed the car door.

Chapter 40

Abby stared at the dark ceiling above her for forty-five minutes, tossing and turning under the warm covers. Moonlight flickered through the backyard branches and brushed bright streaks across the loft's wooden paneling.

Jessica had barely said a word to her on their short drive home from De Lucia's. She recapped her evening in about ten seconds, and then leaned back on the headrest like she'd fallen asleep, not a single word of appreciation for her mother driving into town.

She was supposed to be a professional communicator and influencer, yet she couldn't even persuade her own daughter to safeguard her future. Once again she'd failed as a communicator . . . and she'd failed as a mom. Maybe that was why God took Hunter from her. If she couldn't be a good mother to one child, she would have been a rotten mom to two.

When they drove up to the house tonight, Jessica ran into her bedroom and locked the door. At least one of them could sleep.

Tucking her head under the blanket, Abby closed her eyes and counted a line of plain white sheep, each of them leaping over a hurdle and running away . . . 31, 32, 33. She started to relax until the nondescript sheep began dancing and twirling over the plain hurdle. Then the hurdle transformed into a giant blue jay and flew away.

She sighed as she reopened her eyes. Her brain was much too active for this menial sheep-counting task. She'd have to try another tactic to woo herself to sleep.

The mattress creaked under Abby when she rolled over again. Her body was exhausted, but her mind raced through her long to-do list, items to complete before she officially launched Damian's campaign. She

needed to rewrite the press release, develop a stellar media list, and send the release out.

Killer Whales Vanish from Puget Sound.

That was it!

Abby hopped out of bed. It was pointed and simple. The exact headline she needed. Tugging a sweatshirt over her pajamas, she raced down the stairs to the kitchen table and opened up the cover of her sleeping computer. If Jessica could stay up all night talking to a boy, she could certainly stay up and finish her project. It wasn't like she had any plans tomorrow. Once she sent out the press release, she could sleep all day.

Banging out her frustration on the keyboard, she pounded out the new headline and subhead: *Washington Coast Contaminated with Deadly Toxins, Popular Orcas Disappear.*

Then she revised the words of her press release one last time and printed it on her portable printer to review.

She read her words quickly at first and then she proofed it slowly, marking her changes with a red pen. At least her lack of sleep was a good motivator to get her work done. She proofed it a third time, and then set the paper down by her computer. It was 4:25.

With a second pot of coffee brewing on the kitchen counter, Abby grabbed a bottle of Advil from the cabinet and swallowed two pills. She really should lie back down and try to sleep, but she was so close to completing this project. She glanced out the window and watched the tall grass and cedar leaves sway eerily in the breeze.

Why was she so motivated to rush through this campaign? The timing was certainly right to do it. The whales hadn't returned, and if they were going to speak out about it, they had to do it now. However, if she was really honest with herself, she knew the truth. She was trying to validate her own worth by helping Damian and the whales, proving that she could make it without the umbrella of Nulte P.R.

Pouring the fresh coffee into a mug, she skipped the cream and sugar to maximize the caffeine jolt. With the caffeine streaming through her veins, she could work another eight hours.

She sat back down in front of the computer, opened her Palm Pilot, and synchronized her office Rolodex with her laptop. Plodding through her long database, she marked major media contacts. *The Early Show. 20/20. Dateline NBC.*

She surfed online for contact information on media outlets in the top twenty-five markets, searching for reports and stories on environmental issues and for reporters who'd done their homework on industry pollution, wildlife extinction, and national parks.

She'd gotten used to establishing a few perimeters at the office, clicking a button, and their media software would spit out an updated list for her to use. Now, she was searching, cutting, pasting, and developing most of the list on her own.

She successfully compiled a solid list of 115 contacts. Not bad. Even without a budget, she was going to get some serious media.

She shoved her fingers through her tangled hair and rested her head on her hands. She only needed three more of her contacts before she wrapped up her list. They'd disappeared from her personal Rolodex, but she'd ask Maggie if she could borrow the information.

Blinking, she realized light was shining on the papers in front of her. In fact, the entire table had brightened, and the light wasn't coming from the chandelier above the table. She spun around. The darkness had vanished as the first rays of sunshine crept over the lawn.

She glanced again at the clock on her computer screen: 7:15 AM.

It was 8:15 AM in Denver, and Maggie would be walking into her cubicle at any moment, dumping her enormous purse into the bottom drawer of her filing cabinet and powering on her machine. Did she dare call? It wasn't like Blanche would answer the agency phone. Even on the mornings that she got there early, Blanche always spent at least a half hour engrossed in the morning news.

Abby refilled her coffee mug and stared out the back window at the water. The white-capped crests sparkled in the direct sun and a canopy of fog lingered over the trees. She was so far from the dusty Rockies—removed from the power struggles at the office, unhappy clients, and a boss who'd probably been trying to oust her for years.

Digging her cell phone out of her purse, she dialed the familiar number.

"Nulte P.R." Maggie's voice dragged. She was missing her usual lilt.

"Have you forgotten me already?"

"Abby!" Maggie exclaimed. She hushed her voice. "How are you?"

"I've been shipwrecked somewhere off the coast of Washington."

Maggie managed a polite laugh.

"We miss you around here," she whispered. "Everything's falling apart."

Abby wanted to relish the details but knew instantly that she couldn't. If she wanted to move on, she needed to flee from her anger . . . and the sickly glee of gloating after she'd been wronged.

"I'm sure Blanche has got it under control."

"The strange thing is, she doesn't. She's above day-to-day management, and she doesn't know what to do without you."

"I miss you dearly, Maggie, but this has been a healthy break for me."

"I'd like to ask when you're coming back, but Blanche tells us you're not."

Abby resisted the bitterness trying to seethe through her voice. "It appears that she doesn't need me anymore with all that energetic new blood she's hired."

"She can say what she wants, but I'm telling you straight—we need you!"

Abby smiled slightly as she walked back to the kitchen. Wasn't that the entire reason she'd started a career? Jessica hadn't needed her anymore, Scott was gone, and she'd turned her back on God. Work was something she could pour herself into without exposing her heart. Purpose without commitment. A place to show up every morning and be needed, but no commitment beyond the job. Hopeless, she realized suddenly. She'd been running along avoiding real relationships or a purpose beyond her tedious job. She did need a change.

"I'm calling to ask a small favor," she said.

"No problem. What is it?"

"I'm doing a small P.R. project here—pro bono. I'm missing a few contacts from my list."

Abby heard Maggie clicking on her keyboard. Hopefully she was opening her Rolodex.

"Who do you need, hon?"

"*CNN Daybreak, FOX & Friends,* and *Primetime.*"

Maggie rolled off their names, numbers, and e-mail addresses as Abby scribbled them down.

"You're a gem," Abby said.

"Did you hear about the Duncans?"

"I didn't."

"Heartsong just placed another baby boy with them."

What was that feeling erupting in her chest? Jealousy? She should be happy for them. If anyone deserved a baby, it was Tom and Briana. The baby couldn't have a better home.

"That's great," Abby said, wishing she felt more enthusiastic for the couple.

Then she heard a voice on the other line, and a muffled response. Maggie's hand had obviously covered the phone.

"The witch is in," she whispered. "Better go play my part."

"Thanks again," Abby mimicked her whisper, and then hung up the phone. She typed the media contacts into her Rolodex and was suddenly grateful that she didn't have to deal with Blanche's approval today. This was her campaign. She owned it, and she planned to do it well. With a simple click, she distributed the press release to editors and producers all over the country.

She turned off the kitchen lights as sun poured into the room. She made another pot of coffee for Jessica before heading upstairs to the loft, collapsing into the soft bed. She didn't need to count the dancing sheep this time. In seconds, she was gone.

Chapter 41

"Morning, folks," Damian welcomed his guests over the microphone as he steered the tour boat out into open waters. The boat was more than half full on this Saturday morning, and that was good enough for him.

The sky was slightly overcast, the sun struggling to break through the thick mantle of gray. Damian hoped the clouds would burn off in the next hour or two for a sunny finale to their four-hour ride.

Damian plunged the boat through a bumpy set of waves, saltwater spraying the sides, and glanced into his mirror. He was hosting a small bundle of parkas and raincoats today, and the crowd seemed happy. The adults were chatting casually as the children leaned against the railing, pointing toward the water.

It was a cool day for a ride. If they got too cold, a few people could huddle together underneath the enclosed deck and finish their whale watching through the wide windows.

He'd invited Abby on the ride today, but she'd declined. Sometime he'd ask her what happened to her passion for the water, but the timing wasn't right.

He smiled. After all these years, Abby still looked the same. The same beautiful girl who'd stolen his heart when he was a teen . . . yet the old camaraderie between them had vanished, torn apart from years of experiences and stories shared with others.

Time and relationships had wedged a gulf between them, but they still shared a history together, a brew of stories and memories that no one else could understand. The memories flashed back like rapidly moving slides. Their sailboat toppling far from land. The Coast Guard rescuing them from a thunderstorm. Their lunch off Shaw Island, watching the whales swim by. Hours spent sailing and then splashing into shore to play chess and rummy until dusk.

So much had happened to both of them since the days they were free to enjoy the water like Marc and Jessica did these days.

He thought he'd be able to maintain his cool when he saw her again. He thought the feelings would be long gone. He'd grown up, matured, changed . . . yet he still wanted to take her in his arms and never let her go.

But she'd rejected him so many years ago, and she'd probably do it again.

When Abby got engaged, he chose the single life, and for years, it was exactly what he wanted—a drifter with no commitments, no restraints, just him and the water and an occasional relationship when he spent more than a month in one place. When he moved to Seattle, he thought his single days might be over, but he could never get Abby out of his mind.

The boat collided with another swell, and adrenaline rushed through him as he tried to focus on the ride. He wouldn't contend with an angry sea, not with a boatful of passengers, but irritated waters made his job a bit more interesting. The thrill seekers onboard would thank him for a safe but exciting ride.

"Looks like we're in for a real adventure today," he said into the intercom as the water sprayed the sides again. "But nothing to worry about— just a bump here and there."

A surge of water cascaded over the front of the boat and then streamed its way back. Damian squinted his eyes, searching the horizon again for any sign of life. Not only was he the pilot of this boat, he was the chief entertainer, and he hoped to find something interesting in the water to amuse his audience onboard.

"Approximately 71,000 Chinook salmon run these waters every summer, eating and spawning," he said. "In fact, sea life from all over the region migrate here each summer to enjoy the abundance of food, and this is where we find killer whales as well as seals, sea lions, harbor porpoises, and our famous giant octopus."

They blasted over another choppy wave, and Damian directed the boat west, hoping he could offer this group a glimpse of the whales.

Abby had persuaded him to pursue a media campaign for the whales, but he wished there was someone else to triumph the cause. Anyone would do a better job than he would. He hadn't even been able to make a decent case to the local press; he'd completely botch an interview with national media. But Abby and Marc were both convinced he was the one. Maybe God could use his obsession for sea life to help the whales.

"We've got a sick one," Marc said as he stepped into the wheelhouse and shut the door.

Damian pulled a plastic first aid box out of a drawer. They'd both been trained in rescue breathing, fibrillation, and CPR, but thankfully, the only trauma they'd ever had on board was seasickness. He'd stocked the boat with Dramamine and acupressure bracelets, but once someone was seasick, it was too late to administer that kind of preemptive care.

"You want to steer while I handle it?"

"Gladly." Marc took the wheel as the boat bounded over another wave.

Someone got seasick on the vessel at least once a week. Damian usually delegated this task to Marc, but today he wanted to get out from behind the wheel and breathe some fresh air.

He found the nauseous woman at the back of the boat—the only person lying on the floor, her face a pale shade of green. A circle of curious onlookers had formed around the woman, but no one seemed to be helping her. A man with balding brown hair whispered in her ear, and then turned toward Damian for help.

Damian knelt beside the woman. "Are you her friend?"

"I'm her husband."

Damian ignored his defensive tone. "Is she on any medication?"

"She took some Tylenol this morning, but nothing prescription."

Damian felt her pulse. Slow, but not threatening.

"Did she eat breakfast?"

"No. We were running late."

"Hence the problem," Damian murmured. Never take a bumpy boat ride on an empty stomach.

He directed the man to take one of her arms, and they gently lifted the woman to her feet and escorted her through the curious crowd. Her arms and legs were shaking, and she moaned with every step.

Out of the corner of his eye, Damian saw something black move on top of the water. He stopped and turned his head toward the sea.

Nothing.

The woman took another step. Damian tried to concentrate on her plight, but he stole several more glances starboard before helping her inside. He thought he saw something again.

"Feeling sick," the woman mumbled. He handed her a plastic bag seconds before she heaved.

Damian sighed. Obviously Marc hadn't seen the black sheen across the surface or he would have steered the boat starboard. He almost ran up the stairs to alert Marc, but the woman beside him threw up again.

Damian pointed to the leather seats in the lobby, and the woman collapsed across the row. Most of their seasick guests wanted to jump overboard . . . there was nothing they could do but wait until they got back to shore.

"Is she going to be okay?" her husband asked when they hit another rough wave.

"She'll be as good as new by morning."

The woman groaned in response and Damian assured her again that it was only temporary. Then he backed out of the room before running upstairs.

Taking the wheel from Marc, he steered the boat north, but if the black dots had been whales, they'd disappeared.

Chapter 42

Abby toasted a bagel and slathered it with blueberry cream cheese. She'd yet to receive a single response from her pitch on the dying whales. Not a phone call or an e-mail reply. Not one inquiry expressing interest in her story or even a rejection note. She'd checked her computer over and over during the past three days—the message had definitely been delivered. She thought she'd nailed it, but maybe she had lost her touch. If she couldn't sell a story this big, it was time to retire her career.

She carried her breakfast along with her laptop through the living room. For the first time in two weeks, she actually felt comfortable walking across the floor barefoot. Every inch of the house had been scrubbed, top to bottom. She'd cleaned all the curtains, vacuumed under the furniture, and mopped the hardwood twice. The old home deserved this return to its cozy shine.

She opened the back door and breathed in the garden's sweet aroma. The wind blew off the bay, rousing the flowers to life, their fragrances gusting through the air.

She was drawn to the garden's wild, enchanting beauty. Purple and yellow iris rose to her waist while white clover scattered like snowflakes on the ground. Woven between the vibrant rainbow blend of flowers were hundreds of plain dandelions that had reproduced until they owned her back yard. When she had time, the dandelions would be the first to go.

Abby arranged her bagel and her portable office on the picnic table. She sat on the bench and dialed the first producer on her media list. Enough time had passed since she'd sent the e-mail. It was time to follow up by phone. She planned to contact the entire list this morning, plotting to catch a few reporters drinking coffee in their cubicles and waiting for the next big story to crack. She hoped it was a slow news day.

She listened to the first producer's hastily recorded voice mail message and responded with a succinct message of her own, explaining the story idea and telling him they could get great footage of the island's locals searching for killer whales. Using the past footage of the beautiful whales combined with current shots of the sea's ghostly surface, they'd have a compelling story to both show and tell.

She disconnected the call and took a deep breath before dialing Victor at *USA Today*. She realized suddenly that her stomach was cramped in knots. She hadn't been nervous about pitching media in a long time.

She paused when he answered the phone.

"Hey Victor, it's Abby," she began. "Thanks for your great article on Heartsong."

"Sorry, Abby," he blurted. "Can't talk right now. I'm in the middle of a huge story."

"No problem." She plunged straight into her prerehearsed pitch. "I sent you an e-mail a few days ago about the whales disappearing from Puget Sound. Thought you might be interested in finding out why."

There was a long pause on the line, and Abby thought for a moment that he'd hung up. Then she heard the faint sound of typing in the background. He probably hadn't heard a word she just said. She wondered if she should start her pitch again or say good-bye.

"Victor?"

"Yeah, still here. I got your e-mail, but the story's too cliché for me right now. The 'save the whales' theme has been done a thousand times."

"I know, but this is a completely new angle. I promise it will be a great feature for you."

"Sorry, Abby. Story due in eight and a half minutes."

"Thanks, Victor," she mumbled as he hung up the phone. "Call me if you change your mind."

Pathetic . . . she was pitching the dial tone.

She scratched Victor's name off her list. No big deal, she told herself. It was one rejection. She was used to getting ten or fifteen before she scored a hit. She'd just keep pressing on. Someone would be interested in this story if she stayed upbeat, focused. She had to remain optimistic to make a good pitch.

She dialed the next number on her list, left a message, and then dialed again. For the next hour and a half, she pitched reporters and producers, but not a single person she spoke with sounded interested. A few said they'd consider the idea—the brush-off line that usually meant no.

She cheered herself up with a mental pep talk . . . somebody would call back soon. They'd listen to her message, read the release, and realize this was the story of a lifetime, Pulitzer Prizes and Edward R. Murrow Awards flashing through their heads.

Or maybe they'd already deleted her note after reading the first line.

Her bagel only half eaten, Abby suddenly realized it was an hour past her typical lunchtime. She walked back inside to the kitchen and tossed a few pieces of ham and turkey on a slice of rye bread, smoothed light mayonnaise across the other slice, and smashed the bread together. She held the sandwich up to her mouth but hesitated before taking a bite. She wasn't hungry at all.

She slid the entire sandwich onto a plate and stuck it in the refrigerator. She'd eat it for dinner instead. Right now she preferred to be busy outside.

Slipping on her hiking boots, a straw hat, and a pair of new gloves, Abby stepped back out into the yard. She critiqued the overgrown mess in front of her. She'd carve out a few areas designated for the jungle, transplanting the mature flowers into designed areas that featured the natural beauty instead of letting them all grow wild.

That's what she wanted—tousled wildflower gardens scattered around the back yard and woven through a thick, manicured lawn. Her brother-in-law would probably hate her when he realized he'd have to spend his vacations mowing, but they could actually enjoy the yard instead of hiding out on the porch.

Kneeling down, she plucked out a handful of weeds and tossed them into a giant trash bag. The breeze grew stronger, a pleasant cooling for her steaming face and hands. Sweat poured into her eyes and she wiped it off with her gloves. No one would care that she was streaking black across her forehead and nose.

With her spade, she gently dug into the soft earth and unearthed the roots of several flowers she wanted to replant. She set them into a fresh pot of water and moved them across the yard. They'd already transplanted themselves into her back yard without any help. Surely they would thrive in their new, well-fertilized home.

As she mixed plant food into the soil, she heard a grinding sound, and she turned to watch a lime green Beetle race down her driveway. The car brakes squealed, and Abby braced herself for a crash. Instead she heard the slam of a door.

She slid off her gloves, brushing the sweat and dirt off her face with the sleeve of her T-shirt as she walked to the front of the house.

Practically skipping around to the passenger side of the tiny car was an elderly woman with a stringy gray ponytail, turquoise flannel shirt, and cropped jeans. Her wrinkled face was a ghostly white, but her smile was anything but an apparition. She looked as genuine and hip as Abby had remembered her twenty years ago.

"Abby Taylor!" the woman greeted her, and Abby grinned at the town florist.

"Mrs. Crockett. How are you?"

Abby hugged her, and then apologized. She was covered in dirt, and Mrs. Crockett looked like she'd just stepped out of the shower.

"Now why are you apologizing for hugging an old woman? I don't get enough love these days."

"You haven't changed a bit," Abby said. "I had no idea you were still on the island."

Her eyes twinkled. "You mean, you had no idea I was still alive."

Abby choked on her reply.

"Lighten up, child. I'm only teasing you." The older woman glanced around the front yard. "How's that baby boy of yours? I bet he's grown into quite a handsome young man."

Abby was speechless.

"You were spoiling that baby the last time I saw you. I remember delivering some of the most beautiful white roses not long after he was born."

Abby didn't know how to respond, but gratefully, Mrs. Crockett didn't seem to need an explanation. She'd already slid her front seat forward and removed a floral arrangement from a cardboard box stuffed securely between the seats.

"Well, today I have red roses for you instead of white."

"Really?"

"Seems like that young De Lucia fellow still has a thing for you."

Abby hoped the woman didn't see her blushing when she took the beautiful bouquet. Hopefully, the deep red roses would offset the pink in her cheeks.

The irony struck her. Here she was pruning away her flowers in the back yard and someone was delivering her more. Well, she didn't appear to have any roses springing up out back. These would be a treat.

"Always thought you and Damian were going to get married," Mrs. Crockett continued. "Seemed like the perfect pair, always out there playing on the water or riding your bicycles through town."

"That was a long, long time ago."

Actually, eons ago, Abby thought. An entire lifetime had gone by since she and Damian had been the best of friends.

"Not so very long," Mrs. Crockett said, winking at her as she hopped back in her Beetle to deliver another round of flowers.

As she drove away, Abby wondered if she would ever see her again. She smiled. Mrs. Crockett would probably be delivering flowers when she was 101 years old.

The roses were rich in color and scent. She dug her nose into them and marveled that she could still smell after the myriad of aromas battling for her nose today. Ripping open the little white envelope tucked between the leaves, she read Damian's words in Mrs. Crockett's shaky handwriting.

Thanks for all your hard work. You're the publicity queen.

Years . . . it had been at least ten years since anyone but a client had sent her flowers. And roses? Probably longer than that.

If only she deserved the roses today. With the glory days of her career apparently behind her, she was on the verge of relinquishing her crown.

Sighing, she checked the cell phone in her pocket, but no one had called her back. She escorted the gorgeous bouquet into the house and centered the roses on the kitchen table. Jessica would tease her for sure, but she'd shrug it off. Damian had been very deliberate in his card. The flowers were a simple gesture of thankfulness for her work—sweet encouragement for a friend.

Chapter 43

Marc parked alongside Jessie's cottage and hopped out of the truck.

He'd made a decision. He could tell himself that he just wanted to be Jessie's friend, but he'd be lying. Friendship was the foundation to a good relationship, he knew that, but he wanted them to be much more than friends.

As he walked across the yard, he saw Mrs. Wagner bent over in the garden, her clothes caked with dirt. He moved toward her, but she didn't turn her head. She didn't even acknowledge him with a wave.

He stood behind her and cleared his throat.

"Hello, Marc," she said, but she didn't stand up. Her eyes were focused on the wildflowers tangled around her legs.

"Is Jessie home?"

"She went bike riding this morning." Mrs. Wagner pulled up a handful of weeds. "Didn't say when she'd be back."

Did she forget their date?

Mrs. Wagner lifted her head, her eyes warning him of her strength. Did she think he was a threat?

She pointed at his shirt. "Are you going surfing?"

Marc glanced down at the army green shorts that fell past his knees and a white T-shirt sporting a black Fox logo across his chest. He'd thought his clothes were a good choice for a casual date, but apparently Jessie's mom had a different opinion.

He shifted his weight to his other foot. "I made her dinner."

"Huh," she mumbled.

He eyed the full bag of weeds in her hand. "Can I help you?"

She grunted and tossed him a plastic bag. He knelt down beside her, plucked a handful of dandelions, and threw them in the trash.

"Actually, I'm glad she's not here yet," he said as he pulled another handful of weeds. "I was hoping to talk to you before Jessie and I went to dinner."

"About what?"

"It's pretty obvious that I'm interested in Jessica." He took a deep breath. "And I think she might like me a little, too.

"This probably sounds old-fashioned," he continued, "but I'd like to ask your formal permission to date your daughter."

Mrs. Wagner sat down on a tree stump and removed her gloves.

"I'm glad you brought it up," she said. "I want to be entirely honest with you too."

He wasn't sure that's what he wanted, but he nodded his head.

"Jessica's young, Marc, and she needs to discover what she wants out of life on her own. I don't want her to be confused by a heartbreak right now."

"I'm not going to break her heart," Marc assured her.

"I'm sure you have nothing but good intentions, but your relationship will eventually have to end. I'd rather you take the lead now while you're still friends."

He wasn't sure they were still friends, but he didn't tell her that.

"You don't want us to date?" he asked, and she shook her head. He froze, staring at her in disbelief.

"I don't want to sound cruel, Marc. You seem like a nice boy, and I'm confident that the right woman is out there for you. I just don't think it's supposed to be Jessica. Not right now."

"Is it me?" he asked and waited for her reply. None came. "You don't have to answer."

He heard Jessie shout from the driveway, and he turned around. She flew toward the back yard on her bicycle, her hair soaked and her arms dotted with brown. Throwing her bike on the grass, she jumped off and ran toward them.

This was definitely the woman for him.

"I'm sorry," she said, out of breath.

"No problem."

"Did you collide with a garbage can?" Mrs. Wagner asked as she stood.

"I could ask you the same thing."

"I've been pulling weeds all afternoon. What have you been doing?"

"Playing in the mud." She smiled at Marc. "We don't have enough mud in Boulder."

"Sounds interesting," Mrs. Wagner cracked.

Jessie pointed toward the sliding glass door. "Can you two entertain each other while I jump in the shower?"

"I don't know . . ." Mrs. Wagner said.

"I won't be long," Jessica said as she faced her mom. "Be nice."

Marc grimaced. It was too late for that.

Twenty minutes later, Marc drove the truck slowly toward Moran State Park on the island's eastern shore. He'd spent all morning preparing for this date until Jessie's mom had crushed his plans.

What was he supposed to do? Step one way and please Mrs. Wagner, potentially alienate Jessie, be miserable for life but probably do the right thing. Step the other way and alienate Mrs. Wagner, please himself and hopefully Jessie but probably do the wrong thing. An exhausting two-step with no middle ground.

The sun warmed the cab, and Marc fiddled with his electric window, running it up and back down, the rubber scraping against the glass. Martina McBride entertained them from the stereo, singing soulfully about her daughter's eyes.

"Everything okay?" Jessica asked as a nasally male artist replaced Martina's soothing voice.

"Sure," he mumbled.

"Do you mind if I change the station?"

He blinked hard. "Sorry, I didn't even notice."

Jessica flipped the tabs until she found a soft rock station playing U2.

"Are you going to tell me what's wrong?" she asked.

"Eventually."

He should have talked to Mrs. Wagner before he'd ever asked Jessie out. This was his fault. He couldn't blame her for wanting the best for her daughter. He could never be the kind of man Jessie deserved.

He turned right, and they drove inland, passing red barns, herds of cattle, and boxy white homes centered on large pastures of farmland.

"It's so peaceful out here," she said, breaking the uncomfortable silence.

"Fertile ground," he replied. "Great for farming."

"It reminds me of a field trip I took to Vermont once. It's odd how you can be an entire country away from the East Coast and yet look at the exact same scenery."

And odd how you can be sitting across the seat from someone and feel like you're a world away.

"That's nice."

"Fine," Jessica whispered and stopped talking.

Marc secured his eyes on the double yellow line racing by them, searching for what he was going to say. Without looking over at her, he could feel Jessica seething. He knew he was being rude, but he wasn't sure what to do. Was it right to continue dating Jessie if her mother was opposed to it? Was it right to end his relationship with Jessie when they were becoming such great friends?

Mrs. Wagner was wrong about him and Jessie, dead wrong. Jessie may be searching, but so was he. Why couldn't they search together? Wouldn't it be better if they discovered their future as a team instead of waiting years until they'd both traveled separate roads, too late to turn back? This seemed like the perfect time.

But her disapproval probably had nothing to do with him and Jessie together—it had everything to do with him. Mrs. Wagner didn't think he was good enough for her daughter.

Well, at least they agreed on something. He didn't think he was good enough for her either. He finally glanced over at Jessie, and she was glaring at the window. She seemed to think they could be more than friends, or at least she had given him every sign that she enjoyed his company as much as he enjoyed hers.

But Mrs. Wagner was right. Jessie deserved the best.

Please, God, show me what to do!

Driving into the state park, they passed a peaceful lake on the right and a thick grove of pines on their left. Jessica rolled her window back down, watching the sunlight glitter against the water's glassy surface. Large blankets were spread around its banks as families picnicked and played Frisbee on the shore.

He parked the truck along the road and jumped out.

"Are you hungry?" Marc asked as he grabbed his backpack and strapped it over his shoulders.

"Uh-huh," she mumbled.

She tightened her shoelaces and followed him back on a trail into the lush green. In seconds they were trekking through the magical forest, the ruddy trunks of redwood trees surrounding them. Ivy draped off tree branches above them like giant spider webs, and bright red berries dotted the bushes.

Marc glanced down at the forest floor as they hiked through the trees, each step cushioned by a bright green moss that felt like goose down. Mushrooms sprung out of damp, matted mounds of browned leaves, and a musty aroma wafted through the trees.

He led her down a path that ducked under a canopy of leaves and then emerged at a waterfall gushing over a rock bank and crashing into a quiet stream below. When they hiked down a muddy wall, he paused to take her hand, but he let it go as soon as they were back on stable ground.

Gnarled tree roots were embedded in the dark wall around them, moss creeping up their smooth sides. He almost set up their dinner at the base of the thunderous fall so they wouldn't have to talk, but he led her down the river, away from the water's roar.

He took off his backpack and spread a thin blanket over the dry riverbank, the tip almost touching the creek. Then he slowly pulled their dinner out of his pack.

Aluminum foil covered a half loaf of French bread and a creamy chunk of Brie. He smoothed the cheese onto a rye cracker, spooned a topping of almonds and cranberries, and then handed it to her.

She took a bite. "It's delicious."

He pulled two plastic plates out of the pack and set them on the blanket. On each plate he placed a piece of bread and added slices of chilled roast beef and pasta salad. Next he brought out a bottle of sparkling white grape juice, cushioned in a stained white T-shirt, and he poured the juice into two paper cups. They ate silently for a few minutes, each waiting for the other to speak first.

"What's going on?" Jessica ventured again as she ate a bite of salad.

He sipped his juice, but didn't say anything for a moment.

"The thing is, Jessie . . ."

She set her cracker on the napkin. "You don't have to say anything."

"But I want to be honest with you."

She shrugged her shoulders. "Honesty's overrated."

"You know I was raised a lot differently than you," he said. "Filthy apartment, alcoholic mom, classic case of dysfunction."

"Okay." She fidgeted with her silver class ring.

"Do you understand what I'm trying to say?"

"You're breaking up with me."

"I like you a lot, Jessie." He sighed. "And I'd like to see you a lot more, but I don't have anything to offer you right now."

"That's a lousy excuse."

"I'm a broke student struggling to make it through school, and then I'll be off to some poor country to do mission work. Nothing glamorous at all."

"Did my mom say something to you?"

He hesitated as she searched his eyes.

"She told you to leave me alone, didn't she?" Jessie groaned. "She's butting in."

"Not in so many words."

"How dare she!" She pounded the grass with her fist. "What exactly did she say?"

Marc swallowed hard as he decided to be honest with her.

"She said you weren't ready for a serious relationship, but I think she meant to say you wouldn't ever be ready to have a relationship with me."

Jessica's fingers clawed into the dirt beside her, and she pulled up a stone. She threw it into the river, and then grabbed another rock, plummeting it like the first into the slow moving water. Then she threw another rock and another.

"We don't have to listen to her," she finally said as she wiped her hands

on her jeans. "She has no idea what I want or need in my life. Her only desire is that I do what she wants and needs."

"She wants what's best for you, Jessie."

"I love being with you, Marc." She grabbed his hand and squeezed it. "If my mom would just open her eyes, she could be happy for me instead of trying to tear us apart."

Marc kissed the top of her fingers and gently pulled his hand away.

"You're going to let her win," Jessica sighed.

"We both need to pray about this," he said. "Pray hard that God would have us honor your mother while doing the right thing. I don't know what that looks like, but God can change a person's heart."

"It sounds too easy."

"I think it sounds incredibly hard."

Marc opened his backpack again, pulled out a plastic carton packed with two pieces of chocolate chip cheesecake, and served them.

"Thank you for dinner," Jessica said softly before eating her dessert.

He just stared down at his cheesecake, his appetite gone as he wrestled with his next step. He'd have to win over Jessie's mother before he won Jessie.

How he'd do that, he had no idea.

Chapter 44

Abby set her shovel down and leaned back against the tree. The kids had left more than an hour ago, but she still couldn't get the conversation with Marc out of her head.

None of Jessica's boyfriends had ever asked permission to take her out, but it wouldn't be fair to anyone if she played along now. She had to be honest with Marc even if it hurt. Better that they break up now than when they left the island and everyone was wounded in the process.

She'd done the right thing . . . hadn't she? She'd told Marc he was a nice boy, and she'd meant it. Just because he was nice didn't mean he was the guy for Jessica. He'd asked for her permission, and she'd been honest with him.

But if she did the right thing, why did she feel so rotten?

She sighed, pulled the cell phone out of her pocket, and dialed her sister's phone number. The answering machine took her call.

"Hey, Sis, it's me," she began. "I really need to talk when you have time. I think God's trying to tell me something, but I can't figure out what He's trying to say."

"Abby!" Laurel blurted into the phone as Abby was preparing to hang up.

"Am I interrupting something?"

"I was on a wild goose chase for my purse. Any idea where it is?"

"It's probably buried up in the attic of this cottage," Abby laughed. "You're not going to recognize the place next time you come."

"You haven't burned it down, have you?"

"I came close a few times, but it's still standing. It's been scrubbed from top to bottom, and I threw out piles and piles of stuff you'll never miss."

"Good!" Abby heard a whoosh and hoped that Laurel had landed in a chair. "I could never throw anything away by myself. What's going on?"

"I feel awful." Abby pulled a piece of bark off the tree. "My life is falling apart, and I can't figure out why."

"What happened?"

The impending tidal wave collided with the dam, and Abby's heart broke. Like water gushing through the cracked cement, Abby spilled all the secrets she'd kept so tightly locked inside. She told her sister about Heartsong and her anger toward God and how the memories of Hunter had flooded back to her in a harsh, unexpected way. She told her she'd lost her job and she thought she was losing her daughter as well.

"I've prayed, Laurel, I really have, yet I can't understand what God is trying to do except brand me a complete failure."

"Did something trigger this today?"

"Yes," she paused. "Jessica's new boyfriend showed up, announcing his intentions, and I told him they are getting too serious, too fast."

"Is that true?"

"It's partially true," she offered. "He's a nice kid, but, this sounds awful Laurel, he has a horrible home life."

"He's not the right guy for Jessica?"

Abby sat down under the tree. "I'm all for him succeeding in life, but I want the very best for her, and it's clear to me that this isn't what's best. She won't be happy—not in the long run."

"That story sounds familiar," Laurel said.

"What are you talking about?"

"Didn't Dad say something similar about you and Damian?"

"What?"

"C'mon, Abby, I'm sure you remember. Dad said Damian made a great sailing instructor and friend, but he had no aspirations in life."

Abby quietly contemplated Laurel's words. She'd forgotten her anger at their father when she met Scott. Damian had never pursued anything more than a friendship with her, so she let it go. Her dad had been right, of course. Hadn't he?

"I wonder what Dad would say if he could see Damian now?" Laurel asked. "He probably never imagined that Damian would be a successful biologist."

"He's leading boat tours, Laurel."

"Because he wants to. You have to admire a person who makes a career out of what they love."

"Now we're completely off the subject."

"I don't think you're a bad mother for wanting to protect your daughter," Laurel said. "I just wonder if there's more to your turmoil than a boy."

"Of course there's more. Everything's crashing around me."

"Can I pray for you?"

"I guess."

Abby closed her eyes and felt the breeze on her cheeks as Laurel prayed.

"You're obviously working in my sister's life, Lord," she said. "Please be close to her right now and guide her through this dark place."

Abby waited for a few seconds, wondering if Laurel was done.

"Thanks," she said.

"Tell you what, Abby. I'm going to spend the rest of the afternoon praying, and I think you should do the same. We'll pray together that God shows you what He wants you to do."

Abby didn't feel much better when she hung up the phone with Laurel. She sat down on the picnic table bench to pray, but instead she just stared at the chipped wood on the table. The words simply didn't come. Hadn't she prayed already? Yet God continued ignoring her prayers. If He was trying to tell her something, she wished He would speak loud and clear.

She mumbled a few words, but nothing seemed to come out right. Maybe God would listen to Laurel's prayers.

She debated taking a long jog, but decided she'd pray while she shopped. Her transplants needed more Miracle-Gro, and she needed to get away from the house.

She climbed into the convertible, cranked the top down, and drove toward the small nursery on the other side of town. Was Laurel right about Damian? She thought back to her teen years running free on the island. She'd liked Damian, but she'd never dreamed the relationship would go beyond friendship.

Okay, maybe she had daydreamed about it occasionally, but her dad had discouraged her from getting involved with Damian. Yet even though she knew what he thought about Damian, he'd never been cruel to either of them.

Had she been cruel to Marc? She hoped not—she'd only wanted to do what was best for him and Jessica. If only Scott were here to be the voice of reason, the protector, the bad guy . . . while she relished being the loving mom. She could cheer Jessica on while he reined in her juvenile pursuits.

But Scott wasn't here and she had to wear both hats of Mom and Dad—neither of which she seemed to be doing well.

She prayed softly for guidance as she drove, just a little wisdom on how to convince Jessica to guard her heart and her future. Surely God would be gracious enough to answer that prayer in spite of her anger toward Him.

As she drove through Westsound, she saw a man with a pair of broad shoulders in a white T-shirt walking ahead of her, his rugged dark hair spilling over his collar. She did have a slight crush on him when she was about sixteen, and he was a handsome twenty-year-old sailor. She'd forgotten all that time she'd wasted away thinking about her and Damian's future. Her life would have been much different if he'd shown the least bit of interest in her, but he'd just been a friend.

She stopped beside Damian, and he stepped off the curve.

"Hey, there," he said as he leaned over her window.

"The roses were gorgeous."

"Thanks for working so hard on this campaign."

"Where are you going?" she asked.

He nodded down the street. "To the marina. I needed to get a couple things from the boat."

"I'll give you a ride."

He walked around the car and got inside.

"The kids stole my truck this afternoon," he joked as he slammed the door. "They better bring it back."

She braked to let a crowd of tourists meander across the road as they swung their brightly colored shopping bags beside their hips and gawked at a fleet of yachts sailing by the harbor.

"Any word?" he asked.

She shook her head. She wished she had good news to give him. She wished ten reporters had called her back, begging for a feature before the story got cold. She'd been lugging her cell phone in her pocket for days so she wouldn't miss a call, but the ringer had been eerily silent.

"That's okay," he said, but she could hear the disappointment in his voice. Here was a clear story that needed to be told, and no one wanted to risk telling it. Surely he knew she'd done everything she could do. The media had let him down.

"Sometimes it takes days and even weeks to get a return call," she said. "They've got so much stuff to review."

She dropped Damian off at the marina and turned left toward the nursery before she remembered she'd been praying.

Please, God, she asked as she parked her car. *Please, show me what to do!*

Chapter 45

"What do you think you're doing?" Jessica demanded when she walked back in the door less than three hours after she left. She tried to contain her anger, but she was about to explode.

Abby glanced up from the news magazine. "Did you have a nice dinner?"

"Don't pretend you don't know what I'm talking about!"

Wooden legs grated across the floor as she yanked out a chair, dropped down on the seat, and faced her mother.

"Marc told you about our chat?" Abby set the magazine on a stack of new mail piled on the kitchen table.

"After I begged him, he told me a little. Apparently, in your own special way, you told him to stay away from me."

Abby clutched her hands together. "That's not true. I told him I think it's best if you two remain friends right now so you don't complicate your lives."

"Complicate? Is that what you think I'm doing with my life? I can tell you right now, Mom, this guy is more than a complication."

"He's a very nice boy, honey. I just don't want you to get hurt."

"Could you please explain to me how I'm going to get hurt?"

She cleared her throat. "Remember Jeff Matalin? You locked yourself in your room and cried for three days when he broke it off."

"Thanks for bringing that up."

"And then there was Austin Davenport."

"I was twelve!"

"You were still heartbroken, and if you don't let go of it soon, you're going to grieve the same way when this relationship ends."

"But that's the thing, Mom. This relationship doesn't have to end.

Didn't you know Dad was 'the one' right away? He told me that he knew after the first date that he wanted to marry you."

Abby sighed. "Your dad and I were too young, honey. We should have waited a few years before we jumped into marriage."

"You don't think Marc's good enough for me?"

"That's not it . . ."

"You're not willing to give Marc a chance!"

"Someone has to be realistic about this."

Jessica thought she was about to gag.

"Can't you see his passion for life and his drive to succeed? Marc has overcome huge obstacles to do what God wants him to do. He's absolutely determined to live for the Lord."

"Honey, you asked me to be more honest with you, and this is me being honest. I don't think you and Marc should date."

"It stinks, Mom. It really stinks."

A phone rang, and Abby grabbed for her pocket.

"That's mine," Jessica said and ran for her raincoat. She dug out the telephone and answered before it went to voice mail. If it was Marc, she'd tell him to pack his bags, and they'd run away tonight when her mother was in bed.

"Hello," she said.

"Jess!" a male voice exclaimed, and she almost threw the phone at the wall. Could today get any more awful?

"How are you?" Brett asked.

"What do you want?"

"Someone told me you were out west for the summer, and I wanted to see how things were going."

"Great, Brett. Things are going great."

"Do you miss me?"

What is this? Suddenly, he wants to make amends? She knew that couldn't be true. Even if it was, eons had passed since she'd seen him, and it was too late to turn back.

"Not really," she replied. "I'm sorry, Brett, but I'm dating someone else."

A long pause on the phone, and she wondered if he'd hung up on her. She was about to turn the power off when she heard his voice again.

"I wanted to come visit you this month. Thought it'd be fun to hang out again."

"In other words, you're looking for a free vacation." She wasn't in the mood for subtlety tonight. No more games for her.

"It's not that, Jessica. I really wanted to see you."

"I appreciate it, Brett, but I really am dating someone else. Probably not a good idea for you to show up."

"I understand," he finally said, and she imagined him shrugging off her rejection as he headed out the door to swim. He wouldn't call her again. "I'll see you this fall," he said before hanging up.

Please, Lord, I can't handle anything else today.

She buried her phone in her pocket and joined her mom back in the kitchen.

"Who was that?" Abby asked as Jessica screwed off the lid on a Coke bottle.

"Brett."

"Now he was a nice guy, and he was on his way to being an Olympian."

Jessica choked on her drink. "You hated Brett. Thought he had too much going for him to be with me."

When Abby shrugged her shoulders, Jessica stomped out of the room.

Part 3

[Pain] removes the veil; it plants the flag of truth
within the fortress of a rebel soul.
—C. S. Lewis, *The Problem of Pain*

Chapter 46

Abby woke with a start, grumbled at the morning sun, and rolled over. As the bright rays warmed the loft, she finally let her gaze follow the light outside, the bay glowing with soft layers of pink, blue, and orange.

She grabbed a blue flannel shirt hanging on a wooden peg, wrapped it around her cotton pajamas, and walked outside into the chilly air. Sitting down on a damp boulder, she pulled her knees to her chest and cried.

It hurt! Abby didn't want to let go of her pain—she'd grasped onto it for twenty years to keep her afloat. The anger was strangely familiar, a worn grudge she always blamed when she was mad at God. After all, hadn't He failed her when she'd needed Him most? He'd taken away what she'd wanted more than anything in life. He'd stolen her baby boy.

Don't you still love Jessica when she fails you?

It's not the same, Abby argued. She wasn't God. She couldn't control things around her even when she tried.

But what if I didn't fail you? the voice whispered.

She hugged her legs closer to her, tears falling from her eyes. *Yes, You did! You didn't just take him, You ripped him away.*

In her heart, she knew God had been good to her. He'd given her a beautiful little girl, and He'd cared for her family after her husband died. He'd blessed her with a home and a job and the ability to put her daughter through school.

Yet she clung to her bitterness like it was a lifeline. She knew God was love, but for so many years, she wanted to tell God exactly how to love her. She wouldn't allow God to demonstrate His love in His way. She

243

only wanted to give Him the plan—every detail mapped out perfectly so He could proceed with exactly how her life should go.

Trust Me.

It would mean letting go. Releasing all that pain and anger she'd guarded for so long. She couldn't possibly do that. At least not all at once—the wounds were too deep. If God let her down again, she'd be completely exposed.

The colorful lights in the sky faded into a dull yellow and the air warmed, but she didn't move. She wanted to resolve this resentment here and now before her anger destroyed her and her family.

"I'm sorry, Lord," she prayed softly. "I haven't been the woman that You've wanted me to be."

I can heal your pain.

More than anything, she wanted to let go of this pain. She needed to let it go.

"I don't know why You took Hunter away or where You're taking me now, but please forgive me for not trusting You."

The waves softly lapped against the rocks below her, and a dove cooed in the trees.

"I realize that I may never know why in this life, but I want to trust You, Lord. Please show me how to follow You again."

In her heart, she felt a sharp pain and then an amazing release, like a slow ooze of bitter infection seeping out of her wound. Then it was gone, and the walls crumbled inside.

Tears streaming down her cheeks, she picked herself up from the rock as she whispered a prayer of thanks. She knew God was working at that very moment. He was with her, healing her pain.

As she walked slowly back toward the house, a bed of weeds brushed her legs. For the first time since she'd returned to the island, she didn't care about pulling them out. They could stay there forever if they'd like.

What would God do next?

She'd felt Him for a moment, and she didn't want to let go.

Nine hours later, Abby hummed as she sliced through an organic tomato and arranged the bright slivers on top of a spinach salad for dinner. The house was quiet—Jessica had hidden in her room the entire day.

It was Jeff Matalin all over again. When they broke up, Jessica had given her the silent treatment for weeks even after she emerged from her bedroom for some food.

She placed her salad on the table alongside a tall glass of iced tea and knocked on Jessica's door. When her daughter didn't respond, she cracked open the door and saw Jessica lying on her bed, a pillow across her face.

"Are you okay, honey?" she asked.

The pillow slid to Jessica's belly, and Abby looked at the red smears staining her cheeks.

"I don't want to talk about it right now."

"Do you want something to eat or drink before work?"

"I called in sick."

Abby took a step into the room. "I'd like to talk to you."

The pillow went back over the face. "Whatever."

Abby wanted to hug Jessica until all of her pain disappeared too, but an invisible hand seemed to stop her. The timing wasn't yet right. God needed to mend her daughter's heart as well.

Abby sat down to eat her salad when she heard the musical notes of her cell phone ring. She ignored it at first, relishing the heat welling inside her soul. But it rang again and again so she finally answered it.

"This is Abby."

Someone cleared her throat. "This is Lisa Andrews with *Primetime*, and I'm interested in talking with you about your press release on the dying orcas. Is this a good time?"

Abby sucked in a gulp of air and hoped it didn't sound like a gasp.

"It's a great time." Abby set both her elbows on the table. Midnight would be great if *Primetime* wanted to call.

"We've done some research," Lisa said. "And we think the orca story is an investigative report in the making."

Abby nodded her head even though Lisa couldn't see her.

"I've talked to officials in both the U.S. and Canadian governments, but no one seems to think there's a problem. We want to research the industries along the Pacific and see if any of them are dumping waste illegally."

"Sounds like an excellent idea," Abby said trying to mix the right amount of excitement and calm into her voice.

"We'd hoped you'd agree. As part of this story, we'd like to come to Orcas Island and do an interview with . . ." Abby heard her rustling a stack of papers in the background. "An interview with Dr. Damian De Lucia. We were hoping he'd show us around Puget Sound, and we could get some shots out on the water."

"Definitely," Abby told her. "He'd be glad to do that."

"Wonderful. How about Friday?"

The day after tomorrow? They certainly weren't wasting any time.

"Is that too soon?" the producer asked as she waited for Abby's response.

"No. Friday is great. What time should we be ready?"

"Around eight. We'll fly in first thing that morning, do the interview, take a boat ride, and then we've got another interview in Seattle at four with the EPA."

"We'll be ready."

In under a minute, they arranged the details.

"Thank you," she whispered softly when she hung up the phone. A break in the cycle.

She walked past Jessica's bedroom door and prayed for her daughter as she slipped out of the house and started the car. The drive into town took less than ten minutes, and she parked at the marina. Damian's sailboat was docked in its slip. She walked across the weathered boards to see if Damian was working on *The Drifter.* He wasn't.

She stared at his impeccably clean boat for a minute or so and wondered how it sailed. It had been so long since she'd been out on the water, and she almost longed to feel the wind in her hair again, drifting across the sea.

She glanced down at her watch. It was almost five. Maybe he was at his house preparing dinner, or perhaps he was at his office or the restaurant. She'd check the office first.

Orcas Island Expeditions wasn't far from the marina. The main building stood beside a long dock, a rugged fishing shack with mossy brown siding that looked on the verge of collapse.

She parked the car and walked across the pier, the stench of seaweed and dead fish plaguing the air. Local fishermen had probably just packed up their gear for the night and headed home, the remains of their catch left on the beach for the salty tide to mop.

Abby knocked on the office door.

"Come in," Damian called.

She opened the door slowly, the hinges creaking their greeting. Damian wrote something in a ledger and then looked up.

"Abby," he exclaimed, bumping his legs against the wood desk as he jumped up.

"I have some good news for you."

He slammed the ledger shut. "I'm ready."

"*Primetime* just called, and they want to do a story."

He paused as he digested the news. "A good one?"

"It appears so. They're talking to the federal government and local officials, and they are going to research local industry as well to see if they can uncover the source of the toxins."

"That's great!"

"So you'll be ready to talk to them on Friday?"

He choked. "Friday?"

"You'll be ready." Tomorrow she'd give him a crash course on media training, and by Friday he'd be prepared to regain his reputation and articulately explain his cause.

"Have you eaten yet?" He grabbed his jacket from the back of his chair.

She thought about the spinach salad wilting on the kitchen table.

"I was so excited to tell you that I forgot."

"I know a great restaurant," he smiled.

"Italian?"

"The best on the West Coast."

He held out his arm and escorted her to dinner.

Chapter 47

Stacie Cartwright peered through her dusty blinds and then pulled the cord tight. The sunlight hurt her eyes. Why did it have to peer in at her like a prying eye?

Her hands shook as she collapsed on the sofa and surfed through the four working channels on the old RCA until Wheel of Fortune popped on the screen. She squinted as the lines on the television cracked and squiggled. She couldn't even read the letters turning on the board.

"Leprechaun," one of the contestants yelled, swinging both arms before pummeling Pat Sajak with a hug.

A long time ago, she'd been able to spell words like that. Harder ones, in fact. They'd called her "Queen Bee" in middle school because she'd won so many spelling competitions. Every once in awhile she'd pull out her sophomore yearbook, flip to page 178 and stare at her photo, overlaid with the signature of one Whitman Stakes III. Her fellow students had voted her "Most Likely to Succeed" before they found out she was a drunk. She cackled bitterly . . . she'd succeeded at being drunk quite well.

Someone shouted on the other side of the thin wall, and she heard a crack. Throwing her shoe against the peeling plaster, she hollered at her neighbors to stop or she'd call the cops. A man screamed for her to go to hell.

No problem, she thought and laughed again.

"Cider House Rules," another contestant exclaimed. The bells chimed, and with a flick of her glittering wrist, Miss Fancy Pants flipped the bright boxes and displayed the movie title to audience cheers.

An easy one, Stacie thought. She'd whip all of them someday when she got on the show.

Her neighbor on the other side yelled at her to turn the TV down, but she didn't touch the volume. How she needed a drink! It would stop this pounding in her head, and she'd get some rest. She hadn't been able to sleep in two days.

Winding and twisting, the cramped room seemed to cave in on top of her, and she scrunched her eyes, willing the walls to stand. The bugs had returned, crawling on her neck and arms. She scratched and scratched until her skin was numb, screaming for the creepy things to leave her alone. Why couldn't everyone just leave her alone?

She shut her eyes again. She only needed a few hours of sleep, and then the bugs would go away.

Someone knocked on her door. Stacie peered through the peephole before cracking it open, the safety chain locked and a baseball bat grasped in her right hand in case he tried something stupid.

"Did you get it?" she asked, her voice raspy with desire.

"Right 'ere." The skinny man held up a brown bag. She salivated at the sight.

"You got the card?" he snarled.

She squeezed Marc's grocery certificate through the crack.

"I'll leave this by the door."

"Uh, uh." She flung down the bat and wrestled to open the lock. "Give it to me."

The man glared down at her menacingly when she opened the door, but she grabbed both liters of vodka from the bag and slammed the door shut. He knocked again, but she ignored it. Finally, she had her liquor. She wanted nothing more.

Lying back down on the couch, she gulped the bitter drink until the fog in her brain lifted. Why couldn't anyone understand this was the medicine she needed? Why couldn't her son help her be sane? She sighed. It was really so simple. The alcohol made her problems go away.

The telephone rang, but she ignored it. No one else called her anymore except Marc, and she didn't want to talk to him. Her son always seemed to know when she was drinking. He was a good boy, but he made her feel disgustingly guilty at times. No, she definitely didn't want to talk to him right now.

The phone rang two more times before stopping. She took another long drink of the clear, soothing liquid and felt the burn of it ease down her throat. It raged through her, and she felt its incredible heat. How she loved the heat.

Minutes passed and then an hour. Had she passed out?

The phone rang again. This time she decided to pick it up. She didn't care what Marc thought. She was his mother, after all. He couldn't make her feel bad for taking a couple sips. She just needed a little bit to press on.

"Hello," she babbled into the phone, sloshing the liquid in her hand.

It was a woman on the other line. She couldn't understand her name, but Stacie sat straight up when she said she was calling from Heartsong Adoptions. Stacie coughed into the phone and then braced herself. She knew they would come someday. Yes, she knew. And now they'd finally tracked her down.

She wouldn't tell them a thing. They could try and get her baby, but they couldn't have him. They'd said she could keep him, and it was too late for them to change their minds.

"Ms. Cartwright," the woman said. "The woman who cared for your son when he was born is seeking closure."

"You can't have him," Stacie snapped.

"I understand your fears, Ms. Cartwright, and she doesn't want to take your son away. She only wants assurance that he's okay. She had him for four months, you know, and she's curious to know what's happened to him now that he's become an adult."

"My baby's fine."

Stacie chugged her vodka as she thought back to the day in the hospital when she watched Abby steal away her baby, the worst day of her life . . . the day she thought she'd never again see her son. He'd haunted her the next four months until she couldn't stand it anymore. She called the agency and told them it was time for her baby to come home.

Now he'd probably haunted Abby as well for . . . how long had it been? Oh yes, twenty whole years since she'd become a mom.

"Okay, I'll tell her that he's fine," the voice said.

"Wait," Stacie stopped her. What harm would it cause to give the woman a little information? Just a small clue like they did on the game shows—if she wanted, Abby could solve the puzzle on her own. "You promise you won't take him away again?"

"Yes, ma'am. He's too old for us to take away even if we wanted."

"Too old," Stacie muttered. Her baby was too old. She'd fed him, changed him, made sure he was healthy and well, and now he'd grown old. What did that make her?

"Ms. Cartwright?"

"He's working this summer on Orcas Island." Stacie clutched the glass bottle in her hand. "You know where that is?"

"Yes, ma'am."

"He lives there during the summer and goes to school in the fall. He never comes home any more."

There was a long silence on the phone.

"But my boy's a hard worker," Stacie continued. "I took good care of him."

"I'm sure you did."

"Marcus Scott Cartwright, that's my son."

"You named him Scott?"

Stacie cleared her throat. "Marcus is the name of my grandfather, but Scott was the only dad he ever had."

"You remember his name?"

"Of course I do."

Didn't this woman know how smart she was? She'd thought about Scott and Abby almost every day during the past twenty years, wondering if she'd done the right thing. But she had raised her boy and no one could say he didn't turn out well.

"Ms. Heartsong," Stacie said, a wave of soberness clearing her mind. "Tell them I said hello."

"I can do that."

"And please tell them thank you for taking care of my son."

Stacie hung up the telephone, guzzled another drink of vodka, and hoped that she'd done the right thing. She thought about calling Marc, just to warn him, but she had a new bottle of liquor in her hand. All she wanted to do was drink until it was gone.

Chapter 48

Abby didn't leave De Lucia's until eleven. She hadn't even realized how late it was until she glanced around the restaurant and saw that she and Damian were the only diners left. The kitchen staff was probably saying all sorts of mean things about them . . . whispering, of course, since Damian was the boss's nephew. They probably thought the two of them would never let them close.

Vincent spoiled her with a mound of freshly prepared pasta, dousing it with a homemade red sauce that contained bits of sausage and eggplant and more spices than her tongue could sort. He followed that with a rich tiramisu and cappuccino.

A thunderstorm had moved in over the bay while they ate, a brilliant display of lightning streaking across the water as the evening turned into night.

As she pulled back into her muddy driveway, Abby marveled at how fast the hours had passed. She didn't tell him about the turmoil with Jessica, but they discussed his move back to Puget Sound, the beginning and end of her career in Denver, and the *Primetime* interview on Friday. He promised he'd dive into media training tomorrow.

She ran in the front door and grabbed a towel from the coat closet to dry her arms and drenched hair. The house was dark and still, and she flicked on a living room lamp. She didn't see a light under Jessica's door—she must have gone to bed already. It was strange to be coming home after her daughter was asleep.

She turned on the light in the hallway bathroom and quietly shut the door before scrubbing her face with a coarse washcloth, smearing Oil of Olay across her skin, and then brushing her teeth. Thirty years had erased in minutes as she and Damian relived the stories that colored their pasts. It was comfortable, normal to be with him again. She was 18, eating and chatting with her best friend.

As she walked out of the bathroom, she saw the cell phone next to her spinach salad on the kitchen table. She dumped her salad into the trash and picked up the phone. There was one voice mail message.

"Abby Wagner," a woman began and then paused. "This is Julia Martin from Heartsong Adoptions. I hope you remember me."

Abby swallowed hard. Of course she remembered Julia. The last time they'd spoken, Abby had exploded in a barrage of angry words.

"I'm the director of Heartsong's Seattle division now," Julia paused. "Chloe told me you were asking about Hunter, and I'd like to help you."

Abby braced herself against the kitchen table. Why would Julia want to help her? If anything, she'd thought the woman would do everything possible to ignore and possibly botch her request.

"I tracked down Stacie today, and if you give me a call back, I can tell you what she said."

Abby stared into the darkness, the shock of Julia's words shuddering through her. She collapsed onto a chair. They'd found Stacie!

She folded the phone and set it back on the table. What was she going to do? Just hours ago she'd finally reconciled her pain with God—did she really want to reopen this wound? She wanted to know what happened to Hunter, but what if something bad had happened to him? Would her faith shatter again? Could she really love a God that hadn't cared for her son?

Trust Me, the quiet voice soothed her again.

Slowly, she stood up from the chair, clicked off the kitchen light, and turned to walk toward the loft. There was nothing she could do tonight anyway. It was too late to call Julia back, and she needed to prepare for Damian's training in the morning.

"Hey, Mom," Jessica whispered in the dark. Abby jumped, clutching both fists to defend herself.

"That is so wrong," Abby retorted as she slowly relaxed her fingers.

"I agree."

Jessica flipped on the light before padding across the floor, dressed in

tube socks, a T-shirt, and black shorts. She filled a glass with water, and then she turned the light off as she moved back toward her room.

Abby spoke into the darkness. "I saw Marc tonight at De Lucia's."

"Great."

"When I said you were sick, he almost ran out the front door."

"I'm sure you stopped him."

"Damian told him you needed to rest."

"I don't need rest."

"Listen, Jessica," Abby leaned back against the paneled wall. "I'm sorry for being so harsh about you and Marc."

Silence answered her until she heard her daughter take a deep breath.

"You think you're protecting me," Jessica finally said, "but you're really protecting yourself."

"I don't understand."

"Do you realize the pressure you've put on me over the years? You've had this ideal image of your first child, and when you lost him, you expected me to live up to your fantasy of what he would have been. It's impossible for anyone to do that—especially me."

Abby wanted to scream that it wasn't true. She would never do that to her daughter. Instead she calmed her voice and said, "I never meant to make you feel like that."

"Can you just give Marc and me a chance?" Jessica asked. "He's the kind of guy most moms would want for their daughter."

Abby wrapped her arms around her daughter as Jessica bawled.

Rain pelted the cottage's tin roof and slapped against the windows, but neither of them worried about the storm.

Chapter 49

The thunderstorm blew over Orcas Island by morning, but rain still dripped from the palms of the leaves, a gentle reminder of the raging downpour that pummeled the island overnight. The sweet scents of wild blackberries and strawberries wafted through the trees as Abby snuck out the back door right after dawn. The air was heavy with humidity; her damp hair clung to her forehead.

The picnic table on the porch was drenched, so she covered the wood with a white plastic tablecloth. Buttoning a cardigan over her brown corduroy overalls, she sat down on a bench. Soaking wet! She leaped up, ran back into the house, and rummaged through the hall closet until she found an old beach towel. She rushed back outside and dried the benches before she sat again.

She'd planned to prepare for the interview last night, but she and Jessica were still talking long after midnight. Damian wouldn't arrive for at least a half hour—just enough time for her to collect her thoughts.

With her legal pad in front of her and a pen in her hand, her world seemed right. As the sun slowly warmed the table, she rapidly made notes and decided that working outdoors was much better than slaving away inside her stuffy Denver office. She could almost feel the inspiration in the air.

It would be hard to convince Damian to stay focused, but she'd try. A sincere voice. A succinct message. A compelling story. Damian would have them all when they finished working today.

Abby glanced down at the cell phone next to her notepad and debated calling Julia this morning, but she probably wouldn't be in the office yet. She needed time to prepare for Stacie's response anyway. She'd wait until the reporter left tomorrow; then she'd make the call.

Damian's truck tires crunched through the gravel in her driveway. Abby heard the truck door slam, and she reshuffled her stack of paperwork.

An entire day with Damian De Lucia! Who would have known a month ago that she'd be back on Orcas doing media training with Damian? How quickly things changed.

For a moment she felt like a girl again, waiting outside for her sailing instructor to arrive. During her high school years, she'd spent a half hour getting ready on these island mornings to have her hair and makeup instantly washed out by the wind and ocean spray.

But it had been worth it for Damian.

When did all those mushy feelings go away? Probably soon after her father convinced her that Damian was too restless, too wild for his little girl. The island memories with Damian were replaced with the memories she had of Hunter in the cottage. She'd forgotten all those happy times before.

"Gorgeous morning," Damian said as he sat on the bench across from her and handed her a tall Styrofoam cup.

She smiled at him.

"A latte. Skim milk with a shot of vanilla and caramel."

"Perfect! Thank you." She opened the lid and sniffed. It smelled wonderful "What did you get?"

"Plain old coffee. Black."

"And boring," she retorted.

"It'll wake you up light years faster than that milky stuff you drink."

"I hope it will wake you up," she told him. "We've got a long day of work ahead."

"I'm all yours. Marc is cleaning the office, and I've got a local kid going out on the water with him this afternoon."

"Can Marc handle that on his own?"

One of Damian's eyebrows shot up. "He's a big guy, Abby, and quite responsible at that. I think he can handle it."

"Okay, let's get started."

Damian took a long sip of his coffee. "I asked Marc this morning when he was going to see Jessica again, and he clammed up. You wouldn't happen to know why?"

She cringed. "I've already gotten a lecture from my daughter."

"So, you're responsible?"

"Jessica and I made amends last night. It's fine."

"And you and Marc?"

She shook her head.

"Well, I think you should talk to him too. My guess is that unless you do, he won't ask your daughter out again. He's got too much respect for you."

That was exactly what she wanted . . . wasn't it?

"Why don't you like him?" Damian asked.

Scribbling on her notepad, she drew a huge wave surging toward the rocks.

He stared at her in disbelief. "You haven't become a snob in your old age, have you?"

"It's not that, Damian. Every parent wants the best for their child, and I want the best for Jessica. I don't understand why that's so horrible."

"Has it occurred to you that maybe Marc is the perfect person for her? Have you seen the two of them together?"

"Of course I have," she snapped, waving her hand in disgust. Her fingers slammed into her coffee cup, splattering the creamy brown latte across the cloth.

"I'll get some paper towels," he said as he rushed inside and back out again with a roll, quickly wiping up the spilled drink.

"Thanks," she muttered as he sat down beside her. She scooted a few inches back . . . he was too close.

"All I'm asking is, have you really watched the two of them interact? They're made to be together."

She couldn't say that she'd watched them in a positive light. Whenever she'd seen them, she'd had to prove to Marc that she was in charge. She couldn't be open-minded while defending her daughter.

"You think they're supposed to be together?" she asked. Maybe if she didn't view Marc as the enemy, he and Jessica could at least be friends.

"They've got more in common than a lot of married couples I know," he said. "But more than that, they obviously love being together."

"They're too young to know what they need."

He met her eye, and she glanced away. "Not necessarily," he whispered.

She cleared her throat and moved further away from him. He smelled like spicy cedar wood, and fire seemed to leap from his skin to hers. She wasn't ready for this!

"We better get started." Abby opened a manila folder, pulling out notes she'd made about the project. A wave of nervousness fluttered through her, and she shuddered. This was her career, for heaven's sake. She could easily prepare him for this interview.

"The most important thing is that you don't stray from your subject." She looked up from her notes to meet his eyes. "The producer I spoke with seemed like she was on our side, but that's never guaranteed. No matter what she says, you need to remain pleasant and understanding and if you have to, repeat your message over and over. Never let a reporter pressure you into saying something you don't mean."

"That's easier said than done."

"Yes, but it's important. You found out from the newspaper article what can happen if you don't stay on message, and it's the same for a taped TV interview. They can cut out everything except the clip where you're aggravated or defensive or plain wrong. Don't let that happen."

"This is just for a few hours, right?"

"Exactly. And I'm confident that you can keep your cool."

"I'm not."

"Well, you can."

He threw his coffee cup into the trash. "What exactly is my message?"

"You want to rescue the orcas, plain and simple."

"That sounds too easy," he said.

"It sounds easy, but it's hard to stick to that message and not go down rabbit trails. This is your passion, and we need to work from that solitary topic."

Abby ripped a list of scribbled questions off her legal pad so they could conduct a mock interview. Then she went back inside and carried out a video camera and tripod.

"What's that for?"

"I'm going to record your responses so we can critique them."

"You've got to be kidding me!"

"It's the best way to practice." She set the camera on the tripod and faced it toward Damian before she pushed play. "Better for you to catch any errors now than when we're watching the show on national TV."

He grimaced. "I'd rather you pull a tooth."

"It's not that bad."

He let out a snort.

"All right, Dr. De Lucia." She cleared her throat. "Thank you for your time today. Could you describe the plight of the killer whales around Puget Sound?"

"Yes, Ms. Wagner." He straightened his back. "Usually we have around eighty orcas that call the Sound their home, but every year, the number of returning whales decreases. I'm worried that toxins in the water are killing them off, and someday, not a single whale will return. This year we're still waiting to see them around the islands."

"That's good," she said. "Make it personal, but also make it more definitive. Research has shown that the PCB toxins are killing them, right?"

"Why can't I just tell them the truth?"

"This is the truth with a little finesse."

"This is ridiculous."

She smiled. "Think *Seattle Times*."

"Ouch."

"We need a mix of personal and professional," she explained. "Perhaps say that you are a local who's grown up watching these beautiful whales, and you are also a marine biologist who has studied them. I'd like you to describe the joy of seeing the pods play and interact to personalize it, and then give some statistics to show you're the expert."

"I can do that."

She waited as he described both.

"That's good, Damian. You're going to be a pro at this in no time."

"I'm not going on circuit."

"Of course not, but you'll have the confidence you need if other media calls."

"Can't you do the interview?"

She laughed. "I'm not the expert here."

"I don't feel like an expert."

"Well, let's not mention that in tomorrow's interview."

Damian sighed. "She's going to ask me about my job with the whaling commission."

"Okay," Abby said. "Tell me about your job."

"I regulated the quotas for whale hunters around the world."

"And why did you do this?"

"Because I didn't want whales to be slaughtered en masse."

"So you're an advocate for the whales."

"I'd like to think so."

She scribbled a note on her pad. "Just tell her yes."

The grilling had only begun. She pummeled him with a long list of questions, asking some of them three or four times until he got the answer right. She didn't want any surprises tomorrow.

"And why are you speaking out now on this topic?" she asked.

"The killer whales are being killed," he retorted. "Someone needs to speak out before they're gone."

"And there's your sound bite," she said as she wrote his words in bold letters and underlined them twice. "Say that more than once in your interview so they catch it."

The door slid open behind them, and Jessica stepped out. She wore flag red shorts over a matching red and blue bathing suit and a denim baseball cap. She balanced a canoe paddle and a backpack over her right shoulder.

"What are you kids doing out here?" Jessica asked as Abby turned the camera off.

"Practicing for my interview tomorrow," Damian said. "Your mother is ruthless."

"That's the truth."

"You seem to have survived quite well in spite of her."

"Barely."

Abby cleared her throat. "You both realize that I'm sitting here, don't you?"

"I'm going to paddle around the bay for a few hours before I go to work." Jessica started to walk through the grass.

Abby glanced over at Damian.

"I've got a different idea," Abby said.

Jessica turned around. "You want me to clean something, don't you?"

"No." She paused, contemplating her words before saying them. Then she winked at Damian and continued. This was the right thing to do.

"Rumor has it that there's a young man going sailing this afternoon, and according to Damian, he might need a little help."

"Really?" Jessica dropped the paddle.

"You better hurry or you'll miss it."

"Are you sure?" Jessica asked as she ran toward her bike. She didn't turn back to hear the answer.

"Good for you, Abby!" Damian squeezed her hand. "Good for you."

Chapter 50

The next morning, Damian arrived early at the diner along the water-front. The sky was pale blue and the seas were calm—the perfect day to escort the *Primetime* reporter around the Sound. He crumpled a pack of Splenda between his fingers until the white powder coated his hands, and then he drummed his thumbs against the shiny, waxed table as the beat of an old Beach Boys song pounded in his head.

He shouldn't be nervous—he knew his stuff. He just needed to focus on the topic.

Gray seagulls looped over the tables on the deck below him, begging for leftovers with their piercing scream. Most of the diners ignored the noisy birds, but Damian watched a little boy toss a piece of his biscuit into the air. A horde of seagulls swarmed the family's table, and the parents yelled at the birds to go away. The kid laughed as he dumped half his cereal on the floor behind him, and the birds swooped again.

The front door opened, and Damian turned to see Abby lugging her heavy briefcase into the restaurant. She wore brown pants and a sage green cardigan over a cream blouse. She'd pinned her hair up, but long wisps already escaped over her collar.

"You rob a library?" he asked.

"I dare that reporter to stump me." She dropped the bag on the seat across from him and the legs shook.

"I wouldn't mess with you," he said. "That bag's intimidating."

"Late night?" she asked as she opened a menu.

"Some woman kept asking me the same questions over and over until my head exploded."

"I'm sure she was doing it for your own good."

"That's what she kept saying."

Their waitress appeared to take their order.

"What can I getcha?" she asked, barely suppressing a yawn. The dark lines under her eyes matched the black apron over her uniform. It looked like she'd had a late night too, and a few drinks to go along with it.

"A ham and mushroom omelet," Damian said. "Along with a bowl of oatmeal, a large glass of orange juice, and extra Tabasco sauce."

She finished writing his order before turning toward Abby. "You?"

"Just a bagel with cream cheese and coffee."

"You've got to eat more than that," Damian insisted.

"Okay . . ." She glanced back down at the menu. "A bowl of Special K with skim milk, please."

"Abby!"

The waitress glanced back and forth between them.

"Just a second," Damian said. The girl stepped back, ready to change the order.

Abby put down the menu and met his stare. "I always eat a bagel or cereal for breakfast."

"You're going to get seasick if you don't have something more hearty." He grinned. "Plus . . . I dare you."

Abby ordered two eggs, toast, and bacon. The waitress waited for his nod before she wrote it down.

"You look great," Damian said.

Abby blushed, pushing loose strands of hair behind her ears.

He glanced down at his dark green shirt and khaki pants. "I'm not too casual, am I?"

She shook her head. "You're perfect. A believable expert who's confident enough to wear casual attire."

"You can spin anything, can't you?"

"It's my job." She shifted in the seat. "Or at least, it used to be."

The waitress brought them mugs of coffee and glasses of freshly squeezed orange juice.

"I called Marc this morning," Abby said.

"Bet you got him out of bed."

"He did sound a little groggy at six. I can't imagine why."

"What were you planning to accomplish?"

"I thought he should know you wouldn't be needing his services today since you canceled your tour."

"I told him yesterday."

She dumped a packet of sugar and some cream into her coffee. "But I bet you didn't tell him it was a good day to take out one Jessie Wagner."

"What's going on with you?"

She stirred her coffee. "I'm trying to give God back the stress of staying in control."

The waitress brought them their meals, and they ate quickly. Abby glanced at her watch and pulled her credit card out of her purse.

"We're meeting them in fifteen minutes." She set her credit card on top of the check, but Damian handed it back to her and left cash on the table.

"This one's on me." Damian stood up.

"I can get mine."

"Let's just pretend it's your retainer today."

Abby smiled. "I should be paying you."

"Is this the start of a new career?"

She shrugged her shoulders as she stood up. "I've been thinking about venturing into the world of freelance publicity."

He grinned. "So you could work from anywhere?"

"I suppose."

Interesting . . .

Lisa Andrews was waiting for them outside the office door alongside a giant of a man. Damian had defended himself in a few scuffles around the world, and he could instantly size up an opponent. If this man jumped him, he'd brace himself for the blow.

"Thanks for meeting with us today." Lisa shook their hands with a firm grasp. She wore a black pantsuit with a light blue shell, pearls, and black stilettos. Damian wondered if she'd thought through the implications of wearing heels on a bumpy boat ride.

"This is my cameraman, Ten Carnigan."

Ten acknowledged them with a nod before hoisting up a heavy trunk. When he flexed his bicep, the tail of a dragon tattoo crept under the edge of his worn gray T-shirt.

Abby set her bag on the dock while Damian unlocked the office door.

"Where did you get the name Ten?" Damian held open the door for the man. He grunted, hauling the trunk through the doorway and planting it on the floor.

"One of my five older brothers gave it to me." He opened the trunk and took out a video camera. "When I was about three, people'd ask me how old I was and I'd always say 'ten'—guess it doesn't take a genius to understand why."

"I bet no one ever forgets your name," Damian said.

"Beats a boring name like Lisa." The reporter grinned at him, pushing her blonde hair off her shoulders.

It was going to be a long day.

Abby dug into her briefcase and handed Lisa a stack of articles and other materials she'd compiled.

"Just in case you need any more information," Abby said. "There's been a lot of speculation as to how these toxins get in the Sound, but no one has done a serious investigation."

"We're planning to change that today." Lisa flipped through the stack with her manicured nails. Then she took charge.

"I'd like to ask a few preliminary questions here in your office," she said. "And then we want to go out on your boat and get some footage where the whales normally swim."

"That sounds great." Abby stepped back so Ten could drag in a spotlight and the tripod. Then he set up the camera so it peered over Lisa's shoulder.

Damian checked the front of his shirt and cringed. Smatterings of Tabasco sauce stained the green—it must have flung off the bottle when he doused his omelet. With a grand swoop, he pointed out the stain to Abby while Lisa was stringing her microphone under her jacket. Abby ran to the tiny kitchenette behind the office and returned with a white dishtowel saturated with hand soap and water.

"We haven't even started the interview yet," Abby reprimanded as she scrubbed out the stains, leaving a watermark below his left shoulder.

"Are you going to fire me?"

"It's too late for that." She gently turned his torso. "Sit like that for this interview. Hopefully, it won't look like you drooled on yourself."

"Nice image."

Abby pulled out a jar of powder from her bag along with a brush, patting the powder across his face until he coughed.

"You look good in makeup," she teased.

Lisa sat down across from him and handed him the lapel microphone. He untucked his shirt and strung it up and around his back, clipping it below his collar.

"That's perfect," Lisa told him as Ten started recording. She flipped through her notes and then began.

"Dr. De Lucia, you're concerned about the well-being of Puget Sound's whales. Could you tell me why?"

Damian took a deep breath. "I was born on this island, and I grew up watching these amazing orcas live and eat and play. In the last few years, the killer whales have been murdered, and someone needs to speak out before they're gone."

Lisa nodded her head with approval as he waited for the follow-up question.

"Do you have any idea what's causing their deaths?"

"Toxins called PCBs have been found in the dead orcas."

"And where do these come from?"

"PCBs were used legally until the late 1970s, but high levels of these toxins are still in the Sound."

"Is anyone still dumping PCBs into the water today?"

"I can't speculate," he said even though he was dying to speculate.

Damian watched Abby out of the corner of his eye, and she was nodding. At least she was pleased.

Lisa rattled off a long list of questions, and he answered each one as succinctly as possible. He felt like he was repeating himself, but Lisa didn't seem to mind.

"How does your previous work regulating whale hunters impact what you're doing today?" she asked.

"I've always been passionate about cleaning up our waters and rescuing sea life. My past jobs and current job involve educating the public about whales and fighting against their futile deaths."

Lisa pulled a newspaper article out of her briefcase. He braced himself.

She quickly perused the story. "A Mr. Dantzler was quoted in a recent *Seattle Times* article saying that you're welcome to come check out their factory any time. Have you taken him up on that?"

His face twitched, but he took a deep breath. This wasn't the time to blow it.

"Mr. Danztler wasn't as welcoming in person as he appeared to be in that article," he said calmly.

"So you tried to visit the company?"

"I did, but Mr. Dantzler wouldn't let me test the water."

"Did you take any legal action?"

"I've been too busy searching for healthy whales to mess with Pageant Industries again."

He wondered if this was where she would move in for the kill.

"But if they are fighting extinction, wouldn't it be worth your time to go confront Pageant?"

He squeezed the sides of the chair. "The killer whales are being killed. It's my job to speak out and let the world know about their plight before they're destroyed."

He heard Abby exhale and wondered if the camera caught the noise. Lisa didn't seem to notice. He'd responded exactly how they'd practiced, blowing off the questions about Pageant but not discounting them. Hopefully Lisa would dig a little deeper after the interview.

"Thank you, Dr. De Lucia," Lisa said pleasantly. Damian started to stand.

"Wait a sec, big guy," Ten said. "I need to get some shots over your shoulder."

"I'm going to ask a few of these questions again," Lisa explained. "We need another angle before we move on."

Damian waited patiently and nodded as Lisa repeated several of her questions.

"Excellent job," Abby whispered to him when Lisa moved toward the

window to check her hair and makeup in a portable mirror. Ten packed up the camera equipment by the front door.

"You sure?" he asked as he unwound the microphone.

"You're a pro."

Abby followed him outside to help prepare the boat for their cruise. Her blue eyes reflected against the water and lightened in the sun.

"Can I wear my cap?" he asked as he plopped the navy and gold hat on his head and started the boat engine.

"Do you really need my permission?"

"I thought it would be polite to ask. You prepared me well for today."

"Wasn't sure if you'd be interviewing with a playful seal or a man-eating shark."

"A little of both, I think," Damian said as he eyed Lisa and Ten stepping onto the deck of the boat.

He steered them out into the Sound as Abby escorted Ten to the back of the boat. Lisa stayed in the wheelhouse, standing a little too close to his side. Shouldn't she be back with the camera?

"Ever been to New York?" she asked.

"A couple of times. Too much city for me."

"Something's always going on there."

He looked back at Abby in the mirror. "Something's always going on here too."

Lisa winked at him. "I can see that."

"I didn't mean—"

She interrupted him. "Is this where you usually see the whales?"

"One of the many places they perform." He turned off the boat engine, waves charging them from all sides. "As you can see, they aren't entertaining anyone yet this year."

Lisa stepped outside to make sure her cameraman was shooting the choppy surface. Damian watched out the window as she stepped in front of the camera and probably repeated the words he'd just said. At least, he hoped so. This could be the exact spotlight they needed to make a change.

Ten panned a wide shot across the water as Lisa walked back inside.

"Could you take us by Pageant Industries?"

Damian hesitated.

"You don't need to be in the shot," Lisa said. "I just want some footage from the water."

Damian turned the boat slowly and sped toward the mainland.

The winds had picked up, the seas rougher near the coast. Pageant Industries was a sea by itself—an ocean of cement, metal silos, and steel buildings. Steam pouring out of the stacks, the company appeared cold and dirty. Damian looked for the grey-eyed guy in the dinghy, but he wasn't in sight.

Too bad for Pageant that the man wasn't on patrol, because today's guest could blow a kiss of death onto their front door.

Chapter 51

With backpacks bouncing against their shoulders, Marc and Jessica rode their bikes over a bumpy path a mile or so off the main road. Wind rustled the leaves and cooled Jessica's legs and arms before they stopped at the end of the bike path and parked their bikes in the tall grass.

"We walk from here," Marc said.

She bent down to retie her shoelace. "How do you find these places?"

"I can't stop exploring."

"Sounds like you have issues."

He grinned. "I do."

Jessica glanced back at their bikes before they started their trek through the woods. She thought about asking Marc if they should lock them up, but then she laughed at herself. If someone actually stumbled upon the bikes hidden in the grassy middle of nowhere, she supposed they'd earned the right to steal them.

They tromped along the mossy floor, creating their own trail. The butterscotch scent from the pine trees clung to the breeze and made her hungry for something sweet. Unzipping her pack behind her neck, she dug for her bag of M&Ms, but pulled out her phone instead.

"You brought your cell?" Marc asked like she'd stolen it.

"If you can pack a knife for emergencies, I can bring my phone."

He shook his head as he looked at the natural beauty surrounding them. "It just seems so wrong."

She tucked her phone back in the bag, pulled out the candy, and filled his palm with a pool of red, blue, brown, and green. He flung the chocolate pieces into his mouth.

"Aren't you upset I brought candy?" she teased.

"I'd rather have M&Ms in an emergency than a cell phone."

A branch cracked on their left.

"What was that?" Jessica whispered.

"Probably a bird."

Marc started walking again, but Jessica's legs froze.

"I see eyes," she said. Marc stepped toward where she was pointing and laughed.

"Come here," he whispered as he took her hand. She crept up behind him.

Peeking out from behind a snag was the slender brown head of a miniature deer. When the animal realized they were staring at her, she leaped over the log and bounded back into the forest.

Jessica gasped a lungful of air—she hadn't even realized she'd been holding her breath. She stepped back, but she didn't let go of Marc's hand.

"It looked like a skinny dog," she said.

"Just another one of the marvels on this island."

"I don't know if I can take much more."

"Well, I hope so, because our day is just beginning."

He kept her hand wrapped in his as they continued their hike past a line of glassy tide pools. As they ducked under the spidery branches of a maple, the leaves brushed their backs, and they were covered in forest, light dancing through the tree limbs, stirring shadows across the mossy floor.

"So are you going to tell me what she said?" Jessica asked as they climbed steadily up a hill.

"Your mom?"

"Of course."

He stopped walking and turned toward her. "She said you were free today and thought it might be a good idea if we spent some time together."

"I think my mom's starting to like you."

"It's not about me. She loves you, and she knows that you . . ." his voice trailed off.

"That I what?"

He started hiking again, shadows dancing across the back of his white T-shirt, and muttered something that she couldn't hear. They must be getting close to the water—she could smell salt in the air.

She was about to ask the question again when they emerged from the forest on a tall craggy cliff that overlooked the sea. They secured their packs as they climbed down the edge of the rocky wall until they reached a damp ledge.

"Where's the beach?" she asked as she glanced down at the water about two feet below.

"Gear up."

She dug her wetsuit out of her bag and zipped it over her bathing suit while he pulled tight black booties over his feet and secured his knife in a calf band. Jessica spit into her mask and knelt over the ledge to let the saltwater wash it clean. The tide sledged against the rocks with enough power to jolt her nerves.

She whisked her feet through the surf. "Is this crazy?"

"We'll be fine," he said. "It's an easy climb back up the rocks when we're done."

"You first."

He jumped into the water, and she followed close behind.

Light illuminated the cloudy water under the surface, and she realized they'd descended into a jungle—an underwater forest of bull kelp with towering stalks and golden leaves flowing like long hair from the tips of their bulbed heads. It was eerie and incredible at the same time.

She dove under a canopy of maroon-colored kelp and twisted through the leafy fronds before swimming back toward the surface for air. Then she followed Marc as he maneuvered through the jungle, and they rapidly swam away from the rocks.

The gentle rhythm of the rocking water echoed in her ears. A silvery fish swam by her, and then a school of burnt orange fish raced under her, playing in their glittering back yard. It was magical.

Marc swam to the left. She followed, weaving through the giant stalks until she saw a blood red sea star clinging to a frond below her.

She dove to inspect the star and the yellow snail curled close beside it. She wished that she had a scuba tank so she could explore for an hour without worrying about air.

She whipped her fins to follow a translucent school of fish, but instead of plummeting ahead, her leg twisted behind her. She peered over her shoulder to see what was wrong.

Her right fin was gone.

She brushed a curtain of fronds away from her face and kicked hard to resurface when a slimy arm grabbed her foot. She screamed into the water, but her terror dissipated in the sea.

Was it an octopus?

She thrashed her legs to beat it back, but it wouldn't let go.

God, make it let go!

She flailed at the invisible creature with her arms and legs, but it wouldn't release its grip. Tiny bubbles surrounded her head. She couldn't see. What was happening to her?

Panic seized her, and she twisted and turned to loose herself from the grasp.

She needed air. Now. The surface was just a few feet above her. She had to get to the top.

She whipped the water with her arms, but couldn't move. Just one breath. That's all. Then she'd be free.

One more push toward the surface. Her last push for air.

She couldn't get to the top. Her arms and legs shook out of control as she sucked in seawater instead.

The light above turned black.

She stopped battling for air.

Chapter 52

Abby stood behind Ten as Lisa talked to the camera, the expansive compound of Pageant Industries floating by in the background. Her perfect blonde hair fluttered in the wind, but somehow it managed to land perfectly between takes. She definitely had the face for TV, and Abby had to admit she was good at her job.

Lisa waved her hand as she walked back inside the pilothouse. Abby watched through the window, she and Damian laughing like best friends. Well, she was having just as nice of a time laughing and hanging out with Ten at the back of the boat.

At least she was until he turned green.

The boat bounced across the waves as they rode back toward Orcas Island, puffy batches of white moving in overhead from the west. Ten packed his camera and tripod into his black trunk before sprawling out on the wet deck.

"Are you okay?" Abby asked. She realized how stupid those words sounded when he groaned back in response.

Of course he wasn't okay. His pale skin was the color of seaweed, his eyes glazed over. She hoped he could still walk, because the three of them couldn't possibly carry his massive frame into the boat's lobby.

Abby rushed up to the cabin and interrupted Lisa's lesson on captaining a tour boat.

"The waves don't appear to agree with Ten," she told Damian.

"Seasick?"

"I'm no doctor, but the man looks like a Martian and he's groaning like he's in labor."

"You remember how to steer a boat?" Damian asked Abby as he stepped away from the wheel.

"You're kidding me."

"This is no time for timidity, Abby."

"Okay," she muttered as he raced out the door to assist the cameraman.

With both hands on the waxy oak wheel, she steered the boat straight, not veering from Damian's course.

"You've got a good guy there," Lisa said as she watched Damian and Ten through the glass.

"He's not my guy."

Lisa stared at her like she was crazy. "Then I'd have to say you're fooling yourself."

"What do you mean?"

"It's obvious that Damian is quite enamored with you."

Abby didn't think it was quite so obvious.

"We're just old friends," Abby said.

"Then maybe he's the fool," Lisa shrugged as she stepped out the door to check on the men.

Damian helped Lisa Andrews lift the camera equipment into the taxi trunk, and she slipped him her business card. Ten was in the backseat of the taxi, begging Abby to knock him out. She wished she could make his head stop swimming, but they had all tried to explain to the overgrown man that he would have to wait it out. He said he was going to shoot himself if no one else would do it for him.

Lisa shook both Damian's and Abby's hands, thanking them for the tour. Ten groaned his good-bye through the cracked window.

"I've got several more interviews to do before I finish the story, but the show should air before the end of the summer." Lisa climbed into the cab. "I'll call you when I get an airdate."

Damian and Abby watched the taxi drive off toward the airport.

"Will Ten make it?" Abby asked as they backed away from the curb.

"The plane ride back to Seattle will be murder, but he'll be fine."

Abby slipped off her cardigan and strung it over her arm.

"So . . . what do you think?" Damian asked as they sat down on a bench beside the water.

"You did a great job."

"Thanks."

"And Lisa Andrews had a crush on you."

"Now you're being silly."

Sunlight shimmered across the water in front of them like ten thousand flashbulbs illuminating a dark football stadium.

"You answered her questions with dignity and patience," Abby said. "You didn't give them a bad clip even if they wanted to do a negative story. I'd bet money the *Seattle Times* will beg you for another interview when the story airs."

"I'm not talking to them again."

"I may try to convince you to do otherwise."

"Do you have plans tonight?" he asked.

"Oh, you know, crazy stuff like cleaning out the garage."

"Sounds tempting." He paused. "Could I convince you to go sailing with me instead?"

A second passed, then several more.

"I haven't been sailing in a long time."

"Your life isn't over, Abby."

She stared into the sparkling water. Why shouldn't she go sailing with him? The garage could wait another twenty years or so before she scrubbed it down. After her exhilarating morning on the water, the last thing she wanted to do was go home and clean.

She tilted her head, squinting her eyes like she could read his face.

"What time?" she finally asked.

"Five—and don't eat. We'll have a dinner cruise."

Abby waved good-bye as she climbed into her car and rode home. What did one wear on a dinner cruise? Something warm but not dowdy. Or maybe she should look a little dowdy. She didn't want Damian to get any ideas that she was dressing up for him.

Well, at least she had three hours to figure it all out.

She opened the cottage's front door; the scents of lemony Pine-Sol and 409 overwhelmed her. Hiking up a window, she let the fresh air blow in, the broken screen flapping in the breeze.

She filled up a glass of water in the kitchen before she saw a piece of hot pink stationery propped up on the kitchen table. Jessica had scribbled her a note.

Gone snorkeling with Marc. Work afterward.

Thanks, Mom—I love you.

She walked back to the bedroom, opened the closet, and stared at a row of casual shirts, shorts, old capris, her overalls, and a pair of jeans. She'd packed to live near the water—not to play on it.

She leaned back against the paneled wall of the hallway and looked around at the fresh coat of wax on the hardwood floor, the clean cushions on the couch, and the dust-free pictures and seashells. She pulled out the faded denim jeans and a hooded sweatshirt, held them up to the light, and then threw them both on the floor.

Wasn't there a little clothing shop in Eastsound?

She slammed the closet door and moved toward the front door when the sunlight exposed a layer of dust on the windowsill. How could she have missed that before? She turned to find a clean cloth to scrub it before she caught herself.

What was she doing? This obsession for cleanliness had overtaken her. She could clean the dust when she got back.

Diverting her eyes from the window, she marched with purpose out the front door.

Damian was right—she needed to get a life.

Chapter 53

Marc popped his head out of the water and spit out his snorkel, the sun glaring into his eyes. This bull kelp forest was a haven for him—a masterpiece of God's underwater design and a brilliant hideaway for giant octopus and schools of stunning fish.

Turning his head, he scanned the surface for the tip of Jessie's snorkel, but he didn't see the black straw bouncing across the water. He squinted into the sun, but all he saw was a deep blue. She must be looking at the fish.

He dove under the water to see if she was darting through the shadows, his arm brushing a slippery stalk as he bolted through the kelp. When he didn't see her, he swam back up to look for her snorkel again.

Nothing. Maybe she'd decided to wait for him on the ledge. He turned back toward the cliffs.

Then he saw something floating near him, black glistening in the sun. He raced toward it. Before he reached the object, he realized what it was. Jessie's fin.

Panicked, he plunged deeper, searching for her in the kelp. Past the leafy heads and a school of fish. Past the slimy yellow shoots. Past the edge of the bright light. He still couldn't find her.

He emerged with a vengeance, gasped a deep breath, and dove again.

This time he saw her below him. A dark mass among the stalks, filmy blonde hair flowing like the fronds. She shouldn't look so peaceful! She should be fighting for air.

God, help me!

He didn't ascend for another breath of air. Instead he dove, grabbing the knife secured against his leg.

Jessie's arms swayed with the current, but her right leg was trapped. A sheath of kelp had tangled around her ankle and a broad frond fastened around her thigh. She'd probably kicked in panic until the tentacles ensnared her.

He slashed through the stalk with his knife and whipped his legs, propelling them in seconds to the surface. Bursting his head through the water, he towed Jessie to the cliffs. He dragged her limp body up the incline and set her down on the ledge, her arms dormant on the flat rock beneath her, her beautiful face tinted blue.

He felt her neck for a pulse. A weak heartbeat responded to his touch, but she wasn't breathing. He knelt down, tilted back her wet head, pinched her nose, and blew air between her lips as he watched her chest slowly rise and deflate. His fingers on her neck, he checked her pulse again. Her heart was barely pumping, but her lungs were still.

He breathed slowly into her mouth again. Was it ten breaths a minute or twelve? He couldn't remember. He'd do twelve.

After a minute, he stopped and checked her pulse again—slow but steady. She still wasn't breathing.

How long had she been down there? They'd been a team, swimming together like fish through the kelp. He'd been checking on her regularly, hadn't he? But he couldn't remember how long it had been since he'd seen her last. If it had been over five minutes, her brain could be dead.

What have I done?

He breathed into her lips again and waited. Jessie coughed suddenly, water seething from the sides of her mouth before she gasped for air. Marc checked her pulse again and listened to her breathe.

He dumped the contents of her backpack onto the black stone and dug through it until he found her cell phone. Snapping it open, he punched in 9-1-1, and then cursed into the wind. No service.

He kissed Jessie on the forehead. Then he climbed up the rocks and fumbled with the phone as he raced through the menus to switch the service from digital to analog. He dialed again.

"My girlfriend . . ." he pleaded with the operator. "She was in an accident."

"Where are you?" the woman asked.

"On Orcas Island, the far east side. We've been snorkeling."

"Does she have a pulse?"

"Yes, but I had to give her mouth to mouth. She's still unconscious."

"I'm calling the Coast Guard to get a boat to you."

"She's lost a lot of oxygen! We've got to get her to a doctor right away."

"Don't move," she said. Marc heard her calling a dispatcher.

"I've got a helicopter coming to you," she finally told him. "Should be there in ten minutes."

"Thank you," he heaved.

"I want you to stay on the phone with me," the woman said.

Marc peeked over the edge and saw Jessie lying alone on the rocks. He wished she'd sit up and smile at him. He'd say good-bye to the helicopter and take her home.

But her eyes were closed and her arms strung out lifelessly beside her. She looked . . . the thought made him sick, but she looked dead. Sleeping, he corrected himself. It looked like she was sleeping.

Please help them get here fast.

The operator continued asking him questions about his location as five minutes passed and then ten. A deafening roar whisked over the trees, and he stood up, waving his arms wildly at the helicopter as it circled him twice.

"Do you see a clearing for them to land?" the woman asked.

A clearing? He hadn't thought about it. The dense forest led right up to the cliffs and then plunged into the water below. How were they going to get her into the craft? He should have told the operator to call for a boat.

"There isn't one," he yelled into the phone, the twisting thunder from the blades echoing in his ears. The helicopter passed over him and looped around.

His phone crackled as the operator talked to someone else.

"Can you still hear me?" the woman asked.

"Yes!"

"I'm going to patch you in with the medevac."

"Marc," a strong voice commanded his attention. "Can you go below the rock?"

He looked down and then back up. What were they going to do? "Yes."

"I want you to hang on to her as tight as you can. We're going to land where you're standing."

Marc scrambled down the rocks and clutched Jessie in his arms as the roar of the blades pounded in his ears. The noise was almost unbearable, and he put his hands over her ears, ducking back with her under the rock ceiling to protect her from the surging water and wind. When the waves in front of them rippled back, the contents of her backpack hurled into the water.

Marc closed his eyes as her hair thrashed his face like a whip and prayed that they wouldn't follow Jessie's stuff into the sea.

Seconds later the driving wind ceased with the roar, the rotor shrieking as it whirled down. Someone shouted his name, and he shouted back. In seconds, a woman scrambled down the rocks and joined his side, checking Jessica's heart and limbs.

She took out a radio from her pocket.

"Victim is unconscious but breathing. Broken leg."

Someone lowered a stretcher over the cliff and Marc helped the paramedic strap Jessie on top of it before they lifted her up the wall. The pilot motioned for him to come onboard, and when the door slammed shut, the rotor roared.

They lifted off the ground, the helicopter's nose pointing toward the mainland, but Marc didn't notice when they left the island behind or when they prepared to land. Instead, he focused on the beautiful girl lying still in front of him.

As the paramedic hooked her to a respirator, Marc begged God to save her life.

Chapter 54

Damian held out his hand to help Abby climb aboard his sailboat. After much deliberation at Wanda's Boutique, she chose khaki capris and a lavender cardigan to wear over a yellow cotton shirt. Wanda had told her it was the perfect outfit for sailing—sophisticated, soft, and comfortable.

"It's only right that we go out on the water tonight," he said as he steered the boat out of the marina. "The kids got to play on it all day."

"We spent the entire morning on the water." Abby stood beside him at the helm, waiting for Damian to tell her what to do.

"That was nothing like sailing," he said as the white flap captured the wind, catapulting them forward like a rocket through the waves.

A squeal escaped Abby's lips. She was flying. It all came back in an instant—the thrill, the pleasure, the joy of tearing through the water carried by the breeze.

For the next two hours, they glided across the water as he shouted commands. Her hair whisked wildly around her head as she turned the sail—the lingo returning quickly. She'd forgotten how much she adored this, thrived on it in fact. It was glorious to be out on the sea again, absolutely amazing. A glimpse of God's swift, beautiful hand.

Damian sailed into a serene bay and lowered the anchor over the boat's side. The boat rocked so gently she could barely feel the rhythm.

"Thanks for getting me back out here," she said as Damian unpacked a picnic basket and spread a navy tablecloth across the bow.

"The Abby I used to know wouldn't have waited a month before sailing. She would have run out of the car, stumbled down those slippery steps behind her house, and pulled the boat into the water like her back was on fire. If it's possible, I think she used to love the water more than I did."

"I'm not the Abby you used to know."

"Well, your daughter reminds me a lot of the girl who loved to sail and swim. The girl who swore she'd never leave the sea."

Jessica would probably have a heart attack if he ever told her that.

Damian opened the picnic basket, filling the hull with the aroma of garlic, spicy tomatoes, and pesto sauce. Then he unloaded a stack of warm Tupperware dishes and served her a plateful of homemade manicotti, garlic bread, marinated olives, and fresh greens dripping with balsamic vinegar.

"So tell me, what happened over the years to make you change?" he asked.

"I grew and matured into a responsible adult."

And into a bitter old lady.

"So it's not mature to spend your free time enjoying what you love?"

"It's not that," she replied. "I still do things I love. I read and jog and spend time with my daughter."

She took a bite of the manicotti, the fresh mozzarella and ricotta cheeses melting in her mouth. She never should have served him plain chicken and beans the other night. Next time she'd call a carpenter to fix her house and ask Damian to cook a meal.

"I remember one of the first times we sailed past your house," he said. "You were waving so hard at your mom that you fell off the side of the boat."

She laughed. She'd been completely ridiculous in her youth, and the thing was, she hadn't even cared. Her mom had teased her about the boat plunge for years.

Damian ripped off a piece of garlic bread. "Then there was the time we snuck out for a night swim, and Ed stopped us before we made it to the water, figuring we were up to no good. He threatened to drag us down to jail if we didn't run home. We didn't even say good-bye."

"How could I forget? I got stuck climbing back through the window, and Laurel had to help me get in. We giggled so hard we woke up my parents. They told me to use the front door next time, and then they grounded me for a week."

"Remember the time you—" he began, but she cut him off.

"Hey," she pointed at him. "I happen to remember a time that someone tipped an entire boat over and ruined a perfectly good sail. Your father had to rescue us."

"We were right offshore, weren't we?" He grinned. "We couldn't stop laughing long enough to right the boat."

"Your dad didn't think it was funny."

"When he came to help us, he left my mother in charge."

"Hence the kitchen fire."

"But the show still went on. They never even closed for the renovations."

"We had fun, didn't we?" she asked softly.

"When was the last time you tried something new, Abby . . . took a chance, a risk, dived into the unknown? Stopped working and actually enjoyed the life that God gave you?"

"I guess the answer is tonight." She paused. "Before this, it's been a long time."

They ate quietly as a flock of seagulls flew overhead, their white feathers capturing the sun.

"So are you going to tell me about Hunter?" he asked.

She stared at him in shock at his casual tone. Hunter had never been a nonchalant topic for her.

"How do you know about Hunter?"

Damian had been traveling the world when they brought Hunter to the island.

"Jessica told Marc about him, and he told me."

It embarrassed her to think about what else Marc had told him. She sipped the sparkling white grape juice that Damian had poured into stem glasses.

"Hunter has haunted me for twenty years," she confessed. "It's hard to understand, but he was my son and I lost him. He didn't die, he wasn't buried and gone—I sent him into the unknown with a woman who was a child herself. It's the unknown that agonizes me."

"Do you feel like he's dead?"

She slid her fingers up and down the glass stem and shuddered. "I feel like I killed him . . . It was Scott's decision to let him go, but I should have taken a stand and used every last penny we had to save our son."

"So you're spending the rest of your life shadowed by guilt?"

"He was my baby, and I should have fought for him."

"Why didn't Scott pursue legal action? Surely he must have loved Hunter as much as you did."

She shrugged her shoulders. He couldn't have loved Hunter as much as she did or he wouldn't have let him go.

"He was convinced that Stacie would fight back, and a long legal battle would have hurt Hunter instead of helping him. Stacie never relinquished her rights, and she hadn't abandoned him either, so legally he was still hers. Scott thought the likelihood of her winning the case was fairly high."

"And you disagreed?"

She nodded. "A fair judge would have given him to us. We'd taken good care of him for four months, and Stacie's life was a mess."

He scooped another helping of manicotti onto her plate.

"I've often wondered what it would have been like to have a boy and a girl. The perfect family, you know."

"Sounds like wondering has been your life."

"I thought I had let it go," she said. "Then my boss sprung a new client on me last month, and I went into shock when she said it was Heartsong Adoptions—the same agency that Scott and I used so long ago. Everything rushed back to me, and it's been out of control ever since."

She thought about Jessica discovering the album in the attic, the many questions, and now the call from Heartsong saying they found Stacie. The puzzle pieces were all flying around, and she had no idea where they would land. Was it possible for God to put it all back together again?

"I'm trying to let go of the past, yet it seems like God keeps bringing it back," she said. "I think I've been healed, but then the pain shoots through me again."

"Sometimes the pain is the most unbearable right before a wound begins to heal."

She nodded her head as she gazed out at the dark pines that surrounded the bay. The sunlight danced through the needles, casting fluid shadows across the water.

"The adoption agency actually called me yesterday and said they'd located Stacie, but I haven't called them back yet."

"Why not?"

"I'm scared to death," she admitted. "I'm finally starting to heal, and it would kill me if something awful happened to him."

"I think you should call. Get the closure that you need."

The sun dipped slowly toward the horizon.

"We should probably head back soon," he said. "I don't want to sail in the dark."

She nodded as she bit into the sweet, flaky baklava—the perfect Grecian end to their Italian meal. After they finished, she packed up the picnic basket as Damian rolled up the anchor.

She smiled at him, and he dropped the anchor back into the water, letting the heavy weight fall to the sea floor.

Then he faced her. "If I don't say this now, I'm never going to say it."

Her gut clenched as she looked into his eyes. He was searching, and she was scared to ask what he was searching for.

"I don't want you to go back to Denver." He stepped toward her. "I don't want you to go anywhere."

She braced herself on the side of the boat. "What are you talking about?"

"The thing is, Abby . . ." he began.

She ran her fingers through her windblown hair. Her capris were rumpled, and her makeup must be a smeared mess in the water and wind.

"The thing is . . . do you remember the summer of '77?"

That was the summer she'd discovered that she and Damian would never be anything except friends.

"Vaguely," she told him.

"I came to your parents' house the first day you arrived home from college. I'd just finished graduate school, and I was finally going to tell you how I felt."

Waves swirled in her mind. Everyone had told her that Damian had feelings for her, but she'd refused to believe them. He'd never said a word to her.

"So why didn't you tell me?" she asked softly.

"Your dad told me to go home."

She remembered it now. She'd been so disappointed when Damian hadn't come to visit that year. She'd been waiting, wondering why he didn't show. After a month, she called Scott, the man she'd gone out with a few times at school, and asked him if he wanted to come visit for a week. He came the next day.

"You should have told me," she whispered.

"It wouldn't have made a difference."

"Yes, it would have."

He gave her an odd look. "You and your parents had plans for your life, and they didn't involve me."

This isn't what she wanted. Not now. She'd already had and ruined a seemingly healthy marriage. Right now, she only wanted a friend.

"So much has changed since then," he said. "But I always regretted not telling you how I felt in spite of what your father said."

"I'm going back to Denver," she interrupted. "Next week, I'm going home."

He looked devastated. "I understand."

"I just want you to know that my stay here is short. I've got a house, a life, a job." *Well, maybe not a job.* "I've got responsibilities back there," she continued, trying to convince both of them that she had to leave.

"Your life is just one big responsibility, isn't it?"

A splash rocked the water at the side of the boat. Both of them jerked their heads toward the sound, and a sleek black whale crashed through the surface.

"They're back," Damian whispered.

Two more whales breached the waves, spurting geysers of water into the air. The orcas had come home!

Damian clapped his hands, and she grinned as she watched the

creatures entertain them with their show. He grabbed her, kissed her lips, and then he let go to watch the gorgeous mammals glide around the boat.

Chapter 55

Marc leaned back against the plastered wall of the waiting room. He had bought a can of Coke from the machine an hour ago and cracked it open, but he still hadn't taken a sip.

The helicopter ride to the hospital blurred in his mind. The medic had hooked Jessie up to some machine and poked her arm to insert an IV. He kept hoping she'd wake up as they crossed the water—just long enough to smile at him and then go back to sleep. Just long enough to let him know she was okay.

He'd changed from his wet bathing suit into the baggy pants and T-shirt someone at the hospital handed him after they arrived. Then an attendant told him he'd have to wait in the lobby while they examined Jessie.

The waiting was torture.

He looked down at his bare feet on the linoleum floor. His shoes had blown off the cliff in the blast of helicopter wind.

What had he been thinking, taking Jessie out to the kelp forest? He'd been cocky, plain and simple. He'd wanted to show off his favorite underwater spot, and gamely, she'd played along. He'd overextended them. Pushed her too hard. He'd never forgive himself for what he'd done.

The clock above the reception desk ticked past seven. He'd been there for two hours, and they hadn't told him a thing. The stifling room was filled with injured people, broken bones and bleeding skin, yet he couldn't think about anything else except Jessie fighting for her life.

Help her fight, God. Help her win.

He opened Jessie's cell phone and dialed her home number again. Mrs. Wagner still didn't answer. He'd tried at least thirty times, but nothing. And Damian wasn't answering his office or home line. The only person he'd been able to get in touch with was his pastor in Seattle, and the man had promised not only to pray for Jessie but to move his entire prayer team into action. She needed every one of their prayers.

He dialed again; this time calling Vincent at work. He didn't want to talk to anyone else, but Mrs. Wagner needed to come to the hospital right now. Jessie needed her here . . . and so did he.

The dishwasher answered the phone.

"It's Marc Cartwright."

"Where are you, man?" Phil whispered. "Vincent is flaming mad."

"There's been an accident. I need to talk to him."

"Are you okay?"

"No."

"Hey, Vincent!" Marc heard him yell. "Telephone."

Amidst the clatter of dishes and trays, he heard Vincent shout back. "Take a message!"

"I think you better take it. It's Marc Cartwright, and he don't sound good."

The phone banged against something before Vincent took it.

"I knew this was going to happen," he raged.

"Vincent, I . . ."

"You're fired!"

He sighed. "Have you seen Jessie's mom or Damian?"

"No, but I have a restaurant full of people that need food, and I'm missing two servers."

"Jessie was in a snorkeling accident, her leg got caught in some kelp and she couldn't breathe. If you see them, please tell them we're at Seattle General, in the ER."

Vincent hesitated. "Is she going to make it?"

"I don't know."

Marc hung up the phone before he collapsed into a cramped hospital seat. The emergency room doors flew open and another gurney rolled through the doors. The man on it was screaming at the EMT.

He dialed his mom, and she answered the phone on the second ring.

"It's Marc."

"Hi, honey."

She sounded sober. On a Friday night . . .

"I'm at the hospital, Mom, and I need you to pray."

"What's wrong?"

He looked around the room at a disheveled man who'd brought in his daughter, an elderly woman clutching her arm, and a little boy waiting for his mom. "I went snorkeling today with a friend, and she almost drowned. The doctors are working on her right now."

"I'm coming to the hospital."

He didn't say it, but he knew she couldn't come. She'd already spent her gas money.

"You don't need to come, but I'd really like you to pray."

"I want to come."

"I'll call you back when I know something."

"There's something I need to tell you . . ."

"What?"

She hesitated. "I'll tell you later."

"I love you, Mom."

"I love you too."

He tried to dial Mrs. Wagner again when the phone beeped. He looked at the screen, and the power was almost gone. Just great.

Hopefully Vincent would tell Jessie's mom where they were.

She'd never forgive him for what he'd done, and he didn't blame her. He'd never forgive himself either.

Chapter 56

Like giddy children, Abby and Damian snickered as they sprinted up the stairs to De Lucia's Italian Restaurant and burst through the front door. They nodded politely to the diners before scrambling into the kitchen, searching for someone to tell their good news.

Damian slapped Phil on the back, flinging soapy bubbles across the counter. Abby thought Damian was going to hug the guy, but Phil just stared at him like he'd gone mad.

Turning his head, Abby watched Vincent set down his spoon and stagger toward them, almost like he didn't want them to be there. He probably didn't want them messing with his business, but this news was too good not to tell.

"You'll never guess what we saw!" Damian said.

Vincent didn't answer, his lips pressed together in a grim crease.

"Is something wrong?" Abby glanced around the room. Where was Jessica?

"I've been trying to call you both," Vincent said.

"We've been sailing."

Vincent hesitated. "There was an accident."

Abby's eyes searched the kitchen and dining room for her daughter. Maybe she was on break.

"Marc and Jessica were snorkeling, and her leg got tangled in some kelp," he said. "Marc's with her at Seattle General, in the ER."

The floor disappeared under Abby's feet, the room whirling around her. She collapsed against Damian, and he held her tight.

You've taken my son, my parents, and my husband. Not Jessica too, God. Leave Jessica alone!

"It's okay, Abby," Damian whispered. "She's going to be okay."

"You don't know that!" she gasped. "How do you know she's going to be okay?"

Damian helped her to a chair in the kitchen, and she collapsed.

Was she going to lose her baby girl? God was taking everyone she loved, and she didn't know why. What did He want from her? She'd already given Him everything. Why did He want Jessica? He could punish her for her anger, but her daughter hadn't done anything wrong.

Don't take my girl!

She dug her cell phone out of her purse and saw she'd missed twenty calls while they were out on the boat.

She shoved the phone toward Damian. "Call Marc!"

He checked the phone's directory and dialed Jessica's cell phone number. "It's going straight to voice mail."

Her voice broke. "God, help me."

"I'm calling a friend," Damian dialed another number. "He's got a Cessna on the island, and if he can, I know he'll fly us to Seattle."

"Thank you," she groaned, her hands and legs shaking uncontrollably.

Why couldn't she just faint? If her world faded, she wouldn't feel the pain.

Have mercy on me, she prayed, but she didn't black out.

Plates clattered, pots boiled, and the kitchen staff rushed by her balancing trays of food. It was surreal, waiting here amongst the busyness to find out if her daughter was alive. Her life stopped while everyone else's roared on.

My beautiful girl. It had been ages since she thought about the joyful day Jessica was born. Her labor had been dreadful, agonizing pain that lasted twelve hours as Scott coached her and cheered her on. She'd screamed that she couldn't do it, but he'd told her calmly that not only could she, but she would. Ten minutes later, their daughter was born.

The painful memories of labor vanished the instant she'd held her little girl in her arms. The nurse had washed her baby, and Jessica slept peacefully, cuddled up in a blanket with tiny blonde curls spilling over the sides.

Then she woke up and gazed into her mother's eyes before she cried out for milk. For a brief moment, this baby had erased the pain of losing her first child. Life with Hunter had only been a dream.

How had she let the old pain creep back? Jessica was right. She'd glamorized life with her first child. Hunter was perfect in her mind.

Her little girl could never live up to her expectations. She'd spent her life competing with a dream, an apparition, a brother that she'd never seen. It wasn't fair to put so much pressure on Jessica to be the perfect child and have the perfect life. As much as she had resisted it, Jessica had taken second place.

Damian took her arm and helped her stand.

"He'll be ready by the time we get to the airport."

"Okay," she replied. She wondered if she'd be able to walk across the tile.

Leaning against Damian, she wobbled toward the door.

"Do we need to stop at your house?" Damian asked.

"No!"

They needed to get to the hospital. Nothing was more important than getting on that plane. She had to get to Jessica; her daughter needed her now.

Damian passed every car in front of them as they sped toward the airport.

"Drive faster!" she wanted to scream, but she knew he was already driving far above the speed limit. He could be going a hundred miles an hour, and it wouldn't be fast enough for her.

What was Jessica going through right now? Were the doctors taking good care of her? Was Marc at her side? She was probably looking around for her mother, wondering why she wasn't there.

Tell her I'm coming, Lord. Tell her I'll be there soon.

Damian helped her board the Cessna, buckled her seat belt, and then sat down beside her.

As they took off into the darkened sky, Abby prayed harder than she'd ever prayed in her life.

Take care of my baby, she pleaded with God. *You can have my life, but don't take my little girl.*

Abby and Damian burst through the hospital doors and found Marc slumped in a chair. She grabbed both his arms.

"Where is she?"

"She's in the trauma center, but they aren't telling me a thing."

"I want to talk to a doctor."

Damian swept past them, motioning to a nurse at reception. He pointed toward Abby. "This woman's daughter came in a few hours ago."

Abby moved in behind him. "I want to talk to a doctor now."

The nurse picked up a stack of clipboards and scanned through them for Jessica's chart.

"She's on a respirator," the woman said. "The doctor will be out in a few minutes to give you a full report."

Damian helped Abby into a lobby chair. He sat on one side of her, and Marc hesitated before sitting on the other.

"I'm so sorry, Mrs. Wagner," he said.

"How dare you take her out in that water!"

He dropped his head.

"Don't you know you have to be careful?"

Damian grasped her arm. "He rescued her, Abby."

She thought about all the other awful things she'd like to say to him. She wanted to chew him into shreds and spit him out. But she saw the pain in his eyes, the same pain she was certain blazed through her own eyes, and she couldn't hurt him anymore.

With her trembling fingers, she took Marc's hand, and he squeezed it. Damian took her other hand, and they waited in silence until the doctor called Abby's name.

He was middle-aged with a long blue coat wrinkled over his thin body. Under his black-rimmed glasses, Abby saw brown eyes streaked red. He shook their hands, and they followed him back to a small conference room.

"Your daughter's been stabilized," he told Abby. She heaved a sigh of relief as her pounding heart relaxed.

"Thank you, Lord," Marc whispered beside her.

"We're moving her to her own room right now." The doctor glanced

at his notes. "She'll be in a leg cast for at least six weeks, and we'll need to monitor her abc's for a few days before she can go home."

Tears streamed down Abby's cheeks.

The doctor looked over at Marc. "A few more seconds without oxygen, and she would have gone into cardiac arrest. If her heart had failed, we'd be having a different kind of conversation right now." He tapped Marc's shoulder. "You did the right thing, son."

"Can I see her?" Abby asked. The doctor escorted her back to the hospital room, its walls a plain tan and dimly lit by a corner table lamp.

Jessica was asleep under the pink blanket, her blonde hair matted against her forehead and her pale skin pasty and cool. Abby kissed her cheek and grasped her hand. She looked so peaceful in spite of the trauma that had tried to steal her life. Abby swept her fingers over her daughter's head and pushed back her hair. Then she wiped her face with a warm towel. She'd set up camp on the couch and stay until Jessica was ready to go home.

Kissing her cheek again, Abby tiptoed out of the room and walked back to the lobby.

"Go home," she told the two men.

"I'm staying here." Marc pointed to the chairs in the lobby.

"I'll call you when she wakes up," Abby said, but Marc insisted on staying. She couldn't argue with his resolve.

"I'm staying the night too," Damian said.

She looked at her watch. "You have a tour in a few hours."

"I'll cancel it."

She shook her head. "You have to go."

"I'm canceling it, Abby."

When he hugged her, she realized how good it was to have Damian De Lucia at her side when she needed a friend.

She went back to Jessica's room and lay down on the stiff couch, staring at the ceiling and counting the infamous sheep in her mind. When she opened her eyes in the darkness, she turned and saw the shape of Jessica's body in the bed.

God had rescued her daughter, and she'd be eternally grateful to Him.

Chapter 57

Four days later, an attendant wheeled Jessica through the hospital lobby as Abby waited for her daughter outside the glass doors. Jessica used her crutches to maneuver herself to the convertible before flinging them behind her into the back seat and slipping into the car. Rain pelted Abby's jacket as she slammed Jessica's door.

Her daughter had almost drowned, and the hospital was discharging her without fanfare. Abby had argued with the doctor and appealed his decision, saying three days wasn't nearly long enough to monitor Jessica's condition. The hospital staff agreed to hold her over one more night, but today they prescribed her Tylenol with codeine and told her to go home.

As they drove away from the hospital, Abby peered up at the sea of windows on the brick wall, every piece of glass representing a book of stories—grief, forgiveness, hope, retribution, love, fear, and sad good-byes.

What would her and Jessica's story be?

"A gloomy day for a ride," Jessica said as she pulled off her soaked raincoat.

"You doing okay, honey?"

"Feeling great on this medicine." She paused. "I'm sorry for all of this, Mom." Abby glanced over at her as she pulled out of the hospital's drive.

"For all of what?"

"For causing all this hassle in your life."

"Don't ever think like that again!" Abby reached over and took her hand. "You have nothing to feel bad about."

"Are you mad at Marc?"

"I was," Abby admitted. "But I apologized to him for losing my temper."

Abby merged with the interstate traffic moving north. If they made the next ferry, they'd be back on Orcas in time for dinner.

"I like him a lot, Mom."

"I know, honey."

"He saved my life."

"He's a good guy, Jessica. I'm happy for you."

"Are you really?"

Smiling, she nodded her head. "Yes, I really am. I love you, honey."

"I know, Mom."

"I don't say it enough, though. I almost lost you before I could tell you again."

"I'm not going anywhere."

Abby didn't reply, but she knew that wasn't true. She was losing her daughter this summer. Jessica had grown into a wonderful woman, and she needed to let go—let go of her expectations and her guilt and her own fear of being alone. Yes, Jessica was going someplace incredible, and it was someplace she needed to go on her own.

Her cell phone rang, and Abby answered it as she steered left.

"Hello."

"Is this Abby?"

She turned right onto a side road.

"Yes it is."

"This is Julia Martin at Heartsong. I wasn't sure if you got my message a few days ago."

Abby glanced in her rearview mirror and then looked over at Jessica. She was staring out the window.

"Thank you for calling," Abby said, her voice dragging as she contemplated what to say. "I wanted to tell you how sorry I am for how I acted the last time I saw you. I was horrible."

Jessica looked her way, and she flashed her daughter a quick smile.

"There's no right way to react when an adoption falls through," Julia said.

"Well, I wanted to apologize anyway."

"Apology accepted but not necessary." She paused. "I need to apologize to you too."

"There's nothing you could have done."

"It was the first time I'd had a birth mother change her mind after a child had been placed, and I was at a loss how to respond. I should have told you how sorry I felt."

Abby's voice cracked. "Thank you."

"I made a few calls," Julia continued. "Stacie is still living in Seattle, and she gave me some information about Hunter."

An ambulance roared by as Abby tried to focus. Here it was, the information she'd been wanting for years—an answer to resolve her pain. She did want to find out, didn't she? This is why she'd come to Seattle in the first place, to put an end to the questions that she'd been confronting again and again.

"I'm assuming you still want to know?"

Abby hesitated. "I do."

"Didn't you say you were staying on Orcas Island for a few weeks?" Julia asked.

"Yes."

"Stacie told me that her son is fine, and oddly enough, he's working on the island this summer too."

"Orcas Island?" Her voice cracked. "Are you sure?"

"That's the one."

Could it be?

"Her son's name is Marcus Scott Cartwright. Apparently she kept your husband's name to honor what you and your husband had done."

Abby braked at a stoplight, her hand trembling as she tried to steady the phone against her ear.

Marc was the one! These past weeks of wondering about her son, and there he was right in front of her—helping her with the yard, laughing with her daughter, saving Jessica's life! He had grown up into an amazing guy, and she'd been too proud to notice.

"Thank you, Julia," she finally muttered. "Thank you very much."

"Do you want his address?"

"No, it's an awfully small island."

"I hope you get to give him a hug."

Abby hung up the phone as the light turned green.

Why hadn't she seen it before? He had the same blue eyes and coffee-colored hair that he'd had the day they picked him up at the hospital. The smile—when he smiled at Jessica, it was the same smile he'd given her and Scott when he was a baby, total abandonment of love.

All of these years she'd envisioned him as a baby, and he'd grown into a man.

"Who was that?" Jessica asked.

"An old friend."

Chapter 58

Marc placed a white teddy bear and an envelope on Jessie's bed. He'd labored over the card for an hour, writing words to express how much he cared for her, how he'd never let her down again. She'd assured him that the accident wasn't his fault, but it *was* his fault. He'd swum too far away from her. He should never have left her side.

A huge "Welcome Home" sign hung from the edge of the loft to the top of the screen door. He lit the twelve candles he'd purchased from a specialty store downtown and scattered them around the room. The vanilla and lavender and pine scents made the cottage smell like a garden.

Inside the kitchen, he opened a box of pepperoni and mushroom pizza—Jessica's special dinner request. Another smell to add to the barrage.

He walked back into the living room, sat down on the couch, and looked around the brightly colored room.

Was it all too much? Too little? How do you welcome home the girl that you love? The one who almost died?

He heard the convertible drive up to the front door, and he rushed outside. Jessie was smiling at him from the passenger side, and she looked beautiful. Her hair was pulled back in a ponytail, and he rushed to help her get out of the car. Glancing over at Mrs. Wagner, he kissed Jessie quickly on the cheek.

She squealed when she hobbled through the front door. "Cool decorations."

He shouldn't have put out so many candles. "It's a little overwhelming."

"It's perfect."

Mrs. Wagner came inside the cottage, and he heard her shut the door behind them.

"Do you want to sit down?" he asked Jessica.

"I'd rather go sailing, but it'll be a few weeks."

He took her hand and helped her toward the couch.

Mrs. Wagner cleared her throat. "Before you sit down, do you mind if I talk to Marc alone?"

What in the world?

"No way." Jessie plopped down on the couch.

"For just a couple of minutes." She gave him an odd look. "Then I'll leave you two alone."

Jessie didn't move. "I don't think so."

"It's okay," he said. It couldn't possibly be any worse than what they'd discussed before.

He squeezed Jessie's hand and helped her stand up.

"I guess I need a quick nap," Jessica said, emphasizing the word "quick" as she limped into her room on one crutch.

Mrs. Wagner directed him into the kitchen, and he sat down by the table. She put a slice of pizza on a plate and handed it to him.

"I'm so sorry, Mrs. Wagner," he apologized again. "I'll never put Jessie into that kind of danger again."

"I'm glad to hear that," she replied. "But I don't want to talk about the accident tonight."

He shifted in his seat. He didn't know if he wanted to talk about anything with her tonight.

She opened up a kitchen cabinet and pulled out a plastic bag. Inside was a navy-colored photo album, and she slowly took out the album and set it on the table between them.

"This was my son," she said, opening to the first page.

"Jessie told me about him."

"I loved him very much."

Marc glanced down at the family pictures, wondering why Mrs. Wagner needed to explain this to him now. All he wanted to do was see Jessie.

She turned the page.

"My husband, Scott, and I were desperate to have a baby in the early 1980s. When we couldn't have a child, we decided to adopt. Our agency called and said they had a son for us, and we both fell in love with him right away. The second he looked up at me in the hospital, I never wanted to let go."

Didn't she know that Jessica had already told him the story? Was this her own strange way of telling him to leave her daughter alone?

"Hunter was an incredible baby. He loved to laugh and touch the fuzzy baseball bat his dad bought him and reach out and touch the soft fur on our calico cat. Before my husband died, he prayed every day for Hunter, and I deeply believe that God listened to those prayers. Scott prayed that God wouldn't let go of Hunter and that he would grow into an amazing godly man."

What was he supposed to say?

"I'm sorry that you lost him."

He fiddled with the pepperoni on top of the pizza and picked up the slice to take a bite.

"I'm not."

Marc jerked his head up and met her eyes. "But Jessie said . . ."

"Oh, I used to be sorry, very sorry. But I'm coming to realize why this happened. Why I had to let Hunter go."

"Okay." He wondered how long Jessica was going to be napping. He could use some support if her mother was going mad.

"You see, Hunter's birth mother loved him as much as I did. Her name was Stacie, and after we had Hunter for four months, Stacie decided that she wanted to raise him alone."

He dropped the piece of pizza.

"Stacie's the name of my mom," he said slowly.

Mrs. Wagner nodded her head. "Stacie was young, and her parents had kicked her out of their home when she refused to have an abortion. She didn't want to kick out her son too."

Marc froze in his chair, trying to comprehend her words. What was she saying? That he had been Hunter? That he could have had a mother and a father, a family who loved him, a place to call home.

The realization stunned him.

"It's nice to have you back," she whispered.

Marc tried to speak but couldn't. Instead he gazed at the kitchen wall. He couldn't make sense of all the thoughts swirling through his head.

This was what he'd always wanted! A real, loving family to connect with. An actual mother who cared. Not that Stacie wasn't his mom, but across from him was a woman who fought for her daughter. Fought for what she thought was right even when she was dead wrong. If his mother hadn't taken him back, he'd even have grown up with a dad.

His stomach rolled. Did Mrs. Wagner want him to be excited about this? Sad? What was he supposed to say to this woman who cared for him as a baby? If Stacie hadn't taken him back, he'd be calling this woman "mom."

"And now I have to apologize," she said. "I've been downright cruel to you, and I am so sorry."

"That's okay, Mrs. Wagner."

"No, it's awful, but God's been faithful to me in spite of what I've done. And He's obviously been faithful to you too."

"Yes, ma'am. He most certainly has."

"I hope you and Jessica continue dating. You are the perfect match for her."

God had indeed been faithful to him. He would never have imagined this answer when he had prayed for wisdom.

He stood and gave her a hug. "I'm glad to be home."

Jessica opened her door and peeked out.

"I'm not really tired . . ." She stopped and glanced back and forth at them. "Are you both crying?"

Mrs. Wagner wiped her eyes with a napkin. "We've got a story for you."

Chapter 59

Abby served icy bottles of Coke to Damian, Marc, and Jessica as they hovered around the tiny TV, the hot August sun baking the living room. She'd opened every window in the cottage and blasted two fans on high. Next year she'd install air conditioning in the house, but tonight they held ice packs on their foreheads, moaning about the stifling heat. Three of them were too hot and lazy to move from the couch. Abby was too nervous to sit still.

She and Damian had spent the afternoon preparing a buffet of hors d'oeuvres for the *Primetime* story debut. A half hour ago, the coffee table overflowed with nachos smothered in salsa and cheese, stuffed mushrooms, artichoke dip with crackers, and chocolate-covered strawberries. All their hard work disappeared in minutes when Marc and Jessica returned from their day of sailing.

As she glanced around at the small group glued to the television set, she realized how much God had blessed her. Healing. Forgiveness. A future. And a family to love.

At the end of this summer she'd watched Marc Cartwright with new eyes and realized that she couldn't have done a better job raising him no matter how hard she tried. With God as his father and Stacie as his mom, Marc had grown into a courteous, caring man who'd dedicated his life to Christ. She couldn't compete with that.

Around Jessica's finger was a slender golden band—a promise for the future, a hint of what they all knew would come. God had done the unimaginable. Not only had he brought Hunter back to her, but Marc Cartwright was going to be a permanent part of their family. She now had her daughter and her son.

"Anyone need anything else?" she asked, fidgeting with a plateful of crackers.

"Shhh, Mom," Jessica hushed her. "It's coming on."

Damian reached out and took Abby's hand as Lisa Andrews appeared on the screen—her blonde hair brushed perfectly around her smiling face. Strange, Abby thought. It had been two months since they'd hosted her and Ten around the bay. Two months since Jessica had been airlifted to Seattle. Two months since Julia had called her with the amazing news.

It seemed like a lifetime had passed.

"Orcas come home every summer to Puget Sound, but during the past five years, the Sound has been a dangerous place for these whales to live," Lisa said, leaning against Damian's tour boat railing as Ten skimmed the top of the deserted sea with his camera lens. "*Primetime* came to the Pacific Northwest to find out why."

The show cut to the interview with Damian.

"Our orca population has dropped 20 percent over the past five years," he said. "Someone needs to do something before our killer whales disappear."

"Damian De Lucia is a marine biologist and has studied whales for twenty-five years," Lisa explained. "A resident of Orcas Island in Washington's Puget Sound, he's concerned about toxins called PCBs that are polluting the seas."

"Accelerated levels of PCB toxins have been found in the whales that died, with no other apparent causes," Damian told her. Lisa nodded in response. "These toxins have been banned for over thirty years, and yet the levels seem to be increasing as the years go by."

The story cut to an interview with an EPA representative touting Damian's concerns, and then to the footage of Pageant Industries.

"The levels of PCB toxins near Pageant Industries off the coast of Washington are far above normal." Lisa leaned down to take a water sample. "We wondered if Pageant was partially responsible for polluting the Sound."

"Absolutely not," Colt Dantzler said.

Abby silently critiqued the man's frumpy attire. It was easy to look good on paper, but television told no lies . . . well, only a few lies. She thought Colt Dantzler would be older, more mature, and impeccably dressed, but he looked like a middle-aged guy with no place else to go.

"Damian De Lucia is a washed-up biologist with nothing else to do than complain, even when our company has done nothing wrong."

His statement seemed laughable when Lisa took the water sample to a lab and it tested high.

She interviewed a former Pageant employee who said that the company consistently disposed of untreated sewage. The reporter feigned appall.

Abby had to admit Lisa was good.

She outlined the threats not only to the whales, but to all marine life in the Sound. The camera caught Damian and Abby talking as they peered over the side of the boat, and Jessica cheered her mom's national TV appearance.

"People like Damian De Lucia and Abby Wagner are speaking out for the orcas since they can't speak for themselves.

"The orcas finally returned to the Sound this summer, and they were welcomed home by residents and visitors alike," Lisa concluded. "The question is—will they come back again next year, or is pollution going to force them to flee their home forever?"

The story ended and a commercial popped up on the screen.

"Nice job, Mom," Marc said.

"He's right, Abby," Damian agreed. "This was exactly what we needed to get the Sound cleaned up."

She grinned back at Damian, glad that he was pleased with the work and relieved that the waiting was finally done.

"Who wants a frozen cappuccino?" she asked. Everyone raised a hand. The four of them stayed up past midnight, laughing and talking and dreaming about the future.

Abby woke up the next morning to the ringing cell phone on her nightstand.

"Hello," she muttered.

"Abby, it's Blanche."

She glanced at her watch—it was 7:15 AM. Abby waited for her former boss's snide comment about Abby sleeping in, but Blanche shocked her instead.

"I need you to come back, Abby," she said. "If you take over the Heartsong account, I'll raise your salary and give you another week of vacation. Same position, but more pay."

"What happened to Curtis?"

Blanche cleared her throat. "I had to let him go."

Abby waited for the taste of victory, the rush of satisfaction, the glib feeling of "I told you so," but she didn't feel a thing except sorrow for her discontented boss.

"You could start right away," Blanche continued. "We're moving full speed ahead with the Labor Day event, and I . . . I need your expertise."

Her mind raced with this new possibility. Blanche wanted her back, needed her to help with the campaign. The offer and its ramifications surged through her mind. She'd known firsthand the sorrow of adoption, and now her perspective had been radically changed. She'd love to work with Heartsong again.

But as she looked over the balcony of the loft and through the glass at the glistening waves below, she knew she wouldn't be returning to Denver. Some days she still missed her job and the mountains and her beautiful home, but she'd changed this summer. She couldn't go back to Nulte P.R.

"Are you there?" Blanche asked.

"I'm sorry," Abby replied. "I can't come back."

"How much do you want?"

"It's not about money."

Blanche grunted into the phone. "This is a great opportunity, Abby."

"I know, and I appreciate it, but you were right. I was losing my focus, and I needed to get it back. God's taking me to a new place in my life right now, and I'm enjoying the ride."

"If you change your mind—" Blanche cut herself off. "I'll make it worth it to you if you'll change your mind."

Nothing would be worth it, Abby thought as she said good-bye.

Setting her phone back down on her nightstand, it beeped, and she saw she had voice mail. She picked it back up again—all these calls and it was hardly dawn! A voice told her she had three new messages.

First message: "Hi Abby, it's Harold Rogers from Heartsong. I've been trying to track you down, and then I saw you on *Primetime* last night. The producer just gave me your number.

"Listen, our organization is growing and expanding this fall into international work. I'm canceling our account with Nulte P.R., and if you're available, I'd like you to start back where you left off."

She scribbled Harold's number on the back cover of the novel beside her bed. Yes, she'd take over the campaign—if she could do it on her own and she could do it from here. She'd tell Harold her story, and if he still wanted her onboard, she'd be a ruthless advocate for adoption and the Heartsong agency.

The voice mail beeped.

Second message: "This is Brian Booker from the *Seattle Times*. We'd like to do a follow-up story on Pageant Industries after the *Primetime* story last night, and we want to interview Dr. De Lucia."

The reporter left his work number, cell phone number, and e-mail address so she'd get back to him right away. She smiled. She'd call him this afternoon, if she had time.

Third message: "Abby, this is Stacie Cartwright." She cleared her throat. "Marc gave me your number . . . I hope it was okay for me to call. Since our kids are getting married and all, I, uh, wondered if you'd like to get together."

Abby stared out at the morning sunlight as Stacie paused.

"I'd like to thank you for loving our son."

Epilogue

> And we know that all things work together for good to
> them that love God, to them who are the called accord-
> ing to his purpose.
>
> —Romans 8:28

Four Years Later

Damian steered the tour boat by the beach Jessie named Coral Spit. The packed load of tourists cheered as a pod of six whales breached the water, splashing the passengers when they slapped their black flukes against the sea.

Two more whales had died over the past few years, but the remaining whales continued to return to the Sound. The media had embraced the dying orca story for about six months after the *Primetime* feature, and the national attention inspired Pageant Industries to clean up its waste. The Sound's PCB levels had decreased by a few points each year.

That was all Damian wanted—safe water for the whales and other sea life so they could thrive again.

"We've got a sick one," Jake spurted out as he burst in the door.

Damian sighed. His new first mate refused to help when someone got seasick, saying it made him ill. Damian grabbed his medical kit, leaving Jake to steer, and pushed through the crowd gathered around the poor man at the back of the boat. After all these years, it still amazed him that a crowd would gather to watch someone get sick. It seemed like there was better entertainment on the other side of the boat, especially on days like today when the whales performed. Yet a good bout of seasickness usually stole the show.

He leaned down, checked the guy's pulse, and helped him stand.

This was the first summer Damian had done a boat tour without Marc, and he missed the boy. Marc and Jessie had gotten married two years before, and they'd both graduated from the University of Washington last year.

With their undergraduate degrees under their belts, the kids launched right into graduate school to earn their master's degrees in marine biology. A month ago, they'd flown to a small village in Venezuela to complete their dream internship—studying the effects of pollution on the local fish population.

They'd both felt the tug toward South America during their junior year, so they'd immersed themselves in Spanish until they became fluent. Marc had already started a Bible study in their coastal village, and in her last e-mail, Jessie said twelve Venezuelans were attending. The word was spreading fast about these strange young Americans who loved the Lord.

Nothing could be more perfect for the two of them, but Damian missed them dearly.

In secret, he'd envisioned passing the tour company on to Marc someday. He'd actually hinted about it once, but Marc already knew he was being called far away. Who could have guessed the twists and turns that trip would take?

Damian helped the sick man lie down on a row of upgraded leather seats, and the guy groaned for Damian to take him back to shore. Fortunately for him, the trip was almost over. Damian took over the helm of the boat as he wrapped the tour. Some days he still craved that rush of freedom that he'd experienced working with the IWC, but those days were rare. He no longer wanted to run.

Damian escorted the seasick man onto the dock and helped him sit down on a bench to rest in the shade. Abby yelled his name, and he turned to see her running toward him.

"They got the call!" she shouted.

He hoped his wife wouldn't fall into the water as she raced across the slippery planks. She kissed him as she swirled a piece of paper in front of him, an e-mail she'd just received. He grabbed the note and read:

Hey Mom and Dad!

Harold just called—Heartsong found a baby for us!! He's four months old, a Haitian boy who lost both his parents in a fire. They're bringing him to Venezuela on Monday, and we're naming him Damian Hunter Cartwright to commemorate his family heritage and God's loving and eternal grasp on his life.

We'll call you as soon as our son arrives home.

Lots of love,
M & J

Damian hugged Abby as she cried in his arms. Their grandchild had been born.

Author's Note

I experienced my first panic attack when I was sick last year and couldn't care for my baby girls. Darkness smothered my mind. My heart raced. My hands shook. I was hot. I was cold. I was too scared to sleep. Too scared to move.

Terrifying.

Weeks passed, and the panic returned almost every night. I called out to Jesus, and He gave me hope in the midst of the attacks, but they still didn't go away.

I memorized the first chapter of James, and my mind cleared as I took deep breaths and recited the words of faith in my mind.

But then I would wake up again, overwhelmed by fear. I felt like I was going crazy.

When the weight became too much to bear, I finally begged for help. It was very hard for me to tell others that my mind was out of my control, but I was desperate. My family and friends loved me in the midst of my pain.

The nutrition doctor I visited said I had a classic case of adrenal stress as well as hypoglycemia. I was thrilled to be "classic." A strict diet, rest, supplements, exercise, and a lot of prayer slowly eased my attacks. As I write this, the attacks have yet to return.

Some people need medication. Some people need a diet change. Some people need counseling. Others need rest. And still others, like Abby, may need to release their pain and fear to God even when it means giving up control.

If you are suffering through overwhelming anxiety or panic attacks,

please seek help! No one should have to endure this terror. No matter how embarrassing it may seem, you are not alone.

For more information about adrenal fatigue or to hear about our adoption story, please contact me at mdobson@kregel.com.

Discussion Questions

1. Why was Abby still so attached to Hunter after twenty years?
2. How is the bond of adoption both the same and different from the bond of a mother with her biological child?
3. Why do so many Christians struggle with anxiety and panic attacks?
4. Is it possible to bury pain for two decades and then have it suddenly resurface?
5. Why was Abby's pain so overwhelming to her?
6. How did Abby's secrets affect her relationship with her daughter?
7. What are some of the similarities between Abby and Stacie?
8. Do you think there's hope for Stacie?
9. Damian is passionate about cleaning up the polluted water in Puget Sound to help the orcas and other sea life. What should a Christian's role be in protecting the environment?
10. Should Jessica and Marc have continued dating without Abby's permission?
11. What type of man would Marc have been if he'd been raised by Abby?
12. It hurt Abby to release her anger and fear and the need to control her life. How does God use pain to change and grow the people He loves?
13. What difficult situations has God used for good in your life or in the lives of your family or friends?
14. How can a Christian woman continue to grow in faith even when she doesn't understand the reason for her pain?